Chip Tales

by Walter Block

"Tell me again, GranDad,
how it was back then."

authorHOUSE®

AuthorHouse™
1663 Liberty Drive, Suite 200
Bloomington, IN 47403
www.authorhouse.com
Phone: 1-800-839-8640

First published by AuthorHouse 10/28/2008

ISBN: 978-1-4389-2818-0 (sc)

Library of Congress Control Number: 2008909838

Printed in the United States of America
Bloomington, Indiana

This book is printed on acid-free paper.

Acknowledgments

To Bette, the sharp-eyed expunger of fanciful spellings and grammatical gyrations, always the firm veto keeping some exciting incidents from appearing in these pages.

To Candy, the spark and the spur, without whose encouragement these chips would not have been whittled.

To Wayne, the happy man, the gentle critic who remembers some of our exploits differently but who would have me "not change a thing"!

To David, the perceptive appreciator.

To Chelleye, who honed my hankering and whetted my keyboard blades.

To Ben, who has shared thoughts with me since before he could talk.

To Allison, who rode on my shoulder, patted my flat top, and brightened my life.

To Will, the first responder, the constant inspiration.

To Michael, the thinking one, who bubbles with infectious laughter.

To Luke, the quiet one, who makes and holds friends with all of the world.

To Austin and Weston, horn-blowers and bear-huggers who fished before they were born.

To the nephews and niece, Jimmy, Tammy, Terry, and David, who read and asked for more.

To Christi, the dispenser of critical elixir.

To T, the wholehearted acclaimer.

To John, who beat me to the draw and then helped me pull the trigger.

To Leon, the ever constant friend.

Introduction

These are just a few things I've experienced -- or repetitions of some of the tales to which I was an avid listener in my youth.

My daughter and daughter-in-law, Candy and Chelleye, have prompted, prodded, and/or persuaded me to write them so that their children, grandkids, and progeny-to-come can read or be read such when I'm not around to do the telling.

Candy prompted me with a blank-page book, "A Father's Legacy -- Your Life Story in Your Own Words". But it didn't take. Then, as a father's day gift, she enrolled me in a short writing class. Karen Gleason honed my rusted pens. Reading Ted Gray's memoirs and Ben Green's yarns sowed seeds. Bedtime readings of Kipling's "Just So Stories" to my grandkids inspired. I knew a novel was not in me, but I wondered: Could I spin short remembrance tales?

My oldest grandkids were away at five far-flung colleges. I made a deal with them. I'd e-mail them a tale at a time if they would send me an e-mail informing they had received it and if they would let me know of my errors and weaknesses. Of course, e-mails went similarly to Candy and Chell, David and Wayne. Before long nephews, nieces, and others found out, asked, and were receiving my e-mailed tales -- with the same deal -- "be a critic".

I've tried to be truthful, at least to the extent that I am able.

But as Aunt Beth was wont to say: "you need to know", that all the little bits and pieces of some of these happenings are not included. Some things I have "edited" just to not be too long-winded. And then, some left-out things are details which I can't remember accurately enough to be confident that I'm telling it close to like it was.

I've almost always been aware of my poor memory. Like most folks, my ability to recall has worsened in my later years.

I attribute the life-long memory insufficiency to some happenings which I do remember well enough to report.

Each of these little episodes will probably be told more expansively in various remembrance wisps included in Chips Tales, but in order for you to understand why I might be "corrected" on some of my details in the next few years before I and all those I tell about in the stories are departed, let me briefly give you a listing.

First, sometime around age six, I was swinging, alone under a big old huisache tree, "pumping" as high as I could in a swing my dad had rigged from an old tire casing and an even older hank of rope. When the rope broke I was on an upswing. I made a big swoop and landed on my head. Next thing I knew I was spitting dirt, huisache beans, etc.

Second, not too long after that I was squatting next to the irrigation ditch that ran through the school grounds, launching a little paper boat I had made in my second-grade class. A well-intentioned classmate (I give him the benefit of the doubt) heaved a brick-sized rock. He meant to hit the water close to me to splash me. His aim was second-grade quality and the rock smacked me just over my left ear. Next thing I knew I was being pulled out of the ditch, thoroughly soaked, had a headache and a more than noticeable ringing in my ear.

Third, I was washing my grandad's car, standing on wet concrete, and reached up to turn on a hanging light in the garage. The old light fixture had once had the metal of the twist switch covered with rubber insulation. That the old insulation was long gone had never before been meaningful to me. It took me a while to figure out why I was laying on the wet concrete, but, when I did, I was glad the fall had pulled my hand off the exposed electric switch.

Then there was the time a few years later when I didn't tighten the saddle girt enough on a little short-legged, round-bellied, kid-gentle horse. When the horse decided to go around a bush on one side and I had planned on going around on the other side, the saddle slipped. I parted company with my mount and landed -- wouldn't you know -- in the grit on my designated landing point -- just above that left ear.

I think my hearing loss as I aged is due to a lot of shooting without ear protection, but my memory insufficiency started early on and getting whacked or bopped on the head that many times must have had something to do with it.

There also was the home-made diving bell incident, and the insufficient air supply . . . And the running dive into the creek where it had been deep the summer before, but had been made shallow by gravel fill from a spring rising.

So these are just things I remember -- tales for Chips -- to expose them a bit to "how great it was" when the world was a bit younger.

Contents

Summer of '44

June

The summer of '44 was mighty eventful. That June, July, and August between my junior and senior high school years I hired on as a junior laborer at Laughlin Army Air Force Base.

Recent graduates of DRHS like John Graf, Claude Draper, Johnnie Brinkley, etc, were not quite old enough to be in military service. So they and 16- and 17-year-olds such as Paul Epps, Joe Hollingsworth, and me, were making early contributions to win World War II.

Laughlin's mission was training B-26 pilots. WW II was in its third year. B-25s and B-26s were the principal medium bomber planes by then. The big B-17 Flying Fortress and B-24 Liberator were four-engine, long range, heavily armored jobs. The B-26, the Martin Marauder, with a couple of big-prop engines, top gun turret and tail gunner position, was designed for intermediate bombing runs. But it was a heavy bird. It flew fine with both big motors cranked up. However, if a greenhorn crew lost one engine, it was hard to keep the plane airborne.

Junior laborers were paid at the mind-boggling rate of $1,800 per year. So . . . if we worked a full three months during the summer, those headed back to high school to finish our senior year would have $450, less what we had spent. It was a bunch of bucks to us then.

First off, they had us in for a physical exam. We were all healthy escapees from Wildcat football and track training and sailed right through.

1

Except for Claude. A USAAF corpsman sat him up on a high-legged stool so he could stick a syringe in his arm and take some blood. When they jabbed ole Claude with that needle, he rolled his eyes back and flopped right down on the concrete floor. They picked him up, checked his pulse, listened to his ticker, and decided he would survive. Claude, apologized all over the place, chattering ninety to nothing, telling all the folks in the medical building within hearing distance -- especially his high school buddies waiting in line -- that such a gosh-awful thing had never happened to him before. So they sat him back up on the stool. Stuck the needle in his other arm. He passed out again. Fell off on the other side of the stool. An airman and a nurse caught him that time before he hit the deck. They laid him on a cot, took his blood sample, and labeled him fit to toil for Uncle Sam.

Next came an ear-pounding on the potential damaging effects of the hot Texas weather. They conjured up menacing mental images of federal incarceration, confinement, and long stays in the hoose-gow if we failed to drink lots of water and take gobs of salt pills every time we drank it.

All that palaver about water on a hot June morning had me thirsting for a drink. At our next induction tour stop we spied a water cooler. I sashayed up to that drink machine, turned the little handle, bent over, and took a big swig of mouth-puckering sulfur water. That oratorical spiel about the effects of not drinking lots of water failed to inform that Laughlin didn't have San Felipe Spring water. It was years later before good limestone aquifer water was piped out to Laughlin.

Junior laborers were scattered over the base in various assignments. Most of the young non-military kids I was grouped with were placed either with Aircraft Maintenance or Reclamation.

Maintenance gofers were put to a duke's mixture of menial tasks, but much of their work was in the relative cool of the biggest building I had ever been in -- the big flightline hangar.

Each junior laborer assigned to Maintenance or Reclamation was issued a tool kit. Just a basic kit -- hammer, pliers, screw drivers, open-end wrenches, folding wooden measuring tool, etc. Plus a genuine, bone-handled, three bladed pocket knife -- a war-time jewel hard to come by.

Remember that knife.

For the tools, we each had a tool box. A flimsy war-time tool box hardly worthy of the name.

That dinky, cardboard-sided tool box was painted battle-ship gray. Had big bold, black numerals stenciled on the sides. Everything in the tool kit was etched with the number painted on the outside of the tool box. That number, of course, was assigned to us individually. It's a wonder we weren't tattooed likewise.

At the end of each day, the tool box was stashed in a locker assigned to us in the hangar.

As you might expect, we were threatened with excruciating consequences if we lost the kit or any of its contents. There was one alleviating provision. Any tool damaged beyond serviceable condition while employed in honorable and honest performance of U. S. Government assignments could be replaced. But only if the broken article was turned in with triple-copied, blood-oath, written testimonial documents. And those were the days of carbon paper copies!

Whenever our tasks required bigger, stronger, more serviceable, odd-sized, or specialized tools, we got a request form and trotted over to another building to be temporarily issued the needed gismo. Requirements for odd tools like that didn't happen to guys low on the totem pole very much. But sooner rather than later each of us was sent to the tool supply window for things like left-handed monkey wrenches, air hooks, sky tongs, and other exotics. It was embarrassing to be hoodwinked into asking for non-existing crud, but we soon learned that when sent on a hair-brained search for things like that, it was legal goofing off time.

That enormous hangar building was incredible. On both its east and west sides, the hangar was a two-story structure. Covered by a big arching roof. Both the north and south ends of the building could be closed with big sliding doors.

The bottom and top floors on the east side housed offices and administrative quarters. Entrances to offices on the lower floor were via doors opening onto the hangar floor. Entry ways to second floor rooms were from an open cantilevered walkway that jutted out into the hangar.

The hangar's west side was mostly shops below and supply and parts areas above. Again, access to the second floor spaces was by way of a cantilevered walkway at the second-floor level.

The hangar floor was wide. Two rows of B-26s -- somewhat staggered -- could be inside for service. The Engine Repair line extended the length of the hangar next to the west wall shops.

Most aircraft flights took off into the prevailing southeast wind. Too frequently, a heavy B-26, struggling to be airborne, suffered either engine failure or what the pilots took to be engine failure. Del Rio and Mexico were to the west. The guys at the controls -- usually one was a trainee -- had to: (a) keep going south -- maybe to the auxiliary field near Eagle Pass -- or (b) try to coax and coddle the fuel-laden plane -- sometimes called a Widow Maker -- around to the east, circle north, turn south again, and try to land back on the Laughlin runway.

If the wing with the ailing engine dropped too much in that process, it was almost a given that it couldn't be hauled back up. Crash landings were usually to the south, east, and north of Laughlin.

A belly landing in the brush usually resulted in salvage crews being dispatched. Aircraft remains were brought back. Wings and engines on a big truck. Fuselage and other parts on a bigger truck. Junior laborers didn't go out on gruesome recoveries, but we did assist in the mostly manual, labor-intensive work of retrieving the pieces.

In those days there were no rocket-propelled pilot ejection seats.

An ailing B-26 too low for parachutes to open required an attempted landing of some sort. When the plane couldn't make it back to the runway, most often a belly landing was the option. When the planes went in for a belly landing, pilots -- by rule -- cut the engines, killed the switches, and hoped for the minor miracle of no fire. Even with motors stopped, the big four-bladed propellers were usually still rotating. When the wheels-up plane neared the ground, the wind-milling blades hit first, came unglued, and, most of the time, were sent spiraling off into the hungry hidings of rocks, sage, and prickly pear.

Locating and recovering those big blades was pure-dee mandatory. We might not find other parts, but we didn't come home without each and every one of those eight propeller blades.

Occasionally, shorn blades were extremely difficult to find. It was amazing how far they could be flung and how deep into the rocky soil they could be embedded.

For the junior laborers on those recovery jobs, hunting for those eight blades was one of the less odious tasks. We made a game of it, scattering out and seeing who could find the first one, the last one, the one the most distance away from the wreckage, etc.

July

As stated, the pilots usually cut the switches and doused all electrical circuits before they slid back into or onto mother earth. Nevertheless, when the salvage crew got to the wreck, the first rule was to check the main switch in the cockpit to make sure the power was off. Only then were the salvage teams supposed to approach the downed bird and go about siphoning off fuel, dismantling, etc.

On one of these bring-back-the-pieces runs, when we arrived at the crash scene, the downed plane's wing tanks were leaking fuel on the ground. The crew was rigging hoses to pump it from the plane to barrels in a nearby truck. I was sent up into the plane to look for something. In the cockpit I saw that the main electrical switch was still ON! When I yelled that info out the cockpit window, workers in, around, on top of, and under the aircraft, scattered like a covey of quail. Just flat disappeared! I froze.

Our work leader hollered at me to not touch anything and get the heck out of there. As I am here to tell you about it, you know I executed that command to absolute perfection. Set an all-time record for holding my breath in the process. Someone went in and turned off the switch. The crew reappeared out of the brush, came back, and started pumping fuel and removing wings.

Another twist of the recovery jobs for junior laborers was locating the dumped parachutes. When a B-26 -- which had "Flying Coffin" as one of its nicknames -- slid in, pilots and others on the craft abandoned ship PDQ. It was usually only after they were well away on terra firma that they took time to shuck the parachutes they were required to wear on take off.

Sometimes those hastily abandoned chutes were as hard to find as the prop blades. Most were discarded within forty or fifty yards of the downed Marauder. A few times much beyond that. Usually we found single chutes at all compass points around and away from the plane, but there were times when we found them stacked in bunches or piles. And, more often than not, there was -- not too far from the discarded chutes -- solid and/or semi-solid evidence that excitement of a belly landing in a Flying Coffin strongly stimulated the bowels of airmen.

Along about the middle of the summer, a P-38 Lightning -- a twin-motored, triple-fuselaged, pursuit/fighter -- developed a problem with one of its engines while flying cross-country near our area. The plane came in easily on one engine. Safely landed at Laughlin. The ailing motor was removed. A replacement motor had to be requisitioned from some far off source.

While awaiting the arrival of a replacement engine -- the beautiful little bird rested in that big hangar we frequented. We hovered all about it, admiring its sleek lines, ogling the twin tails, and gawking at the nose ports where the four fifty-caliber machine guns could be mounted.

The original cross-country pilot went on to another site during the wait. When the new power plant arrived and was installed, a survey of pilots then at Laughlin turned up one who was qualified to fly a P-38. Of course he had been daily flying B-26s in his instructor's role at our air base.

Just about everyone who could jar loose from their assignments was on hand to watch the P-38 take off to be ferried to its intended destination. The pilot taxied the little fighter out onto the runway, pointed its nose into the southeast breeze, revved each engine, then gunned both of them, and whisked down the launching path. The plane lifted, the wheels tucked up into the nacelles behind each engine, and the craft began arching up. The right wing dipped. We thought the pilot was waggling his wings in a farewell gesture. But the right wing went too low. Perhaps the new engine had cut out. The pilot -- used to hauling up the heavy wings of a B-26 -- jerked the stick too far left, over-controlled, and the sweet bird flipped over onto its back into the runway. Ugly black smoke spiraled up and marred our bright sky. It was a sad day in Mudville.

Part of the time, junior laborers were assigned humdrum jobs in Engine Repair in the hangar. Mostly clean-up tasks. But a lot of training was devoted to teaching us how to "safety" nuts onto bolts. Never had run into such before.

Seems it is important, especially on an aircraft which might be pounded by enemy machine guns while on a mission, to keep nuts from jarring loose and allowing important thingamajigs to come apart. So, each bolt used on those B-26s had a little hole drilled through it at just the right number of threads from the bolt end. The nuts had six or eight slots cut into the off end. When the nut was screwed onto the bolt to just the right tightness, that hole in the bolt would line up with one of those slots in the nut. Then, you slipped a brass wire of exactly the right diameter thru the slot on one side of the nut, thru the hole in the bolt, and out thru one of the nut slots on the other side. Next came the icing on the cake. You wrapped that brass wire around the bolt exactly the prescribed number of times, twisted the wire ends together a strict number of turns, and bent the wire at precisely the correct angle back around the end of the bolt. And, mister, every dang one of those safety-wired nut-bolt combinations had to pass inspection. The USAAF, War Department, FBI, and probably super-serious surreptitious liquor license revenuers had squinty-eyed jayboes who checked the tensions, the twists, the turns, and the tucks. If you messed up on just one, they never forgave you until you passed inspection umpteen times.

Transportation to and from Laughlin was always a problem during the war. Everything was rationed -- gas, tires, and -- most of all -- cars. About the only civilians able to obtain new cars were doctors. Folks drove and/or rode catch-as-catch-can. Most vehicles were old and weary.

Four or five of one junior laborer group rode with Joe Hollingsworth in a Model T Ford that his step-dad, Seth Galloway, had scrounged from some old barn. It was older than dirt. Three pedals on the floor, spark lever sticking out on the left side of the steering wheel and throttle lever jutting out on the right. Tires were thin enough to see thru. Brakes were shot. Canvas top torn, windshield cracked, headlights askew, one running board was missing, fenders dented. It was a mess, but it had a license, was legal only because they didn't have inspections in those days, and it got us out to the base and back almost every day that summer.

Another small group of junior laborers was luckier. Johnnie Brinkley's dad was the renowned Dr. John R. Brinkley. Johnnie drove an almost brand new coupe to the base each day. I think it was a Chevy, but it might have been a Ford. In any event, it was clean, shiny, and, dependable.

Each day when the five o'clock whistle blew at the base, all the junior laborer types, most of the multitude of civilians, and a lot of the military folks (no base housing then) dashed for the gate -- the base exit onto Highway 90. If you didn't toe the starting line and be ready to go with the whistle, you had a long wait for a lengthy line of vehicles to creep past the gate guards and work their way into the highway flow. A lot of the time, we either just didn't want to fight the crowd or the temptation of ten-cent pints of ice cream at the base PX diverted those of us in Joe's Model T clunker. Johnnie and his load almost always beat us to town.

I don't recall where Johnnie's bunch rendezvoused each morn for the trip to the base, but I met Joe and our crew on Dignowity Street just east of Main Street. It was close to Joe's home and we could wait under the awning that ran along the south side of Burditt's Grocery Store.

That awning also sheltered the produce which farmers and suppliers delivered to Burditt's in the wee cooler hours each day before the store opened.

One morning on a summer day which had every promise of being a real scorcher, the temptation of a bushel of luscious tomatoes was too much for us. We appropriated a dozen or so of the ripest red beauties and left Mr. Burditt a note saying we would pay that afternoon when we returned. When we got to Laughlin, for want of a better place, we stowed the tomatoes under the seats of the old Model T. During the day it got mighty hot in that old black vehicle parked out there next to the flight line. (You remember, don't you, that Henry Ford said his early cars came in any color you wanted as long as it was black?) When we got off work those tomatoes were almost too squishy to pick up.

Lady Luck wiggled her wand waggishly that day. We exited the base gate and onto the highway before Johnnie and his new buggy. When they saw us in the lead of them on the way to the gate, they headed for the PX and ice cream. We chugged west over a little rise on the way to town. About a mile down the road we pulled off in the shade of a big mesquite tree. Close to a culvert.

And there the devil helped us hatch a devious plan.

When Johnnie's car topped the rise to the east, it was easy to recognize. We spread out on both sides of the culvert, three on one side and the others across the highway.

They saw us waiting down the road. Johnnie Boy put the pedal to the metal. If that shimmering cream-colored coupe had been blessed with wings coming down that hill, it would have soared right over us. When he got to the culvert -- which he couldn't go around -- he came lickity-split right down the middle of the road to be as far as he could from us.

We didn't throw a single tomato. Just tossed them out at windshield height.

The splattering splooshes as they swooshed past was splendidly satisfying.

August

Undoubtedly using will-o'-the-wisp reasoning, the deciders and determiners of the destinies of junior laborers sometimes frothed at the mouth with fiendish glee about wicked assignments. Without prior notice, we would be shuffled off to the hinterlands of Reclamation. The folks in charge down there were good people, but they were duty-bound to function within the fetters of weird rules and practices.

The Rec Yard working area had a high fence all around. It was a sort of Parts Purgatory. Salvaged stuff found its way into those confines. Mostly surviving pieces from aircraft, but also office equipment, vehicles, fire and fuel hoses, electrical wiring and connections, and anything some nabob decided was unfit for the purpose for which it was purchased. Unwanteds might be cleaned up a bit, but one way or another they were routed to new life or shunted to non-existence. Engines from the planes that cracked up might be deemed repairable and sent for reconditioning on base or at a location with more sophisticated abilities. Wing tanks and instruments might be salvaged. Some things went to Reclamation and lived on.

But scads of still-good items which some feather-brained jocko ruled were junk were given the proverbial deep six. Even if, in that era of strict rationing and severe shortages, some of those doohickeys might have had use left in them for yokels in the boondocks,

One sad morning an airman drove a small truck into the "Wreck Yard". The truck bed was half full of discards. Among the unwanted was a treasure trove of small tools -- hammers, saws, screwdrivers, wrenches, measuring tapes, etc. Each item may have been flawed. Some badly. Others had only minor faults.

We eyed screwdriver blades you could make as good as new in a couple of minutes with a file or grinder. Hammers with nicked claws or chipped faces still were serviceable in my book. A saw with a cracked wooden handle could have been bound with tape and served adequately for decades. There was a wheelbarrow with a body split that could have been welded into something better than a lot of folks ever had.

Still wet-behind-the-ears in my experience with the magnificence of governmental bureaucratic administrative wisdom and procedure, I wondered a bit too loudly if some of the only slightly damaged items they were about to trash could be obtained -- pilfered, purloined, or purchased. Some hairy, heavy eye-browed, would-be-big-wig growled, "NO". Then he watched me like a chicken hawk over the hen yard until each of those "defective" tools was so badly melted or burned with a cutting torch that they were beyond redemption.

Bitter lesson learned and marked!

However, . . . every happening down at Reclamation wasn't a bitter pill.

Junior laborers and others, both military and civilian, who earned their keep at least part of the time at the Rec Yard were often tasked with removing serviceable parts from planes which survived belly landings largely intact.

One sweltering afternoon, I was sweating and swearing under the cockpit Plexiglas canopy of one of those crumpled but still valuable B-26 hulks, wresting out innards of the plane brains. Among the gismos I was detaching from the instrument panel were switches and dials of the communication system. A pair of headphones with an attached mike hung on one of the knobs.

I looked over my shoulder back thru the plane's bomb bay area. One of my junior laborer buddies was scrunched into the tail gunner's cramped, oven-like cubicle taking a doodad loose.

Still just a playful lad at heart, I put those earphones on my head, held that dead radio mike up to my mouth, and called back loud enough for my pal in the back to hear: "Pilot to Gunner. Pilot to Gunner. Any bandits in sight?"

My equally gallant and courageous friend, with intellectual adroitness, picked up a funnel-shaped object connected to a black rubber tube and responded: "Tail Gunner to Pilot. Bogies coming in fast at six o'clock high!"

Another look back thru the plane startled me. Then, laughingly, I informed my fellow air warrior that -- instead of a radio mike -- he had a relief tube pressed to his lips.

He may still be spitting and rubbing his mouth with the back of his hand when he remembers that war-time juvenile melodrama.

Real drama occurred, however, the clear-skied August day at Laughlin Air Force Base when I fell out of the open bomb bay of a B-26.

No parachute, of course.

Neither of the Martin Marauder's two 4,000 horsepower Pratt and Whitney engines were running. The two big four-bladed props weren't turning. Nothing below but hard concrete.

The next thing I knew, I was looking up at this anxious air force type with twinkling brass on his crisp khaki collar, who was saying: "Are you alright, son?"

Making probably the biggest mistake of my whole ever-loving life, I said, "Yes, sir."

More than likely old Uncle Sam would have been providing for me the rest of my natural born days. I had just frittered away an almost guaranteed life-time pension.

We had been rejoining and re-tensioning control cables which run from the cockpit to the elevators and rudder in the back of the ship. The plane was in the hangar, jacked up abnormally high over the concrete floor so that others working on the brakes could raise and lower the landing gear. While the plane is airborne, the landing gear extends much lower when first lowered. Then the struts compress as the wheels touch down and the weight of the plane bears.

Guys working inside the jacked-up B-26 could climb in and out via a ladder from the hangar floor. But for those agile enough, there was another makeshift way.

The bomb bay doors were open. A metal beam ran along the belly of the plane, from the front to the back of the bomb bay. In flight, this narrow girder was the walkway for a crew to get from one end of the plane to the other. On both sides of the walkway a sturdy strap provided some safety and a "hand rail". The straps were fastened at each end with metal hooks to u-bolts in the vertical ribs in front and at the back of the bomb bay.

Some ingenious fellow had discovered that if the metal hook of a strap was detached at one end, the strap would hang down from the hook and fastener at the other end . . . just about right for a person on the hangar floor to reach up, grab the strap, swing his feet up to the middle girder, and then pull up hand over hand until he could step off onto the walkway.

I was doing that. My body was about horizontal, with a foot on the girder . . . when the metal hook on the end of the strap broke.

By instinctively bowing my back, I managed to keep my head from hitting the concrete too hard, but my back got a real bashing.

The rest of the day my head ached, my back hurt, my neck was sore, and I cussing myself for that dumb response to the big brass officer.

But . . . you guessed it . . . I survived. Lived to tell the tale of my fall from a B-26.

And, say! Do you remember that bone-handled, three-bladed pocket knife issued in my tool kit?

Well, during my deeds of daring the summer of '44 at Laughlin, that remarkable instrument sustained a few injuries. The tip of the small blade was snapped off trying to pry something stronger than it was. The middle blade got a neat round nick in the middle of the cutting edge when I carelessly tried to cut a "hot" electric wire.

And the etched number? It succumbed to natural wear and induced erosion when I was faced with having to turn in that crippled friend of mine for an almost certain RecYard execution.

You may be sad or glad to know this. That knife has lived on. Served well for sixty-plus years.

A special spot is reserved for it in a tool kit in my garage.

But, at this momentous moment . . . it is here beside me as I weave this tale.

The Panther Hunt

One of the favorite tales I heard many more times than once in that delightful atmosphere of rocking chairs and pipe smoke on the back and/or front porches or around the fireplaces of my grandparents' ranch at Bakers Crossing was about "Ole Tim's Panther Hunt".

Depending upon who was telling the tale, some of the small details varied from time to time, but the basic story was always the same.

"Tim" and his wife "Maud" (I've doctored the names to protect the innocent) pioneered a ranch several miles further down Devils River on the southwest side of the river.

Way back in the early days of getting their ranch started, Tim was out by the wood pile late one sunny but cold winter afternoon, splitting kindling for Maud's famous cook stove. He looked up to see one of their newly met neighbors riding his horse up to the yard gate.

I'll just call the neighbor Sam. His ranch house, like Tim's & Maud's was up on the divide a mile or so from Devils River, but on the northeast side of the river.

It was easy to see that Sam was more than some stirred up. He told Tim that he had just come across fresh panther spoor in a sandy drift down along the river bottom near where Dead Man Canyon runs into Devils River.

Panthers (or pumas, or mountain lions, or leons, as they were called just across the Rio Grande to the south) were hard on ranch stock. In those days deer had been hunted down and were not as numerous as they are today. But kid goats, lambs, calves, and colts were a rancher's bread and butter and a panther's prime eatin'. So a roving stock predator showing up on your place demanded immediate attention.

After a spell of serious jaw-boning, the two men decided there wasn't enough daylight left that day to go after the visiting leon. They agreed to meet early the next day down at the river where Sam had found the tracks and droppings.

Way before daybreak, Tim looked at the dipping thermometer, put on a jacket and a heavier coat, stuck a back-strap sandwich in one saddle bag and some extra ammo in another, belted on his bat-wing chaps, slid his 30-30 in the saddle scabbard, crawled on his horse, and headed out to meet Sam.

I should tell you here, that I very deliberately use the phrase "crawled on his horse". You see, Tim, so the story goes, was built low to the ground. Short legs and arms. Not the typical tall, lanky cowboy depicted in western novels and movies. He, like me, cast his eye for stumps, high rocks, and other aids to assist in a not-so-gallant mounting of his trusty steed.

As Tim let his horse pick its way in the cold early morning starlight down the steep canyon trail that led to the riverside meeting place, his mind toyed with some intriguing thoughts.

The meeting place was on Tim's side of the river. Sam had a bit further to go to get there. He had to cross the river upstream from the meeting place and then, had to ride up on a shelf that ran along the river before the trail dropped back down close to the river on Tim's side.

A bit before Sam got to the meeting place, his trail threaded through a thicket laced with catclaw, thorny young mesquites, and a huisatchie or two that had grown up in the fertile soil left by the last river rise.

Tim remembered that right in the middle of that thicket, about half way from either end, a nice-sized oak tree had managed to survive the more recent river floods. That oak tree always bothered riders, because of a low limb that stretched over the trail which forced a man on horseback to duck low to ride under it.

Tim got to the meeting place first and, while he was shivering in his saddle waiting for Sam, those intriguing thoughts turned into an inspiration.

Without really thinking why he was doing it, Tim dismounted, tied his horse, took off his spurs, and jogged down the trail thru the thicket to the oak tree. He climbed up the tree and sat on the limb that overhung the trail.

Soon he heard Sam coming. As was his usual custom, Sam was loudly singing one of his favorite songs -- probably something like "The Strawberry Roan" or "Sweet Bessie From Pike". He was all bundled up against the cold morning mists from the river -- in a woolen coat. The coat collar was turned up almost to the brim of the wide-brimmed felt hat and streams of frosty breath from his lusty singing spewed out and back around his tucked-in head.

And Sam was riding a big flop-eared mule!

The mule saw or sensed Tim on the limb and came to a jarring stop. Without saying a thing, Tim dropped down from the limb, hung by his arms, and churned his boots and little short legs like he was riding a bicycle. Those bat-wing chaps slapped the air right in front of the mule.

The trail was too narrow for the mule to turn all the way around, so he just whirled ninety degrees and started making a new trail through the thicket.

The heretofore cold, still, quiet morning air was pierced with the fearsome sounds of mule braying, limbs cracking, brush popping, clothes ripping, and the awesome screams of "whoa" from the startled singer -- all mixed up with his strangled bellowing of blasphemous descriptions of the loathsome parentage of the mis-begotten mule!

After awhile, quiet returned to the river bottom. But not for long.

Tim heard Sam and the mule returning. He peeked around the oak tree at a scene hard to imagine.

The mule's flop ears were straight up. His eyes were rolling rapidly from side to side. His nostrils flared and slobber dripped from the bit in his mouth.

Sam had lost his big hat and his coat was torn. But he was spurring the mule and he had his rope down and was using a loop of it to whip the mule back up that trail the suddenly strong-minded critter was positively determined not to go. Sam was hoarse and his language was worse, but he was giving the mule lots of colorful encouragement to get his sorry butt up that trail!

Just before Sam and the mule reached the point of their first awesome departure from the trail, the mule made an independent decision to take another previously uncharted route away from the scene of his scare. He made his ninety-degree turn, this time to the opposite side, and carved out a brand-spanking new virgin pathway.

Again, the brush popped and ripped and tore and the mule hee-hawed just as loud, but Sam's croaked curses weren't as easy to distinguish.

Tim had sudden thoughts of the feelings Sam might harbor for him if he survived this ordeal. Coming to a hasty and humble decision that discretion might be the better part of valor, the instigator of the dastardly episode hurried back to his horse, mounted up, and rode down the trail to intercept his friend Sam.

Sam was a determined man. Tim met him once again struggling with his wall-eyed, moaning, trembling mount, forcing his way back up that trail of tears. Sam was almost nude from the waist up. His body was scratched and bleeding. He had lost the rope. His rifle was no longer in the saddle scabbard. But he had found the rifle and was now using the butt of it to encourage the quivering mule.

Tim told Sam that he had heard this gosh-awful, fearsome racket as he approached the meeting place. Sam told Tim that he was just riding along peace-full-like to meet him and when he got to that oak tree in the thicket, that dang panther was sitting on the limb overhanging the trail and had jumped at him and his mule.

Tim choked and gasped and managed to get out words of comfort for his friend. Sam wanted to go to the oak tree and look for the panther tracks he knew were there and go git the critter!

Tim advised a wiser course of action.

He loaned Sam one of his coats and convinced him to go home and rest up before they took up the hunt again. And to doctor the mule as well as himself!

Sam assured Tim that he would doctor that fool mule alright! And learn him a lesson or two in the process.

Tim tidied up the area around the oak tree and went home a wiser man. But he never told Sam all the facts about the lesson he himself had learned. He figured his own good health was in the balance.

The Indian Pony

My granddad, Edwin S. Block -- I always called him Babo -- came to Del Rio when he was ten years old with his parents, Herman and Janie Block. Babo told me that when his family moved to Del Rio, they increased the number of anglo families living here at that time to ten.

Herman Block, a Confederate veteran who served with Sibley's Brigade during the Civil War, moved to San Antonio after the War Between the States. He married Janie Sampson, who was a member of a Carolina family which settled in Austin. Herman Block was the commissary clerk or sutler at Fort Clark from 1865 to 1874. Then, he moved, with his wife and son, to San Felipe Del Rio.

As a child, Babo, with his dad and mother, lived in a small adobe house on a three-acre plot next to the San Felipe Creek (at the east end of a dirt road now known as Strickland Street). There was a barn and a set of pens east of the house on the bank of one of the two irrigation ditches running through the yard.

While he was sutler at Fort Clark, Babo's dad (my great granddad), had enjoyed friendships with many of the officers and men in the cavalry units stationed there.

From time to time, cavalry groups patrolling the western fringes of early Texas to "control" Indians and others who had little regard for the law, would stop over at Camp Del Rio, located on the eastern bank of the San Felipe Creek a bit upstream from the Block home.

At the beginning of one of these patrols, while his troopers were camped on the San Felipe, the officer-in-charge was a supper guest of Herman and Janie. Their son, Edwin ("Babo" to me), soaked up the stories the officer told about his troopers' Indian scrapes.

Next morning, as the cavalry troop rode out on its way west, Babo -- the excited 10-year-old boy -- waved to the officer and his men on the trail of the raiding Indians.

About two weeks later, the army "horse soldiers" returned on their way back to Fort Clark. Again, they camped overnight on the banks of the San Felipe Creek. With them was a herd of horses and mules they had "recaptured" or "recovered" from the Indians.

Once more, the officer supped with the Blocks, and while telling the tales of the Indian encounters, he spoke of a small pony which had followed the horse herd. He said the pony was too small for a cavalry mount. It had no brand. They didn't know to whom it belonged. He asked, "Would Babo's dad let him drop the pony off at the Block's barn in the morning so the soldiers wouldn't be bothered with it any more?"

When the troop left with the herd the next day, one of the troopers brought the pony by and told Babo, "I guess he's yours now."

Need I tell you that Babo was excited? His first, his very own, real live horse! His "Indian pony"!

Babo's dad helped him put the little pony in a pen next to the barn. A shed on the south end of the barn gave shelter from the sun and occasional rain.

Babo tended the pony each day, watering, feeding, and gentling.

Every morning before breakfast he would look out the kitchen window -- to the east, the rising sun, and his pony in the barn pen.

But one morning, after a night which had been bright with a full moon, he looked out and didn't see the pony in the pen.

"Well", he thought, "The pony's just inside the shed or the barn".

So, after breakfast, Babo went to the pen. The pony wasn't in the pen. He wasn't in the shed. He wasn't in the barn.

Babo had an empty feeling in his stomach.

The pen gate and the barn doors were shut, but the pony was gone.

Babo ran to tell his mom and dad the pony was missing.

When, with his dad, they carefully looked in the dust of the pen and outside the gate, they discovered something that made the feeling in Babo's stomach much worse.

Mingled with the pony's hoof prints, but very easy to see, were -- Indian moccasin tracks.

And so they knew.

The Indians had come during the moonlit night.

And . . . they had taken back their pony.

The Screaming Woman

In the olden days, nearly everybody was a story teller. That's how folks "recorded" family histories. That's the way they were able to recall -- after the passing years -- events that occurred even long before they themselves existed. Sometimes humorous, sometimes scary, always worth listening to. Under the evening stars or by the fireside, tales were passed for entertainment. But mainly, lore was "handed down". That's how we know the way it was.

This is one of the stories that Grandma Birdie, my daddy's mother, told her grandkids, sitting in the evening quiet on the back porch or out on one of the lawn benches where she showed us the Big Dipper and Polaris.

Great Grandpa Hart, Grandma Birdie's dad, had an itchy foot. He and his young wife started from the family home on the East Coast of the United States -- one of the Carolinas, North, I think. He moved his family to and across Texas, leaving a daughter married in Del Rio, a son in El Paso, stopped awhile in California, left some children there, moved on north up the West Coast, and finally stopped and lived in Grants Pass, Oregon, where he is buried.

I'm not sure how The Harts traveled during their earlier journey stages, but by the time Grandma Birdie was a little girl of five or less, they were on the move by wagon from South Texas toward Del Rio.

This was during the time between the ending of the Civil War, which motivated Grandpa Hart to move West, and the building of the railroad from New Orleans thru San Antonio and Del Rio on to El Paso and beyond.

In the years between the late 1860's and early 1870's, Texas -- especially West Texas -- was only sparsely populated with hardy folk who mostly lived in small communities. Each village was about a day's travel by horseback from the next closest cluster of cabins. Sprinkled in between the sprawl of tiny towns, living on small farms and isolated ranches, the very toughest settlers scratched out their livelihood.

Indians still roamed the western-most parts of the state. Bad hombres and rustlers and owl hoots living on both sides of the Rio Grande sometimes raided ranches and even small towns. Those "good old days" were rough, rugged, and mostly uncivilized times in Texas.

The U. S. Army had cavalry units -- mostly Buffalo Soldiers -- stationed at far flung forts and camps to help control Indians and outlaws. But military posts were few and far between. Texas Rangers were tall in the saddle when on the scene; but their numbers were not enough and they weren't always where or when help was needed.

Well, sir, about mid-day it was, as The Hart Family in their heavily laden wagon began to ford the Frio River.

There weren't many river bridges in those days. If the road came to a river, there were usually just two ways to get a wagon across. If the water was deep, the wagon had to be floated or carried across on a barge. If the water was shallow, the river could be forded.

To ford a river, the wagon was just driven into the water and pulled across by its team -- IF the river bottom was firm and not too rough.

Grandpa Hart checked the Frio as best he could. The road down to the river on the south side clearly showed where to enter the water. The road coming out on the north side was easy to see. The water was not deep where it flowed over the ford, but it was not clear, due to a rain a day or so before. He clucked and hollered at his team, slapped the reins on their backs, and started his wagon across.

All was well until the wagon reached the middle of the Frio. But smack dab in the middle of the river, the wheels sank into loose gravel. Right up to the hubs on the wheels.

Grandpa Hart tried every way he could think of to get the wagon out. The horses strained. He got out and pushed while Grandma Hart held the reins and whipped the team. He shoveled gravel, threw in sticks and brush and small logs, and for every bit they made it forward, they went deeper.

The sun was moving on down in the Western sky. Just a few hours and it would be dark.

Finally, Grandpa Hart unhitched one of the two horses to ride back for help from a ranch they had passed that morning. He left his pistol with Grandma Hart.

Sitting close together on the seat of the wagon stuck in the gravel bar in the middle of the Frio River, the little girl, Emma Lee Hart, and her mother, who was pregnant with her second child, waited and watched and listened for Grandpa Hart to come back.

A few flies buzzed around the sweating horse. The melodious gurgles of the shallow river flowing across the loose gravel which trapped them were lulling sounds for the little girl. Her eyes were drooping.

Suddenly, the quiet was shattered by a woman's scream.

Grandma Hart and her frightened daughter anxiously looked down the river, searching the trees and brush downstream where the scream had come from. They could only see leaves shifting in the sluggish mid-afternoon breeze.

The first scream had startled them. But a few minutes later, they heard another scream. Louder. Nearer. Much more frightening.

A third scream, closer still, seemed to come from the trees and thorny brush on the river bank . . . just across from them!

The remaining horse of the wagon team, with ears stiffly swinging and eyes rolling, was pulling and jerking against the harness holding it to the bogged wagon. It couldn't get loose. The wagon hardly moved.

Grandma Birdie told us she remembered the crisp click as her mom cocked the big pistol.

They breathed very quietly so they could hear better. They listened, and watched, and waited. The sun was dipping lower. Shadows from the trees on the river bank reached almost across the Frio.

Grandma Birdie, the little girl, could hear her heart beating.

But . . . no more screams.

The wide-eyed horse had stopped splashing and snorting and straining. Its ears twitched back and forth as it looked at the far river bank.

Then, at long last, Grandpa Hart was there, riding bareback on the team horse.

Riding beside him was a mighty welcome sight -- a rescuing rancher, mounted on a big horse. And the rancher was leading a team of mules.

In hushed but hurried tones, Grandma Hart told the men about the screams.

Grandpa Hart squinted his eyes and started looking quickly around.

But the rancher laughed and said: "Ma'am, that had to have been a panther. It was probably just talking to its mate out in the brush."

He said that during the quiet period after the screaming stopped, the panther was probably watching the struggling horse and the mother and child in the wagon. The rancher figured when the beast heard the noisy team of mules and the two men on horseback coming, it just moved on off into the brush. No big deal in those times and in places, he grinned.

After they pulled the wagon out of the Frio River gravel, Grandma Birdie -- your great-great-grandmother -- with her dad and mom, came on to Del Rio where she grew up, married, had a son, and grandkids, including me.

And she told my brothers and sister and me about The Screaming Woman.

So I could tell the tale to you.

And you -- later on -- can tell it to your kids and grandkids.

The Lady and the Lamp

Aunt Beth and Uncle Lucious lived in a house by the side of the road. It was a small ranch house up on the divide by the Pecos River. The divide is the high, relatively flat area between two or more deep canyons. The little-used, two-rut ranch road crossing the divide towards the Pecos vega ran almost right up against the west side of the house.

All that means many things. But for this tale, it is important to note that this young newly-married couple, who had started their married life living in a cave on their ranch, at the time of this tale lived far out in rough, rugged, and remote West Texas. Town was a long way off. Visitors were few and far between.

Starting a depression era ranch in the early 1930's meant that gasoline money was hard to come by. Nevertheless, Aunt Beth and Uncle Lucious drove their old pickup to Comstock almost every Sunday morn for church.

And that meant a Saturday night bath.

Their little house had a screened-in front porch and four rooms: a southeast corner living room, two bedrooms on the west side, and a northeast kitchen/dining room. No closets. But there was a big semi-finished attic which provided storage for clothes, groceries, saddles, etc. The outhouse was fifty yards northwest of the kitchen door and the barn and pens were another fifty yards to the northeast.

No electricity. No hot water heater. No indoor bathroom.

So, for the Saturday night bath -- or any other baths -- water heated in the kettle on the wood cook stove in the kitchen was combined with water piped to the kitchen sink from the windmill tank. In a big wash tub on the kitchen floor.

On this particular late summer Saturday evening, Uncle Lucious bathed first. Then, as it was beginning to get dark, Aunt Beth lit the kitchen kerosene lamp and began her bath.

Uncle Lucious put on his pants and, needing something from the attic, went upstairs in the fading evening light to fetch whatever it was he hankered for -- barefooted, shirtless, and without a light.

The outside kitchen door was in the center of the north end of the house. A rock walk ran at ground level from that door to the stairs to the attic. These steep, exposed steps were outside the house, going from the northeast corner up to the attic door just above the outside kitchen door.

Aunt Beth was just stepping into the wash tub on the kitchen floor when Uncle Lucious, stumbling about in the semi-dark attic, felt a sharp pain in his foot.

Fearing a snake bite, he screeched for Aunt Beth to bring a light.

Having been bitten by a rattlesnake when she was a toddler, Aunt Beth viewed any potential or real snake bite as an extreme emergency. Her reaction was immediate and spontaneous.

Aunt Beth jumped out of the tub, grabbed the kerosene lamp off the kitchen table, ran out the kitchen door, dashed barefooted over to the foot of the steps, and -- without a stitch of clothing, holding the lamp, halfway up the steps -- she saw -- in the little road by the side of the house -- three men on horseback.

She froze. Didn't know whether to go up or down.

The sun was setting behind the riders and she couldn't see their faces, but they were still as statues also. Staring at the lady and the lamp.

Uncle Lucious yelled again for a light.

She ran on up the remaining steps to the attic.

By lamp light, they were able to determine he had been bitten not by a snake, but by a scorpion. Bad, but not death threatening.

Concluding that Uncle Lucious was not about to die from snake bite, Aunt Beth told him about the riders and her spotlight performance on the stairs.

Uncle Lucious anxiously limped over to the attic door.

The three riders were disappearing into the sunset -- silhouettes against the Western sky.

After Uncle Lucious went down and brought her some clothing, a shaken and apprehensive Aunt Beth hurried back down and into the house.

Uncle Lucious and Aunt Beth did a lot of speculating, but they really never knew for sure who the three horsemen were. It almost had to have been neighbors. But, then . . . maybe not. And, if not? Who?

But, whoever they were, those Three Mystery Riders of the West were gentlemen. They didn't tell the tale of the Lady and the Lamp.

And . . . neither did Uncle Lucious and Aunt Beth for a long time.

The Boots

Back in those golden olden days, folks from neighboring ranches in our neck of the woods -- family, friends, neighbors, and hired hands -- would get together to help with the more intensive work that was necessary each Spring and Fall. Oh, there was plenty of work all the time, but in a livestock operation, whether it was cattle, sheep, or what have you, and whether they were avoiding summer heat or winter frosts, they gathered Spring and Fall, and the larger group was able to divvy up the various tasks and do the roundup, marking, shearing -- the whole she-bang -- better that way.

Usually the work started before daylight and went right on through into the dusk and evening hours. But right after the noontime meal, scanty as it might be, there was a short period of rest. After the nap, siesta, forty-winks, or shut-eye time, it was "up and at 'em" for the whole crew, men, boys, ladies, and gals.

Uncle Lucious used to love to tell the story about the time when he and some of his brothers -- Carroll, Sullivan, and/or Charlie -- had more than just a smattering of fun.

When the men folk sacked out -- in the shade, under the shed, on the porch, or wherever -- most of them just snoozed those precious moments with their boots on. In those days boots had higher heels -- to keep a rider's foot from going through the stirrup. Boot tops were almost knee high. Some were pretty snug around the calf, to protect the horseman's legs as he rode through the thorny hills and arroyos of Southwest Texas.

Some of the older men would sometimes persuade one of the young progeny to assist him in taking off his boots so the breeze could cool his toes. This occasionally had an irksome effect on some of the young boot pullers.

One of those keen-eyed boys had observed -- and shared the info with his fellow conspirators -- that one of their uncles always followed an unusual routine when he put his boots back on.

"Uncle Frank", as we will call him for this tale, (Uncle Lucious didn't really have an Uncle Frank, you know) would carefully take off his boots and carefully stand them side by side, always upright, close by his roosting place. When he woke, he never varied his putting the boots on method.

He picked up the left boot, stuck his fingers in the leg loops, and slowly eased that foot into the long-legged boot. Then -- he would stand up, reach down and grab the loops of the other boot without picking it up, lift his foot up enough to clear the high boot top, slam his newly rested right foot into the boot, and then stomp both feet on the ground, the shed floor, the porch or whatever was the surface he was standing on.

Now, please note, dear reader, that this was a far different technique from that followed by most folks back then. Nearly all had learned to cautiously pick up their foot gear one at a time, shake vigorously, and slap hard once or twice to shoo out scorpions and other nasties that might be lurking for a surprise attack. Then you put it on.

On the day of infamy, the Hinds boys lay around where they could keep one eye closed and the other peeled for the anticipated action. One of their number -- he who drew the black bean -- tiptoed up with a coffee can full of water and poured it in Uncle Frank's upright right boot.

Just the right boot. Not the left.

Then they waited.

Sure 'nuff, when Uncle Lucious' dad, Levi Hinds, called that it was time to go back to work, Uncle Frank rolled over, sat up and began his usual unusual booting routine.

When he socked that right foot into that high top boot, a gusher of water sloshed up into his chest and face.

He gasped and staggered back. The bench he had been lying on caught him behind the knees. He fell. The old wood of the bench splintered.

Uncle Frank bounced right straight up -- into a blue haze of volcanic profanity he was shoveling out to the whole wide world of West Texas and Northern Mexico. He had something mighty unkind to say about the perforated purple perfidy of pusillanimous little step ants.

The Hinds boys' plans to keep it cool just evaporated in snorts, gasps, and gurgles of laughter. That ran Uncle Frank's caliber of cuss words up about ten more notches.

Needless to say, it was never exactly pinned down which of those rapscallions was the boot filler.

But Uncle Frank knew it was one of those little "Hinds Hellers", and that they were all in it together.

So . . . being a devious and resourceful man himself -- and -- after all -- kith and kin to those pesky Hinds boys . . .

Well, you know the rest of the story.

And, of course, Uncle Lucious also loved to tell how "Uncle Frank" repaid his nephews.

But, that's another tale to tell.

Ranch Plumbing

Aunt Beth really and truly wanted to rescue her trapped mother-in-law. But she just couldn't.

She was laughing so hard at Scottie Hinds' "situation" that the tears were flowing down her cheeks. She knew she absolutely could not afford to be laughing like that -- or even at all -- when she released Uncle Lucious' short-statured, almost red-headed, usually good-natured, but presently mad-as-a-wet-hen mother from her dastardly predicament.

So, Aunt Beth stood there just inside the screen door of the little ranch house and tried to calm her rampant emotions so that she could run out there to the outhouse and effect Scottie's escape.

As she watched her new mother-in-law's short, freckled arm vainly flailing the air, she knew exactly what had happened.

An outhouse -- or privy, if you will -- that is properly engineered and constructed always has an escape mechanism. But it wasn't working for Mrs. Hinds.

A well-built privy, especially one sprouting out of the flat, rocky, wind-swept terrain of the divide country next to the Pecos River, had to have at least two door fasteners.

The inside door keep was a board pegged to the inside wall with a single large nail. The board rotated on that spike so that it could be swung up and over and dropped into the holder on the inside of the door. That inside holder was fashioned from a short piece of board overlaid with a longer board so that it was a top-open slot the keeper board could fall into. This part of the edifice insured the privacy of the occupant or occupants (for the two-holer or sometimes the even more luxurious three-holer outhouses).

On the outside, there had to be a similar device to keep the door closed when there was no one inside. Otherwise, coons, snakes, spiders, wasps, owls, tarantulas, and other oddly-inclined visitors could be laying in wait for the sometimes hurried legitimate users of the little building. And up there on the divide where the wind blew freshly to fiercely almost all the time, if you failed to peg the door closed when there was no occupant, the best hinges of the time just weren't up to that kind of abuse.

Oh yes, there was also another fastener rigged on some privies by thoughtful folks. Using it, you could prop the door open while you were inside -- for the air conditioning effect. Rarely used in the winter time, but it was quite handy when the sun shone with West Texas intensity in July, August, and September.

You have surely observed what some have considered artful cutouts in the doors and sides of these unique structures. The stars, moons, quarter-moons, and sometimes misshapen squares, rectangles, and even triangular holes in the walls were there for -- you guessed it -- ventilation first -- fancy decoration second.

The opening in the door usually was multi-purposed. It let air in and out all right. But it also allowed the user to see if anyone was approaching. When there were kids around, -- especially mischievous, calculating boy-types -- it behooved all occupants to be alert for chicane trickery.

It's shattering to be jarred from the serene realms of contemplative daydreams by the crash of a fist-sized dirt clod against the wooden side of your protective privacy -- er -- ah -- privy.

The most important function of that hole in the door, however, was to let the person inside unhook the outside latch if it inadvertently became fastened.

All of Uncle Lucious' brothers -- Carrol, Sullivan, and especially Charlie -- took after their dad, Levi Hinds, insofar as their height was concerned. Uncle Lucious and one of the sisters, Alvia Mae, were the recipients of Scottie's shorter Ingram family genes. (Marjorie was in between.)

When the gust of wind slammed the privy door on Mrs. Hinds that day, she was in deep trouble and she knew it. It mattered not whether she stood tippy-toed on the floor or up on the front edge of the plank board seat. She just couldn't quite reach out the quarter-moon opening in the door and get to the latch board that had been flopped over by the tooth-rattling door slam. The piece of wire that usually hung inside which could be used to slip between the door and the jam to flip the outside latch up was somehow missing. She didn't have a clasp knife in her apron pocket. Men and boys always carried a knife that could be used to open the door in similar circumstances.

Scottie Hinds was ranch-raised. After she got excited and all worked up, the volume of her squawks for aid had risen to a marvelously high and sharply inflected pitch. But her yells were, she thought, being carried away from the house by the buffeting spring-time southeast winds.

Finally, when Scottie took off her apron, stuck it through the hole in the door, and started flapping it in the wind, Aunt Beth was enabled -- nay, compelled -- to go out and open the privy door. But she never told Mrs. Hinds how long it took her to do it.

Lots of ranch plumbing was superlatively efficient like that.

Aunt Beth was born and raised at Bakers Crossing. By the time I started roaming around out there in the early 1930's, the original two small rock rooms had grown into a two-story, six-bedroom structure with screened sleeping porches. It boasted a fully functional bathroom.

That lonesome downstairs bathroom was quite small. It had a single lavatory, a solitary claw-footed iron bath tub, and one honest-to-gosh flushing toilet. A wash stand was near the hydrant out on the front porch -- next to the dining room and kitchen. Its two wash basins, lye or lava soap, and towels on the nearby rack served all comers for hand, face, neck, and behind-the-ear washing. Tooth brushing, too.

Sometimes one of the men even shaved there with hot water from the kettle on the kitchen stove and a little mirror hung on a nail in the towel rack post.

But how in the ever-lovin'-blue-eyed world were the occupants of all those upstairs and downstairs bedrooms toilet-accommodated -- especially on cold winter nights?

Well, sir, every bedroom had a fancy or rustic furnishing that had a wash basin, a water pitcher, a towel rack, a towel, a wash rag, and a neat little built-in closet that housed a squatty pot with its lid. Uncle Jim called those contraptions thunder mugs. Uncle Pete said they were jolly jars.

As my brother and I matured to the requisite ages of six or seven -- we developed serious and severe dislikes for those slop jars and we had some descriptive names of our own for them.

You see, Bud and I, as Papo and Mamo's first grandkids to come along, were drafted -- conscripted might be a better word -- into a morning emptying service.

Uncle Jim called us conscientious objectors. When we hinted rebellion, Uncle Pete worried that we might be having chronic constipation contractions. Papo, who always asked us every morning: "Boys, how do your dybogilators groshuate today?" said maybe ours were acting up on us. Mamo sternly explained -- with a sparkle in her eye -- how much good our "duty" did us.

Bud and I lost out on our argument that any "good" we were doing was for a bunch of lazy thunder mug thumpers.

Besides. We just found it mighty hard to believe that some folks preferred using those cold crockery jugs or enamelware containers when it was so much easier and more comfortable out behind the fences in back of the barn.

It also came to our young and sprightly attention, that in the winter time at our grandparents' place at Bakers Crossing there were long spells between baths. To which we did not object. It was ok with us that during the warmer months, the near-by beckoning of the gurgling currents of Devils River contributed to reasonable body washing. Mamo and the older ladies seemed to still be attracted to the bathroom. We kids, the uncles, and most of the aunts used the river.

Come to think of it, I just don't remember Papo ever bathing, but I guess he did. I always liked to sit in his lap. Maybe the Prince Albert smoke from his old crook-stemmed pipe did the job.

After Uncle Pete and Aunt Joy were married, however, I found it -- in those days of my youth -- puzzling that they always took off after supper with a towel, a bar of store-bought soap, and clean duds and hiked way off through the garden and the water lot to a secluded place. Where the river ran swiftly through some shallows. Next to a nice wide area of flat rocks. The water was colder at night. Howsomever, the flat rocks were still warm to be on when you got out to dry off. They always returned late. Squeaky clean and jay-bird happy.

Back when Uncle Lucious and Aunt Beth got married-- in the depths of the depression -- they took up residence on their first ranch out on the Pecos without a lot of comforts and extras. They lived in a cave. It was a wind-carved rock shelter under a bluff on the side of a hill -- probably used by Indians way back in the beginning days. Uncle Lucious rigged a canvas tarp at one end to give a little more protection from the elements, carried a set of bed springs and a mattress in for their sleeping, set up a small cast iron wood stove for cooking, and they made do.

The main problem was the plumbing. The absolute, teetotal lack of it. Uncle Lucious packed water up to the cave every day in a couple of buckets.

After the guy they bought the ranch from scraped together enough dinero to haul himself off to other climes, Uncle Lucious moved their few belongings into the little four room ranch house up on the divide and Aunt Beth had her own kitchen.

But plumbing was still scant. Water was piped via an iron pipe down to the house -- over the rocky mesa from the tank at the barn where the windmill was. That pipe ran more on top of the ground than under it. In only a few stretches was it covered with dirt. More of it than not lay on top of the hard, stony ground -- only covered partly with loose rocks. That single pipe ran water through a hole in the kitchen wall to a faucet over the kitchen sink.

Oh, they had hot and cold running water, all right. Hot in the summer and cold in the winter.

But no toilet or commode. No lavatory. No bath tub. No shower. In mild weather, Uncle Lucious shaved at the wash stand just outside the kitchen. On bad days, at the kitchen sink. Baths were weekly events with a big wash tub on the kitchen floor or up at the barn behind the water tank.

In another Chip Tale -- The Lady and The Lamp -- you'll find a recounting of Aunt Beth's infamous Saturday night wash tub bath.

When they sold their Pecos ranch in the early 1940's and began again the long process of paying out their Devils River ranch, the move was -- of course -- motivated mostly by the chance to have ranching country that was not as rough and hard to work. I think it was also prompted by the newer ranch house having an indoor bathroom.

At the Devils River place, Aunt Beth and Uncle Lucious were living a lot closer to the lap of luxury. That indoor bath room had a lavatory, a commode, a claw-footed cast iron bath tub, AND a tin-walled shower. The shower was a bit narrow. Men bumped their shoulders turning under the shower spray. I often wondered why most of the women preferred the tub.

But again, the water pipe ran from the water tank located near the windmill at the barn. It came a good hundred yards to the house over the divide -- alternately under and over the rocky-soiled surface. During the day, from June to September, water flowing through that pipe from the tank at the barn to the house was solar-heated to near scalding temperatures. At their new ranch, summer bathing was done more often, but usually well after sundown or early in the morn when the water pipe had cooled.

That super hot bath water was a real contrast to their last winter at the old Pecos place before they moved. About mid-November that year they were visited a Texas Blue Norther. The kind old time trail drivers told hairy stories about being caught in.

Out there at the Pecos place, when Uncle Lucious knew or thought he knew that it was going to freeze before morning he would turn off the water up at the barn and drain that long pipe. He didn't do that unless it was necessary to keep pipes from freezing and splitting. It was a chore to cut the water off and draw water at the house in order to have it for coffee and cooking the next morning. Also, it was not his favorite passion to have to get out of bed on a cold morning and trudge up to the barn to turn the water back on.

The first night of this late-fall cold snap caught ranchers all over Val Verde County by surprise. Back then, the nearest U.S. of A. government weather prognosticator worked up on top of the Federal Building in Del Rio. And in those days he didn't send out radio reports.

Uncle Lucious did not expect a freeze. At least, not a hard freeze. So he did not turn off the water and drain the pipe. Just to be safe, however, before she turned in for the night, Aunt Beth cracked the faucet to let the water slowly drip into the kitchen sink.

It was important that the drip be carefully calculated and adjusted. Unless it was a hard freeze, just a trickle was all that was needed to keep water in the pipe from freezing. But the flow had to be kept small -- to conserve water. When the fickle wind failed, the old wooden-vane windmill often had a tough time pumping enough into the tank to water all the livestock.

Sometime before daylight the next morning, Aunt Beth -- the light sleeper -- awoke to the unpleasant sound of water splashing a bit too loudly in the kitchen. She poked Uncle Lucious awake, scrambled out from under the pile of quilts, and dashed to give her precious kitchen whatever aid she could render. As she crossed the linoleum floored kitchen, she choked out an anguished squeal to Uncle Lucious that there was icy water all over the floor.

Water was still dripping from the faucet. But the sink drain which ran through the kitchen wall and over the outside ground to their little garden plot had frozen. There was a solid block of ice in the sink that the water was dripping onto and running off onto the floor.

Aroused from his usual bear-like, winter-time deep slumber by her cry, Uncle Lucious yelled, "Don't turn off the water!"

Too late.

Aunt Beth's instinctive reaction to the sound of water splashing on her kitchen floor was to grab the handle of the misbehaving sink faucet and twist it shut.

Almost immediately she realized why Uncle Lucious had hollered not to turn the water off.

In that momentary blink of time between her jamming the faucet handle as far closed as she could until she tried to yank it back open -- the water pipe had frozen. Solid.

Uncle Lucious had to pack water again.

It was a week before it warmed enough in the daytime for the water pipe to thaw so they could once more have running water at the house.

Pitchfork Fishing

My brother, Bud, and I inwardly groaned and outwardly cat-smiled when Aunt Beth told us at breakfast that, after the morning chores at the barn, we would be going with Uncle Lucious to the garden.

Uncle Lucious and Aunt Beth, as I have told you, or will tell in another tale, began their young married life in midst of The Depression on much less than a shoe string. They first lived in a cave. (But, that's part of another story).

From the start, however, no matter what, they always had a garden.

The garden, of course, was a necessity in those times and in those remote places where they lived. But always, their gardens were truly joyous to them. They craved and savored fresh vegetables and fruits.

It was a different story for Bud and me, visiting them in the summers. For us, the dinner table pleasures were much more than offset by the agonies of weeding, gathering, and, most of all, watering the garden.

This was never truer than at their first ranch, located up on the wind-swept divide east of the Pecos River. The divide is a relatively flat area between canyons draining a hilly region.

The divide's rocky soil was too thin for a much of a garden, but down in the vega -- the bottom land next to the river -- there was fine sandy loam washed up by river rises. So, they had a River Garden.

In those days, their financial condition was about as thin as the divide soil, so funds were not available for sophisticated or costly watering equipment. The garden irrigation system they used was: haul water-filled, five-gallon buckets up, hand over hand by rope, from the river the twenty feet or so to garden level, carry it to the planted rows, and tip the heavy buckets to pour the life-giving muddy Pecos River water slowly (not to wash the soil too much) on or next to the corn, tomatoes, squash, beans, etc.

In the midst of the June, July, and August, the Pecos River vega, can be as hot as it gets in West Texas. And, of course, in those summers visiting nephews were dubiously designated as number one type assistants in this delightful garden watering job.

At the ranch in the early 1930's, there was no electricity and the only communication received from the outside world between rare visits to town came via a battery-powered radio. And they conserved the batteries, so we didn't get daily weather reports or other news. We had not heard of any rains upstream on the Pecos, but the Pecos is a long river, winding its way from eastern New Mexico thru West Texas on its way to its meeting with the Rio Grande.

So, on that clear, cloudless, but relatively cool early summer morning, we loaded the ole pickup with buckets, rope, hoes, a couple of baskets, and a pitch fork and took off.

It all began very pleasantly, bouncing along over the rocky, but relatively smooth divide "road" from the house to the river canyon.

Uncle Lucious always had great stories to tell about "the olden days" and he was a good teacher. Looking back, it's amazing how adroitly he wove the things we needed to know in with the things we wanted to hear. Listening to his tales, back-grounded by the chorus of rattles from the pickup and the tools and gear in the back, the time passed quickly from the barn to the rimrock overlooking the Pecos River.

The road down the side of the canyon wall into the river bottom area -- the vega -- was much rougher, almost tortuous. Once in the vega, though, we had almost a two-rut, mostly sandy highway as the ole pickup carried us upstream beside the river.

It was a surprise to discover the Pecos running several feet high and its waters more than usually choked with mud and trash from some upstream rains we had not been aware of.

About half a mile up the vega, a small, short, no-name creek dumped its crystal clear water a couple of hundred yards from its spring down the bed of a side canyon until it joined the Pecos.

That darn spring water always fooled you. You would ride along, hot and thirsty, come to that beautiful, clear, cool water and flop down on your belly to soak up some it. Then you would spit and mash your lips with the back of your hand, trying to get the sulfur taste out of your mouth. But it was drinkable, and that's more than you could say about the muddy Pecos.

The up-river road to the garden required us to ford the creek (drive across and thru the water), just before we got to the garden.

On this day, when we got to the crossing, the creek, from the river on our left as far as we could see to our right, was absolutely full of fish. Bank to bank, side by side, all headed away from the muddy Pecos toward the clear spring. It looked like we could drive or walk across on the backs of those jam-packed fish. Nearly all of them were carp or buffalo.

Uncle Lucious explained to his goggle-eyed nephews that the fish were packed into the clear spring water trying to escape the muddy Pecos where there was so much dirt and debris that they could only breathe with great difficulty.

He then announced: "Boys, we are going fishing!"

"How?" we wondered. We had not brought fishing gear. No hooks, no lines, no nets, no seines, nothing.

Well, would you believe it? Uncle Lucious started taking off all his clothes, shirt, jeans, boots, even his shorts. He only had on his wide-brimmed straw hat.

I was always astonished when one of my uncles undressed for a swim or a bath in the Pecos or Devils River. Their hands, faces, neck, and a small vee-shaped area at the top of their chests were very brown, from an outdoor life under the Texas sun. But the rest of their body skin was quite white. Uncle Lucious, whose hair had a definite cast of red before it turned grey, did have some freckles, but he stood out like a light-house in the fog that day with nothing else to go with them but that curly-brimmed hat.

"Get the buckets out of the pickup," he said, as he took the pitchfork and walked barefooted over to the creek. "When I pitch the fish out on the bank you boys catch them and put them in the buckets."

He began to make big swooping scoops with the pitchfork under and up through the massed fish in the creek. The fish tried to swim away from him, but there was really no room for them to go. So, although most of the fish he brought out with each scoop fell back into water, some flopped around on the rocks of the bank until Bud and I could get to them and catch them.

Most of the fish we captured were large, weighing several pounds. Bud and I each wanted to catch fish with a pitchfork and Uncle Lucious let us try, but we weren't very good at it.

When we had several fish in a bucket, we would dump them into one of the baskets in the back of the pickup. When we had a basket full, Uncle Lucious laughed and said, "That's enough."

Then the fun was over and we had to clean fish.

Again, Bud and I were students of new learning. Uncle Lucious, explaining once more, showed us that these carp and or buffalo were much bonier than bass or catfish and the best way to prepare them for cooking was to simply cut strips of flesh from between the ribs. So, with his pocket knife, he did so, while Bud and I chunked the unusable body portions into the Pecos for the gar to dispose of.

The garden work was as hot and laborious as always, but it seemed to go faster that day. Uncle Lucious helped us more with the watering, spent less time cultivating, and, after we gathered the ripened garden growth, we went back, over and thru the fish-filled creek, up the canyon-climbing road, and back to the ranch.

Aunt Beth was, of course, amazed at our story of pitchfork fishing.

But she was very much up to the task of turning the unexpected fish bounty we brought home it into the best croquettes I've ever eaten before or since.

(Croquettes, dearly beloved, I've been asked to remind you, are small rounded gobs of fish, coated with breadcrumbs and deep fried.)

The Ice Plant Lake

In 1874 Herman M. Block, with his wife, Janie Sampson Block and ten-year old son, Edwin Sampson Block, moved from Brackettville and Fort Clark to Del Rio. Then, or shortly thereafter, he bought a three-acre plot on San Felipe Creek. It was located at the end of a dirt road now named Strickland Street and was bounded on the east by the creek. One of the Madre Ditch offshoots that exited the mother ditch at Mills Street flowed along the west side of the place. Another ditch, carrying water from the Tardy Dam, ran through the property just above the crest of the creek bank.

Greatgrampa Block's original home was a four-room adobe building. Over the years he expanded it, attaching a bathroom with indoor fixtures for Grandma, constructing a kitchen and dining room, and finally adding a screened sleeping porch. That sleeping porch is an important part of this tale.

My granddad, Edwin Sampson Block, grew up there. He married Emma Lee Hart and they bought the three-acre property her dad and mother, Benjamin T. Hart and Emily P. Hart, had built up. It fronted on Martin Street and was bounded on the south by the Madre Ditch. Babo and Grandma Birdie improved the Martin Street place over the years and beautified the area along and near the irrigation ditch.

Greatgrampa Block gave the Strickland Street property to my dad, Edwin Hart Block, when he married mom (Lois Emeline Baker). So I and my two brothers, Edwin Hart Block, Jr. (Bud) and Lee Sampson

Block, and my sister, Shirley Adele Block, grew up along the sides of and often in the creek and irrigation ditches of Del Rio.

In the early years of my childhood -- the early 1930's -- there was a dam across the creek just upstream of the Academy Street Bridge. Water was impounded and channeled through a concrete flume into The Ice Plant. Ice manufactured at the plant was a wonderful commodity distributed all over our town by ice trucks. Before we had refrigerators, people kept food from spoiling by storing perishables in iceboxes. Chunks of ice went into an insulated box on the top of a furnishing that had another insulated section below for milk, butter, food, etc. The "ice men" had regular routes, just like postmen, and delivered on a regular schedule so folks could replenish the ice for their iceboxes.

When the railroad advanced in sophistication to refrigerated passenger cars and then ice-cooled freight cars, the ice plant turned out big 300 pound blocks of ice in sufficient quantity to cool the folks and the produce transported from coast to coast by the Southern Pacific Railway. The big blocks went into containers under the passenger cars, into hoppers at the ends of the freight cars, and fans circulated air over the ice and into the areas to be cooled.

The best feature of that dam, though, was the small lake it created. Right in my back yard.

Water was backed up and spread over a wide area, mostly to the east, between the dam and upstream some little bit beyond the old iron-framed, wooden-decked Canal Street Bridge.

The banks of the creek were not clogged with the rampant, out-of-control growth of river cane that is now the curse of the creek. We could see all the way over to Plaza Brown from our yard. There was easy access to the cool clear creek waters for swimming and frolicking. Boats and canoes sometimes were rowed and paddled by youngsters and often by fisher folk.

Also, in those days, the neat custom of the siesta was still evident -- even sometimes prevalent. Mothers were mostly stay-at-home moms then and most of them were seriously inclined to this practice. Of course, they had another name for the ritual. It was called "napping".

Shortly after the noon-day meal, -- especially in the summer -- kids were put down for the count. Had to take a nap whether you needed it or not. And, wouldn't you know it? Moms usually had to lie down beside the youngsters to calm them down enough for sleep to come. I just happen to know that Mama also sometimes succumbed to the artful tricks of the sand man. Just forty winks, of course.

One such summer afternoon, with Bud and Shirley, I was snoozing on that sleeping porch which Greatgrampa Block so thoughtfully provided those many moons earlier. Ever so reluctantly, mind you, but benefiting nevertheless from breezes wafting our way over the ice-house lake.

Suddenly, a gosh-awful, ear-jarring noise jerked me right up off my sweaty cot. It was coming from the creek. We jumped up, ran out in the yard, and we could see it. Roaring down the creek, just coming out from under the Canal Street Bridge. Just one tarnation-loud little wooden boat. Going faster than I had ever seen a boat go.

There was only one guy in the boat. Looked like he was in a heck of a tussle with something trying to come over the tail end of the boat. That's where the noise was coming from. The thing hanging over the back of the boat -- half in and half out -- was making all that blamed racket.

The boat ran down the lake -- close to our side -- almost to the ice-house dam, swung left, went almost to the far end of the dam, and turned back up the lake.

Mama was out in the yard by that time and she started waving her apron at the guy in the boat.

That rascal waved back with one hand while he hung on with the other to that thing at the back of his boat. Like he was riding a mean horse. The roaring never let up a lick.

The boat and the guy and the noise maker roared back under the bridge and around the bend of the creek. The noise tapered off and then died.

We looked at Mama, who was still holding her apron, and asked, "What was that?"

"Motor boat", she smiled. "Now go back and finish your nap."

Moms are like that. They think three jabbering little kids -- goggle-eyed over an ear-jarring first time to ever meet up with a motor driven boat -- right in your own back yard -- could just lay down and go back to sleep!

The Mulberry Tree

Let me tell you about the Great Mulberry Tree.

As did most early folks in Del Rio, Great-Grampa Block planted exceedingly well all over his wonderfully sub-irrigated three-acre home site at the end of East Strickland Street down by San Felipe Creek.

There were pecan trees, walnut trees, date palm trees, persimmon trees, fig trees, grape vines, pomegranate hedges, honeysuckle, and mulberry trees.

Of all those trees, The Mulberry Tree was my favorite. It was old long before I came into the family. Located just steps away from the back porch, its broad green leaves were a splendid umbrella. Shady in summer. Light rains didn't penetrate. So, from the time my brothers, my sister, and I were tykes, beneath it there were little roads for toy cars, miniature adobe forts and trenches for tin soldiers, water gun fights, mud pie kitchens, etc.

The Mulberry Tree had a massive, gnarled trunk. Although the tree limbs were relatively smooth, the trunk bark was bumpy. Real bumpy! Big swells and swirls and layers of grayish-brown bark crowded and overlapped from the ground level roots up to about ten feet where most of the limbs started. It was a super place to hide behind in any kind of game -- from Hide and Seek, to Kick the Can, to Capture the Flag, to what have you.

When we were younger, that big knotty trunk was much too round and the lowest branches were much too high for us to climb. But as we grew -- although the tree was becoming bigger also -- we found ways to get up into the limbs.

And there were lots of limbs. Every spring new ones appeared. Every summer, there were bigger and smaller limbs all over the tree for us to climb among.

I was about ten and Bud was eight, when we discovered a secret place -- an inner sanctum -- in that Mulberry Tree! We had not known about it before! The new tender leafy limbs appeared yearly at the upper edge of that big old bumpy trunk. In the center of the tree, larger old growth limbs seemed to become brittle and die. Outer limbs and leaves almost walled off an inner opening on top of the trunk and under the larger limb leaves.

Shirley then was about seven years old and Lee was about four. So, for a spell, Bud and I had that secret place mostly all to ourselves.

Of course, we were absolutely compelled to improve upon our tree hideout.

After considerable conspiratorial cogitation, Bud and I started to very selectively thin dead branches and limbs. We opened inner space; without much damage, in our opinion, to the outer, screening foliage. And, we could do most of it by just breaking off the old stuff.

But, when we wanted to take out some of the live limbs, we hit a serious snag. A parental permission problem. As problems go, permission problems -- especially parental -- are the worst kind for kids.

Mama made scrumptious jelly, jams, preserves, etc. from the grapes, figs, dates, and, other bounty from the trees and vines on Great-Grampa Block's place on the creek. And, as you might have guessed, in Mama's mind, The Mulberry Tree was a fruit tree!

Not even Kit Carson, Wild Bill Hickock or Hopalong Cassidy would have been allowed to lop limbs off of any of those fruit trees! And, even though we ate mulberries, I can't recall a single jar of anything labeled "Mulberry". Never-you-mind, no live limbs off of The Mulberry Tree!

But, we still had the ok to climb the tree, if we were careful not to fall or break off the limbs.

It really escapes me how it happened, but as we clambered around in the upper levels of the tree, some of the limbs and branches in the middle area of the canopy became badly bent, were somehow irreparably bruised, and sometimes --necessarily -- discarded. Only with regret, you understand.

Sometime during the winter after our first summer in the Mulberry Tree Hideout -- with the tree bare of leaves and more open for our investigative inspections -- Bud and I had an inspiration -- a really magnificent idea. There was some old lumber stashed up in the barn loft that wasn't going anywhere and needed to be used somehow.

So hatched The Plan.

After lots of begging, Daddy said we could use some -- just a few -- of the old boards in the tree. Mama said that was ok as long as we did NOT nail into any of the live limbs or the trunk. And, oh, by the way, BE CAREFUL!

So began The Tree House.

First, a few crisscrossed boards laid as close to level as possible in the maze of limbs and branches. It really wasn't very level, but what the heck.

Our classic construction was more or less that of the birds we had watched building nests. Lay a piece of two-by four here, add a piece of one by something there, stick in a chunk under or between this and that to wedge or level . . . And since we couldn't nail into the tree, we substituted by wrapping and tying with old rope, binder twine, cord, even leather scraps.

So The Tree House grew.

Along about July of that summer Bud and I noticed a lot of board ends sticking out into the air around the edges of our tree house platform. It looked jagged; needed tidying up. Permission was granted to take a saw up into the tree to cut off some of the board ends jutting out. No hammer, though. But, TAKE CARE ! ! !

And all went well for a bit. I would saw some and Bud would saw some and we would rest some and talk some and saw some more and . . .

Then, disaster struck a heavy blow.

It hurt Bud more than it did me, of course, but really, it was painful to us both.

At the dizzying height at which we worked, at least a dozen or more feet in the stratosphere, Bud stepped back just one little step to take a better look at our shaping of the perimeter of the tree house platform. And he stepped on a board end we had almost nearly, but not quite hardly, sawed off.

Well, sir, I forgot to tell you earlier that The Mulberry Tree had the most conglomerated mess of big old twisted roots growing around each other and into the ground that you probably ever saw. All around the base of the tree, roots were exposed before they plunged into the ground. And these roots were just as gnarled and bumpy, but rougher and harder than the trunk.

Bud lit smack on the side of his head on one of those rough bumpy roots!

I thought he was killed.

I yelled for Mama. She came out the back door, wiping her hands on her apron, and started screaming just as soon as she saw Bud laying there not moving on top of that pile of roots.

Well, he wasn't killed. Just almost.

By the time they got ole Bud to Dr. Ross's office just three blocks away, he was letting them know loud and strong that he wasn't dead.

As it turned out, of course, he was as hard headed as I had always known. Didn't break a thing.

He was mighty bruised up, though. The outside of his face was chewed up by the roots, but it was the inside of his mouth that was the worst. Didn't lose any teeth, but between his teeth on the inside and the roots on the outside, the inside of his cheek was chopped up more than I can tell you.

I don't recall what they gave him for his headache, but I do remember what the doctor said was the only thing Bud could eat for awhile because of that chewed up cheek. And I remember how it changed our habits for a time.

I didn't understand why, but because of the fall on his head, Mama made me watch Bud all the time to see that he didn't sleep more than normal.

Because of his sliced up cheek, Bud lived on nothing but prune juice for a couple of weeks and he made a lot more trips than usual to the bathroom.

It was late in the summer before we managed to whine, beg, promise, and I don't know what all to get ourselves back up in The Mulberry Tree. But we did. And the next year it began to grow walls and a roof. And it lasted a long time.

The Hooky Player

I do sorta hesitate to tell you this tale. But then, I guess you know by now that all folks aren't perfect. And that includes me.

My elementary school education went right well for the first three or so years. Miss Sweet was my first grade teacher and she could not have been sweeter or prettier than her name. My grandparents were impressed with her because she was the young unmarried sister of Judge Brian Montegue's wife. But that didn't mean a thing to me. I just liked her more than a bunch.

For second grade, my teacher was Miss Carstarphen. She wasn't married either, and she was a really good teacher, but she wasn't as young as Miss Sweet and I missed Miss Sweet.

Then there was Mrs. Lane for third grade. Good teacher. Up on art. I learned about The Blue Boy and the like. Made a wood carving of a deer; on the end of an apple box. I still have it.

Howsomever, when I got to fourth grade, I began to take a good look at my education and decided I could improve on it. Ten-year-olds are prone to such shenanigans, you know.

My teacher that year was Mrs. Payne. Now don't jump to conclusions. Her name didn't have anything to do with the arbitrary and equivocal -- you more level-headed types might call it "unusual" -- tack I decided to take in my quest for learning.

You see, I had been "acing it" those early grade school years. Must have been some slow pokes in my classes. I had never taken home a report card that had anything other than "A's". I was more than mortified when I got an "A minus". It was a walk in the park. And I liked it like that.

But I also like sleeping late and hated to have to hustle my tail to school each morning.

I was living with my grandparents. Their home was right next door to the school yard. All I had to do was hop the fence every day to go to and from school -- morning, noon, and afternoon.

So I hatched up this scheme and told my grandparents that the school had announced a new policy to reward and acknowledge the achievement of outstanding students like myself. The new regs allowed smart kids like me who made all "A's" to only go to school four days a week!

You, of course, will find this quite hard to believe, but don't scoff -- it happened!

My good, trusting, proud as a peacock Grandma Birdie swallowed that baloney "hook, line, and sinker". Babo was doubtful. He asked some pretty pointed questions. I didn't think he was going to go for it, but, amazingly, I suckered him also.

For awhile, things went great. Missed my first Friday and told the teacher the next Monday that I had a stomach ache. Cut the second Friday and gave the teacher another cock and bull story. And, did the same thing for another week or two. But then my balloon popped.

Early in the school day that catastrophic morning, there was a firm knock on Mrs. Payne's fourth grade classroom door. Even before she opened the door I had a sudden hollowness in the pit of my stomach. You of unblemished moral fiber and untarnished goodness might have called it a foreboding. I called it what ever a ten year old kid calls Apprehension of Disaster and Impending Doom.

The door opened. Standing there was the Superintendent of the Whole, Almighty, God-Fearing, and All-Powerful School District! Mr. Bankhead.

Mr. Bankhead was a small man, but he had a humongous reputation. Back in those "good old days", several times a week, twitching ears flinched at the sound of a paddle being applied to some poor kid's rear end. It really echoed in the school building halls. And Mr. Bankhead was said to have a double handled paddle!

Mr. Bankhead asked for me -- Walter Block -- to step out in the hall.

Being a "B" name at the top of the alphabet on the roster, it wasn't unusual for my name to be one of the first called. I waited and hoped to hear him ask Joe Bridges, Tim Cobb, Dick Dudley, Dennis Hart, or some of the other guys in my class to join him in the hall. But he didn't ask for anyone else. Just me.

Later in life I could have handled it better -- been a cool cat. Then I was just plain scared silly.

As soon as I was in the hall, Mr. Bankhead slowly closed the door. I knew I was a goner.

He squatted down on his hunkers and, almost eye-ball to eye-ball, looked at me with icy blue eyes. We were so close together that he had to cock his head back so he could focus on me thru his wire-rimmed bifocals. I know he could hear my heart thumping in my chest!

Then, in a soft voice, he told me that when he had heard of my absences, he had called my grandparents to ask if I had been seriously ill. When they told him how I had tricked them, he told them not to worry, that he would take care of it.

Right there, I knew darn well what "he would take care of it" meant. And I teared up.

Mr. Bankhead told me that playing hooky was sometimes the first step a boy takes as he heads off in the wrong direction. And, he smiled and said he didn't want me to go in the wrong direction. So, would I just promise him that I wouldn't play hooky anymore?

That was the quickest attitude readjustment I ever made.

After that Mr. Bankhead was always top notch with me. And I never played hooky again!

The Wash Tub

Without any shadow of a doubt my grandparents were as good as they possibly get. I'm the obvious evidence to their efforts, and observe how greatly they accomplished.

In Justin Wilson fashion, for my tale telling, I'll refer to my dad's parents -- The Blocks -- as my town grandparents and I'll dub my mom's parents -- the Bakers -- as my country grandparents.

My town grandparents, Edwin Sampson Block (Babo) and Emma Lee Hart Block (Grandma Birdie), provided for their grandkids truly extraordinary things like The Wash Tub, The Sand Box, and The Brick Pile. I must tell you about these simple, ordinary, wonderful things.

On Spring, Summer, and/or Fall days, and under Grandma Birdie's keen and explicit directions, Babo would drag out a big old galvanized wash tub from under the wooden table on the back porch. It had probably been a mighty long time since clothes had been washed in it, but my brothers, my sister, and I happily and often splashed in it during the warmer months of the year.

Oh, we didn't think of it as washing! Heck no! We were creating, crafting, constructing, inventing, and rhapsodizing in the realms of childish mythology and adventure.

That big round wash tub and the wooden apple box beside it under the long wooden table on the back porch were the receptacles of treasures and riches: innumerable tin measuring cups, different sized bottles, multiple and mixed used jars, pound and half-pound empty coffee cans, big and little buckets, old cooking pots, not-so-new sponges, grandma-cleaned tin cans of all shapes and forms, three or four sizes of metal funnels, and a good supply of corks.

On the shaded, breeze-swept, wooden floor of the back porch, located at the southwest corner of the old two-storied house, Babo would hook up the garden hose to the hydrant under the fig tree and fill the tub to overflowing with cool, clear water. In we'd go! One, two, three, or all four of us. Four was some more than crowded, and thus a bit contested, but that was part of the fun.

Just all by yourself, tho, was probably the very best. Then, the imaginations, the mental voyages, the calculations of how many of this it would take to fill that, were uninterrupted and fancy-free.

We had small, simplistic water guns of the time. No plastic toys then. Bet you never had a little pot-metal water pistol, the handle of which was a rubber bulb that, when water-filled and squeezed hard, would blast your friendly foe very effectively.

And when water splashing stimulated a need to do so, we boys could just get out of the tub, walk over to the edge of the porch, and provide the fig tree with an extra-rich dose of soluble weakly basic nitrogenous liquid. The kind all little boys like to share with the bushes. I suspected that Shirley, when she was an elfin sprite, didn't follow girl rules for that situation. Or maybe she did!

Copious splashings and sloshings which escaped The Wash Tub mattered not a whit. They just flowed over to the edge of the porch and off onto the grass. After each wash tub session, it was our prescribed duty to dump water out of the tub, and be sure each container was emptied. The tub was turned upside down to drain. Thing-a-ma-jigs with which we water-played were drained and tossed in the apple box under the porch table.

On cooler days in the Spring and Fall, tho, The Sand Box was a preferred setting. There we dug and shoveled and scooped and did things with sand that rivaled water activities in the wash tub.

The Sand Box was in the back yard between two big huisache trees -- well in range of keen eyes in the kitchen or watchful folks perched on the back porch. The trees were far enough from the sand box that we were only occasionally troubled with their beans or thorns, and they shaded us nicely except for a couple of hours at mid-day.

The Sand Box was located on a cleared area just south of an old water well. The well was some twenty or thirty feet south of the kitchen it had once served. It had been filled and over it was a flat-topped brick and concrete structure measuring about six by six by three feet high. The well cover was both a launching pad for our leaps and jumps into the sand box and a wind-barrier against the cooler breezes of winter blowing from the north.

The "box" holding the sand was made of two by twelve boards; set on edge and, butted each to another, to make a square containment about ten or twelve feet per side. It was, not completely, but quite sufficiently, filled with river sand. From time to time, some helpful soul raked it free of any wind-blown or child-toted debris. About once a year Grandma Birdie saw to it that the sand was sifted through some hardware cloth and a wire screen tacked onto a two by four frame. The living was good there for little kids.

That sand box was the site of unimaginable excavations. Little lead solders fought World Wars in its trenches and the Confederacy Rose Again more than once from behind and within its stick forts. African safaris traversed its sandy deserts. Tired and exhausted hunters sometimes found little oases (created with tin tuna-fish cans buried almost to the top and water filled). Aladdin's magic carpet soared over its dunes. Little cars zoomed its roads. Imagination flourished there.

And then, when we were older, we found The Brick Pile. It was out behind the two-storied garage, under a large mesquite tree, up against the sheltering pomegranate hedge. It had been there for years, but it had been overgrown with grass and shrubbery. Until one exciting day, Grandma Birdie had the yard man expose it and we received her blessing to play therein.

I don't know why Babo and/or Grandma Birdie had saved those bricks. I'm not sure they had a reason, other than to save them for us. But how grand it was when we "found" those bricks! There must have been several hundred of them. Just a mess of regular old red clay building bricks. But that was before we had access to them. After that, it was "The Brick Pile".

Our pretentious and portentous playing projects in The Brick Pile were of longer duration than the splashing dips in The Wash Tub and burrowing digs in The Sand Box. We started out with simple things like just plain brick stacks. Later on, the ways and manners we stacked and arranged the bricks became more complex.

We even progressed to prodigious rows of short stacks that, like a file of dominos on end, could be splendidly spectacular when we pushed over the beginning stack and watched as the multiple stacks in the row tumbled.

The rules established by Babo and Grandma Birdie for our activities in The Brick Pile were also more complex than those we were required to follow for The Wash Tub and The Sand Box.

The Brick Pile, behind the garage, was out of sight of supervising observation sites like the kitchen window or the back porch. Also, since we were older, it was expected that we could and should play more responsibly. Watch for snakes, lizards, scorpions, spiders, etc. Don't build higher than four feet, so we wouldn't be smashed when a pile fell or one of the shaky walls we constructed suddenly collapsed. And -- above all -- don't throw bricks!

Further, Grandma Birdie and Babo had a whistle. A genuine shrill, ear-blasting, triple-trilling POLICE whistle. When one of them blew that whistle, we were to stop whatever we were doing and come out in front of the garage so it could be determined that we were still alive and kicking. If that whistle was blown more than once, we were to come to the house right then and there!

We built our replicas of the Alamo and other fortifications. And, did you know, brick castles are just as challenging to build -- and considerably more durable -- than sand castles? Some of those castles were large enough that we could kneel and crouch behind the walls to repel "the enemy without". Some were more elaborate, but necessarily on a smaller scale for our tin soldiers.

Our miniature mazes were too small for our personal traversing, but someone always came up with new patterns and designs and cul-de-sacs -- increasingly complex and competitive.

Most years, The Brick Pile became almost forgotten during the colder months of the Winter. In the Spring, grasses and vines and fallen leaves were found to have invaded the remains of last Fall's constructions. Therefore -- during those few years of our adolescence -- we quite voluntarily undertook a Spring Cleaning Project. But only for The Brick Pile!!!

And, you may find this hard to believe, but I don't think we ever once, in those halcyon days of our childhood, suspected that Grandma Birdie and Babo not only created and arranged, but schemed, planned, and devised these ordinary, every-day -- but oh so wonderful -- things for us.

The Rubber Guns

Most wars are fought with bad, bloody results. But ours weren't. They were fun.

We were lucky to have been the right age at the right time to really enjoy imaginative, ingenious, and inspired play-gun weaponry -- at the peak of its availability and productivity.

Oh, I know, the paint guns and paint ball projectiles the kids and grown-up kids have today are more sophisticated. But . . .

I'm reminded of Kipling's poem, Gunga Din.

> "You may talk of gin and beer
>   When you're quartered safe out here . . .
>   But when it comes to slaughter,
>   You'll do your work on water . . ."

Today we might say,

> "You may think it quaint
>   When you sling a gob of paint;
>   But in a time gone by
>   Rubber filled the sky."

Severely lacking the skills of a poet, however, let me, nevertheless, tell you about our Rubber Guns.

My dad helped me make my first rubber gun. I thought of him then as a pro. He had real talent. I was eager to improve on that first rudimentary model and wanted his additional help. But after we made that first prototype, he stepped back and only offered advice as I, my brothers, and my friends advanced our rubber gun skills and arts.

A rubber gun is, in its basic form, a stick with a vee-shaped notch on the front end, a right-angle notch further back on the top, and a triggering string or strap tied or tacked on the top.

Our projectiles or "bullets" were bands cut from the rubber inner tubes of car or truck or bicycle tires.

Hook the rubber band in the front notch, lay the trigger string or strap into the top notch, stretch the band back and hook it on top of the strap in the top notch, and the gun was loaded.

Longer spans between the front vee-notch and the top notch(s) require more effort to stretch the band, but the stored energy in the greater stretched band sent it faster and a longer distance when "fired".

Wider bands were harder to stretch onto the gun and had more energy, but broader bands also lost velocity quicker due to greater air resistance when fired.

Thickness, length, and elasticity of the bands varied. We diligently searched and scoured garages, car sheds, back yards, service station junk piles, etc. When you found an inner tube that was just about right, the bands cut from it were treasures to be hoarded.

You always lost some good rubber bands in the battles, but you recovered some choice ones others fired. Enticing a foe to shoot a good quality band that you could salvage was part of the game.

Advances and developments of cars and trucks through the early 1900's were accompanied by similar improvements in tires and tire inner tubes. In the late 1930's rubber inner tubes were just about as good as they ever got. After World War II began, in the early 1940's, rubber became scarce, tires and tubes were mostly synthetic, and the elastic quality needed for good rubber gun ammo just wasn't available for us -- the rubber gun shooters of the era.

As our rubber gun making skills improved, we quickly progressed from single notch, single shot weapons. Just cut extra notches on top, lay one longer trigger strap into each of the notches, hook the first band from the front notch to the closest top notch, the second band over the first band from the front notch to the second top notch, etc. Pull the strap and fire one band at a time -- or two or three . . . a salvo!

Usually we fired only one at a time, conserving undelivered bands for the next opportunity, in case we didn't have time to reload before a confrontation with another friendly foe.

The appearance and functionality of our rubber guns was, as you might imagine, rather directly correlated with the age and experience of the weapon maker.

Early rubber gun versions were typically quite simplistic. An old broom stick with whittled notches was the basis for my first, I think.

Soon we advanced to pieces of salvaged lumber. Sawed notches, we learned, were better than carved. Smoothing the notches by filing or rasping eased the wear and tear on rubber bands. Guns made from better quality lumber began to be shaped more like real weapons.

Not too far along in the development of our rubber long guns came our rubber gun pistols! These had to be from a stick or board shaped more or less to represent both the gun barrel and the grip or handle. In place of a notch on top of the board to which the rubber band was stretched, we usually tied, taped, or tacked a clothes pin on the back of the handle. Squeeze the clothes pin trigger and shoot the band.

We became skilled at sizing and cutting rubber bands of proper widths, from the best tubes, just the right lengths . . . to fit our rubber guns and pistols. Calculating correlation coefficients for trigger configurations, barrel lengths, etc. We emulated Samuel Colt and John Browning, but they could have learned a few things from us, too!

Need I tell you that we had a strict code of rules and ethics for the rubber gun wars? We should have written a book! But, then, our rules changed most every day. Add a new player, new set of rules!

I regret not saving some rubber gun specimens to show you. But, if you ever want to try your hand -- just let me know.

The Golden Egg

When I was a sprout, along in the mid 1930's, every year on the Saturday afternoon before Easter Sunday, the ladies of St. James Episcopal Church in Del Rio would stage a grand and glorious Easter Egg Hunt.

I say "grand and glorious" with intentional meaning. This egg hunt was for kids, but the adults who planned and conducted it were quite dedicated and extremely able. Of course, I wasn't cognizant then of the amount of planning and preparation that must have been invested in the operation, but it had to have been extensive and carried out over an extended period of time to be as effective as it was.

Undoubtedly there were a significant number of ladies involved. One or more of those ladies certainly knew how to plan, implement, and accomplish.

Always a gaggle of goose-bumped kids -- all ages and sizes -- participated and always there was a colorful conglomeration of eggs to be discovered.

All the eggs were hard-boiled chicken eggs, dyed in a great variety of hues, colors, shades, and patterns. No candy eggs in those days! And ALWAYS there was one special egg -- always slightly larger and always dyed a beautiful golden color.

Most of these egg hunts during this era were held in the back yard of my grandparents. The hunt area was about an acre; circumscribed by pomegranate hedges on each side, a low wooden fence separating it from the yard around the house, and a wire mesh fence on the back side which was the boundary between our yard and the public school property. My grandmother had that place tidied to her high standards.

On hunt days, the freshly mowed lawn had strategically located tufts and clumps of grasses which had incredibly evaded the mower. Pruned pomegranate hedges had amazingly been shorn of their usual wasp nests. Most of the shed leaves fallen from the pear, pecan, fig, sycamore, mesquite, huisache, bois d'arc, and other yard trees had been raked, but, again, a few leaf clumps were mysteriously present that day before Easter. Ivy and ground covers growing along the banks of the wide irrigation ditch which ran through the far part of the back yard had also been appropriately tended.

Freshly cleaned large wooden tables and long wooden benches were scattered around the yard.

In the early afternoon, a truck from the local Beadles Ice Cream shop delivered a large commercial-sized container of ice cream, wrapped with quilted canvass covers to insulate the precious contents from the Spring Day temperatures.

And about that time, the ladies arrived and began hiding Easter eggs.

I wasn't always at my grandparents' house during the egg hiding, but when I was, my grandmother saw to it that I stayed in the house. She kept the blinds shut so I couldn't peek out at the hidings. I wasn't to have any advantage over the other egg seekers.

But -- I had found a flaw in one of the blinds covering the kitchen window next to the ice box. The crack -- low, next to the window, unnoticed by my grandmother --provided a boy's-eye-view of most of the back yard.

Of course, you know that I should not have made those frequent trips to the kitchen ice box, shouldn't have squatted down, and certainly shouldn't have watched the ladies hiding the eggs on the fateful day I am about to tell you about. But I did!

You see, there was a special prize awarded to the finder of the Golden Egg!

I never had trouble finding lots of eggs, because I knew that back yard like the palm of my hand. But I had never been lucky enough, or sharp-eyed enough, to be the finder of the Golden Egg.

On this particular day, though, when I was eight or nine years old, I thought I had it made.

Down close to the ditch were a couple of big oleander bushes. These old bushes were eight to ten feet high and some eight feet in diameter. As oleanders grow over several years, new branches come out at ground level all around the outer edges of the bush. Older limbs get brittle and die in the inner, shaded part of the bush. My brothers, my sister, and I had removed some of the dead inner branches. We had hollowed out "secret places" in those oleander bushes.

Well, sir, as I peeked out that kitchen window, I saw egg-hiding ladies going all over the yard, planting eggs in grass clumps, in tree forks, under benches, and . . . danged if I didn't see one lady go right into the middle of one of those oleander bushes!

Soon, kids and their parents began arriving. All the youngsters had an Easter Egg Basket. Some big, some small, some newer and some older -- just like the kids. Some of us had done it before, but there were always newcomers.

The little tads were lined up and given a brief head-start. They dashed around picking up the brightly colored eggs that were in the easy-to-see and easy-to-reach places.

Then bigger sprouts toed the line and, at the signal, scattered toward the fences and the ditch, plucking eggs out of the hedges and tree forks, hidden in the brick pile behind the garage, stashed on both sides of the ditch and even on the wooden bridge that spanned the ditch.

And I . . . I made for that oleander bush.

I didn't go directly to the bush. I didn't want anyone to think I had any secret information or would cheat or anything like that. But I kept my eye on the bush as I zigzagged toward it.

Some of my friends got to the area around the bush before I did, but I didn't see any of them try to go into the little clearing inside. When I got there, I moseyed around and finally slipped between some of the outer branches into the privacy of that inner chamber we had fashioned.

But what a disappointment! No eggs were inside the bush. And certainly no Golden Egg!

So . . . I figured I had been wrong in thinking that was where the Prized Egg had been hidden this time. I scooted off, trying somewhat belatedly to gather a few eggs for my basket.

The hustle and bustle of the hunt gradually died down, as always when most -- but never quite all -- of the eggs had been found. At last, the signal was given for all of the kids to gather at the tables where the ice cream and cake were to be served.

This was the time for those who found lots of eggs to brag and show how many they had discovered. And, if the finder of the Golden Egg had not already loudly proclaimed his or her triumph, the ladies in charge would ask for the lucky one to step up, show off the prize, and receive the reward. But, this day, no one did.

So it was suggested that we scatter again and see if that all-important Golden Egg could be found. When this second wave of seekers swept over the area still unsuccessfully, I saw one of the ladies go into the oleander bush. But she came out with nothing.

No Golden Egg Found and no Golden Egg Prize given. I've often wondered what they did with the prize.

About dusk, that year's hunt came to a pleasant, if somewhat disappointing ending. Full of ice cream, cake, and some eaten hard-boiled eggs -- and loaded with eggs for home, the crowd thinned and drifted away.

At St. James' Sunday School the next morning, there was still a buzz about the unfound Golden Egg. It was the first time it had happened. Did it mean the end of the Golden Egg tradition?

Several days after Easter, as I played about in the yard near the ditch, I noticed an odor. A day or so later it was stronger. Following my nose, I came to the oleander bush. Nothing around the bush but the smell. Nothing inside the bush when I first went in. But the smell was stronger. With a stick, I scraped aside some of the layer of leaves that had escaped the yard cleaning prior to the hunt.

And there it was! The Golden Egg! Smashed flatter than a fritter and stinking!

The lady who hid it, hid too well. She must have covered it with leaves. The first egg hunter dashing into the bush unknowingly stepped on it. Then it was too flat and too well-covered.

But for a long, long time after that, the fate of the unfound Golden Egg and the story of the sneaky little kid who peeked -- and was justly disappointed -- was my private secret.

The Elephant

An elephant! In my yard?

On a hot Fall weekend some seventy years ago, a circus -- small-time by today's standards, but large for small-town folks in those days -- arrived in Del Rio via railroad. During the process of unloading trucks and rolling equipment from the train, some of the vehicles were parked temporarily on several streets south of the railroad tracks.

The sidewalks along the streets were crowded with local folks, young and old, watching, listening, and -- of course -- smelling the animals on the circus trucks. With my brothers, my sister, and other jabbering neighborhood kids, I was about as excited as an eight or nine year old could be.

Best of all, right there on Martin Street, smack dab in front of my grandparents' home, one of the parked trucks -- again, small for today, but quite big for then -- was EXTREMELY full of ELEPHANT.

It probably was a small elephant, but then, to me, it was monstrous.

The high wooden sideboards on the dingy old truck were bulging out around the elephant. There was no top on the truck bed. The elephant's back and head were exposed to the hot Texas sun.

Part of my grandparents' big yard was nicely mown and neatly kept, but some of it was deliberately planted with native grasses, trees, and cacti. My grandmother wanted some of the yard to resemble the countryside around Del Rio as she remembered it when she arrived as a little girl with her dad and mom in the 1880's. Some of the grass in the "natural" area had grown tall and headed out.

The old man in charge of the elephant talked to my granddad, explaining that the big grey animal was hungry, thirsty, tired, and needed to get out of that truck. He asked if it would be ok to unload her and let her walk around the "native" area of the yard and maybe munch on some of the tall grass. The old handler assured that the elephant was gentle. He would stay with her to keep her off the lawn and assure the safety of the mess of gawking kids.

Our street was one of the main traffic avenues between the west side of Del Rio and its downtown business section. Every car and truck that passed by -- and there were a lot of them that day -- slowed for a look at that big, flop-eared, long-nosed elephant. Many stopped. Soon the sidewalks and yard were full of excited kids and noisy grown folks.

Now you surely understand, it isn't every day that out of the clear blue sky in any big, little, or medium-sized town in the good ole U. S. of A. that a real-life pachyderm magically and majestically materializes in your yard. In your dreams, perhaps! But the chances of it really happening are dang near nigh on to none!

So what would you want to do if something like that happened? Record it, of course! Take a picture! Bunches of pictures!

Well, sir, my grandparents had a fine old Kodak bellows camera that in earlier times had produced lots of great family photos. Grandma Birdie dug into a pile of accumulated gear in the hall closet and hauled out that old camera. She hustled outside, blowing dust off, pushing buttons, un-snagging snaps, and cranking out that long bellows camera lens. She staggered -- in her haste -- out over the driveway into the long grass the elephant was pulling and chomping. She, Grandma, that is, began trying to bunch us grandkids and the elephant for the photo of a lifetime!

But, wouldn't you know it? The old film left in the camera for too long in the summers of disuse was brittle. It cracked and jammed when she tried to roll it. The camera was useless!

My sweet ole grandma showed an uncharacteristic display of temper I had never seen before. In frustration, swinging that heavy old camera by its worn leather strap, she bashed it on the trunk of one of the sturdy mesquite trees in the yard. The tree lived on. The camera did not.

And, thus, we had no pictures!

Never-the-less, right there in our yard, for a couple of grand and glorious hours, the elephant grazed on the tall grass, chomped some hay the handler forked out for her, siphoned water with her trunk from a wash tub we filled with the garden hose, walked slowly about, and, of course, answered natural calls of nature.

Monday, at school, first crack out of the box, I was telling my teacher and the kids in my classroom about the elephant in my yard!

Do you think anyone believed me? Heck no! They thought I was spoofing.

Did I have pictures? they asked. Surely if an elephant had visited in my yard I would have pictures!

Well, as you know, I had none.

So, I invited the doubters to come with me after school.

In my yard was all the proof needed.

And, it lasted and smelled just fine for a goodly number of years.

The High Wire Act

As I may have told you, a long, long time ago I lived in a far, far better place.

It was in that wonderful realm of childhood. You know . . . the magnificent smells of grandma's kitchen and granddad's pipe . . . the windmill clanking and the owl hooting -- the river or the creek flowing near by . . . and the spell-binding stories and yarns spun out while sitting in grandma's lap or on granddad's knee. Tales of long ago that whetted your appetite for the quests you would someday make and the worlds you dreamed of going out and conquering.

Any time was a good time to hear stories about the "olden days". But some times were better than others. And some places just seemed to create that mystical aura that evoked bewitching tellings of the big and little episodes of the past from Grampa or Gramma.

With Grandma Birdie, one of the very best of those telling and listening places was in the evening, out in the back yard. Sitting with her on one of the wooden benches. With the smell of the nearby honeysuckle bush and the fragrant trumpet vine wafting in the breeze that arose not long after dark. Sound of crickets. Sometimes a frog croaking down along the ditch.

When she was a lass, Grandma Birdie went to a girl's "finishing school" -- Hollings Institute in Virginia. Graduated in June 1887. They must have slipped her a heavy dose of astronomy, astrology, mythology, and that kind of stuff. She was sharp on stars and planets. Showed us the

Big Dipper. North Star. Mars, the "Red Planet", and Venus, the "Green Planet". Told us how the old Greeks and Romans associated them with War and Love.

And it was out there in the early evening twilight, looking up at the sky as Grandma Birdie wove her magical spell with her enchanting spiel, that I first witnessed The High Wire Act.

Babo and Grandma Birdie lived in a big two-storied house on Martin Street. That house was originally built by Great-Grandpa Hart, Grandma Birdie's dad. After Babo and Grandma Birdie were married, Grandpa Hart allowed his itchy foot to take him, Grandma Hart, and their sons further west on his life-long journey from North Carolina to California and, eventually, Oregon.

In the ensuing years, Babo and Grandma Birdie modified and improved the house, but it was still basically a big two-storied, multi-roomed home surrounded by lots of porches and a fabulous yard. (Somewhere in this gob of tales I'm writing for you, I'll be more detailed about the house.)

The house was set back a good way south of Martin Street. Further south some 45 or 50 yards was a two-storied garage. In earlier times it housed wagons, harness, and I don't know what all.

Back when Great-Grandpa Hart built the place, there was little or no electricity. When an electrical generating plant was built on San Felipe Creek (just downstream from Great-Grandpa Block's home), wiring was strung on poles all over Del Rio and into the old and new homes.

The railroad reached Del Rio in 1882 on its way from New Orleans, via San Antonio, and on to California. It ran through Del Rio just three blocks north of Great-Grandpa Hart's place. All along the main railroad track there were spur tracks. Train engines could pull cars off the main track through switches and onto the spur lines. Switch engines pushed or pulled the cars along the spurs to sidings beside the warehouses that paralleled the train route. Then the cars could be emptied of their goods which were stored in the warehouses.

Those warehouses provided shelter for more than the lumber, merchandise, feed, and other items that were stored in them. Large rats -- warehouse rats -- were always a problem. And the electrical lines strung on poles that networked the warehouses and businesses and homes were splendid overhead highways for those rats in their searches and plunderings.

Just three blocks south of the railroad tracks and the associated warehouses, the Martin Street home of Babo and Grandma Birdie had been "secured" from the rats traveling the power lines. Where the electrical lines passed through the house walls from outside to inside, the wires went through ceramic tubes that both insulated the house from electrical current and were too small for vermin to pass through. The rodents could get to the house on the lines, but couldn't get in.

However, to pipe electricity from the house to the garage, two wires had been strung from the highest peak of the house to the highest peak of the garage. The wires ran along, side by side, about eighteen inches or so apart, 35 or 40 feet above the ground.

One warm evening, sitting out in the back yard with bull bats (night hawks) skimming overhead, darting almost but not quite soundlessly as they swooped after flying insects, -- probably already goose-bumpy from an eerie tale being told -- I looked up at the darkening sky and saw the most bodacious, gargantuan, high-mogombus of all monster rats running along one of those overhead wires from the house to the garage.

He got to the peak at the top of the garage, poked his nose all about, but couldn't get in. Put me in mind me of the wolf and the little pig's brick house!

After sniffing and snuffing up and down and all around, the rat crossed over to the other of the two wires and ran back along that high wire all the way to the tip of the house -- and disappeared!

I never knew exactly how those rats got from the front of the house -- where the wiring entered -- to the peak at the back of the house where the wires ran to the garage. Over the top, maybe? Around the side, perhaps? But the rats found a way!

Well, sir, after having once witnessed one of these big furry, long-tailed rats running along the slender wire so high up in the air, I watched for them! Sure enough, I discovered you could spot them almost every evening as the sky darkened and before there was not enough light to see.

I don't think I saw the same rat every time. Just a new one trying out the house to garage route. But they couldn't get into the garage. So, always out on one wire and back on the other. High overhead.

Now if that were the end of this tale, it would be kinda anti-climatic, wouldn't it?

But, hold your horses there, sprout!

I had a dream!

And in this dream it was me -- not the rat -- that was shinnying along this skinny wire -- high up in the air -- half way between the tip tops of the two-storied house and garage!

But when I looked over my shoulder, there was that dang, grand-gargantuan, high-mogombus of all monster rats snorting and shuffling -- coming after me along that wire.

I kept reaching forward and pulling myself along as fast as I could, hugging the wire with my belly, clutching with my feet to keep from falling. But no matter how fast I went; the rat was gaining on me and just about to catch me with those long, rodent teeth.

Each time I looked back, that rat was closer. He had become rhinoceros-sized and his long, sharp, chisel-like teeth and wickedly curved claws had grown enormously. His stiff whiskers were twitching. His big, bright red eyes were glistening and gleaming.

The ugly ogre kept gaining on me! I could hear him slithering along the wire.

Ole mogumbus stretched his ugly slobbering mouth wide open to take off my legs!

I could smell hot stinking rat breath!

I was a goner!

But wait!

Maybe I had a choice!

I let go of the wire!

And fell into dark and empty void beneath me!

And -- I fell out of my bed!

Every dang time I had that dream . . . I ended up falling out of bed.

Oh, later on, as I got older, maybe just almost falling out of bed! I'd wake and catch myself just on the edge of the bed in the very act of falling.

It was years before I stopped having that dream, but I can remember it all too vividly!

And . . . I don't want to perform that High Wire Act ever again!

Ranch Ball

It was "Ranch Ball". Not real baseball. You'd dub it "two-man" or "broom-stick" or "cow-lot" or even "sheep-pen". And it WAS sorta like ALL of those.

But for us, out on a sheep ranch on the banks of Devils River in southwest Texas in the early 1940's it was a game of championship caliber. Many a serving of peach cobbler or hand-cranked ice cream was won and/or lost on the outcome of those crucial games.

Uncle Pete loved games, especially ball games. We pitched horseshoes or washers, ran races, played tag, cards, dominoes . . . But nothing satisfied Uncle Pete like a ball game.

So he cooked up this ball game that just the two of us -- he being in his late teens and me in my early teens -- could play. It came pretty near being baseball. Abner Doubleday probably would have been proud.

The playing field -- we called it our ball park -- was a sheep pen. About as big as today's average back yard, it was oblong, about forty or fifty feet across and some sixty or seventy feet long. The fence was made of cedar stays, closely wired together, about five feet high.

With baling wire, we attached a couple of five-to-six-foot long sotol stalks to the stays in the middle of the short end of the pen -- the north end. Between the two stalks we wired an old feed sack about eighteen inches wide and two feet long. Similar stalks and feed sacks were set up about two thirds of the way down the right side of the pen. Across the pen on the left side, a single stalk held only a "flag".

The sack wired about shoulder-high to knee-low at the narrow end of the field was "home". The side fence sack was "base" and also the right foul line. The stalk on the left fence marked the left foul line.

Our bat was a broom stick. The balls varied a bit in size and were usually hollow rubber, ole tennis balls, etc. No gloves, of course.

Whoever won the toss was first at bat. The other one-man side was pitcher/fielder. The side "up" had the normal three times at bat. Three outs rotated the sides, nine innings to a game.

To get a strike, the pitcher had to hit the "home" sack in back of the batter with a pitched ball which the batter didn't strike at or missed. A pitch the batter did not strike at which missed the sack was a foul. Three strikes and the batter was out for that time up.

If the batter didn't swing and the ball missed the sack, it counted as a "ball". Four balls equaled a "walk", which also scored a "run". But there weren't many balls, 'cause the batters were almost always swinging at every pitch.

If the batter hit the ball over the fence it was a homer, of course, and counted a "run" scored. If a hit stayed in bounds inside the pen, the pitcher then became the fielder. A batted ball caught "on the fly" was an out. A batted fair ball that hit the ground or the fence before the fielder caught it was a ground ball -- playable.

If it was a fair ground ball, the batter had to run to the base sack on the right side of the field, touch base, and return and touch the sack behind the plate to score.

After a hit, the pitcher became the fielder and could put the running batter out by: (1) catching the ball before it touched the ground; (2) fielding the ball after it had touched the ground or the fence inside the foul lines and tagging the runner with the ball before he made it back to the home base sack; (3) throwing the ball and hitting the runner with it before the runner made it back to home; or (4) throwing the ball and hitting the sack behind home plate before the runner could make it back and touch that sack.

The pen we used for the ball field was located next to the big shed, the hub for most ranch operations. All around the shed were pens. Most were fenced with cedar stays, just like our ball park pen.

The water lots were large pens into which sheep, cows, horses, etc. could access or be driven or kept over night. Long, low, concrete/rock troughs were filled with water for the stock to drink.

The horse pen was next to the water lots. This was a round pen with a fence much stouter and considerably higher then the other pens. It was mainly used for breaking of young horses.

The milk pens were also close to the shed, so it was easy to put out the feed for the morning and evening cow milking chores.

The wide shed roof gave protection from sun (and sometimes rain) to sheep, goats, and men during the spring and fall shearings. It also protected the sacked or binned feeds, tools, saddles, leggings, ropes, and other tack. Hay harvested at the end of the summer was stored in the shed loft and used as needed throughout the entire year.

Our pall park pen was next to the shed on the east side. The shed cast its shadow on that pen in the late afternoons. And that semi-shaded pen was often used to hold some ranch live stock over night.

We knew better than to leave sacks hanging on the fences when we were not using the pen for our ball games. Goats, sheep, horses, and -- especially the skittish pair of mismatched horses used to pull the infrequently-used plow or mower -- were mistrustful of strange things. Sacks moving in the wind might spook stock you were trying to pen.

But, alas, one day we forgot to take the sacks down. Sadly, I must tell you: that was the very day when my granddad wanted -- all by his lonesome -- to put the leery team of horses in that pen.

My granddad, I called him "Papo", kept those two easily boogered horses as a team just to pull the plow and the sickle-bladed mower he used to plant and cut hay. The mare was half again bigger than the pot-bellied gelding. Nevertheless, they made a good team for the spring plowing and late summer mowing. But, because they were so seldom used, they were always edgy when they were brought in from the horse trap for their first work session.

On this fateful day, the first time Papo tried to pen them, the testy team made it right up to the gate of our ball park pen and then the mare snorted, rolled her eyes, turned back, and, with her short-legged partner right behind her, almost ran over Papo.

Papo snapped the stem of his favorite crook-stemmed pipe right then and there.

On the second try at penning the team, the can of Prince Albert smoking tobacco that Papo always carried was jostled out of his shirt pocket when he tried to "turn" the lathered-up critters.

And, wouldn't you know? On the third penning try, Shorty stepped on the tobacco can.

Papo always punctuated his speech with colorful language. The hot summer air was turned three shades of blue on the east side of the shed that afternoon.

By that time, everybody on the ranch -- Uncle Pete, Aunt Joy, Uncle Jim, me, and all of the hired hands within shouting distance -- was out there trying to help pen the lathered-up team.

(Well, my grandma -- Mamo -- was still on the porch, laughing and wiping tears out of her eyes.)

After we took the sacks down, it only took three more tries to get the eye-rolling, slobber-mouthed team in that pen. But that was where Papo had made up his mind they were going to go.

And they did.

Need I tell you? We didn't get to play ball in that pen any more that summer?

The Water Lot

The water lot was a place of fascination, mystery, allure, attraction.

Early on, for me, it was forbidden territory. I was banned from its shaded hillock topped by the two small fenced graves.

The gurgling rapids of Devils River washed the southern edges of the water lot from the low-water highway bridge to the deep, quiet, beckoning pool at its lower end.

I always wanted to go there.

The big two-storied Baker ranch house was next to the water lot. The dwelling had started on the tableland overlooking the river as a two-room rock structure. It had grown to include a large dining room bounded by a kitchen on the south. A "dog trot" hallway separated the original two rooms from the eating area. North of those two rock rooms was another "dog trot" hallway, and then the large living room on the north end of the house. Upstairs there were four bedrooms. Long porches on both levels ran almost the entire length of the house. The front porches overlooked the river and its wide valley. The back porches neighbored the windmill, the water tank, and the car house with its bank of batteries for the Delco and later the wind charger. Between those structures and the foot of the mountain were: the work shop, barn, shed, pens, school house, workers quarters, and, of course, the distant privy.

From the kitchen and the front porches, the water lot was always in sight and sound.

During the Fall roundup, hundreds of bawling ewes were gathered and held there awaiting their turn in the shearing. Bleating lambs joined their mother's deeper toned protests in the Spring in a more intensely strident and discordant chorus. During those times, the water lot was a living and pulsating mass.

The periodic rises and floods of the river usually covered only the lower parts of the fenced enclosure closer to the river. But there were occasions when the angry waters swelled high enough to lap and swirl around those two little fenced graves on that tree-canopied hill tucked in the northeast corner of the watering area.

Papo had a standing rule. Kids were not to play in the water lot. Way over in the far southeast corner of the lot, a gate was nearly always open to permit sheep, horses, and cows to enter from the house pasture to access the waters of the river. Noisy, romping kids in the lot would prevent the animals from coming in to satisfy their thirst.

Also, back then, prior to the virtual elimination of the devastating screw worms, when sheep came in to drink, they could be observed from the house. If infected ewes or lambs were seen, someone closed the pasture gate, stock was herded into the shed pens, and afflicted sheep were "doctored".

Little by little, tho, I was introduced to the provoking, prohibited, enticing water lot territory.

When my mother was at the ranch, she liked to supplement ordinary table fare with salads. There were times when Mama took me with her to harvest sprigs of water cress growing in the shallow eddies of the crystal-clear waters along the rocky banks of the river. Some of those forays were actually in the water lot itself!

The house, outbuildings, and water lot were situated on the tableland at the end of a short canyon -- the House Canyon. As it neared the river, that canyon watershed curved behind the back of the outbuildings, passed by the garden, entered the water lot, split around the little grave-topped hill, and fanned out in gentle grassy deltas sloping into the river waters.

Have I told you that Uncle Jim, the second child of the Baker brood and my mother's oldest brother, had a most 'satiable curtiosity bump?

One early summer day, Uncle Jim decided to try a water well digging technique. A magazine article had titillated his fertile mind and he profoundly concluded that he and his number one nephew should test this ancient method of water sourcing.

(The order of the living Baker children was: Lois (my mother), then Jim, Beth, Pete, and Ruby. Mother married first. As Mamma's first child, I was the first of the nephews and nieces to come along; not necessarily the best.)

Chomping on a chaw of waxy white paraffin, which he habitually swiped in the kitchen from Mamo's canning and preserving supply, Uncle Jim gathered up a crow bar, some rope, and me and we were off on a quest -- to the water lot!

Just inside the east fence, he selected a long, low, and flexible limb of a nearby pecan tree that overhung the bottom of the draw. We cleared a dip in the draw, tossed one rope end over the pecan limb, tied on the crow bar, and started drilling. The springy limb eased the lifting and plunging of the crow bar as Uncle Jim punched it repeatedly into the gravelly soil. I was sent to the river for a bucket of water and we poured driblets into the hole now and then. Each stroke of the bar deepened the hole. We paused to scoop mud, but mostly it just sloshed out as the bar kerchunked into the ooze. And, then, when we were about five feet down, clear water began to work its way up through the brownish goo. Just a bit further and we stopped. And there was a nice little working water well. Uncle Jim pointed out to me that the water level of the well was about the same as the surface of the river.

While we were doing our drilling in the shady coolness of the here-to-fore (for me) forbidden area, I asked about the little graves. Uncle Jim explained that Mamo, my mother's mother, the mother of the five living Baker children, had also borne two babies who died in childbirth.

These two tykes lay under the small mounds in the little fenced area on the top of the hill in the water lot.

During the next couple of summers at the ranch, Uncle Jim and Uncle Pete began my introduction to and instructions in handling firearms and developing shooting skills. When they advanced me to the shooting of a .22 rifle, the practice area was a makeshift range set up in a cut in that House Canyon closer to the foot of the mountain behind the ranch house.

Later I was coached in plinking moving targets. These were empty .22 boxes, cardboard pieces, little dried limbs, and/or cow chip chunks tossed into the river rapids below the low-water bridge. To aim and shoot at these bobbing bits, we sat, kneeled, or stood on the low banks of -- you guessed it -- the water lot.

Now, I've told you all this to set the stage for telling the enthralling tale of my first solo hunt.

Pecan trees and oak trees produce gobs of pecans and acorns. The nuts, the shade, and shelter of the large old trees in the water lot were attractions no squirrel worthy of the name could resist.

Papo and his family had no quarrel with the squirrels over acorns. Pecans were a steed of a different shade. Pecans were a depression era money crop. In those times, every nickel and dime meant a lot. Each fall Uncle Jim and Uncle Pete gathered pecans. Those water lot trees weren't the only nut producers along the river, but they were some of the best and certainly the most convenient -- right there next to the house. So Uncle Jim and Uncle Pete had the delightful chore of keeping the squirrel population in check in and around the water lot.

When they had me shooting safely and well enough, I sometimes got to join them when new squirrels migrated up the river into the water lot and tried to exploit the riches therein. I even scored a kill or two. But I was always under strict supervision. Also, my competitive young uncles said I chattered more than the squirrels did. Sometimes they put me on one side of the tree so the squirrels would scoot around to hide from me and be exposed to their marksmanship.

But there did come that wonderful day when I heard Papo ask Uncle Jim if he didn't think it was time for me to go on a hunt all by myself in the water lot! Papo's casual comments carried a lot of weight.

Joy, rapture, and ecstasy!

Promptly, but still much slower than I would have liked, Uncle Jim went into his room and brought out his old long barreled, pump, exposed hammer .22 rifle. Sitting on the front porch just across the fence from the water lot, Uncle Jim handed me the shells.

I twisted the knob on the magazine plunger, pulled it out until the bullet-shaped hole in the magazine tube under the barrel was cleared, and listened as each separate .22 cartridge slid butt first down that tube and chunked up against the one under it. When the tip of the last bullet showed in the tube hole, I pushed the plunger back in all the way and twisted the knob to lock it.

Papo was sitting there in his rocker, smiling though the smoke of the crooked-stem pipe he always smoked. You do know, do you not, that Papo and I have the same first name and I am his first grandson? Merely in order of birth, of course.

About then, Mamo came out of the kitchen, wiping her hands on her salt-sack apron. It seemed she had a mite to tell her first grandson --me -- about what to do when he got to the water lot.

She specifically stipulated where I was to sit over there in the water lot. Right next to the little graves, up against a big oak tree where I could see up into and all around under most of the bigger pecan trees. Right where she could watch me from the porch!

Neither Papo nor Uncle Jim said a thing while Mamo gave her counsel and advice. They were all in cahoots! I tried not to fidget or squirm. I was about to be turned almost loose to hunt on my own!

After Mamo had covered her additions to the rules of the game, Uncle Jim walked me over to the water lot gate, opened it for me, and closed it behind me.

And there I was. In the water lot. On a hunt. All by my lonesome!

Well, I won't bore you with details of that ole hunt. About sitting smack dab where Mamo said I should and only then jacking a shell into the chamber of the 22. About keeping as still as I could 'til my legs cramped and I just had to move. About listening so hard with my mouth open so I could hear better that I got the dry mouth. And about seeing this squirrel mysteriously appear, peek-a-booing around first one side of that pecan tree and then the other.

But when that rascal did get bold enough to come out where I could see his whole head -- I eased the barrel of the .22 up slowly -- ever so slowly. Lined up Mr. Bushy Tail's eye with the post of the front sight and the vee of the back sight. Pulled the hammer back exceedingly slowly so it wouldn't click too loud. Squeezed the trigger just like my uncles had taught me. Watched the squirrel drop and plop limply into the leaves on the ground.

Mamo cooked my squirrel for supper that night. I thought she would fry him, but she made squirrel and dumplings. So everyone could have a taste. It was a fine meal, with lots of other eats. Oh, also . . . it being a Baker gathering, there was some windy and colorful conversation from some folks who had been watching from the front porch.

I can't quite recall how my squirrel tasted.

But I do remember -- exceedingly well -- my first solo hunt -- and its precise location.

The water lot.

The Choker

The last new car we acquired came with more bells, whistles, gauges, dials, knobs, switches, lights, blinkers, beepers, doodads, and gadgets than "Carter has pills".

(That last reference harkens back to the days when Carter's little liver pills were the preferred over-the-counter cure-all for what ails you before ninety-nine and ninety-nine one hundredths percent grain alcohol based Geritol was the wildest thing folks clamored for down at the corner drug store.)

Nowadays, for me to look up how some new doohickey on our car works, I can spend a long afternoon thumbing through the 524 pages of the manual Toyota provides.

And that brings to mind the 1932 Chevy sedan that Babo herded around the highways and by-ways in and around Del Rio when I was a tyke.

Babo was as good a grand dad as a kid could have. A soft-spoken, calm, easy-going, warm-hearted old geezer who would take me on his lap and tell me fascinating tales of the days when he and his mom rode from San Antonio through the Indian-infested wilds to Del Rio on the stage coach and stuff like that. When I was real little he'd hum me to sleep with tunes like "Sewanee River", "Camp Town Races", and other racy tunes of the day.

He studied and passed the bar exam. But he went into the mercantile business. Did very well until the untimely combination of a drought and a revolution in Mexico made it impossible for the ranchers and others he was carrying on credit to pay their bills and his store went under. While he was prospering, he owned several early automobiles, including at least one big old Cadillac "touring car". Howsomever, his raising as a horse and buggy guy always limited his ability to cope with the more complicated intricacies of autos.

He was, though, a very careful driver. Courteous and cautious, carefully observing the laws of the land, the signs of the road, and the strengths and weaknesses of other vehicle operators. He would nod and smile at others of his older ilk and frown and grumble at the Barney Oldfield would-be whiz-bang throttle-trompers.

One day along about '36 or '37 -- he was in his early 70's and I was eight or nine -- we were heading home, driving down Main Street from some now forgotten venture into the far reaches of northern Del Rio. After he had craned his head to carefully look east and west before crossing the several sets of railroad tracks, Babo stuck his left arm out the open window, bent his elbow, pointed up for a right turn, and swung the Chevy westward into the almost traffic-free stretch of Ogden Street.

And right there! A flash of inspiration sparked my questing young mind.

You see, I'd been wondering about some of those knobs sticking out of the Chevy dashboard!

I already knew about the big black knob with a "V" on it. I'd seen Babo pull it to make the vent just in front of the windshield open to let cooler air flow into the car.

But there were other smaller knobs. One marked "T". Another, with a big "C" on it.

While Babo was tilting his head up to look through his horn-rimmed glasses out the rear view mirror at a car coming behind us, I just reached over and pulled out that knob marked "C" an inch or two.

The tone of the motor changed. The Chevy began to hump and buck and cough.

Babo gritted out a few words I'd never heard him use before as he steered the car to the right.

When he looked to the left as the car behind him passed, I shoved the "C" knob back in.

The Chevy perked right up and cruised quite normally down to the corner of Griner.

Babo forgot to make his turn signal for the left turn on to Griner, but we made the corner ok.

He looked to the left to see if anything was coming our way at the Dignowity intersection. I pulled out that "C" knob again -- further than before. . . . Just see what it would do, you know!

The Chevy wheezed and jerked. Babo learned me some more of his previously unexpressed vocabulary, shoved in the clutch with his left foot, pumped the accelerator with his right, and steered for the pavement edge again. That vein on his head just above and to the right of his eye that I knew bulged when he got excited was bigger and bluer than I had ever seen it.

Just before the car stopped rolling, I managed to push that "C" knob all the way back in and the Chevy came to life with a jerk that almost whipped the steering wheel out of Babo's hands.

I figured the paint would be peeling off the car PDQ from the heat of Babo's wonderfully descriptive phrasing. And there was absolutely no doubt of the super-heated, final and permanent hell-fire and brimstone destiny he was projecting for all cars, car salesmen, and car makers.

When we got home, Babo slammed the car door, took the back porch steps two at a time, jerked the phone ear piece off the cradle, jiggled the lever, growled at the operator, and had some things to say to the folks down at the Chevy shop. And he was madder than ever when they came, looked at the car, and told him they did not know why we had suffered such an experience.

I was so impressed with Babo's linguistic ability that I never did tell him what I had discovered about that "C" knob.

Sorta choked me up, you might say.

Figured I might live longer that way.

Waitin' On A Train

When I was a little guy, Daddy would take me -- and later my brother, Bud, and sister, Shirley, -- to The Depot in Del Rio to wait and watch for the trains. This was before, Lee, our youngest brother, hatched out.

The Southern Pacific Railroad was big in our town. San Felipe Springs put us on the map. In the awesome area of Southwest Texas we were amidst, ranching was long the main-stay of our economy. Grapes, wine, and other agricultural produce grown in Val Verde with the abundance of water from the canal system sustained us. But 'twas the railroad that cast the die that made us a growth town in Southwest Texas.

Long before San Angelo started to bloom, Del Rio was an expanding and welcoming site, first on the wagon trail and then the railroad line that ran from New Orleans, thru San Antonio, to El Paso, and on to California.

In the early 1930's -- my twig bending days -- steam engines hauled long lines of freight cars and both a morning and an evening passenger train -- the Sunset Limited -- went thru our town.

Late in the afternoon on nice days, Daddy would turn our old car into the parking lot off of Ogden Street, just west of the depot. We would wait, watch, and listen. If the weather was a little fresh, we'd sit in the car until we heard a whistle or saw the signals change. Either way, we'd be out standing on the walk or sitting on one of the ice wagons, when the trains pulled in.

Like everyone else in our town who "grew up" with the railroad, Daddy knew what the whistle toots signaled long before the train was in sight. Even before we could hear the whistle, he watched the semaphore arms and/or the lights on the signal towers down the track and could tell which block of track the train was entering or leaving as it approached.

It was mysterious. How did he know? But eventually he brought each of us into the inner-sanctum of railroad lore and knowledge. I lorded it over Bud until he knew. I could look down the track and predict almost as well as Daddy. Of course, in his time, Bud frustrated Shirley until Daddy cracked the code for her.

The engines were monstrous, noisy behemoths, snorting smoke and steam, clanging and hissing, and wickedly wonderful. I was awed. Wanted to get closer. Was afraid to do it.

You must remember: those were the good old days. Daddy knew the engineers, conductors, and brakemen and they knew him. As each of us kids screwed up the courage to do so, sooner or later we were invited by an engineer to climb up into the cab of one of those big black belching beasts. When I got up there, I felt like Jonah must have in belly of the whale. That engine was a living, throbbing, had-to-be-alive being! It was better down on the ground.

But, as the years passed, those big unlovely steam engines I first knew were replaced by bigger and better, stronger and more ferocious locomotives. Sadly, for me, the day came when the diesels were put on the line. It became a different world.

In 1937, I was nine and Bud was seven, Babo and Grandma Birdie took us with them on a three-week trip to California to visit Grandma Birdie's sister-in-law, Della Hart. It was a wonderful revelation of and exposure to the world for a couple of little small town kids.

For me and Bud, the best part was the two and a half day train trip from Del Rio to Los Angeles and the return two and a half day journey. We had a Pullman berth -- air-conditioned. At night Grandma Birdie slept in the lower berth and Babo had the upper. Bud and I squabbled about who would get to sleep in the upper with Babo. Or sleep in the lower with Grandma Birdie and be able to part the window curtain and peek out at night when we went thru towns. We ended up, of course, taking turns. Neither got to see much at night, since depression-era towns between Del Rio and Los Angeles rolled up the sidewalks at night.

Dining car eating was a blast. In the lounge car -- another highlight was chug-a-lugging all the ginger ales we would wheedle Babo out of a dime for.

But the strongest remembrance of that train ride is of Bud and me smashing our noses as flat as we could against the window of the Pullman trying to look out and down into the canyon as the train crossed the Pecos High Bridge. And even inside that steel railroad car and its double glass windows, Grandma Birdie was hanging on to Bud's belt and issuing stern instructions to Babo to do the same for me.

Now you know I've had some other train experiences, one of which is a marvelous train trip through the Rocky Mountains in Mexico. That tale is too long to tell in this piece. I'll bend your mind with the recounting of that fabled adventure in a separate story. But there is one more wooly booger with which I want to wind up this telling.

In the fall of 1945, my first year attending The University of Texas, a grand guy named John Taylor lived across the hall from me in Mrs. Carlson's Rooming House on 25th Street in Austin, just off the Drag and only a couple of blocks from the campus.

John was grand in many ways. For one, he was over six feet tall. I was five-six. Like Will Rogers, John never met a person he didn't like. I don't think anyone who ever met him failed to cotton to him right off.

John hailed from Dallas. His dad was a U. S. of A. postman five or six days a week and a strong Baptist preacher the rest of the time. The Taylor residence in Dallas was on McKinney Avenue. Remember that -- McKinney Avenue.

The weekend the first cold blue norther of the season blew in, John and I sashayed up to Dallas, riding our thumbs. We were lucky catching rides and the last one just happened to be able to drop us off right in front of John's house on McKinney Avenue. Just about midnight.

At that advanced stage of my physical and mental maturation, Big D was as far north as ever I had trekked in the Lone Star state. We were as cold as well-diggers in the Klondike by that late hour, but as we walked across McKinney Avenue I did manage to notice steel rails embedded in the pavement right down the middle of the street. I asked John if it was a train track. He laughed, pointed up to the mess of electric cables strung overhead and explained that it was a street car track. Electric street cars ran on that track during the busy times of the day. Well, I allowed as how I was an old hand about street cars, because I had ridden some of those rascals out there in California back in '37.

We crossed the sidewalk, opened the yard gate, walked about five or six paces, climbed the six or eight steps, and were on the front porch of John's home. Just a hop, skip, and a jump from that street car track. The nice old house had two front doors, each with a large, oval-shaped, etched-glass window fronting onto the porch. The left one was illuminated by lights inside.

John knocked. The porch light came on. His dad opened the left door -- the one with the light behind it-- and we were warmly welcomed into the family living room. We briefly conversed with John's dad, his mom, and his brother Dan. But they had been in bed, it was cold, we were tired, and soon we all headed for the sack.

John and I dove into a double bed in John's old room -- the one with the oval-windowed door opening onto the front porch -- the room that had been dark as we approached the house. Mrs. Taylor piled extra quilts on and soon we were sawing logs, breathing heavily against the welcome weight of all those covers. One thing about John. He slept extremely soundly. We always had a hard time back at Mrs. Carlson's, waking him up in time for him to get to class.

Crash! Bang! Clang! Steel wheels on iron rails! Blue and white lights flashing all around! The smashing blasts of sound and lightning-like flashes instantly signaled to me that a blooming freight train was coming right out of the night --through that oval-shaped front door window -- was going to run smack dab over the bed, me, John, and the whole dang family Taylor!

I lunged against the shackles and chains binding me. Couldn't get loose! I yelled at John to save himself! All hands on deck! Away all boats! Every man for himself! We're lost! Casey Jones is driving his engine, train, and caboose right in on top of us!

John jumped up. I thought he was crying. He was -- laughing so hard he was crying! His dad popped in through the hall door, followed by Mrs. Taylor! They were laughing too!

It was the trolley! The street car, goofus! They start those routes before daylight to carry folks to work even on Saturdays! Metal wheels on iron rails just steps away out in the street sent vibrations all through that old house. Those lightning flashes were big electrical sparks jumping back and forth from the cable above the street car to the long antennae-like rod which gathered the power for the trolley's electric motor!

Years later, when we gathered out at the Briar Patch to cook fajitas, drink suds, and tell a few wild ones, Dan Bus, Allison's and Michael's other grand dad, would predictably rumble into song.

Dan was a dyed-in-the-wool Jimmie Rodgers fan. He invariably started out singing:

"All around the water tank, waitin' for a train . . ."

Always put me in mind of these train tales. Still does.

The Tin Boats

We grew up on the banks and in the waters of the irrigation ditches that vein Del Rio. Fed by the cool, clear waters of San Felipe Creek, these waterways were a childhood and continuing fascination. No mariners ever followed enchanting singing of sirens with greater zeal.

We waded in the waters when the ditches were running during the growing seasons. Sloshed in the mud when the flow was stopped for the annual mid-winter ditch cleaning. During the brief times the ditch beds were dry, they were trenches for our war games. King-of-the hill wars raged on the banks, with the vanquished tumbling down the muddy slopes. Ala Tarzan, we swung out over the mesmerizing waters by ropes dangling from overhanging trees.

And, in a deep, steeply banked stretch of the Mother Ditch behind Sacred Heart Academy, a grand tree extended long limber limbs to which we could leap to from the bank; swinging and swaying as long as possible before losing your hold and dropping off into the ditch -- wet or dry.

We tossed pebbles. Skipped stones. Chunked rocks. Floated folded paper boats. Built tiny cane rafts. Made shingle sailboats with stick masts, rag sails, and string rigging. My infamous fishing career began in these ditches -- catching crawdads with string and bacon bits.

When I was twelve or thirteen, we became boat builders.

I often stayed with my grandparents on West Martin Street. The Madre or Mother Ditch coursed through their back yard. Joe Davis lived next door. Next on the west was Keller's Wood Yard, a source of splendid sounds: smashy-splitting and screechy-sawing. And stimulating, tantalizing, tinctured aromas of sawn mesquite. At dusk, the sky over the then-quiet wood yard was filled with swooping night hawks -- catching insects flying up from the wood piles. And we were often there, shooting pebbles at these low-flying "bull bats" with "shooters" made from rubber inner tube strips and tree branch "y's".

Near the ditch bank at the south end of Keller's Wood Yard was a treasure -- a stack of old, used, corrugated roofing tin. The ten-foot rusting sheets were riddled with old nail holes, but no ship-wrecked castaway ever found more welcomed boat building material.

First, we hammered the jagged edges of the nail holes, to reduce the size of the holes and blunt the sharp edges. Nevertheless, there were cuts, scrapes, and torn britches.

An old two-by-four made a passable boat prow. Leave the 2x4 end sticking up -- to tie to, to be a handle, to look jaunty. Next, bend one tin sheet end around the 2x4 prow and nail it on. Hammer out the dips in the tin at the sheet ends at the bow, but leave the corrugations in the rest of the sheet. Calk between tin and wood with inner tube strips. A square wooden apple box end, nailed and calked to the tin sheet, worked as a stern piece. Paddles were a narrow board for a handle, nailed to a wider blade.

But, plugging those nail holes required real creative engineering.

On the north side of the Southern Pacific railroad yard, near the old steam engine turntable, was a tar pit. Don't know why it was there or what that tar was ever used for. But, on a hot summer day, boat-building requisitioners could chop out a tar chunk, heat it in an old bucket over a little wood fire, and dab the hot black goo into nail holes and other punctures. When the tar cooled, it cured most leaks that weren't too big.

The tin boats were twisty, tho. As they had no gunwales, from a lack of both suitable materials and boat-making knowledge, the corrugations of the tin sheets gave the boats what rigidity they did have.

Getting into or out of the one-man boats was testy. Until your body mass was properly distributed over the inside boat bottom, the craft tried to fold in the middle. The tin sheet sides would wallow out and let a whole lot of ditch water get in the boat with you.

I know you will find this hard to believe, but not a one of those tin boats was ever "finished" to our satisfaction. There were always improvements to be made. "One-ups-man-ship" constantly reared its inspirational head. But each of those boats was ever and always -- in-process, near-finish, or under-repair -- a vessel of beauty in its builder's eyes.

Let me tell you about the wonderful water world of our youth.

Some folks call it a system of irrigation canals, others want to say asequias.

However, these waterways were not dug by early Spanish missionaries like the ones in San Antonio. The early settlers who harnessed the San Felipe Creek waters called our water channels: "ditches". They called it an irrigation system of ditches. We grew up calling them ditches. I still call them ditches.

An amazing amount of pure, clear water comes out of the ground at San Felipe Springs and flows down the creek to the Rio Grande.

People began early to live along the creek, using the waters to drink and wash, to water crops and livestock. Trees grew on the banks and nearby. The town of Del Rio grew close to the creek -- by the river.

And to better use the wonderful waters, dams were built and ditches dug to send the waters all over the green valley -- el val verde -- thru which the creek flows. A little way down stream from the springs, the creek is dammed at the Blue Hole, and there begins the Mother or "Madre" Ditch.

Other dams on the creek -- the Tardy Dam, for example -- channel water into other main ditches. Smaller ditches branch off, following the contours of the land to send water where the planners and builders of the irrigation system knew long, long ago it was needed. After each branching, the ditches become smaller, narrower, shallower.

The mother ditch -- which flowed thru my grandparents' back yard -- was the main water way for us in our tin boats.

When my dad was a boy, on a gentle curve of the ditch, his parents had a "shore" created with a sloped, pebbled beach -- ideal for little-boy toy boats and skipping stones. And this was the principal testing and launching site for our tin boats.

We paddled downstream thru the "exotic" areas of Chihuahua or "The West" of Del Rio. We portaged around some of the street bridges which were too low for the boats and paddlers to go under. Others we could bend over and pole our way thru. In these "western seas", the ditch had been dug thru more undulating terrain and the banks were mostly too high for the boys in the boats to see the "lands" traversed by our voyages.

On the other hand, explorations upstream to the south and east carried us thru the well-tended school grounds, past the manicured banks of the Episcopal Church yard, around the bend of the landscaped Graham property, over the Griner Street "portage", and, most daring of all, thru the long, dark tunnel under Main Street and the buildings on either side of it.

The Main Street Tunnel was long; and, for us, the most rewarding of our expeditions. It was also an outstanding acoustical arena for our barbershop harmony. Paul Eppes discovered and promoted our singing abilities inside the tunnel. More than once, after a passage which would have made any Volga Boatman proud, we had curious onlookers gawking at us as we emerged at an end of the tunnel.

(The Main Street tunnel was shorter then. In the days of our adventurous youth, it went under only the street, the Montgomery-Ward building on the west side, and the Star Store on the east side. Now it extends farther to the east under Pecan Street and behind Sacred Heart Academy.)

When our seafaring ambitions eventually extended to San Felipe Creek, we found the tin boats somewhat less than adequate. Our notably increasing skills as builders and our seafaring sailing talents were not keeping up with our growing bodies and expanding ambitions.

As our means and knowledge permitted, little by little, and, by various hooks and crooks, we advanced to the more sophisticated use of tire-tube rafts, and, ultimately, canoes. But the tin boats and the adventurous voyages of exploration we made in them will always rank high in our memories.

The Cows and the Cats

Blossom was her name. Milk and butter was her game. And, boy, she was good!

That sweet old Jersey cow produced the larrupin'est, lip-smackin'est, bluebell best milk of any of the bovine family that ever was. When she was fresh, her milk was more than half cream.

I don't know when or where Daddy got that old girl. She was in the family before I was.

He'd go down to the barn every morning and every evening, take the cone-shaped metal covers off of the feed barrels, dip tajackly the right scoop-sized proportions of bran and other cow feed rations from the separate bins, stir and mix while he whistled the tunes she and I knew so well, dump the carefully created concoction in her feed trough, and let her in the milking stall.

Daddy always had a bucket of water -- warm in winter -- and he gently washed Blossom's udder and teats. I think she liked that. She'd turn her head, roll one eye ball at him, and more often than not moo a low low. You know that cows low, don't you? When a cow lows, it's usually a mellow, sort of rumbling, way-down, good-sounding, deep tone. Something lower than low flat.

Daddy was a whistler. He could purse his lips and zing out snappy, happy tunes. But when he was harmonizing with Blossom, he whistled out soft notes between his teeth.

121

With his head nestled against her flank, Daddy would sit on his stool, orchestrate a little ditty in time with the plinking of the squirts into the milk pail, and together they filled the barn with melody and the bucket with nature's own nectar.

The only fuss Blossom and Daddy had was with her tail. Daddy had a Flit Spray. He filled the little tank with a good-smelling insect repellant. Right after he washed Blossom's bottom works, he'd pump that spray gun handle in and out and give her sides and legs a good coating of bug dope. It usually kept her from swinging her tail to fight off stinging critters while he milked her.

But I remember a time or two when it was wet or cold and she slapped him on the back of his neck with her tail. The tender aura of the milk stall was shattered with some provocative and profane pronouncements of her impending doom.

Blossom's tail got me in trouble, too.

Mama said she looked out the kitchen door one day and saw ole Blossom moseying along with me hanging onto her tail and swinging back and forth. Mama gently and calmly told me to let the tail go. Then, when Blossom had sedately walked away, I got my britches busted.

When I was old enough to spend some solo time -- without Mama along -- out at Papo and Mamo's ranch, I discovered some new things about cows.

Because Blossom had me conditioned to expect all milk to be sweet and delicious, I wasn't ready for Bitter Weed milk.

Ranch cows look more or less like town cows. They graze around on grasses and succulents, coming in to be fed and milked just like honest town cows. But you can't trust ranch cows! Sometimes they sneakily, slyly, secretly, and surreptitiously slink around the edges of the pasture munching bitter weed. When a cow takes in a chaw of bitter weed, her milk gets awful. If a kid raised on town cow milk swallows ranch cow milk slugged with bitter weed . . . well . . . to use one of Grandma's delicate sayings . . . "It's enough to gag a maggot!"

Daddy never let me milk Blossom. That was his job.

But, out at the ranch . . . When we came of cow-milking-age, my brother, Bud, and I were introduced to the art. Out there, everybody -- especially peckerwood boys -- got in on the act.

When Bud and I were sprouts, our three uncles . . . Jim, Pete, and Lucious . . . were in the process of exiting their teens and entering their twenties. Still had rambunctiousness oozing out.

Uncle Lucious and Aunt Beth were beginning to scratch out their ranching start over on the Pecos. When they came to visit at the home place -- Baker's Crossing on Devils River --, it was always a festive time. Even when chores were to be done, there never was time enough to get talked out.

At milking time, for example, what was ordinarily a do-it-on-your-lonesome job, two or three of them might gather at the barn and the pens. While one took a turn milking, the others would shoot the breeze, trading windys. When they had a couple of wet-behind-the-ears, visiting, town-boy, nephews tagging along, conditions were ripe for plucking.

In the midst of the horseplay during one of those before-breakfast milking-talking-visiting confabs, Uncle Jim was at his turn milking one of the several cows. The youngest uncle -- Uncle Pete -- was teaching Bud and me how to sail dried cow chips over the barn roof. Uncle Lucious, squatted down against the gate post, was, as usual, trying to referee the conflict that was erupting between the chip throwers, the skittish milk cows, and the agitated milker.

While dodging a cow chip that somehow was misdirected by Uncle Pete, I stepped into one of the full milk buckets. Turned it over. Splashed a third of the morning's milk on the ground.

Everything stopped. Uncle Jim gritted his teeth and did some relatively refined and amazingly restrained cussing. Uncle Pete jerked up the bucket, salvaged a smidgen of milk, and allowed as how maybe sailing any more cow chips should wait 'til later . Bud looked shaken. I figured my britches were in for another busting. Uncle Lucious, as usual, just offhandedly commented, "Well, that leaves a half a bucket for the house milk, a half a bucket for Mamo and Aunt Beth to churn. The sanchos are gonna get slim pickins -- only one bucket for the whole bunch."

In the spring, when ewes were dropping newborns, most of the ranch milkings were slated for the bottle-feeding of orphaned lambs -- the sanchos. There's a tale I'll tell you another time, best beloved, about Candy and one of those little sanchos Uncle Jim called Dirty Tail.

Two or three years later, Bud and I were visiting during the summer out at Aunt Beth and Uncle Lucious' ranch on the Pecos. I loved it out there.

The little four-room ranch house had no electricity -- only coal-oil lamps after dark. Aunt Beth whomped up some of the best meals I ever ate on her little wood cook stove in the kitchen. No in-door plumbing except for one water faucet in the kitchen sink. In the summer time the water that came out of that faucet was always hot, because it had to flow down from the tank at the barn. The pipe between the barn and the house was more on top of the ground than under and therefore exposed to the tender mercies of the West Texas summer sun.

The house was up on the divide. The wind blew hot in the day. But at night it cooled to an almost comfortable temperature. Bud and I slept in a double bed out on the screened front porch. Long before daylight each morning, one of us had to pull up a quilt. We would wake to hear Aunt Beth in the kitchen. We really couldn't hear her, but she always had the battery radio turned up so we could hear it. I still remember hearing "When it's roundup time in Texas and the bloom is on the sage . . ."and songs like "The Little Church in the Wildwood".

There were cows to milk at the barn, of course. Morning and night.

Uncle Lucious was not shy in sharing the chores he thought growing kids of our age ought to do. But he was a good teacher. He always thought of novel ways to acquaint you with the easiest and/or best ways to do things. And he made light of the odious, difficult, boring jobs.

He had us doing most of the milking. After we acquired the techniques and our arms and hands became muscled sufficiently, it wasn't really that bad with both of us there to spell each other.

But the cats!

Uncle Lucious and Aunt Beth always had a big bunch of cats around. Uncle Lucious said they kept the barn from having too many rats. Aunt Beth, who had been bitten by a rattlesnake when she was a young girl, said the cats kept the snakes away from the barn and especially the house.

At milking time, however, the cats were pests.

They were always working their way up closer to the guy milking the cows. Of course, we had tested them to see if they could catch a squirt of milk squeezed from a teat in their direction. They flinched when the milk hit them in the kisser, but they licked it off and came back for more.

But it made the cows nervous. They kicked at the cats. Knocked the buckets over. Got all tense and "held" their milk. Became too worked up and began to have loose stools in the milking pen!

So Bud and I devised a remedy.

Uncle Pete had told me that if you tied the tails of two cats together and tossed them over a clothes line you could have a lot of fun.

We weren't after the fun as much as we were interested in trying to discourage the cats from trying to take over the milking pen.

So we cut a hank of binder twine, tied it to one cat's tail, caught another cat, tied the twine to the second cat's tail, and tossed them over a wire that was stretched between two fence gate posts to keep them from sagging apart.

You talk about excitement.

Neither cat could get loose, but they were hissing, howling, scratching, clawing, screeching, and yowling. Just about ate each other up.

It had a visible and reactionary effect on the cows in the milk pen, too. The old hussy in the milking stall broke the strap that held the bar, backed up and stepped in the milk bucket, then snorted around the pen like she had a rocket up her tail end. The heifer in the next pen got all worked up and tried to push out the cedar stay fence. Calves waiting for their turn at the teat leavings were jumping around, kicking their hind feet up at gosh only knows what all. Horses over in the corral ran around rolling their eyes and stomping up a choking cloud of dust and dung.

Down at the house, Aunt Beth banged open the kitchen door and was squalling questions ninety to nothing. Uncle Lucious, without the broad-brimmed felt hat he always wore, came swarming out of the privy from his interrupted morning constitutional.

I told Bud to grab a cat. He told me to go to . . . you know where.

Finally, we each managed to get hold of a squirming mess of cat fur, I cut the twine, and the cats departed the milking pen. Don't remember seeing those two particular cats in the pen any more after that.

Some scratched up and more than a little flabbergasted at how the simplest, most innocent experiments can suddenly and totally unexpectedly go sour, we, each, individually, one-at-a-time, took a paralyzed oath -- that was then the sincerest and utterly utmost kind we knew of -- and promised Aunt Beth and Uncle Lucious we would not test cat theories at the milking pen again.

But all the time we were eating breakfast, Uncle Lucious would get choked up -- maybe from all that dust in the horse corral -- and turn away to have a strenuous bout of coughing. Strangely enough, Aunt Beth also seemed to have some trouble breathing and had to hide her face in her apron a time or two while she got hold of herself.

Also, they said they'd have to have a talking with Uncle Pete.

The Deer Feeder

One Sunday morning in late August of the year 1939, '40, or maybe even '41, Uncle Jim was sitting in one of the rocking chairs on the front porch of the ranch house at Baker's Crossing and, looking out and down at the field in front of the house next to Devils River, he said: "Let's build a deer feeder, Walt, and hang it in that pecan tree in the middle of the field".

Well, sir, we did. And I have a hankering to tell you about it.

I need to stick in a little background info here, so that you see it from the perspective of the 12 or 13 year-old lad I was at the time.

This was in the latter years of the Great Depression and just before the beginning of World War 2. Money was scarce. Recreational opportunities were few and far between for most folks. Family gatherings with some fried chicken and wet-sack-cooled watermelon were prized. A place to hunt and/or fish was high on anybody's list. Both for fun and table fare.

Sundays at the ranch were usually rest and guest days. There were always the daily chores that must be tended to: milking the cows, feeding the horses, slopping the hogs, gathering the eggs. But for the most part, it was a day when some of the family from town or another ranch in the Pecos or Devils River area would come to visit. When they did, they usually came by the post office in Comstock and picked up the mail and the Sunday paper.

Reading the Sunday paper on the front porch of the ranch on Sunday mornings was a unique experience. While the ladies finished up in the kitchen, the men would start the "reading" on the shaded and breeze-cooled front porch.

There was always a bit of friendly and jesting competition between Uncle Jim, Uncle Pete, Papo, -- maybe Uncle Lucious -- for the different sections of the paper -- especially the funnies. By tradition, I guess, whoever got the comics would start reading out loud. By the time you got to look at that paper section, you already knew the whole story depicted in the Kats and Jammer Kids, etc.

Uncle Jim was an avid reader. So I don't know whether he got the idea about the deer feeder from something he read in that Sunday's paper, from the latest copy of Popular Mechanics, from an issue of National Geographic, or it just came to his mind. But he gathered up this eager young nephew, headed to the workshop behind the house, and we went to work on a deer feeder.

Now you know without my having to tell you, there weren't any motorized deer feeders in our part of the world in those days. We -- Uncle Jim mostly, of course, and me "helping" -- made it from scratch. Well, almost.

First we cleaned an old five-gallon oil can. As I recall, it originally made its way to the ranch filled with motor oil -- Magnolia, I believe. It had served many subsequent uses between its arrival and the day we converted it to a feeder. It was square, not round. The bail was bent. The wooden handle for the bail had long-since said "good-by". It was made of tin, not plastic. This was a long time ago, you must remember.

In the middle of the flat bottom of the oil can, Uncle Jim punched a hole and then carefully enlarged it with tin snips, making it about as round as a silver dollar. (Silver dollars then were larger than the ones we have now.)

Then he got a section of the newspaper and started measuring, drawing, and cutting until he fashioned a lid large enough to fit over the top of the can with about three or four inches of over-hang on each side.

Next he flattened the paper lid on top of an old piece of roofing tin and traced the paper pattern onto the tin. Then, the tin snips went to work (I helped here) and after we riveted the edges together, we had a cover for the feeder to keep its contents dry from morning dew or occasional rain.

Scooping a couple of coffee cans of corn out of the bin in the barn from which the horses were sparingly fed and salvaging an old frayed rope from a peg in the saddle shed, we headed for the field.

The triangular field ran about three quarters of a mile along the river before the ranch house. At the south end, it apexed just upstream of the highway bridge over the river crossing. Devils River was the field's western edge. The fenced road from Comstock to Juno -- once used by army cavalry, wagon trains, stage coaches, etc. and still, at the time of this tale an unpaved dirt road -- bounded the field's east side. A fence ran across the north end between the river and the road.

The pecan tree we were to use lay midway between the river and the road, a hundred yards or so northwest of the front porch of the ranch house.

I still didn't know how Uncle Jim intended to control the flow of corn from the bottom of the feeder. To me it seemed it would all run out too quickly.

But, in the field, he cut a small limb from the pecan tree and trimmed it so that he could stick the butt of it into the hole and about a foot up into the feeder. He snipped and left a small branch on the limb so that when inserted into the feeder it would keep the "trigger" from coming out. Leaves and smaller branches were still attached and hanging down below the feeder.

Throwing the rope over a big limb of the pecan tree, we hoisted the feeder with its corn and "trigger" into the tree just high enough that deer could walk under the rig and brush against the "trigger". Movement of the trigger branch by the wind or by a deer walking under would cause the part of the limb in the feeder to move and dispense driblets of corn between the hole edges and the triggering limb. After some adjustment, the rig worked well.

It was hung from the tree in a brush-screened location where it and the area below it could not be seen from the road. But from the elevated front porch of the ranch? From the still higher front porch on the second floor of the ranch house!

In those days, does could not be taken. Neither could spike bucks. But as you may have surmised, from the rocking chairs on the porches that fall -- after deer season began, of course -- there were sometimes observed beneath that early, primitive, but very effective deer feeder -- does, spikes, and even mature and legal bucks.

The Traps

Episode One

When I was a tad, one of my ambitions was to be a trapper. Why? Because my granddad, uncles, and even my grandmother (Mamo) told neat stories about trapping and head-lighting exploits. Especially when I was sitting in a comfortable lap in front of the fireplace or on the shady porch. The bent twig growing into the big tree thing, you know.

Mama took her kids -- me, Bud (Edwin Hart Block, Jr.), Shirley, and, later, Lee -- to the ranch -- into the family folds and traditions -- for at least a part of each Christmas. During the depression years of the thirties, gifts were usually small and few, but much love was shared.

When I was five or six, at the gala (for us) Christmas Tree at the ranch on Christmas Eve, Santa rewarded my super good behavior with a greatly desired pair of almost genuine cowboy-style gauntlets.

Gauntlets, you know, are gloves with long cuffs to protect not only hands but much of the forearms. The cuffs extend up over the end of long shirt or coat sleeves and shield the wearer from thorny brush, insects, and dirty stuff.

In my mind right then, Tom Mix himself couldn't have had a better pair of gloves. It mattered not to me that, rather than the leather composition of the gloves and cuffs of the stars of the silver screen, my palms and fingers were covered with dark-colored warmly-woolen fabric and that the lengthy cuffs with the star printed on them were of some material akin to oilcloth.

I was puffed-up proud of my cowboy-cuffed gloves! And I was bodaciously tickled the day after Christmas when Uncle Jim invited me to go with him to run part of his "short" trap line.

Each winter Uncle Jim had two trap lines. The long line had many traps, ran from the river up one canyon to its head, crossed over the divide, and came back down another canyon to the river. It required most of a day to run. The short trap line had fewer traps -- near the house along the river and the foot of the hills. It could be tended after the morning chores and before noon. The trap lines were run on alternate days, first one, then the other.

Trappers are like cooks. Success secrets are seldom shared with others. Often one of the best-kept trapper secrets is how he makes his stink bait!

Varmints must be lured to set traps to be caught. When a trapper catches several animals, he has a heavy load to pack back. So what he starts out carrying must be compact and light. To keep from hauling a burdensome and stinking mess of old meat scraps, etc. for bait, the trapper usually concocts some concentrated, usually very smelly bait which he totes along in a small bottle or jar. A smidgen of stink bait is placed in back of a set trap so that a curious fox, coon, or ringtail investigating the inviting odor, will walk over the trap, step on the trigger, spring the trap, and become part of that year's fur catch.

On this, my introductory trap run, the first trap was in the field just in front of the ranch house between the highway and Devils River. Uncle Jim carried a replacement trap to substitute for one he thought wasn't working right. Carrying his trap bag, I tagged happily along, wearing my new cowboy gauntlets, of course.

The trap bag had small pieces of newspaper to cover triggers of the set traps, a pair of pliers, some wire, an empty tin can with small holes punched in the bottom to sift a light layer of dirt on the paper over the trigger, and, that all-important small bottle of stink bait.

Somewhere in the process of replacing the old trap with the new one, Uncle Jim broke a small stick, opened the bait bottle and dipped the twig in the stink bait. The odor wrinkled my nose. He handed me the stinky twig to hold while he put the final touches on the set trap.

I was in awe -- watching him wire the trap chain to a drag limb, mash the trap springs, and set the trigger. Then he eased the set trap into a small depression under a bush, and sifted dirt on the paper scrap over the trigger.

Until he asked for the bait twig, I was not aware that, while watching him, I had unthinkingly repeatedly transferred the smelly little stick back and forth from one gloved hand to the other. That warm and fuzzy, formerly pleasant smelling fabric covering my fingers had soaked up that smelly, juicy goop on the twig like a sponge.

With smiling consideration, Uncle Jim told me that I had just become the most odoriferously little would-be cowboy-trapper in the whole of the Wild and Wooly West. Not only did my gloves stink, but when I took them off, I stunk too! We both knew that Mama would be unhappy -- with both of us!

Quickly and thoughtlessly, I did what little boys do. I wiped my hands on the seat of my britches. Compounded the sorry mess! But . . . - - -

Like I've told you ere this, ole Uncle Jim was a thinker. On his considered advice, I scooped up handfuls of dirt and rubbed my gloved hands together. It helped, but not much. Then we went to the river and I washed the gloves and my hands. Squished mossy mud and pre- and post-rinsed. Some better? Or were we just getting used to the odor? Or maybe it was becoming a modified odor? By that time, it was hard to tell.

All the way back to the house, I plucked sagebrush leaves and wrung my gauntleted-clad hands desperately together. But when we stepped up on the porch, Uncle Pete smelled us coming and after that everybody in Val Verde County knew about this smelly little kid and his trap-bait-flavored gloves.

Mama was even madder than I figured she'd be. At me. At Uncle Jim. At Uncle Pete. At Papo, when he laughed. And when Mama was mad, Mama was bad news.

For that year, at least, my trapping career had come to screeching halt. But, as it turned out, there was a next time.

Episode Two

The next event that significantly stands out on the horizon of my increasing mastery of the trapping art happened some four or five years later, again during a Christmas vacation period at the ranch. I was then about 10 or ll years old. Basically just a town boy who visited at the ranch of his grandparents in the summers and during holidays.

The HOUSE at the ranch was the improved original structure located at Baker's Crossing. At that time it was occupied by my grandparents, (Papo and Mamo -- Walter H. Baker and Lois Selema [Lem] McLane Baker) and their son, Jim.

A mile north up the road was the former home of Mamo's parents, the McLanes. After their passing, and after Papo and Mamo's second son, Pete, married Aunt Joy, this small house was remodeled and became the home for Uncle Pete, Aunt Joy, and, in time, their children: Michael, Judy, Norman, and Molly.

There were barns, sheds, pens, waterlots, etc., at both locations. But, due to the lay-of-the-land, it was easier to drive and work sheep in the pens at Uncle Pete's house. Therefore, much of the ranch day-to-day activity started and/or ended there. Which meant that at the beginning of most days, those at Papo's house would go to Uncle Pete's place.

One bright and shining, clear and cold, winter morning, Papo, Uncle Jim, and I were in the pickup, driving to Uncle Pete's.

The road we followed parallels Devils River. A quarter of a mile up the road from Papo's, there was a large pecan tree in the right-hand lane. The tree was at the foot of a fair-to-middlin' draw that ran westward from the hills down toward the river.

Uncle Jim had a trap set in that draw, about twenty or thirty yards east of the road fence. I had been with him to that trap before, but on this morning, when he stopped the pickup, he said: "OK, Walt, run up there and check the trap."

With a sizeable lump of apprehension crowding my recently eaten breakfast, I hopped out of the pickup, climbed the fence, and went up the draw to check the trap.

And, WHOA!

The biggest and most ferocious-looking fox I had ever seen, alive or dead, was in that trap! He was NOT glad to be there and NOT glad to see me!

I hollered back to Uncle Jim and Papo: "BIG FOX in the trap."

Uncle Jim yelled back: "Is he alive?"

I assured them that this Fox was very much alive.

"So get a stick, Son, knock him in the head, and bring him out and we'll reset the trap later", Papo called.

I had heard grownup folks talk about something being easier said than done. I learned the meaning of that saying that very day.

Armed with a hefty stick, I tried to get to the fox. He did not cooperate! He stayed at the end of the trap chain, and when I got close, he rolled his lip up and showed his teeth. Did you ever get to count the teeth of a big worked-up fox? Close up? While he was still alive?

That fox had a real mean-sounding, nasty, hissing growl. When he turned his back and neck hair wrong side out, he scared the bejeebers out of me.

I got a bigger, longer stick.

That snarling fox backed further away in the brush and I couldn't get to him. Didn't want to get to him. I figured if he decided to come my way, that chain was way too dang short.

Every now and then Papo or Uncle Jim would call out and ask how I was doing. I swear it sounded like they were choking when they asked. I know they couldn't have been laughing, because they had to know that I was having a real serious time in that thicket with that overgrown, teeth-gnashing fox.

Finally, reluctantly, I yelled to Papo and Uncle Jim and told them I couldn't get to the fox because he was backed too far into the brush and he dodged my stick every time I tried to smack him.

I heard the pickup door slam and the fence squeal as someone came over it and then Papo was there, smiling through the tobacco smoke of his crooked-stemmed pipe. I suddenly understood another phrase: "A sight for sore eyes".

Papo just took my stick, grabbed the end of the trap chain, stepped in and whacked the fox, and that was it.

He helped me get the fox out of the trap and we went back to the pickup.

When Uncle Jim looked at the fox as I heaved it into the pickup bed, he said something about what a big "boar" fox it was.

When Papo talked about this little event later -- and it seemed like almost everybody and his cousin had to be told about it -- I wondered why he seemed to entitle the story: "Walt and his 'Gentleman' Fox".

I didn't think that fox was a gentleman! I had other names for him.

Episode Three

Then there was the time a couple of years later that I was running some of Uncle Jim's traps on my lonesome during the Christmas Season. He was feeling puny from a bout with the flu and, after making one round with me to show me where the traps were, he let me run the short trap line for several days. He helped with the skinning, since I had almost no experience with such.

Uncles Jim and Pete had tutored me with .22 rim fire rifles and I had done some shooting under their supervision in the summers, using old Prince Albert cans as targets in the canyon area behind the house. We also "worked on" river turtles, which were supposedly detrimental to fishing. We would sit on the bank and when a turtle popped its head above the water to get some air, we'd try to hit those small marks.

The best practice came with tossing empty cardboard .22 cartridge boxes and cow chips into the river below the bridge. The water was swift and shallow; the rocks on the bottom caused lots of surface waves. The fast current and undulating, pitching targets were great sport and the bets made on our results either doubled or eliminated some daily chores. I lost most of the bets but the fun . . . the fellowship . . . the training . . . was priceless.

Seriously cautioned by Uncle Jim, I was permitted to take his .22 pump when I ran his trap lines that year. Care came first, but I was also to avoid shooting fur bearers, because any cut or hole in the hide would lessen its value. I was only to use the .22 for skunks caught in the traps or if a snared hog had not managed to free itself.

One day I came upon a trap in which a large and very much alive coon was caught. This big fat coon had a thick winter hide that would bring a lot of money. He had pulled the trap, chain, and drag deep into a catclaw thicket.

I tried to get to him with a club, but he had me just about as buffaloed as my Gentleman Fox. I wasn't so much afraid of him as worried we would tear up his hide while I was crawling in there and trying to bash his head. He was big. He definitely didn't like me coming in there after him.

So, I sat down and cogitated about it. I had heard it was possible to shoot a trapped coon in one eye and, if you lined him up just right, have the slug come out his anus without any new holes in his hide. So I decided to try.

I moved around and he kept looking at me and finally I had a perfect alignment. I squeezed off the shot, hit the coon dead center of one eye, and killed him dead. And I'll take a paralyzed oath if the outside edge of the emerging bullet hole wasn't a mere three-quarters of an inch from the outside edge of his back side portal. Measured before and after he was skinned!

Uncle Jim and Papo were proud of me. But Mama fussed because I had been gone so long and she had been worried about me. I tried to tell her it took considerable time to come up with that Davy Crockett type solution and line that coon up for that shot! She threatened to veto any more solo trapping for me that year, but finally relented.

Episode Four

My trapping career really did start a distinctly definite declining downhill slide a couple or so years later.

The house at Baker's Crossing is located on the western edge of a relatively flat alluvial shelf that fronts on Devils River. Behind the house were: a workshop, car house, school house, workers' house, shed, barn, and pens. Just in back of the pens at the barn and shed, a mountain rises abruptly.

When you climb that mountain there is a splendid view of several miles of Devils River. The Baker's Crossing bridge is just downstream of the house. The view upstream takes in the river field in front of the house and several fenced areas between the river and the road all the way past Uncle Pete's house and north-northwesterly up toward the Hudspeth ranch. Below the bridge, the river alternates between nice, relatively deep and slow moving pools and shallow rapids. It meanders away to the southeast, going past Uncle Bill's (Will Baker) old place, the old cabin where Papo's dad (Dave Baker) last lived, and past the ranch owned by Papo's cousin, Alva Baker and his son A.O.

Uncle Jim had several traps set out on that mountain. One was just under the rimrock and almost directly over the house and pen area. Something had been caught in that trap and, in dragging, the limb wired to it had been broken into pieces too small to impede another varmint trying to get away.

That trap was in a mighty fine location -- a nearly vertical crevice in the base of the rimrock. It was deep enough to put the bait behind the set trap under the small tree growing in the very back of the crevice. It was narrow enough that an animal sniffing at the bait would almost certainly step onto the dirt-covered trap trigger.

When I reset the trap, I couldn't find a suitable limb for a drag. Instead, I wired the end of the trap chain to the little persimmon tree in the back of the vee-shaped crevice. I didn't know enough about trapping to realize that a caught animal could more easily tear loose when tied to a solid object.

After wiring the chain to the tree, I put the pliers back into the trap bag. Then, stepping on the trap springs, I pushed down the trap jaws, and set the trigger. Next, I laid the trap jaws flat, placed the set trap in a depression in the crevice, eased a piece of paper over the trigger, and began sifting a light layer of dirt on top of the paper.

The dirt sifter I used was fashioned by Uncle Jim from an old tin Lipton Tea can. It was square, not round. The bottom had several holes punched with a small nail. The flat can sides were worn slick and shiny.

The late afternoon winter sun was about to drop behind the hills across the river. It was cold.

Particles of dirt had almost covered the paper over the trigger of the trap, when . . . ZAP!

I was dinked by a dastardly, dangling, ding-a-ling of destiny!

The sifter slipped out of my numb fingers!

I grabbed to catch the can before it hit the trigger and sprang the trap. Too late!

The trap jaws snapped up, knocking the slick-sided can out of the way, and catching three fingers of my right hand! After some raw, crude, unrefined, amateurish but heart-felt cussing, I tried to un-trap the intrepid trapper. But I had a real bad problem. The trap was wired to that tree.

The crevice's rock walls were too close together for me to get more than one foot at a time on the trap springs. I couldn't open the jaws without depressing both springs. One foot and the left hand didn't work either. The trap chain was too short for me to stretch my left hand or a foot to the trap bag which held the pliers I needed to cut the wire securing the chain to the tree.

I looked down at the ranch yard far below. Now and then, someone walked from the back porch to a car or an out-building. I swallowed my pride and began yelling. But an updraft blowing up the mountain side prevented those insensitive and uncaring people down there from hearing me.

Then I thought about the flat, shiny sides of the sifter can. I hooked it over to me with a foot and, ala Boy Scout training, started flashing reflections of the setting sun -- to get attention of somebody in the yard.

But no one noticed. They didn't care about me trapped up there on the mountain side -- in plain view -- that any half-brained child could see!

But, wait! Someone, I think it was my brother, Bud, saw a flash. He waved.

I waved back. And yelled, and gestured, and cussed, and cried.

After an eternity, someone else noticed and called Uncle Jim. Then Mama came out and joined the gawkers.

They yelled at me -- that it was getting late and I should come on down because supper was about ready!

After I kept making big swooping gestures for someone to come up to help me, they did send Bud up -- to tell me to get my tail on down the mountain.

He handed me the pliers. I cut the wire holding the trap to the tree. We got me out of the trap, got a stick for a trap drag, reset that dang trap, and went down the mountain.

My career as a trapper went slithering downhill with me.

The Hay Maker

Well, yes, now that you mention it, I did make some hay in my time. Like that pound of dirt you eat before you die. Or "into each life some rain will fall". That's how I feel about hay making.

In my "hay days" -- not "those good ole days", but the ones "making hay" -- I was a twig being processed by my elders into the mighty oak which you undoubtedly know me to be.

Back then, the Baker ranch operation was a sheep and goat business. Game was not yet a money crop. Goats were primarily for mohair and to a lesser degree marketed for carbito and carne de chivo. Sheep were for wool; but a secondary product was lamb, as most male yearlings went to the dining table for their ultimate place on serving platters.

The horses on the ranch were work animals. The few cows were for milk and butter for the folks of the family and to feed dogie lambs which had lost their ewes.

Those animals, except in the dry spells of drought, subsisted by grazing and browsing.

Horses and cows also partook of natural bounty in the pastures, but to be effectively productive, their diets were supplemented. Especially in the winter months when green growth was not as easily found or as nutritious.

Therefore, Papo (my granddad), his sons (my uncles), the grandkids, and even the nephews were sometimes workers in the fields -- the hay fields. Hay makers. Whether we wanted to be or not.

Before the '32 Devils River flood, "The Field" between the highway and the river in front of Papo's house had a goodly layer of fertile soil. Pecan and oak trees had shaded and protected man and animals for countless years as they came to drink and rest. Animal droppings added to the richness of the soil. Original grasses, and later the planted crops, thrived.

Much of that area known as The Field was devoted to growing and harvesting hay.

After the '32 flood, few big trees remained. Most of the top soil was gone. Hay production was scaled back to the few productive acres less eroded in the northeast corner of The Field. The hay crop from this smaller plot was not enough to tide the ranch's horses and cows over a full year. More hay production was needed.

A mile up the road from Papo's house at the crossing was the cluster of barns and pens and the remaining small abode of Grandpap McClain. When Grandpap (Mamo's dad & one of my great-granddads) grew too old to live there by himself, he moved down to the big house at Baker's Crossing. After Uncle Pete and Aunt Joy married, Grandpap's Place was fixed up for their home. The rustic little cabin was gradually and continually improved. In my teen-age, young, and unworldly view, it was a delightful dwelling in a beautiful location.

Grandpap had worked a large garden area just southeast of his yard. After the '32 flood, part of it was retained by Uncle Pete as a garden, but most became the ranch's number two hay field. For a number of years prior to the restrictions imposed by diminishing health and advancing age, Grandpap had been "designated person" supervising the gardening and also the hay making for the Baker Ranch. Gradually and ultimately, Papo assumed that role.

After the '32 flood washed away the hydraulic pump that had been embedded in concrete footings in the foot of the rapids in Devil's River at the upper end of The Field, the hay crops were dry-land operations.

But, there was always a hay crop, large or small; depending upon how much rain fell during the summer. That crop was ever and always due for cutting in the late summer -- when I was out of school. And, therefore, available!

As you know, the 1930's were depression years. Hard times. Folks had to make do with what they had. New equipment and machinery was scarce as hen's teeth. The Baker hay making was a labor-intensive, sweaty, sore-back job.

How the seeds were planted, I really don't know. I was usually still in school in the late spring, so I don't have personal memory of the planting of the hay crops.

Papo used a team of horses to pull the plow and turn the soil. This same team also pulled the mower when the hay was ready to cut. That team worked well together, got the job done, but there was no beauty in their appearance. Ben Green couldn't have traded them for doodley squat!

Papo walked his long legs first behind the plow and later behind the mower. Neither of the rigs was a riding contraption. (I told you it was a tough job.)

The mower was a sickle-bar thing-a-ma-jig. The bar and its slicing blades stuck out to the right side and cut a swath about five or six feet wide. Papo started at one corner of the field, clucked at his horses, and followed the team around the outside edge of the planted area, cutting about five feet into the standing hay stems.

Down at the next corner he reined his team around a right-angle turn and mowed a five-foot chunk of the next side of the field. Then at the next corner, right-angle turn and cut along that side, and finally, around the third corner, cut a swath, and back to the point of beginning. Just kept going round the field that way, hollering "gee" at every corner, with the uncut area gradually getting smaller, until he finished in the middle of the field.

As a tad, I wasn't expected to be much help. I was just a tag-a-long, enjoying watching Papo cut the fields. I was beguiled by those green leafy stems and their mop-top reddish-brown heads of grain all falling in a wave like a row of dominoes.

As the cuts diminished the standing, shading, covering cane, all kinds of critters -- rabbits, snakes, rats, pole cats, and other varmints -- would scurry to the inner area in the uncut cane. But sooner or later they made a dash for the edge of the field and uncut growth. If they lit out early, they didn't have to scoot too far in the open. But if they waited, there was more territory to cross before they got to the safety of the cover outside the field.

Good snakes and harmless snakes were just fun to watch. Bad snakes, rattlers mostly, were exterminated. Rabbits -- mainly jack rabbits -- were fair game, 'cause in Papo's eyes they competed for the same grass and forage that fed his sheep and goats. Rats darted in and out under the cut stems and leaves and grain heads lying on the ground and were hard to kill. But live or not, we wanted all the critters out of the field, because . . .

We did not have a team-drawn rake. At least not in the times I remember. The hay was bundled, not bailed. There was no hay bailer. The men and larger boys would walk along, reach out with both arms as wide as you could, dig your hands into the cut cane laying on the ground, and bring all you could gather that way into a bunch. Pull one of the "ties" looped over or under your belt, tie the bundle. Move up and do it again, and again, and again.

For "ties", sometimes we had binder twine. Early on I became a binder twine cutter. Papo or one of the uncles measured off a length on the pickup tail gate and I cut twine to those specifications. Had to be accurate. Too short and the guys tying would fuss. Too long and Papo scolded 'cause we were wasting twine, twine cost money, etc.!

But some years were leaner than others and there were those times when we either didn't have any binder twine or we ran out before the job was done.

Then, one of the uncles would cut long green Spanish dagger spears, remove the sharp barbs on the end, and slice the leaves in long thin strips. Again, too thin and the strips of dagger would break in the tying process; too thick and the tying job was much more difficult. Also, much of the time, the length of the dagger leaves was not great enough to tie a bundle with only one strip -- two had to be tied together, which meant two knots per bundle.

The sap in the green dagger leaves was hard on your hands. The men's hands were calloused and tough and sometimes they had gloves. The kids who were supplying the dagger ties usually had softer hands and, in those days, seldom had gloves.

After it was bundled, the sheaves of hay had to cure -- lie on the ground in the field for a time; dependent upon how much sap was in the canes and whether there was rain or dew that kept the bundle from drying sufficiently. Always, at least one turning had to be done. That meant going back in the field, walking along, stooping over, lifting each still semi-sappy heavy bundle, and turning it over so that the other side would be up and exposed.

After several days, again depending upon the weather, when the bundles were judged by Papo to be rid of enough moisture, we went back into the fields and shocked the hay.

First, one sheaf or bundle was set upright, butt end down, grain pods on top, and held in place -- usually -- by one of the "fortunate" nephews. The rest of the crew picked up the nearest bundles and -- one by one -- stood them the same way, leaning them just slightly against the center bundle. Each sheaf supported the shock. The angle of leaning was critical. Each sheaf must angle in from bottom to top. Outward angled sheaves fell. Stacked too straight and the shock might topple. Too much angled in and the base of the shock was too wide and the hay would not continue to dry as it should -- rain and dew would not be shed well.

There was some rule of thumb about the size of the shock that I never fully understood. But I know it was important, 'cause Papo fussed if it didn't look right to him!

AGAIN, after a period of more drying in the shock, when Papo deemed the hay in the field was ripe and ready, we were extended the exquisite experience of unlimited joy, rapture, and ecstasy of loading the hay into the pickup and bringing it in to the barn.

First off, colonies of enterprising wasps never failed to find those hay shocks to be enticingly attractive and protecting shelters for their late summer communal berthing and hatching. Not big nests, usually, but those devils got angry when disturbed. Scorpions just naturally flocked to the stacked bundles. Centipedes were right at home in the dark, damp dirt at the bottom of the shock. Tarantulas. Met my first vinegaroon there. Always found snakes.

Stooping, picking up the heavy bundles, and hoisting them into the bed of the pickup was toilsome, hot, sweaty, late August work. Riding on top of the hay loads from the field to the barn was almost fun. But when we got to the barn the ultimate, supreme drudgery began.

The dry, dusty, scratchy hay had to be picked up and manually tossed up overhead to the loft of the barn. By hand. Each bundle. Every bundle. All the dang bundles . . . . . .

If there was a better part of this job, it was up in the loft. We did a lot of chore-swapping, job-jockeying, assignment-engineering, and downright finagling to get the loft duty.

Up there in the loft, right under and next to the corrugated-tin barn roof in August, catching the bundles and tossing them into space-saving layers was hotter -- much hotter.

But if you were on the lower end of the action, throwing the hay up to the guys in the loft, there was just no darn way to keep the leaves and chaff and dust and bugs from falling back on you. In your eyes. Down your collar. Up your sleeves.

It was sneezy, teary, coughing, itching, cussing torture.

And this mild, meek, and gentle description doesn't even take into account the grasshoppers, katydids, millipedes, lizards, spiders, and other lively and squiggly things that somehow always got to the barn with the hay.

Up your sleeve. Down your shirt collar. Even up your pants leg!

Yet, at the end of the day, there was usually mitigating and almost justifying compensation.

Not always, but more often than not, we quit early enough in the late afternoon to go the river and take a swim.

Cool, clear, water!

The Road Off

Back in the early 1940's, The Road Off was not there. It did not exist. That's when Lucious and Beth Hinds sold their Pecos River ranch and bought their new spread on Devils River.

When World War Two created the need for more flying and air space for the training of pilots for the U. S. of A. Army Air Force, the feds bought a chunk of level land south of the Southern Pacific Railroad track and east of Del Rio so they could carve out Laughlin AFB. Most of that land had been part of a ranch owned by Gilbert Marshall.

Mr. Marshall then bought the Pecos River Ranch which Uncle Lucious and Aunt Beth had been working and improving from the time they married. He hoped to mine the bat guano in a large cave near the Pecos. At that time bat guano -- droppings -- brought high dollar for fertilizer.

Uncle Lucious and Aunt Beth had been building up and paying off their Pecos place from the time they first moved onto it and temporarily lived in a cave on it. With funds from the sale of that Ranch, they made the down payment on the Devils River Ranch.

When they moved -- lock, stock, and barrel -- onto the Devils River Ranch, it had no Road Off.

To get from the divide overlooking the river down to the vega or from the river banks up to the divide, there was only a very difficult trail.

That "trail off" was used in those days by . . . coons, ringtails, fox, deer, goats, javalinas . . . and . . . probably back in the really olden days . . . by panthers, bears, badgers, Indians . . .

But for sheep, this trail and others like it were only seldom used routes to or from the river. Sheep opted to take the "trail off" only when sorely pressed or urgently prodded.

Right-minded, rider-less horses rarely figured they needed to leave the divide or come up from the river. If they did, they made a long roundabout trek into or out of one of headers that permitted easier access to the long canyons. They just didn't like to use the "trail off".

Horses with riders could make it up or down. But only with tarnational difficulty. And then only with the rider dismounted, out front, and pulling on the reins a good part of the way. Sometimes it took two people to get a horse up or down -- one in front hauling on the reins and the other working the horse's rear end over with a sotol stalk.

The newly acquired ranch had a small house out on the divide. The divide is the relatively level, mountain-top area between canyons that run drainage to the river. The new place also had a car shed, a big tin-roofed shearing-shed/barn, and some shaky cedar stay pens.

The windmill at the house/barn location was called the House Mill. When the wind blew tolerably -- water was pumped for about a third of the ranch area -- the folks and the stock in the House Pasture.

The East Mill was also on the divide, about half way between the house and the river. The stock in the Big Pasture watered at the East Mill or at the river. In the bad times when the wind didn't turn the windmills enough, folks, stock, and wildlife watered at the river.

So that this tale will be easier to tell, I'll talk about the work done on the new ranch as if it were only done by Uncle Lucious. But please know that when there was work to be done -- even hard, physical, down and dirty manual work -- it almost never was something he did alone. Aunt Beth was always there, either working directly or in a supporting role. From time to time, as they could afford it, wets, braceros, and other hired laborers were employed. During the war years hired labor was hard to come by.

Having no kids of their own -- visiting nephews and nieces, grand-nephews and grand nieces helped out in the summers. Friends, preachers, fellow parishioners, and a multitudinous hodge-podge of others were afforded the opportunity to lend a hand now and then. The lure of hunting and the promise of an easier way down to the fishing were heady enticements.

Early on, sheep and goats in the Big Pasture ranged all over the ranch -- up on the semi-level divide, down in the twisting canyons, and along the winding river. But without mounted-rider access to and from the divide into the canyons and river vega, it was very hard to work the stock. It took several years of labor before Uncle Lucious managed to fence those two large pastures into easier-worked, smaller areas from which stock could be rotated for grazing.

The "trail off", using Aunt Beth's legendary jargon, "needed to be" converted into The Road Off.

The ranch had some three miles of Devils River waterfront, running upstream from the mouth of Dead Mans Canyon to beyond the mouth of Dark Canyon. The Gillis Ranch was downstream. Tom and Myrtle Brite's spread lay upstream.

Another inspiring factor prompting the conversion of the "trail off", as you may have guessed from other Chip Tales, was: Uncle Lucious, Aunt Beth, and members of their extended family -- Hinds, Bakers, Blocks, etc. -- all held fishing -- especially Devils River fishing -- as being close to traipsing in the promised land. Better access to the river was doubly necessary.

Those early fishing trips on the Hinds Devils River Ranch were more than just a mite laborious. You really had a burning desire to go fishing if you signed on for one of Uncle Lucious' outings.

From the Hinds Ranch house, a fair-to-middling, rutty ranch road wandered between the sotol, prickly pear, lechuguia, and occasional clumps of grass on the divide -- first northeasterly, then snaking along about two miles southeast to the East Mill. As the crow flies, the East Mill was roughly a mile and a half southeast of the ranch house.

An even more rudimentary road twisted from the East Mill toward the river over the rock ledges of the divide flats. After that jarring mile and a half journey, you arrived at a point on the edge of the divide overlooking Devils River. There, about a half mile upstream from the mouth of Dead Mans Canyon, the "trail off" dropped down.

War Department, Corps of Engineers, U. S. Army maps record that overlook at about the 1,600 foot level. The noted elevation down at the vega is about 1,200 feet. The "trail off" crawled down the face of that 400 foot drop. Not straight down, but darn near.

In the beginning, it was mostly day fishing. Folks rode horses or bounced along in a pre-war era pickup to the overlook and then climbed foot-back down the trail. Climbed down and climbed up. The climb down was bad news. The climb back up was burning Hades.

You carried all your gear down. Gear and the fish you wanted to bring out, you grunted, groaned, and clumsied up that trail of sweat and tears . . . wondering every step of the way why in the ever-loving, blue-eyed world you were doing that to yourself.

As they worked and improved the new ranch -- tending, doctoring, and shearing the flock, fixing fences, repairing roads, greasing windmills, cleaning tanks, patching water lines, scrubbing water troughs, filling feed troughs, and other must-do tasks -- Uncle Lucious and Aunt Beth allotted as much time as possible to the creation of The Road Off.

Building fences and roads on ranches along the Pecos and Devils Rivers is rock work. Rock Work. Mostly crow bar work. Posthole diggers are people, not tools. You slammed that crow bar into the mostly solid rock. Tried not to let the bottom of the hole get too rounded or the hole defeated you. Scooped rock chips and dirt out with your gloved or ungloved fist or maybe an empty tuna fish or coffee can. A lot of the time even a crow bar won't do the job. Much of the work was done with a masonry drill and a sledge hammer. On rare occasions, dynamite was used. Not often. Too dangerous. Mighty expensive.

The Road Off was built that way.

A crack in the rimrock at the overlook was gradually widened and sloped. Below that gap, the trail curved down, first to the right, and then back and forth across the face of the hill. Ledge by ledge, the path zigzagged, between boulders and jagged rock chunks dumped down from the decomposing rimrock by the wearing elements of wind and rain, heat and cold.

With crow bar, drill, muscle, and sweat, Uncle Lucious and helpers chipped and flaked away the bigger ledges. Fragments and rubble were shoveled and tamped to level the sharper and more abrupt slopes. They filled and smoothed with caliche and gravel until, at long last, folks could walk down, rather than climb. The trek out was a lesser monster than before, but still an agony.

After years of plain old hard, back-breaking work, Uncle Lucious and Aunt Beth and others working stock and tending the ranch could get from the divide down to the river and back out with less concern for their early demise. Roundups were easier. The world was rosier.

Fishing trips became less physically demanding. We could load our gear on horses or mules and ride in and out. But we were still limited in what we could pack in or out. Creature comforts for the lesser warriors were not yet at hand. Aunt Beth could do those trips like picnics in the park. Other ladies fared not so well, if they went at all.

Sometime in 1945 or 46, Uncle Lucious got hold of an army surplus, four-wheel-drive weapons carrier. I think it was a weapons carrier. It might have been a command car. He was an artist with a cutting torch and welding rig. By the time I first saw the four-wheeler in the summer of '45 or '46 he had modified it considerably.

The improvements on the trail done to that time plus that four-wheel drive buggy allowed a change in the name of the "trail off". From then on, it was The Road Off.

Along about then, a hand-cranked concrete mixer was semi-permanently set up on the edge of the overlook. Pickup loads of sand and gravel from washes in Dark Canyon were transported to the mixer. Water from the East Mill and sacked concrete from town were hauled to the mixing site. Little by little, a concrete ramp was created. It sloped down the gap gouged out of the rimrock and curved around to the right just under the worst of the ledges.

With the concrete ramp, the road was a piece of cake -- for the four-wheel weapons carrier. But it was still a white-finger-nail experience that scared the bejeebers out of lots of folks the first time they went off the hill. Or tried to drive out.

The first time Mama and Clarence went fishing with Uncle Lucious and Aunt Beth after the ramp was built, we drove down The Road Off without much fuss. Mama was an old ranch-raised gal. On the way down she only warbled a little waspishly about the steep road and acknowledged the gargantuan amount of work it obviously had required.

Howsomever, as we herded that old weapons wagon back out, Uncle Lucious was driving, Aunt Beth was in the outside shotgun seat, and Mama was perched right where they wanted her -- in the middle of the front seat, both knees straddling the double-stalked gear shift. Clarence, I, and some others were back in the bed of the carrier.

As Uncle Lucious started the pull up the lower end of the steep concrete ramp he had that old buggy shifted down into grandma -- its lowest and most powerful gear. As we climbed up, he gradually eased off on the accelerator and the growling and grunting old surplus motor began to grind slower and slower. Chugging up the incline, that old mechanized mule was making sounds like it was gasping its last. Mama progressively began leaning forward until her nose was almost touching the windshield. She was more than some round-eyed. She was reaching ahead and pulling on the dashboard as we began to agonizingly creep around the curve just below the rimrock. Then Uncle Lucious calmly pressed the foot feed, gave the ole bus the gas, it came to life like a goosed gosling, and we zoomed right on out the narrow crevice in the rimrock and up into the bright and shining sunshine. Mama exercised her innate, native-born, ranch-bred, rough-raised, and well-honed vocabulary. Rasped Uncle Lucious' ancestry real good.

As time passed, continuing improvements on The Road Off made life better on the ranch. The fishing trips morphed from those early one-day-only affairs, in-and-out, quickie affairs -- to camping weekends -- to the first slab-sided cabin. That cabin was upgraded nearly every year until it was carried away by one of Devils River's infamous rises. A second cabin was constructed on higher ground --a few steps farther from the river. It also matured into a more comforting shelter.

In the late '40s and early '50s Leon Walton and I on several happy occasions found our way out to fishing's Valhala at Uncle Lucious and Aunt Beth's place. I'll bend your ear in other tales about some of our escapades on the river at the bottom of The Road Off. But, let me wind up this telling with a word about how our first happy venture there began.

Leon, as far as I know, has never owned a new car. Not a brand-spanking new car. He obtained good serviceable vehicles and wore them out. Still does.

On this occasion, we were driving along, happy as just-hatched June bugs, in a long-nosed old Chrysler. The ranch road over the divide had been considerably improved since Uncle Lucious and Aunt Beth first acquired the place. Still, Leon babied the eight-cylindered old black beauty along, wary of the lasting quality of its old and thin tires over those sharp rocks.

When you first drive up to the lookout on the rimrock just before plunging into The Road Off, the view is spectacular. It inspires. Down there below, Devils River is laid out in its entrancing magnificence. Looking left and upstream you can see beyond The Chute (the location of one of the tales you have yet to encounter) to The Falls (another tale site). You gaze right and downstream and see the clear waters flowing through pools and flashing through rapids, curving off eastward. Right in front -- it is simply gorgeous. Elegant. Dazzling. A scene any artist would be challenged and privileged to paint. Just across, from the rimrock down to the river, the hillside, is crevassed and etched and carved and covered with the sparse, stark, spiny, spiked, flora of West Texas.

As most drivers do, when first cautiously approaching the overlook edge, Leon stopped the car. We just gawked at that gorgeous splendor. After awhile, Leon eased his foot off the brake, toed the accelerator, and started to drive on. Suddenly, he stomped on the brake pedal, clenched the steering wheel, jerked up the emergency, and gasped a shuddering "WHOA!"

The long, black hood of that eight-cylindered automobile seemed to be jutting right out into thin air. He couldn't see where the road went.

My telling him to "just steer down and to the right" was not quite enough. He backed the car up until he could see the edge of the rimrock and the gap with its disappearing ramp. Stopped the car. Set the emergency brake. Got out. Put a big rock in front of one tire and another slab behind it. Then he walked to the edge of the overlook. From there he could see the entire layout of that awesome ramp and the whole of The Road Off. He studied long and hard.

Finally, he slowly drove down, hugging the old car up against the craggy rocks of the hillside, scraping fenders, first on the right and then on the left.

We camped and fished all weekend. Had a bodacious blast.

Leon fretted the whole time about whether the old Chrysler could get us back up The Road Off.

But we made it. With all our gear, a nice mess of fish, and some unforgettable memories.

The Vest

As you probably know, I like vests. I have a lot of vests. I wear vests. One of Ben's friends even called me "Grandpa Vest", to distinguish between me and Ben's other grandad, John Graf.

But my first vest was my best vest. I made that first vest. Not entirely from scratch, but almost.

It started out as an old blue denim navy fatigue shirt I latched on to after the end of World War 2.

I was coming along in my development as a fisherman. Luckily, I had access to some of the best fresh water fishing in the whole wide blue-skied world. Devils River.

Folks in my family had been living on and fishing the clear, clean, cool, fish-filled waters of Devils River for many years before I was turned on to it. Most of their fishing efforts had been for catfish -- with trot lines and throw lines. Bass, for the most part, were caught with poles and lines baited with minnows. Some bass seekers, but not many, were casting with lures.

When I stepped off into the honeycombed channels and pebbled pools --into what was then essentially a virgin river -- I was the one hooked.

With my friend Leon Walton, I was not long in sensing that to wade the river was the best, the very best, way to fish Devils River.

But to wade and cast with rod and reel, we needed to tote along several types and colors of lures. Just carrying two or three stuck in a hat band didn't cut the mustard.

Early on we found that metal band-aid boxes were great for stashing extra lures in pockets. You didn't get hooked and the containers didn't come apart when they got wet. But there simply were not enough pockets in ordinary shirts and pants. Most of the time, in the hot West Texas summers, we really didn't even have any shirt pockets, since T-shirts were the norm for us.

That old navy fatigue shirt had two large-sized pockets. Just two, tho. And it was long-sleeved Denim. Hot in summer.

So, I cut off the sleeves and used the salvaged material to make extra pockets. Now the vest had four front pockets, sized just right for a couple of lure-filled band-aid cans each, and two larger pockets low on the back side for a bulky item or two.

The vest was beautiful. Not the way it looked. The way it functioned! When I wanted to change a lure while I was waist deep or more in the river, it was much easier to take off the lure I had been using and swap it for one stashed in one of the band-aid cans. During an early vest test run, as I waded upstream in water up to my arm pits, it was startling to look back over my shoulder and see half a dozen of my lures floating away behind me!

After swapping one lure for another, I had failed to close the lid on the band-aid lure container when I stuffed it back in one of the vest pockets. And then, having waded into water deep enough to cover that pocket, six or so unsecured floating lures were just bobbing away. If I hadn't glanced back, I would have lost a batch of my artificial baits. I retrieved four or five. At least one sinker "got away".

So, as soon as I got home, each pocket of the vest was enhanced with two or three grippers at the top edge. Didn't have any material left to make pocket flaps, but just the grippers worked ok to keep the containers in the pockets. And besides, I could put grippers on with a hammer and a punch. Easier for me than needle and thread.

From time to time, the vest was improved. A loop was added. With the rod butt in a vest pocket and that loop around the upright rod, I could free both hands to take off lures and add replacements.

Every now and then, if the water was shoulder high or so -- that's about five feet deep on me, best beloved, -- I might catch a bass big enough to give me trouble landing it. Thus, a snap pilfered from an old fish stringer was run through one of the grommet holes sewn into the ole navy vest and I could attach the lanyard of a small fish net.

I snapped a Boy Scout knife to another grommet hole. Sometimes tied my fish stringer onto still another. Earlier, I had rigged the knife, stringer, etc. on my belt. But now with the vest, I figured if I stepped off into water too deep or current too swift, I could shuck the vest and attachments easier than separate weighty things on my belt.

As I aged and the vest aged, I thought about adding pockets inside the vest. But I was growing and the vest wasn't, so I let that idea go.

The vest served me exceedingly well for many years. The blue color faded until it was almost white. At long last the innumerable, lengthy exposures to the Texas sun and wind and rain thinned and weakened the fabric until; sadly, it began to have a tendency to tear.

In time, other folks discovered how useful fishing vests could be. Commercial versions began to be available, even in the West Texas hinterlands. Eventually, I acquired a store-bought fishing vest. Had more pockets, but 'twas seriously lacking in chutzpa and character.

I did not intend to totally abandon my faithful old friend, my home-made piscatorial compadre, my first fishing vest . . . It deserved to be preserved.

But somehow, somewhere, sometime . . . it was mislaid. I really don't know what became of it. I miss it, but I remember it well.

The Box

They don't build fishing boxes like they used to.

In my mid-teens, I had limited money, but was badly bitten by the fishing bug. With a pre-war metal casting rod and a second-hand reel, I needed some means to tote the hooks, lines, sinkers, and few lures I was accumulating.

My earliest fishing was in the irrigation ditches that vein Del Rio. Didn't take long to upgrade to traipsing along the banks of San Felipe Creek for our early bait casting expeditions. Hauling the small amount of fishing gear needed to creek fish was rather easily accomplished via foot-back or bike-riding.

But when it came to longer Devils River excursions, it was a steed of a different shade. It was a lot further to the river. Motorized vehicles and gasoline were difficult to come by in the latter depression years and during WW2. Devils River fishing necessitated plans to stay a while and required a better way to pack fishing gear than an old canvas bag.

My first portable box for fishing gear was made from old wooden apple boxes. It was heavy. Awkward to use. Garish to the observer. How-some-ever, it was quite serviceable to a young beginning fisher-lad.

Best of all, except for some brow-furrowing cogitation, plenty of piscatorial planning, and more than a middling amount of unskilled labor, it didn't cost much. Which was a very important factor when I put it together some sixty years ago.

In those days, just about all apple boxes were made of wood. The sturdy cardboard boxes of today were yet to come.

Most apple boxes had a solid piece of wood at each end. If it wasn't a single wooden piece, it was not more than two pieces; firmly stapled together. There was a similarly shaped divider in the middle of the apple box. These box ends and dividers were each about 12 inches square and about three-quarters of an inch thick.

The sides, bottom, and top of the apple boxes were wooden also; thinner, longer, narrower, slat-like pieces of wood.

The fishing box I made was a vertical stack of four layers or tiers. Each layer had as its bottom one of the square apple box ends.

We trimmed three quarters of an inch from two sides of the apple box end that was the basis for each of the tier bottoms. Then, we nailed strips of that thickness on the four sides of the remaining square piece to form each tier. But the strips were as long as the original apple box ends and thus overlapped at the corners of each tackle box tier.

The sides of the top three layers were three inches or so deep, outside measurement, making the inside depth just over two inches. Each of these three layers was divided into sections using thinner wooden strips from apple box sides. The sections were sized to fit lures of varying lengths and widths. Usually each section held a single lure, sometimes two.

The bottom tackle box tier or layer was an inch deeper to accommodate larger gear such as floats or stringers; and it was divided into larger compartments.

The top of the fishing box was made from another apple box end, but not trimmed; ergo, it was wide enough to cover the four tiers under it.

The four layers and the top were fastened on one side with small brass hinges and on the opposite side with a couple of small screen door hooks. Hinged and hooked sides were alternated so that if all the hooks were unfastened at the same time (a disaster that never happened, thank goodness), the whole rig would look like an accordion.

To lift and/or carry the box and its contents, a brass u-shaped door handle was screwed to the middle of the tackle box top. Unfortunately, it was not quite wide enough for all four of my fingers, making the box a bit awkward and tiresome to carry for long distances. And, I must tell you, some of the places we fished on Devils River in those days were not easy to get to.

Originally, dark green porch paint on the outside and inside kept the wood of the box more or less water resistant. Later in the life of the tackle box, it got a few dabs of other-colored paint sloshed on for semi-camouflage -- and to make it easier on the eye.

This ole wood tackle box served well for years, first as my one and only fishing gear box and later as an auxiliary or spare. It was eventually replaced by a G.I. surplus steel tool box, which, in turn, was succeeded by store-bought aluminum and plastic tackle boxes.

Somewhere along the way, in one of our several movings from one home to another, the old green, weather-beaten, banged-up, wooden, apple-box-based, tackle box which served so well to help usher me into the wonderful world of fishing disappeared.

Like my first homemade fishing vest, I do miss that homely old handmade fishing box.

The Phantom

Paul was the best curly haired oboe player in the band. 'Course, he was the only oboe player in the band.

The oboes sat next to the flutes and the bassoon section. Since we only had one flute player and no bassoon, Paul and I sat near each other -- at first.

Howsomever, over our span of high school years, I advanced from third chair Second Cornet, to second chair, and then moved up to first chair and finally up into the First Cornet row.

Paul just got better and stayed in the middle of the band where oboes are hard to see and even harder to hear.

I used to kid him that, with his dark brown curly hair and that oboe in his mouth, he looked like one of those Greek myth satyrs. He didn't like being compared to a half goat.

We were also science class lab partners. We liked our young, attractive science teacher. Miss Lee was a gift to us from the war effort. Her family, like Paul's, was in Del Rio because her dad was in the service at Laughlin Army Air Force Base. She was fresh out of college and stirred up strong feelings in her students in biology and chemistry -- boys especially.

Paul lived over on Edna Street, about two blocks from the high school -- as the crow flies. By road, it was a lot further. But Paul and the other kids on Edna had hacked out a trail thru the dense, devilish snarl of mesquites, catclaws, huisaches, and other misbegotten thorny brushes that had been allowed to flourish on the neglected lot right next to St. James Church.

I lived with my grandparents, next door to the school yard. I just jumped the back fence to go to school -- first grade all the way through high school.

Besides Miss Lee and mangled music, Paul and I shared another mutual interest -- picture shows.

Down on Main Street, in between the grocery stores, drug store soda fountains, Kress and Woolworth dime stores, pool halls, haberdasheries, and auto supply places, we had -- before the war brought Laughlin and all its people -- two movie theaters. The oldest, the Strand, was where I was introduced to Johnny Mack Brown, Tarzan, Buck Rogers, Jungle Jim, and other Saturday afternoon delights. The Princess came later. It was first class -- had a row of seats with hearing aid plugs for folks like my grandmother. When the Strand burned, the Rita was built in its place. After the Laughlin service guys came, a couple of other flick houses were added, but they were always crowded with smokers.

Sometime along in '44 or '45 Hollywood bigwigs cranked out a then-new version of The Phantom of the Opera. Claude Rains played the phantom. It was supposed to be real scary.

Well, sir, after supper one warm Sunday evening, Paul and I met on the lawn at St. James' Episcopal Church and walked over to the movie house to see this well-publicized cinema attraction. About two hours later we emerged on Main Street.

Later, Paul would be an officer in the U. S. Navy, woo a lovely French lass, marry her, bring her home to the U. S. of A., and have a fine family. But that Phantom movie almost rang his bell.

As we came out under the marquee lights, I thought Paul's curly hair looked a bit straighter. Not standing on end, exactly, but definitely less flexed. My hair couldn't get straighter, but I sure cropped up with goose bumps when we turned the corner out of the Main Street lights and started down the dark of Greenwood Street. A weary street light on

Griner Street just cast eerie shadows. Way on yonder past the church on Las Vacas Street was the flickering of an even poorer excuse for a street lamp. In between it was full-grown night time.

At the church lawn, we normally parted for Paul to take the trail thru the mesquite thicket to his house. I had to jog across the school yard, jump the back fence, and sprint to the back porch of my grandparents' house.

But Paul wanted to talk -- about the phantom and the labyrinth under the opera house. Looking over at the shadowy school grounds and beyond, I was thinking we had a pretty good set of dark and tangled turns of our own. I was glad I didn't have take Paul's creepy, devils-clawed corridor to get home. You had to slow down going thru those barbs and thorns or you'd lose some hide.

We probably talked over an hour -- in the dark, but in the familiar old church yard -- on the grass beside the irrigation ditch. Rehashed tricks the phantom pulled. As we chewed the fat, the darkness got thicker. Over in Greenwood Park -- across the street in the school yard -- in the menacing thicket next to us -- shadows moved. Only rustlings of the evening breeze, of course.

We both had homework still to be worked over for Miss Lee's attention. But Paul just wouldn't haul off and say it was time to split. Never knew him to be so jabber-jawed. Every time we got close to shutting it down, he'd come up with a wicked twist the phantom had made. That, of course, needed more of our profound discussion.

When we said adios, there were no "ifs", "ands", "buts", or "maybes" about the need for my dash across Griner Street to be world class fast. To avoid any late-night, mid -1940's Del Rio traffic, you know! When I looked back, Paul had vanished into the maw of the mesquites.

That puny light from those distant street lights barely slowed me down for the fence. I dodged past oleander bushes and honeysuckle vine shadows, lit the after-burner through the field, zoomed up the back walk, soared over the porch steps, slipped my key into the old back door lock slicker 'n greased owl stuffin', and was inside. In my absolute best record time.

After tossing and turning and tussling with that blasted phantom most of the night, I dragged myself into chemistry class the next morn, bleary-eyed and bushed. Paul looked wrung out, too. Scratches on his face. Band-aid on his hand. His beat-up condition perked my curtiosity bump!

"Make it ok thru the thicket?" I asked, as we eased into seats in Miss Lee's class.

Paul rolled his eyes, leaned over, and, in a hoarse whisper, he told me:

He was hot-footing it thru the dim, snaky windings of that thorny tunnel-- hands in front to ward off spiked branches. Eyes peeled wide for any thing! Mouth open so he could hear better!

About half-way thru, he slowed for a narrow turn. As he stepped around -- something on the ground beside the trail moved!

He jumped back! Two shadowy creatures! One half naked? A Satyr???

The Thing reared up and hissed at him! "Git!"

Paul may have exaggerated a mite as he told me how perfectly every part of his body rose to meet that challenge. He bolted past the hissing critter and lit out for home.

He thought he knew every step of the way thru that mesquite maze. He traveled it twice a day to and from school. But that night he could hear hoof beats behind him -- gaining on him!

He cut some of the trail corners too close. Snagged his shirt. Scratched him up some. He tripped on roots that were not there before. Fell twice. Skinned his knuckles. Banged his knee.

His mom was in the kitchen when he banged open the back door and skidded across the linoleum. She dropped a bowl in the sink and the crash just accelerated Paul into the living room. Paul's dad ripped the newspaper he was reading when he jumped out of his easy chair.

It's not easy to give an out-of-breath explanation about a meeting in the dark with a mythological satyr! Even to your own mom and dad! Paul said his dad went off to bed muttering about suspected "mendacity".

All night long Paul worried about critters that might be in that thicket right behind his house. Next morning he hung around for some other Edna Street guys to cut thru on the trail with him.

When they passed the spot of his nocturnal encounter, he found some cigarette stubs, a handkerchief, and a couple of other things that convinced him that the apparition which had accosted him was probably just a G.I. a long way from home and a warm-hearted gal smooching in the tulies.

"That dang Phantom sure got my goat last night. Scared the britches off of me," Paul grinned.

The Diving Bell

I had some great friends. Leon introduced me to fishing and skillfully shepherded my learning of that subject. Raymond and I collaborated, using his dad's workshop and all the great tools therein, to make rudimentary electric motors for our high school physic class. And Paul and I made a diving bell.

In other tales I'll babble about my experiences with Leon, Raymond, and others, but for now, let me tell you about the diving bell. As we wade through this, you might find this a little technical, but stick around. The ending is or was . . . if not interesting, then close to unsettling -- at least for me.

It was during that all-too-brief 1944 summer between my junior and senior years in high school, when, Paul Eppes, John Graf, "Johnny Boy" Brinkley, Joe Hollingsworth, I, and other high school-aged boys, worked as junior laborers at Laughlin ARMY Air Base.

Almost every hot afternoon after work and especially on weekends, several of us would go swimming, either at Moore Park Swimming Pool or in the cool clear waters of San Felipe Creek Blue Hole.

About mid-June that summer, Paul and I somehow, one way or another, became the possessors of a 14 gallon barrel. Neither of us had ever seen or heard of a 14 gallon barrel before. Lots of five gallon grease buckets, 55 gallon oil and gas barrels, etc., but this odd 14 gallon container was new -- to us.

One or the other of us, however, had stumbled across something in Popular Mechanics Magazine, an old Tarzan movie, or some science fiction book from our wonderful old Val Verde County Library that caused us to start thinking about being able to swim around and see things under water.

That 14 gallon barrel seemed just the right size for us to turn it into a diving helmet. A custom-conversion, you might say.

This was just a small-sized barrel. A kind of reddish-orange color, as I remember. Flat on both ends, with curved sides that had a couple of encircling raised and rounded ridges.

We planned ever so bodaciously. Paul, who later was to become an architect, made perspective drawings. I would add ideas, we would cuss and discuss, and he would redraw. The arguments were forceful, but friendly.

First, we turned the barrel upside down, relocating the opening to the bottom. And, of course, the opening had to be enlarged for a diver's head and shoulders. So, we removed part of the former top which had supported the barrel lid.

Then we cut curved sections up the sides, to allow lowering the helmet-to-be over the diver's shoulders. Used an old hack saw and a file for this work. Broke a lot of hack saw blades. Began acquiring new sets of blisters, then calluses, on our hands.

Our fitting tryouts resulted in scraped and scratched shoulders and sent us looking for something to pad the edges of the shoulder cutouts. Rubber products were almost impossible for civilians to obtain during the war. This necessitated "mid-night requisitioning" of some old family garden hoses, which we cut, split and, with great dexterity (albeit some difficulty), wired in place to pad the shoulder openings.

Next: cut the window opening. With a brace and bit and less than sharp drills (we had no electric drill), holes were worried through the metal barrel sides every inch or so; then enlarged with a small file for cuts to be made between the holes using hack saw blades. By this time the ancient hack-saw had succumbed to our unbridled enthusiasm and heroic efforts, so, we wrapped one end of a saw blade with rags, but still got blisters.

Among some of the new materials developed to meet the needs of the war was Plexiglas, used extensively for the curved canopies for aircraft. In some manner, ever to be cloaked in mysterious mists of memory, we obtained a scrap piece of this amazing stuff. It could be formed when it was soft. And after a lot of dipping in near boiling water, we managed to bend and shape it so it fit the curvature of the barrel over the window cutout.

We drilled holes in the barrel and matching holes in the piece of curved Plexiglas, cut pieces of old tire inner tubes to go between the metal and plastic to seal the opening, and, using some newly found and liberated little bolts which had nuts which could be "secured" so they didn't work loose, bolted the Plexiglas onto the barrel.

Knowing we did not yet have an under water air supply method, we never-the-less had to try the helmet out at the Blue Hole. We discovered faults which should have been obvious to any hare-brained six-year-old.

First, the air-filled, un-weighted helmet floated. To get it deep enough under water for the person in the helmet to see through and test the window, one of us had to push the barrel down on top of the diver.

Second, immersed in the Blue Hole, the masterfully crafted, beautifully curved Plexiglas, which had been okay with air on both sides, severely distorted underwater vision. Things were just too out of focus to be tolerated.

So, back to the drawing board.

To remedy the initial underwater vision flop, we decided we needed a flat-surfaced window.

Our solution: one of those 5 gallon grease cans.

In those days, some five gallon grease cans had four sides and a flat bottom. Trimming a can to needed length, we cut out curves in two of the can sides to match the outside curved side of the barrel. A square opening in the bottom of the can about an inch inside the side/bottom rims was then covered with a FLAT piece of Plexiglas, sealed with inner tubes strips, and bolted on with the neat little bolt and nut combos to that one-inch flange.

Fastening the five-gallon window piece to the 14 gallon barrel was, however, a mind-bending problem. We didn't know how to weld; couldn't afford to hire a welder. We considered flanges bent from the can and bolted to the barrel over inner tube strips, but while that might have worked for the two flat sides of the can-window, it would have been almost impossible for the two curved sides.

So, we soldered the can-window to the barrel-helmet.

Our soldering was a mess. We didn't have an electric soldering iron. We used a cumbersome old wooden-handled soldering iron which had to be fire-heated. It was slow. The resulting seams were sloppy. But it was nearly watertight.

To keep the helmet on the wearer's shoulders while under water, we first considered fastening the helmet to the diver's belt. As it turned out, it was fortunate that we dumped that idea. Instead, we twisted a wire around the barrel above the lowest of the two raised ridges and tied some old discarded lead window weights to that wire.

The air supply problem mighty-nigh stumped us. With our far from unlimited financial means -- and the lack of suitable materials during the war-time period -- , we could come up with nothing better than just plain garden hose to pipe air to the helmet. Raid number two on the shrinking family garden hose supply.

To connect hose to helmet, we scrounged an old brass water faucet which had -- until then -- evaded war-time scrap metal drives. With our rag-wrapped hacksaw blades, we gnawed off the female end of the faucet and attached the male end to the helmet. Had to get help to fasten it to the barrel. I don't remember who did it for us, but because of the brass, it couldn't be either welded or soldered; had to be brazed. This brass coupling allowed attaching the "life-sustaining" garden-hose air-pipe to the helmet.

Temporarily liberated from my grandad's '32 Chevy, a tire pump -- the kind you hold down with two feet and push the plunger up and down vigorously with two hands, both arms, and all your back -- was nominated to push oxygen from earth level atmosphere into the marine depths for our diving bell's intrepid occupant.

To convert the jerky tire pump gulps into something like a constant flow, we attached the air impeller to a five-gallon can. We planned, with great expectancy, to regulate the release of something like a steady flow from the air can via the garden hose to the helmet.

Our "constant flow" control valve was another engineering feat accomplished by means of a salvaged item -- a natural gas valve. Soldered it also to a hole cut in the side of the air can. The fitting between the air-can gas valve outlet and the garden hose was another ultra skillful achievement, but I disremember tajackly how we pulled it off.

Never-the-less, we finally were ready for the first genuine, for-real, UNDERWATER TEST DIVE at the Blue Hole. We flipped to see who would dive and who would pump. I won, put on the weighted helmet, and waded into the clear water.

It was great.

Distant, swimming fish. Treasures on the bottom waiting to be harvested. A couple of "doubting Thomas" friends dove off of the Blue Hole bridge and were porpoising up and down, watching my underwater act.

The sound of the air hissing into the helmet behind my neck was reassuring when I first was completely submerged. But . . . but . . . the dang viewing lens of the helmet was fogging up. I tried, but couldn't get a hand up into the helmet to wipe the lens.

Belatedly, I came to the labored realization that I could no longer hear the air hissing into the barrel-helmet thru the intake opening. Then, it seemed that my chest was heaving . . . and felt like it was being squashed. And . . . I was trying to suck in more air.

I pushed the weighted helmet off and struggled up to the surface.

Paul was there. He pulled me up on the bank.

It wasn't hard to conclude that our air supply system was not tolerable . . . really bad!

Well, sir, we didn't really decide then and there to scuttle the diving bell project. We just put it on hold, while we figured out a better way to get air to the diver.

All during our senior high school year, Paul and I planned, plotted, drew, and re-planned. But we never got around to actually doing anything to modify and improve our diving rig

The next year we went off to be roommates in the ivory-towered realms of higher learning. And sometimes -- not often, but every now and then -- we'd reminisce about that darned diving bell. It was ever a future project waiting for us back home.

That ole diving bell/helmet -- we never did really decide just what to call it -- gathered dust in the back corners of my garage for years. Somehow, it can no longer be found.

It's one of those warmly remembered little episodes of camaraderie out of my past that were . . . almost nearly but not quite hardly.

The Devil's Camp

I didn't miss the river 'til it was gone. The lake killed it. At least a good part of it.

Deep down under the cool blue waters of Lake Amistad is a fabled and fabulous fishing hole that now only lives in memory. You should have seen it.

Before Diablo (later re-named Amistad) Dam uglied up the fishing, Devils River had already been plugged up for hydroelectric purposes in three places. Those dams provided folks in our neck of the woods some fine fishing. Just a hop, skip, and a jaunt up stream from where Devils River ran into the Rio Grande, a low dam contained a pond for the Steam Plant. Five miles further up the river, a concrete wall was jammed between solid rock canyon walls, creating Lake Walk. This body of deeper water extended some six miles to the third barrier, Devils Lake dam.

Texas doesn't have a lot of public land. But if you can get yourself to the edge of most Texas rivers, at bridges, crossings, or dams, you are in public domain. If you stay in the river bottom, you can lollygag to your heart's content up or down stream to partake of the aquatic pleasurings.

We were fortunate in having access to a key to the locked gate in the fence that was the boundary of a semi-developed batch of cabins which had been built on the higher levels above Lake Walk dam. The enclosed area had some "grass lands" on which a small bunch of tired horses enjoyed the semi-retirement of their owners and themselves.

One of the very best places to dunk yourself into the blissful blessings of ole Devils River was the spillway just below the Lake Walk dam.

Back in the '40s, when my friend, Leon Walton, was morphing me and a few other high school aged guys into what some dim wits might mistake for fishermen, the demands for electrical power were much, much less than they are today. Most of the electricity generated by the waters flowing thru the Devils Lake and Lake Walk dam turbines was needed at night -- for lighting. Extraordinary electrical current needs for air conditioning -- cooling and/or heating -- were only gleams in the eyes of engineers and power company gurus. In those days, water releases from the dams during the daylight hours was minimal. At dusk, the turbine gates were opened, and water outlet flow below the dams gushed

During the day, fishing below the dams was good to great. After dark, it was bodacious.

One long mid-summer weekend -- 'bout '45, I think it was -- Leon, Morgan, Bud, and I got our duke's mixture of piscatorial gear together, scraped up enough coins for Mexico gasoline, piled in Leon's dad's old 1930 Chrysler, left the world behind us, and lit a shuck for our favorite fish camp spot below Lake Walk Dam.

A third of a mile or so below the dam, the nicest little spring ever to please your eyeballs gurgled up betwixt the roots of a young pecan tree that had survived the last river rises. A washed out, deeply rutted, rocky road curved down off the hillside almost to the river. There had been a country club building on the flat at the foot of that road until the Flood of Thirty-Two washed it and its surrounding mott of oak and pecan trees right on down to the Gulf of Mexico.

That once-upon-a-time road was so far gone it was more than the gutsy old Chrysler could cope with, so we parked up on the hill, shouldered our GI surplus folding cots, grub, and fishing gear, hiked down to the spring, and set up camp under the little pecan tree.

For Leon, Morgan, and me -- 17-year-olds who had just finished our senior high school year --that fishing trip was a final fling together before we either went into one of Uncle Sam's armed services or spread our fledgling feathers off to college. My brother Bud was two years younger.

In previous outings, we had hatched up a game plan for those good-for-what-ails-you times when we could get together and fish more than a day or so at the river.

The first rule was: bring bait! Frogs and/or perch caught down at the creek, crawdads from the town ditches, chicken innards from Burditt's Meat Market or The Border Grocery, etc. Second rule: when we got to the river, make a stab at setting up camp. Third rule: hustle to set out and bait at least a couple of trot lines and some throw lines. After that -- about dusk -- we would gather to eat stuff we had brought, cast some in the spillway outflow below the dam, and then -- Rule four: run the trot lines about midnight. Then we caved in at camp until daylight.

Before breakfast, three of us would run the trotlines, and then come in to eat whatever the designated breakfast cocinero had ready. The rest of the morning was for bass casting in the low daytime currents below the dam or fishing off the top of the dam into the lake in front of it. Depending upon how much trotline bait we had, we might drag a seine up some of the shallow rock channels of the river for perch, minnows, hellgrammites, etc.

A little siesta after lunch made up for sleep missed with night time fishing, but there never was enough shade under that little pecan tree for four cots 'til the sun sank behind hills to the west.

Mid-afternoon we got out the perch rigs. Always needed trot line appetizers, you know. Four guys with worms, grasshopper legs, fish scraps, etc. dabbled on pee-waddly-sized hooks under cork bobbers in sunbathed spots next to a shady bank. Nearly always caught a bucket-full of perch -- lots of them as big as your hand. No self-respecting night-prowling catfish worthy of the name could pass up bait like that!

About sundown we re-baited the trot lines. Next came supper. Such as it might be.

Then, after some casting in the gloaming for bass, it was serious fishing time in the spillway.

When the lights were coming on in town, the dam honchos revved up the turbines in the power house of the dam. That surge of water was a fish magnet. Small fish and other appetizing morsels washed through the dam's turbines almost always brought catfish -- large and small -- up the river and into the swift spillway currents. Folks jostled and jockeyed along the narrow, slick, acutely sloped rock ledges to get to positions where they could cast way up into the first water coming thru the dam.

When you caught a fish, it usually required working your way back out of your attained casting spot to a less hazardous place so you could land, unhook the fish, and put it on a stringer. When you did, you lost your place and all the rest of the guys moved up to a more favored niche.

Winding up our after-dark-doings that first evening, we were tired and about to head down the river to camp. Morgan was whipping his casts into the dark spillway waters with an old, short, crappie rod that had lost at least one of its guides. He had a big clunker of a reel that had no level wind and only a piece of leather fastened on one of the cross bars to keep your thumb from smoking when you got a big one on. The reel had some good strong line, but not much of it.

Bud and I had reeled in. Leon was lifting the minnow bucket.

Morgan whooped! He had one on!

The weak beam of my old Boy Scout flashlight on the surface swirls in front of Morgan showed his line zipping UPSTREAM right into the strongest flow of the spillway.

"Got a granddaddy!" Morgan squalled.

"Naw. Just a big ole gar," Leon snickered.

Slipping, sloshing, and sliding into the edge of the water on the slick rock bank, Morgan was heaving and hauling and playing whatever he had hooked. But mostly just with his arms. That stubby crappie rod wasn't helping him much. His thumb was clamped down on that leather pad! He didn't have much more line to let out! Looked like the fish was going to land Morgan.

Then the critter on his line changed its mind about going up into the strong current. The line went slack. The fish was coming downstream. In swift water. As it passed him, Morgan knocked skin off his knuckles cranking that squeaky reel. The line wadded up on one side of the reel's arbor.

Morgan started saying downright unkind things about numb butts who would leave you in that kind of lurch.

Suddenly, in the weak beam of the flashlight -- about six feet in front of Morgan -- the big, flat, long-whiskered head of a whopper catfish came up over a ledge into the clear shallow water near the bank. Morgan back-pedaled. Almost dragged the cat out. But then slipped. Fell right on his butt. Kept the rod tip up, tho. The fish thrashed his tail, soused Morgan with water, and turned away.

All three of the slack-jawed scoffers who had witnessed that "gar" turn into a bucket-headed catfish came to life. We ran around Morgan -- Bud to the left and Leon and me to the right -- flopped out into the shallows, surrounded that big splashing catfish, herded it away from deep water, and somebody, somehow, just shoved it -- sliding on the wet, slick rock -- right up there beside Morgan.

Leon grabbed the fish by his lower jaw.

As we staked out "our" trophy cat -- all jabbering that he was at least a 20 pounder -- Bud laughed, "That's the devil's own fish!"

Well, sir. -- and Leon was squatting at the river's edge washing his hands of fish slime when he spied a dang snake swimming along unconcerned-like in the shallow water -- heading right in towards us.

"Snake!" "Where?" "What kind?" "Moccasin!" "Get some rocks!"

That snake was just sashaying along in the shallows over the sloping rock bank like he owned the whole river.

Leon picked up a big cantaloupe-sized rock, held it out at arms length, and just dropped in on the snake's head.

I turned, found a couple of good rocks, and whirled back to do battle.

When I turned away, of course, I shined the light away from Leon and the snake. When I turned back to enter the fray, we saw that blamed snake coming out from under that big rock. He was swinging his head back and forth real mean-like. Coming right toward Leon. Like he didn't take kindly to having a big rock dropped on him!

Leon tried to get space between him and the snake. His turn to slip on the slick rock! Fell right into me. We both went down. The light rolled off out of reach. My good old buddy Leon and I were down in the dark, sliding around on the slick surface, stepping on each other, scratching and clawing, trying to get a toe hold to get away from that snake!

Morgan found the flashlight and shined it on the snake. Heck! It was just moving feebly.

The big rock would have smashed the moccasin's head if it had not been cushioned by the shallow layer of water in which it was swimming. As it was, the blow was enough to addle the reptile and its wildly swinging motion towards us was probably death throes. We finished it off.

"Devil of a snake," someone mumbled.

Back at camp, we shucked wet shoes and duds, eased our bods onto those old folding cots, and -- as gangling galoots whose bellies always thought their throats were cut -- opened up that big, wide-mouthed, two-gallon-sized jar of orange-slice cookies that Leon's mom always provided for our campouts! Mrs. Walton was all right!

Right up at the top of those rules we had devised for our outings was the iron-clad, blood-oath provision that we only opened the cookie jar -- when the whole gang was present -- after each meal and just before we turned in. The number of cookies each could take was calculated so that the cookie supply would be strung out to last the whole time we were in camp.

As we munched orange-slice delights there by the spring -- almost at the riverside -- the wind died and hoards of ferocious, mean-spirited, Attila-the-Hun mosquitoes launched an attack.

So we moved.

Just picked up our cots and carried them about half way up the road where we were up out of the riverside reeds and tall grass. What little breeze came along helped keep the mosquitoes at bay. The cots were rigged for bug nets, but we didn't have any. But, covered from head to toe with ragged old sheets such as our folks would let us pirate out of the house for camping, it was hotter, but bearable. Soon, snores joined the skeeter chorus under the cloudless, star-bright sky.

Leon heard it first. He kicked my cot with his foot and whispered, "What's rattling the pots and tin dishes down at the spring?"

We all sat up. I shined the light down at the foot of the pecan tree -- and there it was!

A big, black, bushy-tailed, white-striped, skunk!

When the light hit him, he pulled his head out of the cookie jar and stared up at us with beady black eyes.

"Who left the lid off the cookie jar?" Leon rasped. No one 'fessed up. It would have been a hair short of signing your own death warrant to admit it.

"Two whole days of cookies were left in that jar," Morgan moaned.

We chucked rocks down close to the pecan tree. Not to hit the skunk. Just close enough to convince him to depart the premises! That arrogant old rascal meandered off along the river bank, waving that big black, white-striped tail.

Eventually, well past two in the morning, the grumblings subsided and we slept again.

Then . . .

I came up gasping ----- convinced that all hell was breaking loose right then and there!

Sparks slashing and flying. Rocks ricocheting across the ground under the cots. Loud stabbing snorts belching on all sides. Sulfurous fumes. Big black forms running over the rocks and gravel. I grabbed the flashlight again -- and . . .

After things quieted down, it wasn't tough to figure out how it happened.

It was the bunch of horses that we had seen grazing on top as we drove in. They had come off down the road to water at the river. Probably were working their way around the interlopers snoring away in their accustomed pathway. Somebody flopped a corner of his sheet or made some other abrupt or noisy stirring. Spooked the bejeebers out of that horse herd. Startled snorts. Sparks from metal shoes sliding on the rocks of the road. Lunging forms as they whirled away.

Those fumes? Well, you know what happens when a horse with a full belly gets spurred or startled!

Hard to say whether the horses were more jangled than we were.

"This is the devil's own place!" Bud sputtered as he jerked up his sheet, turned over, and tried to go back to sleep.

The rest of the weekend went more or less like always before. We caught fish, got sunburned, fought mosquitoes, missed our cookie ration, had a heck of a good time.

We came back often -- together and/or separately.

I'll spin you some more yarns about other happenings at other times at that wonderful place.

But after that Summer of '45 trip -- before Amistad covered it up and afterwards -- we always referred to that campsite -- at the spring, under the pecan tree, beside the river -- as --

The Devil's Camp.

Unbalanced Line

My football career did not come the easy way.

In fact, I was about as laid back and offhand in staking my claim to gridiron fame as "Wrong Way Corrigan".

You remember "Wrong Way Corrigan", don't you? A few years after Charles Lindberg's epic solo flight across the Atlantic, this guy Corrigan filed a flight plan to pilot his single engine crate from the east coast to points westward. He landed in Ireland and always claimed he just headed the wrong way.

To most discerning folks, it was less than an eye opener early in my life that I would not grow into a behemoth basher and/or dashing dervish in the athletic arenas.

So, I didn't!

Starting out in the first grade as the shortest in the class, after multitudinous appearances in front of the full length mirrors of Grandma's double-doored wardrobe, the situation had not altered an iota by the time I got to junior high school.

My friend, Leon, ("Muscled up like a stud polecat", as Uncle Pete would say.), was blessed with a physique that coaches drool over. He thought that because I could almost hold my own with him in our marathon Monopoly contests, I might survive on the football field.

In grades 7, 8, 9, and 10, Leon and other friends of like mentality and inclination acquired the knowledge and skills -- late August to Mid-November -- to block and tackle, punt and pass, strive and strain for the glory of the Maroon and Gold of ole Del Rio High. I watched.

If I wasn't watching, I was listening, since the practice field and Cowboy Park, where good Wildcats did and died for ole Del Rio, was just across the fence from my grandparents place. Coaches always are asking for MORE from their players. A lot of the time, for reasons I have yet to figure out, they encourage yelling. Probably drowns out some of the more anguished groaning.

By late summer of 1943, manpower needs of the U.S. of A. in our world-wide war effort had siphoned off most of the older senior-type guys who before that had hung on in high school to revel and excel in gridiron glories, etc.

I think Leon sic-ed the coaches on me. I held out until three weeks after the first football game. Then I folded. In the fall of my junior year in high school, I went out for football!

But I was late, don't you see? All the other guys had been through "conditioning". Worst of all, they had suffered through those chalk board sessions where you were supposed to be vaccinated with the Plays in The Play Book. I did not know those plays. No one took the time to fill-in this Johnny-come-lately bumpkin. They had other fish to fry. Or footballs.

I was the red-letter goofus. The dummy. The dimwit who ran left when the play was to go right. I didn't even know the number of the holes in the line. Did you know that football lines have holes in them? Numbered holes!

I did learn something in practice about blocking and tackling. Not much, but something.

Every game I had my special place -- way down at the end of the sideline bench. After half the season was gone, I had a nice collection of splinters. I was ready to say, "Adios".

Then came our annual game with our cross-town rival, San Felipe. Somehow in that titanic struggle, we got ahead in the final quarter.

Coach Jimmy Jacks, way down at the other end of the bench, waved at me. I waved back.

Coach yelled at me. Coach Jacks was a good yell coach. He sent me in as a sub. On defense, of course. That way, my not knowing the plays couldn't be too disastrous!

Did I tell you that the position which I was supposed to play was called "guard"? On offense, guards need to know the plays so they can guard. On defense, they mainly plug the holes in the line and just get run over by juggernauts and rhinos.

So, I go in as Del Rio's defensive right guard against the Mustangs. They break huddle and come up to the line. I line up just where Assistant Coach Clyde Bradley taught me to -- in the gap! In between San Felipe's center and their left guard.

Leon was supposed to be next to me, playing defensive left guard. 'Cept he wasn't next to me! He was about two yards over to my left. It was what Coach Jacks later called a hole you could drive a freight train through. My pal Leon acted like he was mad at me. For some mysterious reason he kept yelling at me -- "Shift! Shift!"

I didn't know you shifted on defense. I thought that was an offensive maneuver.

The Mustangs snapped the ball and their confused ball carrier tried to run over me. Got tangled up with some of his players and me and went down. For no gain. The fans in the stands roared.

San Felipe huddled again.

Leon was mumbling something about being unbalanced. I told him I thought he was too!

The purple and gold team came out again. The center gave me a nasty look. Their line dropped into a three-point stance. I dug into my defensive gap position -- right between their center and their left guard.

Leon moved off to the left, leaving a bigger hole in our defensive line, and started squalling at me again about shifting! I was starting to worry that he had been hit too hard.

I stayed right where Coach Bradley had taught me. Right smack dab between their center and the guy on his left!

The San Felipe ball carrier tried to bulldoze me again.

I had learned some the first time he did it, and I tried to scare him with one of those yells the coaches were so gung ho about. He just closed his eyes and clobbered me. I couldn't have gotten out of his way if I had tried. He fell and the Cowboy Park crowd roared again.

Leon was jabbering worse than ever about an unbalanced line! I was spitting dust and telling him I didn't know what the heck an unbalanced line was.

About that time, danged if San Felipe didn't come out again in that weird set up with four linemen to the right of their center and only two on my side.

That Mustang play caller had the bit in his mouth. Amazingly, they tried to run to the weak side the third straight time. More amazingly, I was in on the tackle the third straight time! The crowd roared again -- louder. I liked that sound, but my busted lip hurt too bad for me to get all pleasured up over it.

Coach Jacks and Coach Bradley spent a little more time with me in practice the next week.

Mostly they explained what an unbalanced line was!

I played defense some in every game the rest of that fall of '43.

In the summer of '44, Coach Jacks accepted a commission in the Navy. For the '44-'45 school year, we had a new coach, Herman Gibson.

Well, sir, in the fall of my senior high school year, I really got into football. In those chalkboard sessions I learned every position. Every play! Moved to left guard that year and played in every game on both offense and defense. That was the way it was done then.

Coach Gibson didn't know much about his players at the beginning of the football season. He opted to have a different set of team captains each game. At the end of the season, rather than at the beginning as it is normally done, the Wildcats elected the two season captains.

In November 1944, Leon and I were elected captains of the football team.

But that one game against the Mustangs was the only time I ever met an unbalanced line!

Hunter's Choice

One of the best things about hunting is: you must make decisions. My grandad said when you're 16 it makes your mind grow. Of course, at age 16 and a half, it slipped into my thinking that one of the worst things about hunting is: some decisions conjure up consequences you'd rather not remember.

In the days of my youth, hunting was NOT a money crop. Texans hunted for table fare and/or joy for the soul. But most town folks of what was then the largest state in the union experienced the enchantments, frustrations, and rewards of hunting by invitation. If you were not one of the better-endowed gentry or lesser-fixed kickers, you probably only had chances to hunt because a relative, friend, or kind-hearted property tax payer asked you. Host compensations came from thanks, infrequent gifts, or -- usually -- a bit of the venison or part of the game taken on the outing. Those who could often returned the favor with hunting or fishing on their place, or some kind of needed service. Visitors often brought food, etc.

Well, sir, early one frisky December Saturday morning in the Fall of '44, I and two of my 16-year-old friends, Leon and one who shall masquerade under the moniker of Melvin in this tale, were on our way for a day's hunt at my grandad's ranch at Bakers Crossing.

During the war years of the early '40s -- times of severe rationing and shortages -- and especially by 1944 -- my parents and grandparents in town did not have a vehicle they could spare or that they cared to subject to the stress of a 100 mile trip for our hunting trek. The first 30 miles to Comstock was on paved Highway 90, but the 20 miles from Comstock to the ranch and 20 miles back to Comstock were via an unpaved and not well-maintained road. Melvin, who will be called Mel hereafter, was similarly handicapped.

But Leon's dad had a 1930 Chrysler and had the skills to maintain it. If we could scrape up the coins for Mexico gasoline, Leon could sometimes spring that old long-nosed, black, thin-tired car for our infrequent fishing and hunting jaunts.

The timing of our arrival at the ranch, we thought, was critical. Not just for the success of our hunt, but perhaps even more importantly for the Saturday evening dates for frivolous festivities each of us had with delightful lassies back in town. Mel was downright antsy that we get back early. He had at long last wrangled a date -- his first with her -- with the girl of his dreams!

We needed to get off from the ranch house and on the hunt PDQ after breakfast. Now you may wonder at this, dear reader, since most of what you take into your consciousness in this day and time through books, movies, television, etc. would have you believe that it's necessary to be out on your stand or stalking quarry at or before the crack of dawn.

That wasn't the way it was in those days at my grandad's ranch, or with any of my uncles. Papo didn't hunt anymore, due to a crippled shoulder acquired when a big tree he was chopping down fell the wrong way. He did care that we should leave on our hunts in time to be successful, but he purely enjoyed talking and visiting around the fire place on those cold hunting mornings.

Uncle Pete usually pushed to get away as soon as possible, but he wasn't going with us on this particular hunt. Uncle Lucious always tried to start out shortly after the morning meal, but, if he was not to be the group leader, he wanted to make sure everyone knew the plan and the lay of the land. Uncle Jim was sort of scheduled to be our main host for this hunt, but -- when it came to hunting -- he was the most laid-back of the uncles; with him, we left when we left, got back when we got back, and most of the talking was done en route.

We figured we had our arrival at the ranch timed about right as we dropped down the highway curve just past Camp Hudson and drove over the road graded across the jumbled rocks left by rises of the river. Just ahead was the one-lane, low-water bridge that crossed Devils River in front of Papo's big two-storied ranch house.

Then -- this big boar coon -- headed home from a night of fishing in the river -- sashayed across the road in front of us and hoisted his handsome hide up into a puny little stand of river willows.

"That's a Thirty Dollar hide!" I blurted, in one of my rare fog-minded moments.

Without further ado, Leon screeched the old car to a halt, we three big game hunters piled out, scooped up some hardball-sized rocks, and surrounded that little clump of twigs. About the second or third volley of rocks, the coon was terminated, and the jabbering trio of Neanderthal type high school seniors was arguing whose chunk had kayoed the critter.

Well, as we should have known, all that yelling, whooping, and rock bombardment had more than just alerted the folks finishing their breakfast at the ranch house on the other side of the crossing. So up drives a pickup with a grim-faced Uncle Jim. But his frowns changed into smiles as he recognized us. "Thought you boys were a bunch of road hunters!" he exclaimed.

"Well, we kinda were," I confessed. "But not after deer. Just thought you might like to add this fur to your take of hides you have waiting for the fur buyer."

About then, the consequences of our coon conquest dawned. We had to skin that blamed coon -- and stretch his hide -- before we could leave on our hunt. That little bobble threw us over an hour late on our timing for getting off on the hunt. Mel was muttering and moaning mushy-mouthed things about half the morning being wasted.

Those were the days of not only gasoline, vehicle tires, and all kinds of shortages, but also before folks began to have four-wheel-drive vehicles. Most of the hunting done by Uncle Jim, Uncle Pete, and/or Uncle

Lucious happened while they were tending to ranch work. To get to the windmills, tanks, fences, and to work the stock, they were usually on horseback, rifles in saddle scabbards. On those occasions when they went hunting solely for that purpose, they usually went foot-back. Rifles were usually carried, few slings even. Ammo tucked in a jacket pocket. Stockman's pocket knife in a hip pocket or home-made belt sheath.

And, oh yes, clean, thoroughly washed salt sacks. Folded. Tucked under your belt.

If a buck was killed close to the house, it might be field-dressed and then carried in to finish the skinning and butchering. If it was killed not too far out, the hunter might come back, saddle a horse, and go pack the field-dressed deer in to finish the rendering.

But when it was expected that one or more kills would be made any significant distance from the house, then the plan called for the deer to be butchered at the site of the kill. The meat would be brought home in the salt sacks. Bringing in the sacked tender loins, back straps, shoulders, and hams was a chore, but much easier than hauling a whole carcass.

Somewhere around nine o'clock Papo finally dropped us off at the mouth of a wide canyon about a mile up river from the house. No one had a watch, but Mel had ingested copious Boy Scout lore. He was reporting real regularly his estimates of the time by the height of the sun and the length of the shadows. Uncle Jim allowed as how he was impressed with the accuracy of this oft offered observation. It was the way he kept account of the passage of time also.

We hunted hard up that long canyon, heading mostly east -- away from the river. Uncle Jim had the right side low and Mel the higher level and the headers on that side. I walked at about the same level as Uncle Jim, but on the left side. Leon stayed roughly abreast of Mel on the upper trails of the left or north side. Most of the deer we saw were well in advance of us, climbing out of the canyon up to the divide.

About noontime we gathered at a windmill and ate lunches we had brought. Mel conferred with nature and opined that if we kept the same schedule on the way back to the ranch house it would work out about right for us to get back to town in time for us to clean up and pick up our dates.

We crossed over the divide, dropped down into the upper reaches of another big canyon, and hunted back westward toward the river and the ranch house.

A nice buck jumped up. Leon, Mel, and I smoked him as he ran through the brush in the bed of the canyon. I worked the bolt of my grandad's old 30-40 Krag and got off about two rounds. Mel and Leon, from their higher positions, fired two or three times each. The buck stumbled but kept going around the foot of the hill. Uncle Jim found blood just beyond where the deer slowed and we knew he was hit. So we trailed him.

And that had Mel mumbling and muttering again. Trailing a wounded deer slows a hunt like you wouldn't believe! The way Mel was carrying on, you'd have thought Leon and I were the only ones who could have wounded that buck.

But we found the deer. Butchered him and divided the meat between the salt sacks to even the load to pack in. All that while, Mel was recalculating and announcing how close it was going to be if we were to make it back to the ranch and depart for town on time.

After a little confab with Uncle Jim about the route and distance back to the house, Mel wanted to trade positions with me. The guys with the higher routes had to walk further and faster to keep up with the fellows on the lower paths. The trade was reasonable.

But before long it was evident that Mel was moving on ahead faster than the rest of the group. Anything he jumped, he might get a shot at it, but the rest of us would not be in position to shoot.

At first Uncle Jim was amused and commented that Mel was a little too anxious to get to his date. But then we all began to be irritated when we saw Mel tossing rocks in the brush way ahead of him. A whole lot ahead of us. That rascal was spooking anything someone might want to shoot at before anyone had a chance.

By the time we got to the ranch, Mel had his gear in the car and was standing by it ready to go.

Uncle Jim quietly said that Mamo (my grandmom) had supper on the table and would be offended if we did not eat. I was glad Mel noted his tone and breathed a big deep sigh.

We washed up at the wash stand well enough to pass Mamo's supper-table regulations and ate a hurried snack at the big table in the dining room. There was a lack of the usual conversation.

As we were going out to the car, the beginning evening twilight was slivered by moonlight coming over the mountain in back of the house. Before we left, Uncle Jim quietly told me to come back soon and bring Leon.

Probably out of concern for Mel, Leon pushed the old Chrysler faster than normal along the twisting gravel road toward town. It did appear that we might get back to Del Rio not more than an hour or so later than necessary to pick up the dates. But I was worried ole Mel was going to break one of his jaw teeth with all his grinding and growling.

And then . . . as we were headed up a steep, wicked curve around the side of one of the lesser mountains of old Highway 163, we had a flat. The right rear tire just gave it up.

Mel was out of the car before it came to a halt, dragging one of the bedraggled spares Leon had stashed in the rear of the old car. I dug out the jack. Leon chocked a front AND a back wheel. Mel fiercely pumped the jack handle. Leon hefted the big lug wrench with the four opposing sockets, found the right sized socket, and shoved it on a lug nut.

The nut wouldn't turn. The wrench just slipped. We struck a match and . . . found that the old wrench was not only worn and but it was cracked. Mel had to try it. He did. The lug nuts wouldn't budge for him either.

A dazzling ray of moonlight was shining down on us there on that cold and lonely road when we heard a car coming up the hill and around the curve behind us. Mel ran around the Chrysler to flag it down. Leon and I heard him talking and explaining. Then a door slammed and we heard the car driving off.

As we poked our heads over and around the long, black hood of the Chrysler, Mel leaned out the window and shouted back to us, "I'll get my dad's car and be back for you - - - after I pick up my date!"

After a spell of unbelieving silence, Leon and I just sat down and laughed.

We got some bailing wire out of the Chrysler's jumbled back compartment, wrapped loops around the cracked socket, twisted the heck out of the wire ends, slipped a dime or a penny (I forget which) into the socket, hammered it onto the lug nuts and managed to change the tire.

When we got to Comstock we dug up some coins, used a pay phone, and called my date. Explained to her what had happened and asked her to call Mel's date and Leon's date.

A couple of miles before we got to Del Rio, we met Mel coming to our rescue. After he waved us down, we stopped, and he pulled up behind us. His hair was all slicked down. He had nice clean duds on. Smelled like Allspice and Brilliantine! But he was alone.

"How about your date?" we asked.

"She'd already left with when I got there," he reported. "She thought I stood her up!"

Leon and I hurried home, cleaned up, picked up our dates, got chewed on for being late and missing some of the good times planned, but after a frosted root beer at Brock's, we survived.

Mel lived over it also. But he never did get another chance to take out that girl.

Like I said, the consequences of some hunting decisions can be brutal!

The Quixotic Quest

As you read this bit of irrelevant and inconsequential remembrance, you might cast your mind's eye on cerebral images of a younger me. In the struggle of threading these words around such mental impediments, doubts of my veracity and honest-to-gosh truthfulness may interrupt the creation of wholesome concepts of my athletic accomplishments. I pray not.

Just as he did with my introduction to the finer facets of fishing and the belated and less or more abbreviated formation of my football fervor, my friend Leon Walton enticed me -- in the midst of my senior year in high school -- into trying out for the Del Rio High School Track Team!

Documented history of heroic track and field achievements from ancient Greco-Roman times right up to the spring of 1945 was not then, nor is it now, congested with stories of five-foot-six, 135-pound winners.

At the outset I did not aspire to great success. It was just that most of my DRHS male friends went "out for track" after football season. Football in the fall and track in the spring. The only basketball court in Del Rio was an outdoor, multi-pitted, asphalt-surfaced job which about fifty guys crowded onto the last fifteen minutes of the noon lunch break. Baseball was a work-up game we played with maybe those same fifty frustrated guys bumping around on the playground "outfield" trying to catch a fly so they could have a turn at bat.

I simply wanted to "try out for track" so I could be with the rest of the guys.

Coaches Herman Gibson and Clyde Bradley smiled in a sort of kindly and understanding way and signed me up. Maybe the investment of threadbare track shorts, a pair of well-worn track shoes, and a set of war-time warm-ups could be justified by my youthful exuberance.

But it soon became apparent that the number-one problem I posed for the coaches was in deciding where I fit in the track program.

It was a no-brainer who to assign to the weight events. Leon and Gene Salmon had the shot put and the discus positions cinched. Joe Hollingsworth and others had the dashes -- the 100 and 220 slots -- sewed up; and, with others, had a corner on the relays. Morgan Locke and some other distance guys owned everything from the mile on. Billy Hayes headed the hurdle squad. Lewis Jeffers, etc. handled the pole vault.

I was about the only senior trying out who couldn't find a slot, niche, or position. With the juniors and a few sophs, I dabbled without distinction in nearly all of those activities.

After about three weeks, Coach Gibson curled his arm around my slumping shoulders one afternoon, and allowed as how he and Coach Bradley had been watching me practice and had come to the conclusion that I should focus on the 880 -- the half mile!

I deemed this delightful news. It might have been worse, you know.

I could have been relegated out among the fever trees on the banks of the great, grey-green greasy Rio Grande, dodging Bi-Coloured-Python-Rock-Snakes with the rest of the cross country runners. "Cept that DRHS didn't have cross country competition in those days. So, I quested onward in another episodic saga of my legendary jousting with windmills.

Casting my doubts aside, I squared up, buckled down, and set about trying to improve my starts, my stride, my breathing, my endurance, and -- most certainly -- my finishes. After a bit, although probably no one else noticed, I began to perceive improvement in all of those areas.

In the spring of 1945, DRHS didn't have school buses or any other kind of buses to haul would-be athletes to out-of-town events. Back then we were even more distant than we are now. Gas and tire rationing had been in effect some four years. When we attended competitions in far-flung sites like Eagle Pass, Uvalde, or (gasp) Hondo, Del Rio contenders rode in vintage vehicles of parents, teachers, coaches, etc. Most of those old clunkers were 1930's era sedans. Mr. Walton, Leon's dad, had an old flat bed truck that he used to haul scrap iron needed for the war effort. He made it available when he could. It was slow and we had to get out and push to get up some of the hills, but we got there. Then it was not only not illegal to pile kids in the back of pickups and trucks, it was what most families did -- out of necessity.

Needless to say, we didn't attend many track meets -- in town or out of town. We couldn't get to theirs and they couldn't get to ours.

All those late winter and early spring afternoons, we competed against other teammates and tried to improve on our times, heights, and/or distances. We were aiming for the district track meet, which would be held in Uvalde in early May.

To keep us competitive and probably to narrow the numbers of those for whom transportation would have to be provided, sometime along in mid-April Coach Gibson posted minimum times, distances, etc. which had to be met by those who would get to go to the district meet.

I don't recall exactly the minimum he set for the 880; probably about two and a half minutes. I just remember it was theoretically attainable, but almost impossible for me or any of the misfit Wildcat half-milers to make. We were slow, you know.

But we strained, trained, and -- the weekend before the district meet -- attained. That is, two of us made the cut.

Thomas Rose, a junior, and I qualified to run the half mile at district. Old Dunk (Thomas' nickname in high school from some unfathomable source) and I were happy as two blind hogs in a loblolly wallow. We knew we didn't have a chance of winning, but, by golly, we were going!

Back in those golden, olden days, it was traditional for the high school seniors in our part of the world to have a Senior Picnic sometime in May of their senior year. It also was a mystifying practice back then that each DRHS Senior Class had four Junior Class "sponsors". These Junior Class sponsors -- two girls and two boys -- were elected by their other Junior Class members for these honorable and exalted assignments.

Whatever it was that the Junior Sponsors were supposed to do somehow escapes me after all these years, but I do "recomember" that they were present at each and every senior class event and function. Dunk Rose was one of the Junior Sponsors for the '45 Seniors.

Well, sir, the Friday before the 1945 district track meet, nigh on to all of the DRHS seniors, their class moms (who fixed the larruping good eats), and the dads (who hauled us in those vintage traveling machines) had a tee-totally delightful, lip-smackingly delicious, and pluperfectly scrumptious picnic out on the banks of Devils River at the Steam Plant. And, as the customs of those times required, the four Junior Sponsors were also very much in presence.

The Central Power and Light Company (colloquially referred to in local lingo as the Cedar Post and Lamp Co.) had three dams sprinkled along the course of Devils River. The first of these backed up the waters of Devils Lake. The second impounded Lake Walk. The Steam Plant dam was closest to the confluence of Devils River with the Rio Grande. These dams were the sources of electrical power for Del Rio and, during the war, Laughlin Army Air Base. The clear water backed by the Steam Plant dam was relatively shallow, but great for swimming and boating.

From the time of our mid-morning arrival at the Steam Plant that Friday until our mid-afternoon departure for the trek back to Del Rio, we Seniors and our four Junior Sponsors bathed in the chilly river waters and basked in the bright and shining May sunshine. Most of that time the guys were shirtless -- the better to enjoy spring breezes and demure gazes of dainty damsels.

Would you be surprised to know that upon arising Saturday morning for the trip to Uvalde and the District Track Meet almost all of the seniors on the DRHS Track Team were badly sunburned? When the individual cars began arriving at the Uvalde High School track, the facial complexions of Coaches Gibson and Bradley rocketed to shades only slightly less intense than the lobster hues of the contrite tricksters.

Immediate and emergency digging into the skimpy war-time medical supplies of the DRHS athletic department turned up some sticky ointments and stinking gobs of gook that we smeared on our faces, necks, legs, arms, and chests. A yellowish concoction called Ungentine did a whale of a good job of separating us from the wrinkled-noses of the other track teams. Joe Hollingsworth had some Zinc Oxide he used for his always sunburned nose. He and some others of our track squad sported Mohawk haircuts. With those hairdos, white smears on red faces, and yellow crud on crimson torsos, we were a real stand-out bunch.

At first Coach Gibson and Coach Bradley were so angry they said the guys with the bad sunburns just absolutely could not compete. Then they must have decided that it was better to laugh than cry. Rather than getting to do full warm ups for our events, we were directed to "go sit in the shade and drink plenty of fluids"! All of us felt bad -- physically and mentally. I think we all resolved to bust a gut trying to do better than our best to make up for our negligence.

When the starter's gun popped for the 880 to begin, I'll be a poisoned pup if Dunk and I both didn't get the jump on a conglomerated, duke's mixture of half-milers from other district schools.

Just as he always had done, Dunk pulled out in front of me. I stretched my stride maybe a tad more than I ever had before, bumped my pace up a notch, flared my nostrils wider, and tried to keep up. I knew I was "putting out" more than I had ever previously. I figured I would play out before the end.

At first, ole Dunk was moving on out ahead of me! So I just cussed myself for that picnic dissipation, and thought: "Danged if I let him run off and leave me!"

I could hear runners' cleats behind me. I expected them to pass me. Around the whole first lap, Dunk was still out in front. I was maybe a shade closer behind him. Those guys behind us were gasping just like I was.

On the back stretch of the last lap, the gap between me and Dunk began to shrink. Little by little. Then, perceptibly. Astoundingly! Noticeably! In all our practices, I had never beaten him!

We rounded the last turn. I swung out and passed Dunk. His sun-scorched face looked plumb wrung out. Sick, because I was passing him? Or, had we both enjoyed too much picnic fun?

The pesky drumming of cleats and those panting gasps behind me sounded right on my butt.

I tried to open it up more. It wasn't there! But . . . I wasn't sagging as bad as I thought I would!!!

The little black and white Kodak photo that was snapped as I crossed the finish line in first place was of a worn and weary warrior. But a win is a win, right?

Dunk and I, second place and first place 880 district winners, bounced blissfully up to San Angelo the next weekend with puffed up egos. To participate in the bi-district track meet.

And, you know what? They had something we country bumpkins had never heard of -- HEATS.

We thought it was hot enough in Uvalde after our Steam Plant bake!

Busted our bubbles, it did, when neither Dunk nor I placed in those San Angelo heats!

We watched the 880 finals, checked the winning times against our times in the district meet, and decided that all the other track coaches in our district had done just like Coach Gibson: Put their strong guys in the weights, their sprint studs in the dashes or relays, the distance people in the mile, and all their just plain wannabes (like me and ole Dunk) in the district half mile event.

But, what the heck? We got little silver track shoe pins as "DRHS Track Lettermen"!

Had a barrel of fun doing it.

Along with the rest of the guys.

And that's all we wanted to do anyway!

The Bare Hunt

Day One

Under a dark and starry sky, we crossed over the bridge through the Rio Grande's mists into Mexico before dawn that first week in December 1951. At a small cantina on the far side of Acuña, our sleepy-eyed guide was waiting as planned. At mas o menos 5:30 a.m., he tossed his war bag into the one-horse trailer we pulled. The trailer was loaded with odds and ends of camping gear, a mish-mash of groceries, brim-full jerry cans of gas, etc. The guide mumbled a frosty "buenas dias" from the depths of his turned up collar, and crowded in with us in the work-wearied Plymouth suburban.

This was a jumped-up hunt -- but for me, the hunt of a lifetime.

A few years earlier, a cash-strapped guy needed bail money for a border area escapade. He offered to sell his membership in a hunt club which had a lodge high in the tall pine region of the mountains of Mexico. Jim Riggs couldn't turn down the chance, so Jim loaned the needed cash and ultimately kept the membership.

Jim had gotten in a couple of great bear hunts there. Good guides. Horses and gear furnished. Adequate lodging. More than passable grub. Lots of bear and deer.

Then, the owner of the Mexican hunting Shangri-La fell from favor with Mexican governmental honchos and that area of the State of

Coahuila was arbitrarily decreed to be under a hunting moratorium. Preservation of endangered species or something like that.

Jim and his local hunting friends were devastated. But . . . again, fortune smiled.

Wesley Stiles was a U. S. Immigration official who had a private enterprise side-line activity. He was a significant advertiser -- "The Bible Man" -- on XERF, the infamous high-powered Acuña radio station utilized by the notorious goat-gland surgeon, Dr. John R. Brinkley. Mr. Stiles mentioned to the operator of a thriving saw mill located in the Sierra del Carmen hunting lodge area that he had a friend (Jim) who was mighty discombobulated by the hunting ban. The mill owner graciously extended an invitation for Jim and some friends to visit for a "camping trip" -- and, of course, to bring what arms might be anticipated to be needed for protection from marauding osos o leones (bears or panthers).

So, we had crossed the border at a very early hour with our weapons of protection layered beneath bed rolls and small stuff in the back of the Plymouth.

The Suburban's pale headlights searched for chug holes in the gravel road as we headed at first in a mostly northerly route, following somewhat the west bank of the Rio Bravo. Wisps of river fog hung in low places along the way. Condensation from the five of us clouded the inside of the windshield. Jim opened vent windows despite our bilingually diversified chorus of complaints about the cold.

This was it. The Great Bear Hunt. Ahead lay a whole week in the majestic bosom of the Sleeping Lady Mountains -- the Sierra del Carmen.

The "road" we traveled out of Acuña was puro mexicano -- pitted and painful. Our first night's destination was the sawmill high in the mountains. Huge trucks hauling lumber from the mill in the mountains and its curing yard on the eastern plain to retail outlets in Acuña churned and gashed the mostly bone-dry but sometimes inundated road. When ruts became too deep for the high-clearance trucks to avoid dragging bottom, they simply moved over and made a new "road". Herding the two-wheel-drive heavily-loaded 1949 Plymouth Suburban and its attached one-horse trailer, Jim had to try to keep one wheel on the high center between the ruts and the other tire on the nearest road edge. We stopped often to pry and pound dented and bent under-parts back to functional status.

By noon we were headed roughly west, traveling through a pass in the Serranias del Burro -- the Burro Mountains. It was a low range of lesser hills that lay mid-way between Acuña and the del Carmens. Open-range cattle gathered at a small lago about halfway through the pass. We stopped for sandwiches and coffee. More ducks than I had ever seen scattered the surface of the little lake. Quail abounded in the short, cropped grass and thorny brush around the shores. But, alas, not one of us had been foresighted enough to bring a shotgun. This was a bear hunt. A thirty-caliber rifle thing.

Sometime about mid-afternoon, our "road" made a sudden dog-leg turn. Jim had to stomp on the brakes with both boots to keep the suburban from plunging into a gouge some overloaded lumber truck had gashed out during one of the wet spells the desert infrequently entertains. As we scraped ourselves off the dashboard and the back of the front seat, we were flabbergasted by screeching and wailing brake sounds and shouted Mexican lingo. The northeasterly wind which had been buffeting us all day shrouded us with a sight-robbing cloud of dust.

When the air cleared somewhat, we found we were surrounded by six uniformed Mexican rurales. All pointing pistols or rifles at us. It was a queasy moment.

In answer to the shouted questions of the Mexican jefe, our guide gushed out a string of rapid-fire Spanish that was impossible for us gringos to get a handle on.

But the ominous, menacing, and dawgone scary guns were lowered some and a slower and more comprehensive exchange flowed between the officer and our guide. Finally, the rurales began to smile, then, with our guide, broke into laughter.

It seems that a Mexican patrol had been chasing us in their vehicle for miles. Unknown to us, they were right on our bumper, just about to catch us, when we came to that screeching halt. They barely avoided the rear of our trailer. They thought we were candelilla wax smugglers. Candelilla wax was highly sought after during the WWII war years and afterward. The candelilla wax plant grows mostly in the Chihuahan Desert regions of West Texas and Northern Mexico.

Late that afternoon we drove into the lumber mill curing yard. Crisscrossed stacks of lumber covered a large area on the flat just east of the del Carmen range. The sawmill had no kiln. After cutting, the lumber was hauled down from the mill in a high mountain valley to the curing yard to be air-dried. It took longer, but the dry, hot air of the Chihuahuan desert on the east side of the mountains sucked the moisture out of the new-cut wood very efficiently.

The jefe at the curing yard was expecting us. The rotund, short, friendly, mustachioed Mexican firmly insisted, despite our protests, that we leave the Suburban and all ride in his Jeep. So we removed the cans of gas which were to fuel the return trip, added our gear which had been in the Plymouth to the heavily-burdened horse trailer, and hooked the trailer to his open Jeep. Then the four of us, holding our guns which we did not want to bounce around in and probably out of the trailer, squeezed into the back end of the Jeep. Our guide sat up front in the shotgun seat next to the driver

The drive from Acuña to the curing yard had been tortuous. The ride from the curing yard to the saw mill laid that earlier, irksome little cacti and rut jaunt in the shade.

Six well-fed guys -- and their gear -- jammed in a Jeep that is crowded with four. At first, holding on to the runty little vehicle, the guns, each other, and odd and ends of gear trying to part company with us and/ or our motorized mule, kept us from focusing on the extraordinarily beautiful and extremely hazardous route we were traversing.

The light was fading, but the view -- when we could take time for it -- was spectacular. The road was one sharp switchback after another, constantly climbing at an amazing angle. The driver was, without a doubt, hell-bent upon setting a world-class record.

The Sierra del Carmen is a 50-mile-long limestone plateau -- a sky island rising some 9,000 feet from the desert floor. The top of the plateau in most places is about 8,000 feet in altitude and covered with high elevation conifers.

The four-wheel drive gears screamed through quick up and down shifts. Tires that were in firm contact with terra firma growled and ground only at a slightly lower pitch. Tires not tenaciously clawing at Mother Earth covered trailer, Jeep, and occupants with dust, dirt, rocks, and assorted spewed debris. And all the time, the skilled driver was jawing non-stop in Español with the guide.

And honking the squeaky Jeep horn! With good reason! As we caromed around the hairpin turns, clawing our way up the mountain, we had more than one close, almost fender-to-fender meeting with huge, horn-blasting, monstrously-loaded lumber trucks hurtling down the road.

At one point our driver paused near the road-edge to point out -- far down in the gorge below us -- one of the Caterpillar Company's larger pieces of road building equipment -- crumpled and lying on its side like a discarded child's toy.

"What happened?" we asked. "Todos muertos", the driver grunted tersely and sucked in air between his clenched teeth. And there, in the on-set of darkness, we then understood why our driver had insisted we all ride IN the Jeep and not in the trailer.

As the Jeep carried us higher, the vegetation changed from desert scrub plants to increasing interspersed growths of evergreens. The upward angles of the road began to modify. In the evening twilight we saw that we were driving through slopes studded with large tree stumps. Soon we were in the midst of some of the biggest pine trees I had -- to that time -- ever cast my peepers on.

I had just not anticipated those big trees! From Del Rio, we looked across the Rio Grande and enjoyed the view of the "Sleeping Lady Mountains". The outline of the del Carmens we saw from there quite effectively conveyed the thought of a reclining buxom lass. But from that distant view point there on the international border, on the cusp of the Chihuahuan desert, it was hard to imagine that those softly curving mountains were almost lushly covered with big, tall pine trees.

Finally -- finally -- we loosened our frozen grips as the road topped out. The weak Jeep headlights scanned around. We made a shallow descent into a grouping of rough-hewn buildings -- the mill, the pond, worker cabins, and the warm mess hall.

The early-winter ascent from the desert floor to the high mountain valley in which the mill was sited had been accompanied by a substantial drop in temperature. But our reception was warm -- in English, Spanish, and Tex-Mex.

The mill manager, with courtly politeness, welcomed us. He had received radioed information of our trip. As we were introduced, he did a double-take when he heard my surname. "Mr. Block? From Del Rio?" "Was your grandfather the administrator of the government programs there during the depression years?"

I said that I thought that was correct.

"Well," he said. "No mentiras, Mr. Block!"

Then I did a double-take. What the heck did that mean?

When he perceived, with obvious surprise, that I did not understand, he explained.

My grandad, E. S. Block, when he oversaw the government relief programs in Del Rio during the 1930's, would ask questions of each person applying for assistance. When they replied, he would ask, "Es verdad?" (Is that the truth?)

And they would respond, "Es verdad. No mentiras, Mr. Block." (That's the truth. No lies, Mr. Block.)

Sometime late in that decade, a Mexican radio personality, in an amusing broadcast parody, used that expression: "No mentiras, Mr. Block." It was familiar to many of the citizens of Coahuila and it became an oft-quoted response tossed into their lighthearted conversations when veracity was doubted.

(That was my first hearing of the expression and its background. Since, in these fifty-six years between then and this writing, it has often been addressed to me by some of my Spanish-speaking friends. Less frequently, as the years pass, of course.)

After the warm welcome, we enjoyed steaming bowls of guisado, frijoles, and hearth-hot tortillas. Shortly thereafter, we unrolled bedrolls in one of the cabins and did not need anyone to rock us to sleep.

Day Two

The next morning was cold and cloudy. Vapor curled up from the surface of the pond that supplied water for the workers at the mill and for the steam-driven mill saws.

This was the day a Jeep was to haul us and our trailer of supplies several miles to the south of the saw mill. Our hunting guide was to meet us there. He would bring riding and pack horses, saddles, tents, and other camping gear. Then we would saddle up, and with our paraphernalia on the pack horses, trek up a tortuous trail to higher elevations to set up camp in the roving grounds of our intended quarries: oso negro de Mexico -- the black bear of Mexico.

As we walked to the dining hall, there were smiles and nods from workers standing in occasional daubs of sunshine. Straw sombreros topped friendly faces and colorful serapes draped from their shoulders almost to their ankles. They heeded not the sharp, high-mountain valley winter air, even though they were shod only with leather sandals.

Right after a lumberjack breakfast, the cooks dispatched a goat which was to be part of the workers' noontime meal. As they slit the young goat's throat, every drop of blood was captured in a tin pan. We asked what they would do with the blood. The mill foreman smiled and told us it was for the blood pudding to be served at mid-day. He watched as he told us.

Then he asked if we would like to sample some blood pudding left over from the day before. How could we refuse? It was unique. Cold and very jellied on that frosty morn. But smooth and . . . sturdy. My grandad would have dubbed it "stick to your ribs good"!

We found our trailer hooked to an older Jeep. Another driver -- who was also a very loquacious tour guide -- was waiting for us and we bounced off down a logging road.

With one less passenger than the evening before, the broadest -- in the shoulders, of course -- of our bear hunting quartet was nominated to sit in the shotgun seat. The less than commodious rear Jeep area was left to the remaining three of us. Bill started up a halting, stumbling Tex-Mex conversation with the driver beside him. The three in the back, Jim, Jack, and yours truly, cocked one ear at a time in the cold morning air and tried to listen, while holding tenaciously to the bouncing vehicle, and gawking at the unfolding vistas through which we were passing.

We were headed south. Still high in the mountains, but on a two-rut logging lane in a meandering valley that snaked back and forth in new-growth pines along the lower edges of higher mountain slopes. The westward elevations to our right were much higher.

About mid-day, we arrived at the site where our hunting guide was supposed to meet us with horses, tents, and other camping paraphernalia. The cloud deck above us had lowered. It was starting to mist.

Our hunting guide was obvious by his absence.

The wordy Jeep driver said not to worry. The guide would be along. Unhooking our trailer, he jockeyed the Jeep around, waved a gloved hand at us, and drove off back to the saw mill, trailing odorous little clouds of dirty smoke from the old Jeep exhaust pipe.

And there we were. Smack dab in the heart of the wild and wooly, wooded Sierra del Carmen -- the Rocky Mountains of Mexico -- a hundred plus miles from home and nobody there but us chickens. Or at least -- I felt a mite chicken-lonely at that moment.

While we waited for our hunting guide, we split up and each walked off to taste and test the country. We agreed to be away no more than an hour and then return to the trailer. Grand scenery, plenty of game sign, but no one found anything worth popping a shell at.

Howsomever, right then and there I learned something. It has served me well all my life.

Sort of off-handedly, I opted to climb what seemed to be a not-too-high hill -- just to get a better view from the higher elevation. When I got up to where I thought the top would be, I looked up and the dang hill still went on further up. So . . . I climbed up to that new "hill-top". Only to discover again, that there was yet another ascent to be made to reach what -- from that new position -- now appeared to be the top. That process went on for about five layers of mountainside until I finally ran out of time, gave up trying to reach the top, came on back down, and returned to the trailer.

And that's the way it has always been. When I think I am about to reach the top, or the apex, or the goal, I find there is still more climbing to do! Get discouraged -- give up -- and you never reach the top. But, if you keep on trying, even if there always seems to be more of the hill to climb, you usually keep finding new vistas and greater opportunities.

The sun began to dip behind the western mountain tops a couple of hours into the afternoon. The early December temperature started dropping in our valley.

Sometime after mid-afternoon, a guide did show up. Not THE GUIDE. A guide. Turned out this was the real guide's son. His dad -- el padre, the senior, the bear-hunt guide -- had been mysteriously delayed and would not be there until the next morning. Because we couldn't quite fathom the linguistic intricacies and nuances needed to figure out the wordy mumbo-jumbo perambulations with our version of Tex-Mex, we began to suspect that maybe our trip might be sorta jinxed.

It for dead certain looked like we would camp right where we were for that night. In the cold. Without much ready-to-eat grub. And -- with only rudimentary camping gear.

The son-guide had materialized on the scene only with his caballo, the slicker and bed roll tied behind his saddle, and the pistola stuck in the wear-polished holster on his hip.

Oh, yes. He was also accompanied by a big, yellow-colored, short-haired hound dog.

Well, sir, we decided we had better get a little serious about finding and killing a deer for supper. Bill, with his scoped, bolt-action .270, and Jack, packing his lever-action, open-sighted Winchester .348, departed on that mission.

Jim had made broad, brassy, darn-near-bragging claims about his cooking proficiency, expertise, finesse, and know-how. Also, he had honchoed the gathering, collection, packing, and bringing of the sack of flour, bucket of lard, salt, pepper, chili powder, and a conglomerated assortment of spices, sauces, and condiments. He was, therefore, unhesitatingly dubbed as the jefe cocinero (chief cook) to get things ready for a hearty savory something supper made with the venison our duo of past and proven experienced hunters would surely bring in.

I, due to the dubious distinction that back home in Del Rio I was the scoutmaster of a Boy Scout troop, was nominated and unanimously elected to rig a make-shift shelter under which we could sleep, protected from the cold mist and probable rain. As we had been depending upon promised tents from our Mexican hosts for this "camping trip", the only thing we had brought that came close to real tents was a couple of World War One era shelter halves.

After some head scratching, the best make-shift protection I could fashion was to button the ENDS of two shelter tent halves together to make a long, low lean-to. That, I hoped, would cover our heads and guns. Lower torsos would have to trust to bed rolls in the surplus thick canvas WWII G.I. shelter bags we had brought.

First Jack came in empty handed. Then, as light was fading, Bill straggled back without having even seen a deer.

Our young Mexican son-guide must have sensed our anxious thoughts of belt-tightening.

Or maybe he was also hungry.

The young hombre who was subbing for his dad made it known to us that he only was armed with a pistol. But, if we would lend him one of our rifles, he would be back shortly with some camp meat.

We promptly displayed the two modern, scoped, bolt-action .270's, Jack's older open-sighted, lever-action .348, and my long-barreled, open-sighted, bolt-action, Spanish-American war era 30-40 Krag. Told him to take his pick.

He reached for the .348. Opened the action. Checked the round in the chamber and the three in the magazine below. Nodded his head and started out.

"Wait," Jack called. "Take some more shells. You may need more than four."

The young man smiled, shook his head, said, "Es bastante," and disappeared into the brush.

A few minutes later the .348 roared. We grinned at each other and began stoking the fire. Then we heard another shot. But . . . no more after that.

Shortly, our hunter walked in with the Winchester in one hand and a small deer ham in the other.

We hurried Jim through the supper fixings. No time for frills. We were just hungry. The tender, young, diced venison and pan gravy went down mighty easy.

After we ate, Jack asked the guide how he liked the .348.

"Muy bien. Pero, . . " And he told us that his anticipation that the heavy-slugged gun would kick hard made him flinch the first time he pulled the trigger. He missed the first shot, but levered a round from the magazine and killed the deer with his second shot.

"Was it a buck or a doe?" Jack asked.

The guide held both hands over his head with the fingers curled.

Bill shook his head and laughed. "Nah. You killed a doe."

With a smile that was almost a smirk, the guide reached in his pocket and pulled out a bloody testicle.

We all laughed.

While the fire died down, we pumped the son-guide for information about the country, the bears we were going to hunt, where we would go to set up our hunting camp when his dad came with the horses and camping gear, etc. He said he thought we were late. It was December and the bears had mostly gone into hibernation. Well, dang!

Stumbling around in our Duke's Mixture of languages, the son-guide told us about the panthers -- leones -- he and his dad had killed. Since he didn't pack a rifle, we asked him how he managed to kill panthers.

Oh, easy, he said, pointing to his big yellow dog. Seems when his dog treed the mountain lions, he'd go under the tree and shoot the critter with his 38 caliber pistola.

"How many have you killed?" we asked.

Mas or menos veinte, veintidos. (More or less 20 or 22.)

By that time the mist was falling heavier. We made for the make-shift shelter to turn in.

We all crawled into bed rolls and stuck our heads under the pup-tent lean-to. It was crowded, with five, but the thin old canvas did its job. We lay snugged in a close row -- heads up-hill -- on a slight slope above the heaped bed of coals of the slowly dying fire.

Boots were stacked next to the canvas to divert rivulets from trickling down. Guns were laid on the boots to keep them as dry as possible. Coats were rolled up for pillows. The tent kept the drizzle off our heads. The thick GI shelter bags (not sleeping bags) kept our bed rolls and bods dry and warm. My glasses were safe in one of my boots.

The flickering and dying fire danced now and then above the bed of coals and embers, casting shimmering shadows on the tree trunks and undergrowth on the other side of the little clearing.

I was dozing off, savoring the smell of wood smoke mingled with odors of the pines, listening to the irregular drippings of the accumulated mist softly plopping from the tree limbs above us down on the shelter-half over me. And then I saw him. Or her. Or it!

Across the clearing, soundlessly slinking from shadow to shadow, was a genuine, real-live, dry-mouth, heart-thumping panther! A big MEXICAN LEON!

The hairs on the back of my neck stiffened.

I held my breath and gritted my teeth as I reached over my head, worked that old, long-barreled 30-40 around, slid it down and propped it up on my foot, eased the bolt back, brought a shell up from the magazine into the chamber, and closed the action. Squinting with my next-to-worst near-sighted eye, I aimed awkwardly at the creature crossing just twenty yards away, began to gently squeeze the trigger through its long military trigger creep . . . and . . . the fire flared a little and revealed -- only the guide's old yellow dog.

I dang near went ahead and shot that hound just for scaring me so bad.

Day Three

Next morning, the real guide showed up. Our hunting guide. With four saddled horses, two horses with pack saddles, two tarps, and NO tents. Todo. No mas. That's all.

Our plans to climb higher to our permanent camp meant colder temperatures. The misty conditions at this level might turn into winter rains, sleet, and/or snow up another 500 or more feet. No tents was a definite downer.

Almost as bad, the riding saddles he brought were Civil War vintage McClelland types. McClellands are old time cavalry saddles -- nearly all wood, little leather, open slot down the middle to favor the horse's back but not the rider's, open iron stirrups. Most importantly, each of these saddles brought for us had only one girth. No back girth.

McClellands are two girth rigs. On those old saddles, the front strap holding the saddle on the horse is located far forward. That is acceptable if it is offset by the rear girth under the horse's belly. Without a rear girth, the saddle kicks up. Especially on a down-hill passage, tipping the rider up over the horse's shoulders can be literally very upsetting.

So it was decision time.

We had already lost half a day waiting for the hunting guide, the horses, and the tents which did not come. Delaying more for better gear would eat up too much of the little time we had left for our hunt.

We opted to go with what we had.

The son-guide departed, but left the yellow hound dog with his dad, the hunting guide.

Stowing food, Jim's precious condiments, ammo, sleeping shells and bedrolls, toilet paper, extra socks, and other essentials in the tarps on the pack horses, we mounted up and headed out. And up. The guide, the hound dog, the two pack horses, Jim, Bill, Jack, and, Tail-End-Charlie -- me.

A little south of where we had pitched our lean-to for that one-testicle, hound-dog/panther-scare first night on the hard ground of Old Mexico, the guide reined his horse to the right, westward, and upward. The trail was an easy climb for a short way.

Then it began to switch back and forth up a continuing series of ledges to breaks and flaws in the rock formations where the horses could lunge and grunt up to the next level.

As we continued zigzagging higher . . . working our way up the EASTERN slopes of the del Carmens . . . it got colder, the air cleared, and we enjoyed an awesome display of nature's beauty.

On the WESTERN side of the mountain range, moisture-laden air from the Baja de California and the Pacific was being pushed by prevailing westerly winds over the peaks of the plateau. As the clouds reached the upper edge of the eastern slope which we were scaling, the white, heavier-than-air mists poured over saddles and depressions in the lower heights, and flowed downward toward the valley we were leaving. Like cream from a pitcher. Three or four rich, velvety, bubbling, streamers of mist were roiling down the steeper slots, tumbling and cascading as the narrow confines widened -- spreading, thinning, intertwining and lacing into the green, pine-studded canyons.

We topped out and rode another half hour across undulating highs and lows of the mesa-like mountain crests, through the spicy pungency of the pines, until we came to a small stream meandering along up there near the top of our world. Further along that little waterway we came to the cup-like glade to which the guide had been leading us -- our permanent camp site.

First off, we built a make-shift, one-of-a-kind, jim-dandy shelter to shield us from the mountain winter elements. Well, maybe . . . semi-protect us. Almost.

In that clearing, slightly uphill from the little stream, we patched together a roof of sorts from the tarps. Rigged upper side-walls from the shelter-halves and some blown-down logs. Fashioned reasonably functional lower walls of shingled layers of leafy limbs.

Jack said it looked like it was built by a Genghis Khan yurt maker. But it really was more like a Baker Tent -- sloping top, vertical sides, short back. A bit of a canvas over-hung the semi-open front -- facing the fire and cooking area down toward the creek.

I must sadly report, however, that in keeping with what was in those days considered almost mandatory practice, we "trenched" around the bottom of the back and side walls. It worked ok for us. But by now, a whole layer of mountain has probably eroded away from that thought-to-be proper protection from the snow and rain.

On the downhill side of the stream, properly secluded by a fringe of undergrowth, we dug, fabricated, and assembled a latrine of the first order. It even boasted a seat comprised of a smooth limb set on a couple of forked limbs stuck in the ground. The GI folding entrenching tool was stuck close at hand for individual flushing. The essential roll of tissue was on a stick, covered and protected by the empty coffee can in which it had journeyed with us across the Chihuahuan wilderness and into the enchanting bosom of the del Carmens!

Jim directed the placement and details of the fireplace in front of the shelter. Bill had killed a young deer. So Jim, with intermittent assistance from wood gatherers, fire builders, and careful critics, began whomping up his promised special, delectable "comida" for supper. We each understood the time-honored custom of careful commentary about the cook's concoctions. One false slip of the lip and that cook no longer had those chores, but his critic acquired them.

Our first surprise was the suspicion, and then confirmation, that our flour sack had been splashed with spray from leakage of one of the spare gasoline cans with which it had been riding in the trailer. We ate pan bread and gravy prepared with that flour for the rest of our trip, but it always had a gasoline taste. I don't think it bothered us as much as it seemed to rankle the guide. And that yellow hound dog always wrinkled his nose and snorted before he wolfed down the leftovers he got after our meals.

Jim's main dish was an eye opener. And a tear maker.

That old story about "Hell in Texas" and how the devil made things so tough . . . How "the red pepper grows on the bank of the brook and the Mexicans use it in all they cook"! Well, you ain't tried nothing yet 'til you singe your tongue, sear your sinuses, and sauté your epiglottis with Jim's amalgamated appetite agonizer. Probably the only reason some of us didn't then and there inherit all of the cooking duties for the rest of the trip was our inability to catch enough air to formulate the phraseology. Gasps and coughs, wheezes and whoofs, were punctuated by some belated "Whooees!" And then we were too out of breath and sore-tongued for further refined, serious, or jocular jousting.

I noticed Jim was a little light on the fork draw himself. The old guide smiled and shook his head as he wallowed a big chunk of Humble Oil Company-flavored pan bread around after each bite. I thought he set his tin camp plate out for the hound dog kinda early. And that hound beat a little trail back and forth between that pan of Jim's specialty and the creek before he licked the platter clean.

Next morning when we got up, the guide had coffee made and breakfast ready for us. And danged if he didn't take a notion to do the main-dish cooking for all of the meals for the rest of the trip!

But, we still had the clean-up to do after the meals. And that led to the contest.

Day Four

A light frosting of snow awaited us when we crawled out of the sack to tackle our first day of real bear hunting.

Jim and the guide jawed back and forth in Tex-Mex and Spanglish. Bill, Jack, and I blew on the rims of the tin cups of coffee, slurped noisily, and tried to make sense of what the two were hatching up.

The plan worked out was for Bill and Jim to head north, hunting along trails that paralleled the stream, then split east and west short distances, find clearings to overlook and watch, and not long after mid-afternoon meet back at the stream and hunt together back to camp.

Jack and I were to hunt south along the mountain valley the same way. Staying in the high valley through which the stream ran, returning to the waterway and along it back to camp, no one should get lost.

The guide? Oh, he and his yellow hound dog watched the camp, loose herded the hobbled horses, shooed away any leones or panthers or buggers. He grinned a toothy "adios" from beneath his bristly mustache, raised his grimy right hand, and promised to have bastante comida ready and waiting for our hungry return about sundown. I don't know whether the upheld hand was a good-by wave, a blessing, or signification of an oath attesting to his assurance that he would have supper fixed and Jim would not have to mess with it.

It was a grand day. Spectacular forest glades. "Beautimous" evergreens. Nostril-flaring, head-clearing, aromatic fragrances. Smelled good, too. Plenty of bear and deer droppings. In the lee of bushes, where the light snow had not fallen or in the sunny spots where it had melted away, we found other scats, some of which I assumed might be panther mess. But nary a real live bear.

When he got back to camp that evening, Jim had a tale to tell.

He and Bill had come to a fork in a game trail. One way led around the hillside. The other began angling up through the big pines to higher ground. They decided that each of them would separately go a short distance along those paths so they could cover more territory to maybe scare up a bear. Bill opted to take the low road. Jim took the up fork.

As Jim slowly and cautiously moved up -- stopping, listening, scanning -- he began to feel strangely uncomfortable. Something inclined him to keep looking back over his shoulders, at the trees he had already passed, down the way he had come. At one point he found a pile of bear droppings almost in the middle of the trail. He stepped on it lightly to test it -- see how old it was. It was dry and obviously days old.

As the trail twisted higher through the trees, Jim felt more and more ill at ease. Finally, even though the trail ahead looked promising and interesting, he abandoned it and retraced his way back down.

When he came to the spot where he had stepped on the bear scat, he was astonished to find a fresh steaming pile of manure almost on top of the old pile with his footprint on it. And it wasn't bear droppings! Had deer hair in it!

It didn't take any Einstein thinking for him to figure out that he was more than likely being stalked by a curious or maybe hungry panther as he lollygagged along that trail.

So he hot-footed it back to the fork in the trail and was more than moderately cordial, warm, amiable, and friendly in his greetings when Bill showed up.

Supper was ready. Fried venison, Dutch oven pan bread, gravy, and frijoles! That pot of beans was seasoned just taste-bud-tingling good. Darned if Jim didn't admit he could be persuaded to let the guide handle the cooking as long as he wanted to.

In planning the trip, we had agreed to take turns washing the skillet, Dutch oven, coffee pot, and eating gear -- even gathering the squaw wood and tending the fire. After we ate each evening, and took care of those chores, we lazed around the fire, playing Scratch Your Yatchee with a handful of dice.

I disremember after all this time which one it was, but Jim or Bill one had a .22 caliber Colt Woodsman pistol stashed in his bag of possibles.

That night, Bill and Jim got into a little hoo-rawing discussion about who was the best pistol shot.

Jim's dad was a U. S. Marshall, had been a Texas Ranger, etc. Jim allowed as how he had the genes and knew dang well he could top Bill in a match. Bill expressed a modest amount of pride in his sharpshooter ancestry also, and challenged Jim to a contest. It got serious enough that they bet the loser would do all of the winner's camp chores for the rest of the trip!

Being as it was almost mid-December, the days were almost as short as they get. We were in the midst of the thick darkness of a pine forest, so it took some thinking to come up with a way to run a shooting match that would be a true test of the combatants' abilities. But Jack offered a solution.

Bill took off his grey felt hat, pinched his thumb and forefinger on the brim, and took a stance. I hollered, "Pull!" and he twirled the hat up into the darkness above the firelight. When it came back down where we could see it, Jim aimed and fired four rounds.

Bill walked over, picked up his hat, and poked his fingers into a couple of .22 size holes.

So Jim took his wide-brimmed, dark-brown Stetson and spun it swooshing way up out of sight. When it came slid-slipping down like some skedaddling alien extraterrestrial unidentified object, Bill didn't even shoot.

Jim claimed a win. But Bill cried foul. Said he couldn't see that dark hat in the poor light and wanted another chance. Jim grinned and said, "Aw, go ahead."

But when Jim went over to pick up his hat and throw it up again, Bill protested some more. Said he wanted to throw up the hat so he could better know where it was coming down. Jim shrugged and agreed.

Bill picked up Jim's hat, quickly crushed it into a big felt ball between his two ham-like fists, pitched it up out of sight while Jim was squalling

"No Fair!", and, when it came almost straight down to him, he blazed off every round in that little semi-automatic pistol.

Jim always swore that Bill was still shooting when the hat hit the ground.

Bill never let on like his play was anything but simon-pure, but he finally agreed that the contest might be a draw because of the darkness. So nobody won or lost any dishwashing chores.

But, ole Jim sure had an air-conditioned hat the rest of that Mexico outing. Never did let us count the number of holes in his lid.

Day Five

Because we had all struck out the day before -- didn't see hide nor hair of anything like Old Oso Negro -- the guide said he thought the bears must have all crawled into their holes for the winter and were already hibernating.

But, he said if we rode across to the western edge of the del Carmens, and went down to warmer desert level on that side, we might find bear still feeding on the prickly pear tunas they skillfully and nimbly harvested and ate to lay on lard for their winter naps.

This time the guide led us. We rode, not hastily, but at a right steady clip over trails he knew until we came to the escarpment on the northwestern rim.

It was a bright, clear day. The guide pointed out -- way off in the distance, almost directly north -- what was definitely a road. He said that road was on the American side of the Rio Bravo -- across the Rio Grande in the Big Bend Park -- about 50 miles north.

And then he pointed down to the green prickly pear flats on the brown, sandy desert plain below us. Way down. Way down a steep-sided mountain!

That trail down was much more precipitous, sheer, and abrupt than the one we had climbed up on the east side of the del Carmens. Most of the way down, we could not ride the horses. The rear-girth-lacking McClelland saddles would have just tossed us off over the horse's head. What little we did ride on the way down, we were standing in the iron stirrups on either side of the horse's nose.

If you can't ride your horse down, you have to lead him. If you don't lead him down, you sure as heck can't ride him back up. And it was a long way both down and up.

The excitement of leading a horse down a steep trail is also greatly enhanced by the shower of rocks the slipping and sliding horse kicks down on you. And by the thought of how flat you would be squashed if your caballo and that dang wooden saddle fell on top of you. Every time the horse has to jump down a ledge behind and above you, you screw your head down tight on your shoulders and cringe. And scoot to get out of his way before his momentum brings him to you, over you, and beyond you.

Down among the prickly pear, there was no doubt that the bear had been harvesting pear apples there. In addition to the easy-to-identify droppings, there were tufts of hair caught on pear thorns. Bear hair!

As we rode along the crisscrossed trails tromped through the tall, thickly thatched cacti forests by bears and a host of other critters, we sometimes could not see the heads or even the hats of the other riders ahead. That was some mess of prickly pear.

It was sunny and hot down there. We shucked coats and tied them behind the saddles.

But the bear were not there that day.

The climb back up to the plateau was long and hard. We were pooped, saddle-sore, slumping, frustrated, tired, and hungry as heck.

When we got back to camp, two young Mexicans and their horses were waiting for us.

They had a folded paper -- a note. Addressed to "Mr. Block".

It was written by the saw mill manager. The penciled message briefly informed me that my grandmother had been hurt, was in bad shape, and I was asked to return at once. The two horsemen would lead me back to the saw mill by a more direct and shorter route than the one we had followed to get to our camp site.

There were only a few minutes of daylight left. I asked if these guys had any lights, a flashlight, a lantern? They shook their heads. But they seemed confident of their ability to get me to the sawmill.

After a little confab with Jim, Jack, and Bill, I left all my gear except my hat and coat with them, climbed back on my tired horse and departed with two young caballeros with whom I could barely communicate leading the way into the dark forest full of lions and bears.

I had a quirky thought about how Red Riding Hood should have felt, going through the woods to Grandma's house with the wolf out there somewhere.

The Night Ride

For a short time, there was enough light that my guides had the horses moving at a trot. I tee-totally utterly despise and hate to ride a trotting horse! But it quickly got too dark to continue at that pace. I was too upset to be either glad or sad about the slower gait. It was clear and cold. Now and then, crossing small clearings, I could see stars twinkling above. There may have been some moonlight, because I could sometimes see moving shadows of the riders leading me. But I don't remember seeing the moon.

Most of the time, I could not see well enough to give my horse any guidance. I just let him follow the two riders on their horses ahead of me. My horse was tired from the trek to and from and down and up the western escarpment to those prickly pear flats. I had to keep thumping his ribs with my heels to stay with the two guys ahead.

I worried -- about how far ahead they would get or how far behind I might lag before they lost me or I lost them. I worried about Grandma Birdie. She was almost ninety. What had happened to her? How bad off was she? How far did we have to go to the escarpment? How would we get down in the dark?

I worried about Babo's 30-40 Krag that I had left behind. Would my friends be able to get it back with them to my granddad?

How was I going to travel after reaching the saw mill? The Plymouth had to be left for the others.

At long last my guides halted.

We were at the edge of another steep trail. Way down below, I could see a few twinkling lights. One of the horsemen said something like, "Molino." I asked, "Saw mill?" "Si, Señor." We were looking down at the saw mill. Way down. But the lights were close enough that I conjured up gut-churning, apprehensive thoughts about how steep that trail down had to be.

The guides began to ride down. I had to follow.

I was surprised that my horse started off down that dark trail without a heavier dose of encouragement. I guess that old caballo, like all horses when they get close to the barn, wanted to "go home" -- after those two horses leading him down to his feed at the sawmill. Either that, or he was just plain dumb. That notion chilled the cold sweat I was oozing even more. That's all I needed -- a dumb horse.

But he was a better horse than I thought.

I couldn't see well enough to dodge the limbs my mount took me under -- certainly not well enough to judge when there was a ledge or a turn or something we had to go around.

All I could do was try to watch and not get too far behind the dim shapes of the sombreros bobbing ahead. Lunge down, twist around, disappear, show up to the left, switch back to the right, down again -- in an endless succession of rocks rolling and falling, horses snorting nervously, unseen tree limbs trying to take away my hat and knock off my glasses, etc.

If the horsemen in front turned, I got ready to turn. If they suddenly dropped down, I gritted my teeth and got ready for my horse to hop down to a lower level. Sometimes he hesitated to screw up his courage for the dropping lunge, sometimes he didn't.

I remembered my grandad telling me one time that horses could see better at night than we could. That ole horse packing me down the trail to Dante's Inferno sure proved Papo right on that one! I started giggling and right then and there named that cayuse "Dante"!

And that sorry, misbegotten McClelland saddle! I almost went over the horse's head a dozen times.

But the riders ahead kept moving right on down. Riding on down. Acted like they wanted to get the heck on home. Didn't let on like they had any idea about waiting. I shoved my stirrups up by my horse's nose, leaned way back over his rump, and hung on.

My horse must have thought I was trying to pull his mane out. I had a fist full of it and was pushing back trying to keep the saddle from sliding down over his head -- and me with it, of course.

I really didn't think we would get to the saw mill all in one piece! But you knew all the time that I had to -- so I could be here to tell you about it.

At the sawmill, they had heard us coming off that mountain for an hour or so -- listening to the rocks the horses kicked loose rolling down ahead of us.

The kindly old gentleman running the place had a Jeep, a driver, and a thermos of hot coffee waiting for me. I almost hugged him. I did thank him very sincerely. And thanked the two young fellows who had lead me that far. Then I piled into the Jeep -- and had another cold, fast, screechy, and scary ride from the saw mill all the way down to the curing yard.

At least I could see the road just ahead. I could tell when we were about to swing around one of those hairpin curves. But my empty belly churned when the puny Jeep headlights stabbed out into the void of darkness over the absent mountain side. I remembered that Caterpillar Company bulldozer laying way down in the canyon bottom.

We didn't even stop at the curing yard. Just waved to a couple of guys who opened gates for us and bounced on out across the nighttime desert floor.

My Jeep driver made lots better time on the log truck deep-rutted desert road than we had on our way in. Probably because he just hit the high spots. It was a tooth-jarring, hang-on-with-both-hands (no seat belts in those days) ride. Not much chance for conversation -- in any language.

As we were racing along through the dips, swales, and undulations of the passage through the Burro Mountains, we rounded a dark curve just about at that little lake where we had lunch on the beginning day of our hunting trip. Suddenly, we saw the lights of another vehicle flash from down the road ahead.

And there they were. Uncle Lucious and Aunt Beth. Waiting in their Ford coupe. Right there in the middle of a winter night in a bunch of cactus-covered mountains in Mexico!

There's no way to describe my feelings right then.

They told me that Grandma Birdie had fallen and broken a hip. Most likely had suffered a stroke. But she was going to still be there when they got me home.

I gobbled down a sandwich, had some coffee they had brought, tried to talk to them a little, but slept most of the way as Uncle Lucious skillfully herded the Ford over and around the obstacles of the rutty road back to Acuña and Del Rio.

Jim, Jack, and Bill broke camp, retraced their way back to the trailer, experienced an exciting ride back to the saw mill and down to the curing yard and the Suburban, and got home -- without even seeing a bear. And my granddad's 30-40 made it back also.

And, so you see, the title to this tale was not spelled incorrectly. It was a bare bear hunt.

But, it was the best bare bear hunt I ever made.

The Sling

Back in my day, if you really wanted to do some honest-to-gosh deer hunting in the rocky and rugged hills, draws, headers, and canyons of Val Verde County, you did it with a sling.

Out in the boondocks -- the remotes of Southwest Texas along the Devils and Pecos Rivers -- a sling was almost a necessity.

Oh, I never envisioned my self as a David. And there weren't any Goliaths around. But more often than not, a sling meant the difference between a good and a bad hunt.

That whirring sound as the thongs whizzed around your head and the rock zipped off more or less toward your intended target might not have been melodiously tuneful to whitetails hunkered down in a sheltering thicket, but it was a honeyed hum to a short armed hunter like me.

Now I don't mean to imply that we had any big wig notions that we could put the quietus to some ole trophy buck with a sling. But a whistling chunk of spinning limestone coming in on top of a whitetail holed up in his clutch of catclaw, Spanish dagger, mesquites, cedars, and/or scrub oaks could bring most shy critters out in the open PDQ.

We weren't much for sitting and waiting for the deer to come to us.

The best hunts were those where we walked the canyons and jumped the deer.

Pockets of brush down in the draws, up in the headers, off the points, under the rimrocks . . . that's where the deer lay up during the day. That's where we eased up as near as we could without spooking them so we could have a closer shot when they came out.

If you were slow and quiet, they might just step out into a clearing or jump up on a ledge to look around. That's the deal you wanted.

But deer are darn smart. When they hear or see you a long way off, they usually slip out before you get near. If you pussy-foot up close before they know you are coming, they either bolt or hunker down. When they squat in a clump of brush too far away or too much above for you to chunk a rock to run them out . . . then you haul out the sling.

Ordinarily, we tried to cozy up on the places where deer might be laying up. Uncle Lucious, Uncle Jim, and especially Uncle Pete were better than good at this. They cogitated where the quarry would be. The wind, lay of the land, time of day, light conditions, humidity . . . even phases of the moon . . . figured in their calculations. Mostly, they were real close to the money. Either they were -- or they had you -- in a nigh-on-to-perfect position to shoot when a buck showed.

But there were times when you wanted to get close enough to do your imitation of a deer snort to spur the rascals out of a rock-ribbed, tangled cedar mott and you just couldn't get close enough to do that.

That's when you reached in your pocket for your equalizer. You know, just like the one you see in the Sunday School drawings where that little kid is facing that big, bearded, muscled-up, armor-clad, galoot with the oversized toothpick in his hand.

Pretty much like those from times past, our slings were just two thongs and a cup-like pocket to hold the rock.

But just any old sling won't do. Like other weapons or tools, the more you can fashion it to fit you and the use you intend for it, the better.

Keep it small enough to roll up and stick in your pocket and tough enough to handle the ammo you figure on finding on location.

All kinds of thongs have been tried. A couple of good leather boot laces are hard to beat.

The cup or pocket should be sturdy, but flexible. Too weak and it tears or wears out quickly. Too stiff and your rock falls out, sometimes zooming off toward one of your hunting buddies or the window of your pickup. An old boot tongue works well.

Tie the thongs to holes punched in the cup. Most folks use only one hole on each side of the cup. Some try a two-hole rig on each side to get the cup to pucker and hold the rock better. But you can't have the cup hold the ammo too securely.

One thong should have a loop at its end, to go around the wrist of the throwing arm. The free end of the other thong is held between the thumb and forefinger and released at the proper moment to send your projectile on its way. Some hunters don't use a looped thong. They just hold the "keeper" thong between the "bottom" three fingers and the palm of the throwing hand. It's a simpler rig, but it's harder to use.

The length of the thongs almost always requires some experimentation.

Longer thongs mean a bigger wind-up throwing arc. The release is not as quick, and you need more room to twirl your throw, but that larger arc gives the missile more energy and causes it to travel faster and further.

Shorter thongs are easier to manage. You get less distance out of your throw. But, for me, accuracy was easier to come by.

Throwing techniques vary.

Taller, longer-limbed throwers swing a big arc around their head a time or two and cast the rock as it comes almost horizontally around toward the object they are facing. Shorter guys like me tend to modify . . . swinging first horizontally, but releasing after an overhand uppercut at the end of the throw. That uppercut lets the rock start on its way from a higher point. It also serves to better aim the missile.

Of course, when you stand on the edge of the rim rock and want to heave way the heck out to that thicket down there in the bottom of the canyon, you can use an underhand, lobbing release that arches your rock high up and out . . . to come down almost vertically into the thicket. Accuracy isn't desired as much as effect.

Besides deer, you may, of course, bring out javalinas, coons, fox, rock squirrels, cows, sheep, goats, buzzards . . . sometimes even an armadillo.

It just chokes you up to think how a peaceful snooze on a cool fall afternoon in the sheltering shade of a mountain laurel can be shattered by a fist-sized rock smashing down thru the leafy limbs and splattering on the rocky ground there beside you.

Howsomever, I have to tell you -- even a good sling doesn't always do the job.

Like that time we were hunting out at Hinds Ranch on the Pecos.

Uncle Lucious had worked hard to make a wonderful dream come true. The ranch his dad and mom -- Levi and Scottie Hinds -- started in 1916 had been left to their children, Lucious, Carrol, Sullivan, Charlie, Marjorie, and Alvia Mae. Uncle Lucious almost persuaded his brothers and sisters to set up a trust which would have kept that ranch for all of the descendents to have a place to camp, hunt, fish, and enjoy forever. But only half of the signatures needed had been secured when Uncle Lucious had a heart attack and passed away.

Later, but before the ranch was sold, Wayne, David, and I were out there one bright and shining fall day hunting the big canyon that ran the length of the ranch to its intersection with the Pecos River. We were using the old Ford Bronco Aunt Beth liked to hunt out of.

David and Wayne gave me, the old timer, the easy side of the canyon.

I drove to a place up on the divide where I could walk off to a point on the rim rock, and watch them work the headers and hill sides across from me. The canyon ran in a big curve around my point. It had taken them most of two hours to ease around the thickets, climb up to the headers, chunk the draws, and make their way around the big arc of wondrously beautiful rocky cuts and undulations. The sun was behind me. The ledge I sat on was still damp with dew.

I used my sling to drop some rocks out at some distant spots in the canyon as the boys began to come around. But mainly, I just sat huddled up against the piercing gusts of the north wind out there on a flat rock, drinking coffee out of my thermos, and watching them with my binoculars. Of course, I was glassing around all the time, watching for deer that might be trying to slip away around the curve of the hillside ahead of them.

Down below me -- a sheer drop of maybe 200 feet -- was a little clump of brush tucked into a small depression. I had looked it over when I got to my perch. From time to time, I eye-balled it. But nothing stirred the whole time I had been sitting above it and slinging an occasional rock way out over it and into the canyon beyond.

I didn't want to toss a rock directly into that little brush clump below me until the boys were around far enough that, if a deer came out, they could have some shooting. If something did come out of it, in about one jump it would be around the hillside from me and I would be lucky to get even one shot at it. But when they were in position across the canyon, Wayne and David would be able to shoot if a high-tailing deer tried to go either up or down the canyon.

Finally, one of the boys waved to signal me to start walking on my side of the canyon . . . on down toward the Pecos.

Well, sir, when I got up, all that coffee I had swallowed needed to be jettisoned before I started my walk.

So, I set my binoculars on my rock seat, leaned my rifle up against the bigger rock that had been my back rest, stepped over to the edge of the rimrock, and started tinkling. The wind was just right to carry some spiraling, sparkling droplets into that little clump of brush way down there.

One of the nicest sets of horns I had seen in a long time came busting out of that tiny thicket.

My jaw dropped. I reached for my gun with one hand. Tried to zip up my pants with the other. Kicked my thermos. Heard it crash in the rocks below. Snagged my binoculars just before they went off to perdition. Grabbed a sotol stalk to keep from skating off the dew-slick edge.

The dang deer insultingly flicked his big white flag as he went around a curve of the hillside.

No body got a shot.

The boys said it was the best buck they saw all day.

They also said that dance I did out on the edge of that ledge was the best show they had seen in a long time.

The Canoe and the Chute

Soon after I raided Grandma's sewing basket for bent pins and thread to start my fishing career -- grub worms for bait -- irrigation ditch silver sides my intended prey -- my friend Leon headed me for higher piscatorial levels. We went from minnow hooks and split-shot lead sinkers (Ridley's Western Auto) to perch poles and cork floats (Ledbetter's Firestone Tire Store). Then drooled over treble-hooked dijacks (Russell Hardware) and jointed bass lures (Brian Kelley's).

"Outdoor Life" stories whetted our appetites. "Field and Stream" how-to articles honed our hankerings. Big windies at the Buckhorn Barber Shop zeroed us in on good local fishing spots. We turned wooden apple crates into wooden tackle boxes. Stitched extra pockets on surplus Navy fatigues to make fishing vests. Little by little, we upgraded rods, reels, lures, and gear to better fit our improving skills.

Leon was resourceful. He was always eager to try new water. Nearly every time we went fishing, he had new techniques or equipment to make it easier, more enjoyable. During those war years of rationing and shortages, he scrounged up the transportation we needed to get out to Lake Walk or places on Devil's River.

When it came to us that we needed some sort of boat to run trotlines, he located an old rubber raft. We no longer had to wade neck-deep along the multi-hooked lines.

Later on he showed up with a fair-to-middling, second-hand, green, canvas-covered canoe. That canoe opened up lots of possibilities.

Instead of traipsing along the river banks, to set out and tend trotlines at dusk, midnight, and dawn, why we could just paddle our bods, gear, bait, and catch from one pool to another! Then cruise around the pools, casting to the sweet spots.

So, we loaded up his 1930 long-nosed, black, Chrysler sedan and headed for some canoe-style fishing at the foot of The Road Off on Uncle Lucious and Aunt Beth's place.

That green canoe was a heavy rascal. But we were high school foot ball types. We hoisted it up, turned it upside down, and lashed it to the car top. Those good old cars had sturdy bumpers front and back. Tied the prow of the canoe with some of our older trot line cordage to both ends of the front bumper. Tied the stern to the back bumper ends.

As you may know, The Road Off is a steep goat trail that Uncle Lucious morphed into a one-lane belly churner. It hugs the cliff on one side and falls off almost straight down on the other side to a jagged mess of boulders and broken rocks blasted off to make the road.

Just after we drove off the edge of the divide, curved thru the rimrock cut, exited the concrete ramp, and hit the really rough spots, the old trot line cord securing the stern of the canoe to the right rear bumper snapped. The back end of the canoe slid around left toward the chasm. Leon stomped on the brake! Hauled up the emergency! Stopped the old Chrysler on a dime. That stop jerked the rear end of his canoe way out to the left over that awesome rock pile below. Standing on the brake pedal with both feet, Leon, in one of his resourceful tones, said: "Walt, you hafta get out and retie the canoe."

"Whada you mean, me?" I spluttered. "I can't get out! You have this side of the car jammed up against the cliff over here. There isn't even room to climb out the window!"

"Crawl over the seat. Get out the left door." Leon grunted. "If I let up on the brake this car is gonna start on down and I might not get it stopped!"

Once in a while, Leon can be darned persuasive. I bellied over into the back.

When we went camping-fishing in a vehicle, Leon and I cared for creature comforts. Never took a tent or a kitchen sink. But . . . cots, bed rolls, mosquito netting, pots, pans, skillets, seines, trot lines, rods, reels, cane perch poles, tackle boxes, minnow buckets, paddles, first aid kits, canned sardines, jars of Leon's mom's orange-slice cookies, cans of Eagle Brand Milk and assorted eats for two growing boys. All that was in the back seat area, since the old Chrysler's dinky trunk barely held the two thin-skinned spare tires we always hauled just to be safe.

As I wormed my way, I switched stuff from the back seat to the front area I was leaving. When I moved or moved pieces of that load, the canoe screeched overhead and squiggled over, out, and toward perdition. Leon had his teeth clinched, nostrils flared, and was kinda snorting.

When the left rear door popped open, I slid out. Missed the running board with one foot. Caught a frazzled line tied to the canoe tail with one hand. Teetered with a tip toe digging into the rusty remnants of the old running board and the other leg swinging out in thin space. Hauled myself back. Leon did not one time ever cuss. I did. For both of us.

With the canoe retied, we went on down The Road Off to the bottom, unloaded the canoe, our gear, and made a few stabs at setting up our camp. Then we launched the canoe.

There are two good-sized pools of water on the stretch of Devils River that bounds Uncle Lucious and Aunt Beth's ranch. Between those pools the river flows through a cut -- maybe thirty yards wide --carved in the solid rock by the forces of nature. When the river is at or below normal level, the total flow goes through this cut. Leon and I called it "The Chute".

Even at its normal flow rate, the volume of the river compressed into the restricted fifty yard length of the channel created a strong current between the rock banks. And the uneven bolder strewn bottom tossed significant surface waves and swirls at several points.

Since we had the canoe, our plan for this trip was to set out two trot lines. The first would run from the upper end of the upper pool down to a Sycamore Tree that was Aunt Beth's favorite shade-covered, daytime fishing spot. A second trot line would be set out in the lower pool. Then we would fish for perch off the ledges and seine in the shallows to get trotline bait. Late the first afternoon we would bait the trot lines, run them once about midnight, and again after sunup the next morning.

With the canoe, we figured on the chore of putting out the trot lines being lots easier than it had been. By paddling to the upper end of the upper pool, we could let the current drift us downstream as we played out lines, swivels, hooks, drops, and weights with not a lot of effort.

But how to get the canoe from the lower pool to the upper pool? The Chute was in between.

"Think we should portage? Carry the canoe around The Chute to the upper pool?" I asked.

"Naw. Two huskies like us can paddle up that little way, no sweat!" Leon replied.

At that time, I was not yet a full-fledged, certified, genuine, shirt-badged, water-front canoe- instructor graduate of the Boy Scouts of America Aquatic School. Not being of French-Canadian fur-trapping, voyager extraction, Leon also was some lacking in canoe lore, logic, and learning. "J-strokes", "cross-bow, push-a-way, draw strokes", etc., were in books we had not yet read.

So we just hopped in that green canoe, me in front, Leon in back. Took the doodads we needed to set out trot lines. Plus a rod, reel, and a home-made wooden tackle box apiece -- so we could chunk likely lures at those spots just too temping to ignore in the upper pool.

Things were not totally hunky-dory as we paddled country-style across the upper end of the lower pool. Our stroke timing was ragged, but we did have it about half figured out that, if we both paddled on the same side, that round bottomed canoe wanted to ship water in over that side.

As we started up The Chute, we found the current stronger than expected. Not more than a couple of canoe lengths into the struggle, we were grunting, puffing, and really digging in with our paddles to make headway. It was hard to keep in the center and away from the rough rocky banks of the narrow water passage. The aquatic aura of that green canoe paled some.

Then, just as Leon was reaching forward to take a big paddle bite to get us past a bad spot, a tricky wave came along. Instead of getting his whole blade into the top of the wave, Leon plunged his paddle down into the trough or lowest point. With only half a paddle in the water, his humongous stroke swished mostly air. The unexpected lack of resistance caused him to lunge far over to the right. The canoe shipped a big slosh of water.

Leon went over the side, but in the tradition of "one hand for the sailor and one for the ship", he grabbed his straw hat with one fist and clomped onto the canoe gunnel with the other. As he sank below the foamy surface, he pulled the canoe side down. Another big wash of water swept into the canoe's belly.

Exercising tremendous foresight, I grabbed my glasses with one hand and my hat with the other and let the devil of the river take the canoe as I joined Leon in the drink. Wooden tackle boxes tumbled about. Rolled up trotlines floated out, then -- pulled down by their sinkers -- sank. One paddle went port and the other starboard. I vented some more choice expletives. For both of us.

Rods, reels, and tackle boxes stayed in the canoe. But some of the tackle box fasteners had come open and lures were sinking and/or floating away. In and out of the canoe!

We jammed our hats back on and, with the half-swamped canoe, paddles, and some floating lures, we let the current carry us out of The Chute and into the calmer waters of the pool beyond.

We swam over to shallow water, towing the water-filled canoe.

We looked at each other.

I laughed.

Leon sobered me up with his tart assessment of all the hard-come-by fishing stuff that was on, in, or under Devils River.

Our biggest loss was lures which had tumbled out of those wooden tackle boxes. Some of the screen-door hooks on those home-grown tackle boxes had opened in the swamping. Lures were bobbing off down the river. Non-floaters were on the river bottom, either in The Chute or washed into the pool below.

We splashed downstream to the narrow channels and shallow rock ledges, salvaging floating gear as it came along. Next, dumping the water out of the canoe, we paddled around, picking up lures, bobbers, etc. lodged in reed clumps and on just-below-the-surface honeycombed rock tops.

Then we started diving.

The rest of that stand-out-in-memory outing was spent mostly in diving in the clear waters of the pool at the end of The Chute. From mid-morning to mid-afternoon the next day, with the sun right overhead, we could see a big portion of the river bottom. But there were lots of rocks and rock channels in the river bed. And for me, under water without my glasses, things were murkier than ever.

With a lot of work, we recovered maybe half of the non-floating lures and other items that came out of the tackle boxes.

It was one of the few times that we came home with less than a bragging load of fish.

Some sixty years later, after college, after his careers as a science teacher, football coach, farmer, furrier, husband, dad, serious fisherman, super-successful trophy buck hunter, and owner of a variety of boats, Leon became -- and is today -- a talented collector of antiquated fishing tackle.

More than once he has clucked his tongue, pursed his lips, and sighed, "Walt, do you realize the value of all those old-time triple-dijack and fifteen-hook lures we lost? They probably washed down Devils River into the Rio Grande and right on out into the Gulf of Mexico! Why, today they'd be worth mucho dinero -- a tidy fortune!"

The Hitch-Hiker

I hopped the Austin city bus out on the Drag, rode down to 6th and Congress, caught the South Austin bus out to the city limits on the San Antonio highway, and stuck up my thumb.

Less than a dozen vehicles of various vintages and makes passed before this brand spanking new, bright and shiny 1945 Chevy coupe slowed, pulled off the pavement, and stopped just down the road. Any new car, in the fall of 1945, after four years of war-time rationing, was a captivating sight.

The lady driver looked back thru her rear view mirror; then she waved for me to come.

Jogging to the coupe -- ditty bag in one hand and jacket in the other -- I began to wonder as I noticed the medical symbol on the license plate.

The VERY attractive young woman-- driver and sole occupant -- reached over, cranked down the passenger side window, and asked, "Where you headed?"

"Santone, ma'am, and then west to Del Rio", I replied.

"You a UT student?" she asked. "Yes, ma'am," I answered.

She arched an eyebrow, smiled and said, "I'll take you as far as San Antonio. Hop in!"

Flabbergasted at my good fortune, I slipped into the passenger seat and tossed my bag on the floorboard between my feet. The formerly just plain ole Texas bright and shining day was sparkling. The lady booted the Chevy onto the highway, tromped on the accelerator, and zipped up to and beyond the speed limit in record time.

She asked me my major and classes. A wet-behind-the-ears freshman, I was enrolled for the short 1945 September-October fall semester. As we made introductory remarks, I noticed that she was repeatedly flicking her big green eyes from the road ahead to the rear view mirror.

"Traveling with other cars, ma'am?"

"No. Just watching for the highway patrol," she grinned nervously. "I stole this car."

I gulped. My turn to look over my shoulder out the rear view window.

She went on, "My husband's away. I got lonely and bored. I 'borrowed' this car from the doctor who lives next door. So I could go see some friends in Santone. This new Chevy was just sitting all alone in the doc's three-car garage. Left him a note. Told him I would bring it back Monday. But I didn't talk to him first or get permission to use it. He could have called the law. They might be out looking for me."

I figured she was joking. But she kept one eye on the road ahead and one on that rear view mirror. Had me super jumpy by the time we got to San Antonio. I asked her to drop me off on North Broadway. At the first city bus stop. You must remember: I was a mere 17-year-old, fresh-out-of-high-school country bumpkin at the time.

I caught the city bus to downtown SAT, transferred to a west-bound out to the last stop on West Commerce at 24th Street, and hoisted my thumb again.

Saturday morning traffic -- almost bumper to bumper -- whizzed by for a good twenty minutes. Then a battered old blue car rattled to a stop after it passed me. I hurried up to the passenger-side window and saw this big, brawny Mexican-American driver. Had a bushy black, mustache that drooped around the edges of his mouth. When he grinned, he showed about as many shiny, gleaming gold teeth as ever I saw in one guy's mouth.

"Where you goin', boy?" he wanted to know.

"Del Rio," I said.

"Just goin' out to the Kelly turnoff, but that far out you'll know most of the cars are heading' on out of town."

So I jerked a couple of times at the door handle, finally got it open, dusted off the seat, and climbed in.

"Play football?" he wanted to know.

"Yep. In high school last year. Now I'm at The University in Austin!"

"Muy bien", my husky and jovial driver-host beamed. He began a non-stop chatter of sports-related trivia as he herded his old Ford down the highway. And . . . then . . .

His big, hairy, muscled hand worked across the seat to my leg! That was mucho mas friendlier than I wanted, and I said so.

I began to size him up in a whole new light. Could I handle him, if he got mean? But by then we were close to his turn-off. Just before we got there, danged if he wasn't petting my thigh as he jawed his steady stream of jabber.

But he stopped at the Kelly turn-off. As I scooted out, he said: "Well, some do and some don't."

"Better luck next time!" I shouted, as he drove off waving back at me.

I decided it might be wise to exercise a little more judgment in selecting my rides. Started eye-balling vehicles a lot more keenly as they approached . . . trying only to signal that I was hitch-hiking if the vehicle and/or the person or folks in it looked ok. That was hard to do. Everybody was whizzing by zippity-do-dah without giving me much chance to check.

I began reassessing the merits of hitching a ride. The world might not be exactly the oyster I had conjured up in my youthful imaginings. I began toying with the idea of flagging down the next Painter Bus for the remainder of my trip home.

I was walking on westward, looking back only when I heard the approach of a big vehicle, when this neat, early '40's Mercury sedan stopped a little past me. The driver looked back and waved.

I trotted up to the car, looking it over dubiously. The driver was thirty-ish, clean-shaven, neatly dressed, sported a nice copper-tone tan. "Want a ride?" he asked.

"Maybe," I said. "Right now I'm waiting on the bus to come along."

He said, "Well, I'm a driver for AAA. Some Mexico vacationers stayed last night in Eagle Pass. The lady didn't discover that she had left her purse at the hotel until they got to San Antonio this morning. They have AAA insurance and called our office. Hired me to go down to Eagle Pass, get her purse, and take it back to them. If you are going to Uvalde, I can take you that far."

My day was suddenly brighter. This guy looked solid as the Rock of Gibraltar.

We had a nice conversation as we drove along. He was very attentive to his driving. His steering wheel had a lot of slack in it and required a firm two-handed grip. I began to relax.

As we neared Uvalde, my driver had a sudden thought! He said that, while he had intended to leave Highway 90 in Uvalde, go thru La Pryor, and over to Eagle Pass, there was a newly worked road from Brackettville that now offered another option. He said, if I wanted, he could go that route and drop me off at Brackett.

That was forty miles closer to home, so I thanked him and began to day dream about my plans for the rest of the weekend.

Now I really do know you will find this hard to believe, dear reader. Because I did too!

Not long after we headed out Highway 90 from Uvalde, my super friendly driver reached over and flipped down the sun visor in front of me. Attached to it by clips and rubber bands, was an envelope. He tossed the envelope in my lap, reached back to grab that wobbly steering wheel, and said, "Those snapshots might be of some friends of yours!"

I opened the envelope and out tumbled a bunch of photographic surprises. The kind you could -- in those days (and probably now) -- find street hawkers pushing in the border towns of Mexico. Males and females, in assorted stages of nudity, engaging in diverse sexual activity.

My recently sensitized and already trigger-happy alarm went off.

I stuck the envelope and its contents back behind the sun visor, turned it back up, and told the driver none of those weirdoes were acquaintances of mine.

Shortly beyond the Nueces River, this American Automobile Association driver began to yawn. Claiming he was sleepy, he asked if I would drive. My alarm bells wailed a shriller tone. But it was still thirty miles or so to Brackettville. I didn't want to get out and try to hitch a ride at that particular local, so I told him ok. I was boogered and darned apprehensive, but I had a plan.

Mr. AAA slouched down in the passenger seat, closed his eyes, and for a brief spell I thought he really might be going to sleep. Then his left arm flopped over on the seat toward me.

Well, sir, that little Mercury suddenly had plenty of pep. The foot feed was mashed down to the bottom notch almost one hundred percent of the rest of the way to Brackett. The play in that slack steering wheel had us bouncing all over the road. Those front wheels shimmied, shook, and shivered. The tires stayed on somehow, but we must have thrown a bucket of bolts as we hit the high spots on ole Highway 90.

This was happening, you will recall, in the days before seat belts for US of A cars and pickups were required or even available. That AAA rep literally had to hang on with both hands to keep his bouncing butt in the seat. His healthy tan yellowed a shade or two. Never said a word, tho!

I jockeyed the Merc to a dusty stop under one of the big shady oak trees across from Fort Clark in Brackettville, stepped out of the hot and pulsating vehicle, thanked him for the ride, and he disappeared down the pike to Eagle Pass.

I dug around in my pocket and found a spare nickel. Spent it on a coke at the gas station (this was before they were called "service stations"), walked west a bit, sat down on my bag under another shady tree, and waited for the Painter Bus which I knew was due along in about an hour.

In a little bit, a vintage pre-war-era jalopy rattled by, slowed, stopped, and backed up to where I was perched. I didn't even get up.

The wrinkled, old brown-skinned driver leaned across, smiled out the open passenger window, and offered, "You want a ride, son?"

"No thank you, sir. Waiting on the bus."

"Aren't you Edwin Block's son?" the old fella asked?

"Yes, sir!"

"Well I used to work for your granddaddy. Come on and I'll take you home."

And he did. Right up to the front gate.

So . . . it wasn't too bad an ending . . . to a remarkable and well-remembered day.

But it was the end my hitch hiking.

Speedy Bob

When football season rolls around, you never can tell what's going to pop into the mind of an old moss back. Take my hallowed career as a headline earning gridiron stud at The University of Texas back in '45, for example.

Oh, I know you immediately conjure up a Joe Bifspic rain cloud over your fevered and furrowed brow with that reference. You probably harken back somewhere into the webbed recesses of your various, assorted, and diverse recollections and . . . rather than my moniker . . . you come up with fellas like Bobby Layne. Or maybe Doak Walker. But Doak played for SMU.

Okay, okay. There was that guy Layne, alright! Fresh out of the armed services, he was. But he just stole the show on the varsity squad. I, on the other hand, won laurels on the lesser manicured, johnson-grass-tufted intramural playing fields on Speedway, next to Gregory Gym.

In September 1945, Buddy Graham, Paul Epps, and I shared a corner room at Mrs. Carlson's rooming house on the corner of 25th and San Antonio Streets -- one block west of the Drag.

About the third day we were there, Buddy and I traipsed over to Memorial Stadium to eye ball an afternoon practice session of the Texas football team. We harbored sneaking suspicions that we, as recent graduates of Del Rio High and illustrious first string guards on the Wildcat team the previous fall, might just try out for the Longhorn team.

I weighed 135 pounds . . . more or less. Buddy jiggled the scales around 150. About a ten minute visit cleared it up for us. Texas had guards who weighed about 100 pounds more than we did. The tackles were even bigger.

Right then and there, but with wounded and aching hearts, we started looking for an intramural team which might be in the market for laudable pigskin skills such as ours.

It had taken us only a short time after our early September enrollment at UT to realize that the scanty budgets we were stretching would not allow us the luxurious consumption of meals at the University Commons.

Boldly following directions painted on a catchy sign stuck on a stick at the corner of 25th and San Antonio, we sashayed around the corner and down a couple of blocks. There we found a marvelous institution heretofore unknown to we wayward wanderlings from the West Texas hinterlands. A boarding house. Thereafter we took our noon meals there -- family style. I could tell you a lot about those good eats, but that's a tale for another time.

Among the hungry throngs reaching across for the overloaded bowls and platters of stick-to-your-ribs, finger-licking-good grub that only briefly appeared on that groaning table each noontime was a hefty honcho named Raborn. This guy was loaded with gobs of football terminology which he splashed liberally into any conversation started by anyone, anytime, anyplace.

Didn't take long for Raborn to reveal that he was a gifted sports writer for The Daily Texan. What's more, he was the organizer and manager of -- according to him -- the A-number-one touch football squad that was going to win the UT men's intramural touch football trophy that fall!

We asked if he needed a couple of real horses to bolster this gosh-awful-good team he was so lathered up about. He allowed as how we could try out for his team that very afternoon.

We made the team. Raborn's Red Raiders.

Most of the guys practicing for this two-hand-touch, nine-man-team of pigskin proficiency were like Buddy and me, former high school players who loved the game but were never going to make it on any college squad. But we did have some good players.

Sonny Rooker was the quarterback for the Gulfport, Mississippi Air Force team during the war. When he returned from the service that fall, he tried out for the Longhorn varsity team, but was injured before the season started. He opted for intramurals to provide him an outlet for his athletic talents.

Rooker could throw passes a country mile -- with pinpoint accuracy. And any receiver who button-hooked just beyond the line of scrimmage would find a ball at his nose that would knock him down if he wasn't ready to catch it. He could have laid ole Bobby Layne in the shade.

Raborn's Red Raiders had a simple but efficient series of plays. We practiced and honed our timing. And we won games.

In high school, mainly because of my small size and my near-sightedness, I didn't cut the mustard as a ball handler. But in the touch football game we played at Texas -- there was no tackling -- body blocking was very limited -- I could wear my glasses!

Being able to see, I caught Rooker's passes!

You might find this hard to swallow, but I did well enough in a couple of games that Raborn, in his sports column in The Daily Texan, mentioned me. By name! Even had a headline story. "Speedy Bob Block . . ."

Ole Raborn goofed on the most important part of the story -- couldn't get my name right!

But we won often enough that at the end of the season we were eligible for the playoffs!

Then we were disqualified!

Some snake in the grass reported to the intramural officials that Sonny had tried out for varsity! That made him ineligible. And, since he had played in all our games, that made Raborn's Red Raiders ineligible.

Well, we survived that blow.

Don't know what ever became of Raborn. Sonny graduated. He was very much involved in the intramural program at Texas, and eventually he became the Director of Intramurals, a position he held for a long time.

Years later, in the fall of 1977, some of us from Del Rio managed to latch on to five tickets for the Texas vs Baylor game at Memorial Stadium. It was the year after Darrell Royal retired. Fred Akers was the new coach, Texas had won every game that year, and was ranked number one in the nation. But we needed one more ticket for our group.

Dan Bus, an orange-blooded ex-student and as staunch a Longhorn supporter as Texas ever had, was the editor of the Del Rio News-Herald. I was moaning to him about our need for one more ticket to the game.

"If one of you would like to have a side line pass," Dan said, "my brother-in-law runs that part of the show and he probably can arrange it".

Man! A chance to be on the sidelines at a Texas game!

So Dan called his in-law and, sure 'nuff, we could get that sideline pass. Dan set up a meeting in Austin before the game so we could get the pass, be briefed on how to use it to get in the stadium, and learn what game-time deeds of daring a sideline pass might impose.

"What's this guy's name?" I asked.

"Sonny Rooker," Dan said.

So, after a lapse of almost 30 years, I met Sonny down on the back side of the 40 Acres, got the pass, received my instructions, and had a short time to rehash the old intramural days.

The pass was a card on a cord that hung around my neck. I was to be an assistant to a press photographer who would roam the sidelines. "Just stay in back of me and don't get in the way!" So, the whole game that guy with the big camera roamed up and down the east sideline, snapping his shutter and cussing folks who got in front of him. And me behind him.

I mentioned that Texas was ranked number one, didn't I?

The west sideline is the home team sideline.

It came to me down there on that west sideline that five-foot-six ain't gonna position you to see much of the action on the field -- not when trying to look over all the Texas coaches, Texas subs, the chain-gang, more officials than I ever knew were used in a game, student team managers, assorted cheerleaders of both sexes, umpteen Texas Highway Patrolmen, numerous Austin police, a sprinkling of Texas Rangers -- might even have been some game wardens -- all jockeying around for sideline turf.

At half-time, we got shoved aside by horn blowers, flute tooters, drum beaters, flag bearers, drum majors, and drum majorettes. From two of the biggest bands in the State of Texas. And Big Bertha! There was the cannon at one end of the field and Bevo at the other. Each with a contingent of cowboys, rustlers, and other hustlers with chaps, spurs, bandanas, and Stetsons.

Furthermore, because it was a game with the number one ranked team in the nation playing, we had more dang photographers and photographer assistants vying for a place to take pix than Carter had pills.

Meantime, up in the stands, in addition to our bunch from Del Rio, Hiram and Betty Joyce Johnson, folks we knew from forever, were among the Texas Exes viewing the game.

After the game, Hiram told me he was somewhat discombobulated to look down there on the sidelines at a Texas football game of national prominence and see someone he thought looked like Walter Block.

Hiram refocused his binoculars and zeroed in on this phenomenon.

Then he exclaimed to Betty: "By Golly! That IS Walter Block down there ON THE FIELD!!!"

I always knew someday I'd achieve recognition on the Texas football playing field!

It was just a tad slow in coming.

Oh, yeah. Texas won, 29-7.

The Christmas Visitor

Back in the fall of '53 I think it was, Bette, Candy, Wayne, and I, moved into a small, almost-brand-new home in Woodville, Texas. The young couple who had built it had suddenly moved and we were fortunate in seizing the opportunity to rent the house.

It was picture-perfect for us. Located on the northwest edge of Woodville, it was only steps away from open fields. Shortly after mid-day the yard began to be shaded by the large pine trees across the road which curved in front of the house.

Candy was two and a half years old. Wayne had been born just down the road at the Woodville Hospital the last day of May that year.

Living right behind us was a wonderful neighborly family, the Maclins. They had a passel of kids, the youngest of which was Rose. Rose was a few months older than Candy and the two little girls latched on to each other like the stripes on a peppermint candy stick.

Soon after Thanksgiving, Candy began prompting us about a Christmas tree. Rose, a paragon of senior wisdom, had been rhapsodizing of Christmases Past and conjuring up visions of the approaching visit of the bearded one and his team of reindeer.

And, it wasn't really too difficult to get Bette and I into the mood. It's a fine feeling to be young, married, and the parents of two beautiful sprites.

So, I began to cast my eye on trees to fit the need. In the piney woods of East Texas that was not a major problem.

Bette concentrated on decorations. That wasn't too much of a mind bender either. We only had a few. We would have to augment. But with simplicity as a theme, Bette formulated our plan of action.

First, we had to dig out the couple of strings of lights, garlands, and a smattering of hanging baubles we had stashed away in the garage closet.

Ergo, one bright and shining, crisp and invigorating Saturday morning in early December, Bette and I sashayed out of the kitchen and into the garage on this mission of exploration and adventure.

For the ensuing drama of this tale, you should remember that Bette was a lithe and lovely lass of a mere 21 years. Ole grandad here was at that time still a flat-belly of 25.

This nice new little house had a feature which had not before been our pleasure to partake of: an attached garage. Some of our other quarters during those first few years of our wedded life had afforded covered or enclosed vehicle parking places, but none to that point had provided the luxury of a garage as a part of the house.

It was delightful -- especially on a rainy East Texas day -- to be able to walk out the kitchen door into the garage, open the garage door, and drive off without getting soaked in the process.

Also, prior to moving into that house, we had always been wanting in storage space. Not that we had that much to store. But early houses just didn't have adequate built-in closets. Wardrobes. Trunks. Attics. Few closets.

This house, however, had closets in all bedrooms, one in the hall, and a super-duper closet in the garage.

That grand closet ran almost the length -- one whole side -- of the garage, from the counter-weighted vehicle door at the front to the small door that opened to the back yard. Only the space needed for the kitchen door into the garage interrupted its awesome capacity. And,

I'm here to tell you, it had three -- count 'em, three -- closet doors strung out along its length. Each closet door opened into the garage!

There were, I confess, a couple of minor drawbacks. First, the garage closet did not yet have any shelving And, second, the entire interior length was uninterrupted by dividing walls or partitions. Thus, when you began to search for stuff, if you hadn't been extremely organized in stowing things therein, it was a mess to find what you wanted.

When we moved in, we had been very hurried. Sizable stuff not needed immediately went topsy-turvy into that gargantuan closet. Small items went into its spacious maw in containers of multiple sizes. Things got piled on top of things, ad infinitum.

So it was with our Christmas decorations.

We began pulling boxes out of the closet. As you can imagine, none were marked, so each had to be opened to discover its contents.

Groaning and grumbling, I muscled stuff out of the closet and onto the garage floor. Bette opened first one box and then another, looking for the Christmas things. Half the garage was littered. I was perspiring and opened the back door for some cool air.

Up to that time, it have not occurred to us that living on the edge of the woodlands, we had been leaving our garage doors open in the warmer fall months for air circulation and inviting who knows what creatures of the countryside to wander in.

As I hauled out box seven or eight, a mouse, which undoubtedly had merely slipped in to enjoy our offered hospitality, decided I was rearranging its adopted abode more than it could tolerate. Our little visitor streaked out of that box and began zipping, zigging, and zagging from one box on the garage floor to another in an urgent, frenzied search of a better hiding place.

Bette squealed a screech that acutely assaulted my eardrums and jumped -- flat footed -- right off of that garage floor in one beautiful arching leap that deposited her onto my startled torso with her legs wrapped and locked around my waist and her arms clinched around my neck. My head was squashed against her bosom.

I staggered around, stumbling over boxes, trying to avoid falling. Bette frantically twisted back and forth trying to keep the mouse in sight and repeatedly screamed: "Kill Him!" "Kill Him!" "Kill Him!"

In the startled suddenness of the moment, I really did at first desperately try to look for the little critter. But, I could only see to the left. Bette's bodice blinded me to everything on my right. My glasses were askew and my nose was squashed around and I could only breathe out of the side of my mouth!

And, then, I began to laugh. And I needed air more than ever!

Whereupon, Bette, with great emphasis, began to say naughty things about me. Not the mouse! Me!

Finally, I was able to convince my athletic, agile, and nimble spouse to ease her strangle-hold grip on my head so I could see to turn without crashing down amidst the maze of boxes and scattered objects around us.

There was, by then, of course, no mouse to be seen.

That modest little creature -- for whom I had suddenly developed unexpected affection -- had adroitly, with utter decorum and infinite consideration, excused itself from that hubbub of squealing excitement and consternation.

Using some salty sea-faring language, my lovely burden directed me to tote her to the kitchen door. I can attest with absolute exactitude that she didn't touch the garage floor! Not one tippy toe!

She kept the kitchen door closed until I found those Christmas lights and ornaments, put the boxes back into the hall closet, and shut the outside garage doors.

Sam's Hardware Store in downtown Woodville was still open Saturday afternoon and I bought mouse traps.

Since then, in the cool fall days as Christmas approaches, fond remembrances of our little Yule-tide visitor somehow trigger irresistible urges and impulses . . . to tell this tale.

And Bette still fusses at me when I forget to close the garage door.

The Dipsy Doodle

One Fall weekend, circa 1950, Bette and I -- young, not too long ago wedded, and full of vim and vigor -- were visiting at the ranch at Baker's Crossing. It was a nice sunny day, neither too hot nor too cold, great for being alive and being out in the country.

About a month earlier a nice rain in the Devils River watershed had resulted in a moderate rise of the river. Uncle Jim suggested we walk up through the field in front of the Baker ranch house, look at river changes caused by the little flood, and check the camp sites.

The camping areas were scattered about, under large shady pecan trees in the field between the river and the highway. They had been woefully needed sources of added income during the depression years and still were often in use. Folks from all over came out and rented camp sites to be able to fish and swim in the river. Or just to escape the hustle and bustle of town life.

Usually campers left the areas in good shape, but some surveillance was needed. When garbage barrels filled they must be hauled to the dump and emptied. Ant infestations attracted by food residues required treatment. Wasp nests in the surrounding brush were camper hazards to be dealt with.

So, off we went on an anticipated pleasurable inspection jaunt. Because we would be walking along the river bank, I took my rod and reel and a couple of favorite fishing lures.

Crossing the highway to the gate in front of the house, we walked up the road which ran up the middle of the field to its upper or north end. The fence at the north end of the field stretched from the road to the river.

The fence met the river at the lower end of a run of rapids. Long ago, when my mother and her brothers and sisters -- Uncle Jim, Aunt Beth, Uncle Pete, and Aunt Ruby -- were kids, there used to be a hydraulic pump installed at the lower end of those rapids which, using only the flowing river water pressure, shoved water through pipes to irrigate hay and crops that were gown in the field. (A hay story will be told in time.) The 1932 flood, which washed away most of the pecan and oak trees in the river basin, took that pump out.

Below those rapids the river broadened into a large pool in which most of the camper/fishermen set out their lines. At the downstream end of that "upper pool", the river narrowed. Below the "narrows", there was a smaller pool. It was shallower and less wide than the upper pool. It continued to the rapids bridged by the highway. The current in the "narrows" between the pools was strong, but there was enough depth that a boat could usually be rowed or paddled between the lower and the upper pools. The "lower pool" was also good fishing water and absolutely great for swimming.

The small flood or rise before our visit had "cleaned" the river. Moss, reeds, lily pads, etc., -- even the watercress that momma sometimes harvested for salads -- and all trash and debris had been scoured away. But there had been time enough for the mud and silt stirred up by the swift currents to settle. That day the river was running clear as crystal.

As we walked back along the river bank, Uncle Jim, Bette, and I could see fish swimming in the clear water. Our footsteps along the river edge seemed to alert fish that would swim out from undercuts in the bank and "idle" a few feet away. There weren't places for them to hide that they usually had.

I cast my lures out to the very visible fish, but my offerings were just ignored. After their dashes from under the river edge, they would seem to loaf along in the clear water and watch us -- as we were watching them.

But then, as we neared the lower end of the upper pool, we spotted about six bass hovering together some twenty feet or so out from the bank. The biggest bass in the group really got my attention. It was much larger than the others. We guesstimated that bass to be about a three-pounder plus! I got all steamed up!

I just about worked my arm off casting the best lure in my tackle collection out before, behind, and beyond that little school of fish. All to no avail. Until finally, that big rascal just couldn't ignore my wriggly little lure prancing in front of his nose.

A Dipsy Doodle, that lure was. My most absolutely favorite bass-catching bit of enticement! It was just the exquisitely exact shad-color for Devils River -- a kind of semi-shiny, greenish-grey. The bright metal bent-just-right blade on the front caused it to shimmy real perch-like. Usually bass had a hard time leaving it alone. The two treble hooks -- one under the belly and one at the tail -- perfectly portrayed flashing fins.

Ole Bruiser Bass struck! I could see it and feel it. That bass grabbed my Dipsy Doodle, and I set the hooks. I thought I had him.

But he made a quick run and jumped right straight up into the air. At least a foot completely out of the water! At the top of that leap, that dang bass shook his head so hard that it not only snapped my line, but he threw that lure back at me! He did!

The lure hit the river bank just in front of my feet. Then, as we gasped in awe, it rolled into the river and tumbled slowly down in the clear water to the river bed. There it lay, at least ten shivery cold-water feet below.

I was sick. Not only a great bass lost, but my favorite lure gone as well. But, I could see my Dipsy Doodle down there on the bottom! Maybe. . .?

I was working up the gumption to shuck my duds and dive to salvage my treasured lure -- in that water that I could sense must be getting colder by the second -- when Uncle Jim came up with a better idea.

We walked to the house and told the folks this fabulous fish story. Then Uncle Jim went out to the shop and found a little horse-shoe shaped magnet.

Back at the river, that tiny magnet on the end of my fishing line snagged the metal blade and the hooks on my Dipsy Doodle slick and neat. That lure grew old and battered with me during many of my later heroic piscatorial feats.

But that's not the end of this tale!

Many years after I almost tragically lost but so fortunately recovered my Dipsy Doodle -- after the gargantuan Diablo Dam was constructed, damming the Rio Grande, Pecos, Rio Concho, Devils River, and other tributaries into the magnificent reservoir of water now called Lake Amistad -- a friend -- Jim Latham -- who had a summer-time job at one of the marinas at the lake told me of a happening that whetted my fishing appetite.

Standing at the end of the boat dock that summer day, an apparently inexperienced, inebriated, intoxicated -- possibly even drunk -- fisherman was casting out away from the boats with a super-duper fishing rig. At the extreme end of one of this guy's casting lunges, the rod slipped from his hand and the whole rig zoomed out into the blue depths and deep down into Davy Jones' Locker.

This unfortunate would-be fisherman and his friends instituted a titanic effort to recover his lost fishing rod and reel. They loudly bemoaned the likely loss of what they described as an A-Number-One and costly rod and reel. They cast repeatedly, but unsuccessfully with weighted hooks and other contrivances into the estimated double-fathom depths. (In case you didn't know, a fathom is a sea-faring term which we old salts understand to mean a unit for measuring six feet of depth in water. In case you did know, I humbly and sincerely ask your forgiveness for my doubting your extensive knowledge!)

But, back to the tale.

After a prodigious amount of recovery effort and a majestic mangling of the Lord's English -- also threw in some semi-Spanish and a Latin phrase or two, I was told -- this woeful crew abandoned the salvage operation and left on their long, winding way back to the hinterlands of West Texas from whence they had come to cast their nets, barbs, and lines into our sweet waters.

And you know what I immediately thought of when I heard this harrowing tale!

Dipsy Doodle.

Tucked away in a corner of our garage was a humongous magnet -- a recovered and coveted relic of some massive machinery used in World War II. With (a) that big magnet, (b) a spool of nylon parachute cord (another WW2 surplus item), and (c) what we judiciously considered to be an ample supply of libations, Bette, Jim, and I headed for the marina dock and OUR salvaging.

Driving out to the lake, we had, in keeping with our natural, native, and innate abilities, excitedly discussed the problem and exquisitely developed a system of solely scientific methodology that would strictly, simplistically, and singularly stick to a strategic and successful search.

It was probably around eleven p.m. when we got to the dock. Warm summer night, but cool breeze wafting along the lake shore. The marina was well lighted. A night watchman, with whom Jim was acquainted, after hearing our mission, allowed us to go out to the end of the dock and begin our quest.

Following our plan, Jim and I heaved that magnet, tied onto the end of the parachute cord, into the lake. Each toss was angled to a slightly different spot. Then we would pull in the cord, hand over hand, dragging the magnet along the lake bottom back to the dock. The watchman watched with interest, then amusement, and finally, bored with it all, he moseyed off.

Bette carefully and considerately kept me, Jim, and herself from succumbing to that dreadful malady locally known as "dry mouth". In short, she superbly and with great sophistication sipped and tasted -- sometimes more than once -- the contents of each opened container before Jim and I quaffed it.

Most of the recovery drags of the magnet netted zero results. A few metallic objects were pulled in. After uncounted heaves, hurls, and hand-over-hand hauling in that wet and slippery nylon line, our enthusiasm began to wane.

Noticing -- with concern -- that we were nearing the bottom of our sustaining ice chest, we were approaching a time to call "Uncle".

And, then, lo and behold, as the magnet emerged from the dark surface of the water -- there it was! A lure -- magnetically held by its metal treble hooks.

We weren't too impressed with that dinky, muddy lure. It was of a garish color seldom seen or used in our part of the world. But, tied onto that fishing lure was a line. It was mottled colored, alternating dark and white, less costly, but obviously a new line.

Sooo, we hauled in the line. At first, it seemed weightless. Then we could feel something. As we pulled, whatever was on the mysterious end of the line snagged on something in the depths a time or two. Careful -- it might break!

Suddenly, the bright metal eyelet at the tip of a casting rod came up out of the inky lake. Our excitement and expectations zoomed.

Cautiously, we eased the rod tip to the edge of the dock, and, just using the tips of our fingers, lifted the rod and attached reel out of the dark water.

And . . . had a good laugh . . . and . . . drank another Big Orange.

It was a nice rod and reel. I used it as a back-up over the years. But not the expensive rig of our imaginations and hopes. Just a basic fishing tool.

A treasure recovered from Davy Jones' Locker. By Dipsy Doodling!

The Lion Hunt

When Wayne was a little guy, I used to call him "The Happy Man".

I think he got that bubbling personality from his grandmother, Julia Bird.

Bette's mom was always whistling, smiling, purring little chuckles of laughter, coming up with perky sayings, telling little tales of light and cheerful happenings.

We'd be driving down the highway and she'd see a bunch of cows in a pasture and invariably say: "Boy, those are pretty cows. Don't they have such sweet and pretty faces? I wish I had them and that farmer had some more!"

Or, as a lady who never indulged in more than half a cup of beer, she'd occasionally, on a really hot day, be persuaded to down a small swig. Then she would delicately cover her lips with her finger tips; emit a small burp, giggle a little, and say, "That's the best part."

I'm almost positive that she was the first one to start calling the two little sprouts, Wayne and his cousin Terry, who were so often happily playing together, "The Gold Dust Twins". The boys twitched with delight when she'd use that reference. It was years before they saw a copy of the washing powder advertisement which gave Grandmama Bird the inspiration to dub them such.

One of the stories she loved to tell -- one that always caused her to end up laughing so much she had to wipe the tears away -- was about The Lion Hunt. It went sorta like this . . .

Not long after breakfast one warm day back in the summer of '57, she asked Terry: "Where are you off to this morning?"

"Lion hunting," he casually replied, as he gathered gear and paraphernalia out of the toy box.

She watched him add his little hecho en Mexico hat to his regular garb of t-shirt, khaki shorts, and boots. Next came sun shades, a belted-on, almost-leather holster and cap-gun pistol. Finally, he slung his double-barreled rifle-shotgun on his shoulder, crammed a handful of cork ammo in his pocket.

"Forgot your bandana," she smiled, tucking it under his straw sombrero to drape over his neck.

The five-year-old big game hunter waved coolly to his grandmama and his 14-year old sister, Tammy, as he stealthily stepped off the back porch, squinted his eyes, crouched into a stance, and began his hunt into the primordial wilds of the big yard.

"Don't go too far," Grandmama reminded.

The big old yard, which was so carefully planted and tended in years past, had been neglected for some time before Jim and Julia Bird moved to that house. On that fateful day, however, the area around the house was in a recovery phase.

The lawn was mowed. Flower beds were weeded and watered. It might have been noted that some of the oleander bushes, honeysuckle vines, and fig trees were overly bushy. The pomegranate hedge that ran along one side of the yard was definitely overgrown.

When I was a lad living there with my grandparents many years before, that pomegranate hedge, with its bright red flowers that heralded the appearance of those ruby-hued globes of sweet, juicy goodness, had been one of my hunting ground boundaries also. But my prey in the bushes of that era was yellow jacket nests that I could shoot down with a BB gun. Got stung, of course.

Back then, Dr. Davis, one of Dr. Brinkley's surgeons, lived on the other side of the hedge. I was quite attracted to the Davis family. There were three beautiful daughters, Ruth, Ruby, and Leonora. I was smitten by Leonora. She was only six or seven years older than I. The youngest of the family, Joe Harley Davis, Jr., was a free-spirited boy a couple of years older than me.

The property edge was a picket fence on Joe's side of the hedge. Joe convinced me that we needed a gate between our yards. So we scrounged some pliers and cut a few strands of the picket fence wire at an almost wide place between a couple of the pomegranate bushes in the hedge. When Grandma Birdie found that gap in her hedge and the hole in the fence, I was almost permanently banished to the boondocks. She had the fence fixed, but there was always a noticeably thin place in the hedge where our "gate" had been.

The Davis family was long gone when Terry started out on his hunt. At that time, the place next door was the home of some folks who were often absent. They had a big dog -- large German Shepard -- to help guard their place when they were at home or away.

Grandmama and Tammy watched the little big game stalker as he started creeping around the oleanders, past the honeysuckle and trumpet vines, and began working slowly and cautiously along the hedge. Terry's narrowed eyes darted left and right. His double-barreled pop gun was gripped across his chest at the "ready". A cork was firmly jammed in the end of each barrel. He was deep in safari land.

Grandmama quit the back porch, went back into the kitchen to concoct fried chicken and dewberry cobbler magic, but glanced out thru the screen door from time to time to check on the jungle scenario.

Tammy retreated slightly from her self-appointed duty to watch out for her little brother, and became absorbed in the enchanting empires of her book.

Terry methodically moved past the clothes line poles, and slipped into the "passage" between the big fig tree and the hedge. And . . . then . . .

Terry squalled -- like a cat with its tail smashed under Grampa's rocking chair.

Tammy dropped her book.

Grandmama's spoon clattered into the sink.

Tammy darted out the back door a step ahead of Grandmama.

Terry was streaking back to the porch stammering: "Lion! . . . Lion!"

And out there, where Joe and I had thinned the hedge, a big, brown, growling German Shepard had his nose up to the fence.

Terry's double-barreled big game gun-- unfired corks and all -- lay in the dirt by the fence.

That evening, when Granddaddy came home from work, Grandmama told him about the lion hunt. Then, she had to phone her daughters -- Terry's mom, Lois, in Austin, and Wayne's mom, Bette, in Dalhart. Each time she told the story, she got tickled. Laughed 'til she cried.

Tammy was upset when she heard her Grandmama laughing as she told and retold the story. She didn't want her little brother teased about his encounter with the dog.

Terry says he still doesn't cotton much to some dogs, but mainly he just wonders where the heck Wayne was. "Why didn't he have my back?"

The Weather Balloons

Weather balloons always fascinated me.

When I was a kid, each morning, afternoon, and evening, the weatherman up on a deck on the top of the three-storied Federal Building in Del Rio would release a balloon.

The Federal Building was located at Main and Broadway streets about two blocks east and a bit south of my grandparents' home on Martin Street. The prevailing wind was from the southeast, so the balloons would, more often than not; sail almost directly over us as they gathered altitude. We would stop playing in the yard to watch the balloons sail over us.

As I recall, in the "early days" of these balloon flights, nothing was attached to the balloons on the daytime launchings. But after dark, there appeared to be a light of some kind hanging below them.

Sitting out on the sleeping porch, enjoying the evening breezes that began after dark, listening to Babo or Grandma Birdie tell tales of the olden days, we would be awed by the illuminated balloons as they climbed up over us on their way Westward.

Day or night, the weatherman observed from the deck on top of the Federal Building. I assume he calculated wind speed and direction. Later, after some technological advances, there was usually a folded parachute suspended a foot or so below the balloon and a "little black box" hanging a couple of feet further down. I think there was some sort of radio transmitter in these "black boxes" which sent back information on temperature, air pressure, humidity, and such.

When launched, the balloons were wrinkled and shaped like an inverted pear, but, of course, as the gas that lifted them expanded at higher altitudes and with less pressure, the shape became more globular until eventually they burst and fell.

In addition to being enthralled by occasional news stories of balloons, parachutes, and black boxes returned from great distances, etc., I was also sometimes given to wondering if anyone ever shot one of the balloons down! In fact, I toyed with the idea of doing just that, but never thought it should, could, or would happen.

After many years and much more technological development, the weather service moved from the top of the downtown Federal Building to a site on the western edge of Del Rio at the Municipal Airport.

Weather station employees and most of their sophisticated instruments were housed on the fringe of the airport in a small one-storied office structure next to the accessing street. The top of this building was festooned with many short, tall, and odd-shaped antennas sticking up in the air to receive weather info from the balloons and from other weather stations.

The new weather station also included a small, domed radar atop a lesser structure about twenty yards to the east of the weather office building. The base of the radar building was square and had a large garage-type door. A weather balloon was inflated the proper amount in this room under the radar dome, then the garage-like door was raised, the semi-filled balloon with its attachments was brought out and launched from the relatively windless area between the two structures.

One windy Spring day, as I was driving past the "new" weather station in my little pick-um-up truck, I achieved one of my life-long ambitions!

A couple of the weather station folks had just launched the late afternoon balloon. Apparently a strong gust of south-easterly wind had unexpectedly snatched the balloon and sent it sailing almost horizontally to the northwest. Before the balloon and its dangling parachute/radio box could rise high enough, the wind pulled the trailing lines and hanging gear across one of the antennas on top of the office building.

The semi-inflated balloon was swinging around like a snorting mustang, trying to pull loose from his tether. The vital weather instrument antennas on the building were being jerked first to the north and then to the south and were in danger of tearing away.

Two weather station people with anxious agony on their faces were in the road just west of the weather building, and one of them was trying to shoot the balloon down with a pellet gun!

Man, that's what I always wanted to do! So I stopped my pickup and hurried across the road to watch.

We could hear the pellets hitting the balloon, but they did not seem to be penetrating. As the balloons rise and expand, the sides become thinner, but at Del Rio ground-level, the plastic skin was thick. The pellet gun had to be laboriously pumped up for each shot. The antennas were bending and loosening.

I remembered the .22 pistol in my pickup. I asked the weather station guy who wasn't shooting the pellet gun if they would like to use my .22.

"Quick! Go get it!" he exclaimed.

I ran over to my pickup, and came back with the Ruger. When I tried to hand it to them, one yelled, "You shoot it. Just hurry before it tears up the whole weather station!"

I didn't wait to be asked twice! Although the wind was whipping the balloon at the end of its unaccustomed tether, it was a fat target and I put a couple of rounds thru its sides. But four small 22 caliber holes weren't letting the balloon gas out very fast.

Then the weather guy suggested I shoot repeatedly at the bottom of the balloon where the cords were attached. After about six shots concentrated there, the balloon fabric began to tear, the inflating gas whooshed out, and the rig collapsed onto the roadway by my pickup.

The weather folks thanked me.

But I thanked them much more profusely, assuring them that I had always wanted to shoot down a weather balloon but never thought I would get a legally-authorized, federally-blessed, US of A government-endorsed, bonafide chance to do so.

The Dunlay Hunt

Jack was a shore 'nuff first class outdoorsman. He had TWO Cadillacs. Used the new one to pull his boat trailer, but did usually ease off full throttle and go in the older one when he expected to haul back a field-dressed deer or two.

About mid afternoon one cold rainy Fall Friday, Jack called and said, "Let's go hunting." Then, and to some considerable degree still, that music played sweetly to my ear.

"When?" I asked.

"ASAP, right now, this afternoon," he laughed.

"Where?" I asked. "Dunlay," he said.

"Where the heck is that?" I sputtered.

"You haven't hunted, if you haven't hunted at Dunlay," he snorted.

We lived in Del Rio, prime white tail country. Dunlay, in small print on the Texas map, is over a hundred miles east, between Hondo and Castroville, in urban San Antonio's backyard. Jack was right. I had never hunted in or near Dunlay.

Seems some San Antonio friends with a lease south of Dunlay had pumped Jack up on their big bucks, invited him to hunt there that particular weekend, and . . . bring along any friends he wanted.

"It's been raining all week," I reminded.

"Due to stop this evening," Jack shot back. "There's a cabin we can sleep in tonight. If you want to go, call Jerry. Jim and I will pick y'all up after five."

I scooted home, changed jeans and boots, grabbed my gun, ammo, knife, cap, an old fleece-lined jacket, and a sandwich. A few minutes after five, the four of us were headed east in Jack's older Cadillac, with the sun already setting in a clearing sky behind us.

Less then two hours later, thanks to Jack's lead foot, we turned south off of Highway 90 onto a narrow, paved road I had never noticed before on all my trips thru Dunlay. Six or seven miles further south, Jack herded the Cadillac west across a squishy bar ditch and through the gate of the "lease".

The muddy road to the "cabin" wasn't too bad. But the cabin was a bit less than Jack had described. Not quite first class.

You need a good mental picture of this "cabin" structure to really appreciate the rest of this tale.

It was one wooden room on short mesquite pilings, built to house ranch hands not long after the Civil War. One door on the west side, one window on each of the other three sides. Most of the wooden shingles were still in place, so drips inside could be dodged. No ceiling, no electricity, no running water. In a corner was a bed with a set of wire springs on the slats, but no mattress or covers. One semi-square, rickety wooden table. Two spindly chairs with genuine but ragged rawhide seats, an old less than sturdy nail keg, and part of a wobbly wooden box completed the furniture inventory.

The "source" of heat was a flat-topped iron stove from that civil war era. Pieces of stove pipe were piled in a corner, long ago unattached from the piece still piercing the roof.

With flashlights, we checked for uninvited critters. Found nothing alive except a dinner-plate-sized wasp nest high up under the shingles. The cold had the wasps in a state of near hibernation, all huddled together, without movement. We decided they posed no threat.

But the cold, wet night air wafting through some of the broken window panes was less than welcoming.

A few pieces of bark in an inside corner and under the house next to the doorway was evidence that someone had stocked fire wood once upon a time. But nary a stick was remaining for us.

Outside, everything was soaked from the week-long drizzles. We gathered bits of old boards and some scattered twigs and found a chunky piece of tree stump that looked like it had been used for a chopping block. But it was all soaking wet.

After several less than Boy Scout skilled attempts to light a fire in the stove, we regrouped and ran a systematic and diligent search, inside and outside, for means of igniting the wet fuel. And, voila!

One of our hunter-gather group found a banged-up rusty bucket in which some providential soul had left old, used, black-as-the-ace-of-spades motor oil stashed under the house.

Before anyone could say, "lickity-split" or "Jack Robinson" or anything like that, our fortuitous finder splashed more than a child's portion of the used motor oil on the wet wood in the stove.

And, Eureka! First crack out of the box, with a flick of a cigar lighter, that motor oil was flickering up a real promising flame. Before long the wood began to burn.

Did you know that burning motor oil smokes? It does. Thicker, denser smoke may come from other flammables, but I doubt it.

We opened the door and all three windows and that did help to get the smoke out. And the cold in. But we dast not let the "fire" go out!

Swiftly, nimble minds set numbed fingers to inspired attempts to rebuild and reattach the shattered stove pipe columns to the remaining piece in the roof. But we were short at least one piece of stove pipe. The black oily smoke gathered under the roof. Soon it was settling around the would-be breathing orifices of our bodies.

Well, sir, about that time someone miraculously found an elbow of stove pipe that we had heretofore not found in the dark of the cabin corner. We reconfigured that stove pipe into an "ell-shape" that routed most, but not all, of the motor oil/wet wood smoke out the window closest to the by-now almost glowing stove.

Fear for the survival of the cabin began.

Of course half of the window had to be open for the pipe to extend out of it, but, how fortunate we were, that exiting window was on the south side of the cabin and the wind was from the north.

So, with a combination of the ell-shaped stove pipe out the south window and a partially open window on the north side, we mastered -- very nearly -- control of the smoke. But with some sacrifice of in-the-cabin temperature control. Survival of the cabin began to seem possible.

You may be surprised when I tell you that by this time, it was past midnight. How time does fly when you're having fun.

With the aplomb of a born leader, Jack suggested that, since most of the night had slipped away, and we needed to be on the hunting stands before daylight and -- due also to the scarcity of sleeping facilities -- we should just gather at the table and play cards until it was time to hunt. Jack had a deck of cards. Jack always had the cards.

Along about midway through our poker and match-stick game, the little glowing, smoking, civil war vintage stove was working so efficiently that -- despite our unique ventilation system --it began to be warm enough in the cabin that we loosened and/or removed some of the coats that had been so needed earlier. I tossed my fleece-lined old coat on the bed, making sure the inner side of the coat was up so it wouldn't be on the rusty and cobweb-laden bed springs.

A couple of hours before the anticipated Saturday morning dawn, having eaten less than copiously through the busy tribulations of Friday evening, hunger became a serious topic.

Jack remembered that there was a small "café" in Dunlay which, during hunting season, opened early to feed cookless hunters like us.

So we flung on the coats, sloshed through the mud from the cabin to the Cadillac, and headed to town for grub.

It fell my lot to open the gate to the paved road. I was in the midst of that muddy chore when I became quite acutely aware of several sharp, stinging pains in my back and the nape of my neck. I didn't know what was stinging me, but a decision to shuck my coat came quickly.

In the light of the Cadillac headlights I saw a dozen or more sluggish wasps emerging from the fleece lining of the coat. The smoke had dropped them from that big nest above the bed. Those that had landed on my coat were still cold benumbed and had crawled into the fleece. My body heat, though, had warmed them and my movements had stimulated and/or irritated them into action.

With agility likely seldom ever witnessed before, my three friends found wasps on their coats also, but none had crawled into linings or warmed enough to start stinging. I alone had been the anointed one.

Ridding ourselves of uninvited wasps, we drove in to Dunlay for the promised manna -- huevos rancheros. Only to find a notice on the door of the darkened building that informed of some happening that required the absence of the cook/proprietor until later in the morning! Well! Perdackerdee!

We held a council of hunt. Decision: we had come too far and endured too much to go home empty-handed. We would make a hungry morning hunt and then skedaddle for eats on the way westward toward home.

Back at the lease, Jack said he'd drive about half of the way to our hunting stands and we would then walk. Well, sir, just about half of halfway to "stands", the old Cadillac was hub deep in mud and no longer a viable means of transportation. We were wishing for a Jeep!

So, we began walking to the stands. By that time, it was threatening rain again, so we each either put on or packed our rain gear.

Oh, did I tell you? Jack always went first class. For this hunt, he had a brand-spanking-new, stiff-as-a-board, bright-yellow, guaranteed-water-proof, rain suit -- separate top and bottom. He decided that he should put it on before he started to walk so that he wouldn't make so much noise doing so at the site of his stand.

I want you to absolutely and truly know that Jack tried to control it, but with every step he took -- each time one leg passed the other -- those stiff yellow leggings rubbed against each other and spewed a SWISHing sound that any flag-tailed, wide-eyed, nostrils-flared, ears-up deer in four hundred yards could hear. Our giggling whispers to Jack for him to try to be quiet and his indignantly sputtered responses only added to the pre-dawn chorus.

Twice, as we walked, we heard deer snort. The swishing and muffled laughs were spooking them. The pungent smell of burned motor oil smoke may have had some mild alarming effect, also.

Not too far along, we walked by an old windmill. Its tail was tied back. The windmill was braked and not turning. I decided it was just about as good a stand as I was going to find that morning. And I had to get away from that swishing.

With unloaded rifle, binoculars, fleece-lined and suddenly bulky coat, I climbed up the ladder to the platform beneath the mill vanes and tail. The others, after watching to see I made it to the nest I had chosen, walked on. The swishing sound gradually diminished.

As daylight came, I glassed the area I could see. We were in a large pasture, wooded with mesquites and a few oaks and some other smaller trees. There were large cultivated fields to the south. The trees prevented me seeing beyond them to the east. As it became brighter, I located Jack in the fork of a scrawny mesquite tree to the north. Jerry and Jim were somewhere in the tree-studded lease pasture, not in my sight.

Jack was decidedly not comfortable in that tree fork. He changed his perch several times, but was not still enough to hunt successfully. He was, undoubtedly, worried and fretting about the bogged Cadillac.

Intrepid and thoughtful leader that he was, it was not too long before I saw him climb out of the tree and begin walking back. He had removed and was carrying that yellow rain suit.

When he got to my windmill, Jack told me he was going to walk to a nearby farmer with whom he was already acquainted and ask for help to extract the mired Cadillac. He suggested we stay and hunt until he came back or honked for us to come to the car.

He found the farmer, who, with his tractor, aided Jack in getting the Cadillac back on solid ground.

Shortly thereafter, it being about mid morning and the sun more than very well risen, Jack tapped on the horn.

We regrouped, drove to Hondo for heroic portions to break our fasts, and then headed home to Del Rio, taking turns poking the driver to keep him awake.

No deer taken. But a good time to remember. And what a story to tell!

Almost as good as the one about the time we went fishing with Jack and his NEW Cadillac at Falcon Lake. We swamped the boat and it sank to the bottom with all six of us aboard.

We all survived that time, too, but that's another true tale to tell.

Falcon Fishing

Do you remember a verse from that old cowboy song, "The Old Chisholm Trail": "Ole Ben Bolt was a blamed good boss, but he'd go to see the girls on a sore-backed hoss"?

Well, ole Jack Davis was a blamed good boss all right, and I want you to know that he went hunting or fishing in a Cadillac. He had two. On this beats-all-other-fishing-trips tale that I'm about to tantalize and titillate you with the telling of, he took both of them.

'Twas nigh on to fifty years ago. Not too long after Falcon Dam was constructed on the Rio Grande down below Laredo and Zapata and shortly before Diablo Dam was finished just above Del Rio. ("Diablo", as you may know, was a singularly appropriate name, since that dam is located just below the confluence of Devils River and the Rio Grande. Be that as it may, some ivory-towered nabob changed the name to "Amistad", so's not to offend dainty -minded folks.)

Jack had recently acquired a scrumptious wooden-hulled, twin-motored boat he thought needed an outing. He was mighty proud of that boat. All equipped for water skiing, lollygagging, and just about any kind of fishing you could put your mind to. He was especially prone to brag on those two big, bodaciously powerful motors. And he surely did admire those custom-installed "automatic" transom bailers.

Jack was the chief high mogul of the American National Insurance Company district office in Del Rio. I and a motley crew of other would-be agents were learning tricks of the trade under his tutelage.

Jack regularly came up with motivational plots and ploys to spur us to greater achievement.

With his new boat, it was a natural for his high-geared brain to latch on to the idea of a weekend of fishing and camping for his staff members who met policy sales quotas. White bass were running up the Rio Bravo and Falcon, 'tho still filling, was already a hot spot for trolling.

Right after lunch on a Friday in the middle of a windy March, eight or so of us headed south. Five or six were with Jack in his OLD Cadillac, to which was hitched that brand new boat trailer. Another two or three of our crew tagged along in a pickup belonging to one of the agents.

The pickup bed was chuck full of ice chests, fishing tackle, bed rolls, and war bags of most of the eager-to-be-inspired fishermen of the expedition. Among that mess of gear, I had tossed an old, but still serviceable Baker tent salvaged from Boy Scouting days.

That tent was to shelter Jack's wife Dorothy, and Bette, Candy, and Wayne. They would follow later in the NEW Cadillac when the kids got out of school and the ladies got off work. The guys were to "rough it" -- no tent -- just bed rolls, ground cloths, etc.

In the OLD caddie-led convoy, we zipped down Hiways 277 and 83, scooted through Laredo, buzzed San Ygnacio, and slowed in Zapata to find a grocery store. Just west of Zapata, we located a boat ramp, and picked out a lakeside camp site on the arm of a small inlet.

We were perched on the northern side of a little peninsula. The waterway in front curved east and then back around westward to the lake. We were in the lee of the strong south breezes that swish through south Texas in the spring. But we had easy access to the lake.

While Jack and the guys launched the boat and set up camp, I took the pickup back to Zapata to stock up on grub, essential bottled libations, and lots of ice. By the time I got back, some of the crew were agitating to get out on the lake and start fishing.

Hurriedly, we set up the Baker tent and stowed the Jack's new store-bought set of shiny aluminum cooking gear -- to be all ready for the ladies and kids.

That eye-pleasin' boat could only haul six at a time, so we flipped to see who would go out first. The others would have to bank fish until the boat got back for a second lake trolling sashay. The coin toss put me in the first bunch. At the time, I thought my luck was good!

As soon as the boat load of raucous rowdies rounded the point and headed out into the lake, it was obvious that we could only troll headed north -- up the lake. The strong shore breezes -- where hills, trees, and brush impeded air flow -- swelled to full-blown winds out on the open lake. Wind-pushed south-to-north waves were almost white-cap size.

Some of us had doubts about trolling in water that rough.

"Not to worry," Jack lightheartedly opined as he tipped up a big insulated mug of Texas Tea (as he called it). He assured us lubbers that the seamanship acquired during his sojourn in the U. S. of A. Navy during the last past great global conflict and the nautical qualities of his boat were much more than equal to the task.

Barnie Barnett and I sat in the two back seats just forward of those big motors. Dutifully following our intrepid leader's directions, we opened tackle boxes, rummaged around for enticing white bass lures, rigged for trolling, executed flawless casts to opposing sides, and almost forth-with, immediately, and without delay had two lines trailing in the choppy waters.

With lines out, Jack slowed the boat to a fast trolling speed. Mark, note, and firmly establish in your mind that pace. Even at a fast trolling speed, the following waves pushed by that south wind were slopping water over the transom and into the boat!

The sturdy stern of this all-round, do-everything, good-looking, wooden boat had been cut low to accommodate those honcho twin motors mounted on the back! It was disheartening to note that there was no false transom to keep the water coming in over the stern from filling the boat!

We waited not one little bit in alerting Jack about that water washing over the stern! But he laughed, took another swig of that Texas Tea, growled another "Not to Worry!", and assured us that -- when he shoved throttles, and revved up those whopper motors, the boat would jump up on a plane -- and those "automatic" bailers would suck the water out of the boat lickety-split.

Well, sir, Cap'n Jack knew where to put the boat to hook fish! Almost instantaneously, both Barnie and I got strikes and each had a fish "on". And splish-splash, at least three other casts from over-eager fisher-agents plopped into the white bass mother lode on all sides of the boat.

But -- we were still making knots -- the big, deep-throated rumbling motors were pushing the boat too fast!

We yelled at Jack. He cut the engines to reduce the drag on our lines so we could reel the fish in.

By then, my fish had already aqua-planed over Barnie's line and Barnie's bass went the opposite way, and both our lines were instantaneously tee-totally tangled!

A couple of other lines got snarled also. Guys were snapping, snarling, and cussing in the boat!

Standing up so he, as captain of the craft, could keep the foul-lined and foul-languaged fish landing operations under close observation, Jack nursed his drink with one hand and the two motor throttles with the other, slowing so we could recover our lines and fish.

And -- as you are right now conjuring up in your fertile mind -- the boat's stern was still to the south, the waves were running north, and wave after wave of water was coming in over the cut-down transom of that glorified wooden boat like you wouldn't ever want to see it.

These simple facts were relayed to our skipper -- non-stop. Loudly!

"Not-to-mind", he gently assured us. "Just get the lines in. I'll crank 'er up and the automatic transom bailers will suck all that bi-national agua right on out."

Eye-balling that rising tide IN the boat, Barnie and I got the whole caboodle of our tangled lines and flopping bass gathered up and dumped it into the surging mini-ocean between us. Most of the other lines were hastily hauled in also.

"We're in! Get 'er goin', Skipper!" Barnie shouted.

Jack, the Skipper, shoved his throttles. Both big-muscled motors roared. The boat surged ahead.

Like a garbage scow!

Loaded with lard-ended fisher folk, ice chests, water ski equipment, tackle boxes, and sloshing water in the boat, that massive-motored, maritime marvel could NOT get up on a plane.

And, if the super-craft couldn't get up on a plane, those super-duper bailers couldn't bail.

Those wonderful bailers were brass tubes thru the transom -- below the water line. The outside end was fitted with a soft rubber sleeve. With the boat moving rapidly through the water, the "venturi" effect created a semi-vacuum, sucking water out of the bilges.

But -- if not moving, or not moving fast enough, the rubber sleeves -- by design -- collapsed and sealed the outside end of the tubes!

Those big ole motors were straining to push the boat up on a plane, but with the added weight of water in the hull, their effort produced: (1) a big bow wave, (2) a gargantuan following frothy mountain of water just aft of the depressed stern, and (3) MORE water was coming in over the transom!

I squalled at Jack. "The mis-begotten boat is sinking!" (Actually, I described the boat more aptly.)

The captain of our boat -- and I was thinking at that instant, maybe the captain of our fate -- was standing erect and tall, one hand on the helm, the other pointing a half-empty mug of Texas Tea at a bunch of weeds sticking out of the water in front of us -- a mere hundred yards from the eastern (U.S. of A.) shore line.

"Gonna beach the boat," he mumbled into the mug as he skillfully steered to the tuft of tules.

Cucumber cool, our dashing skipper nonchalantly put the boat's nose up into that wad of weeds on top of what used to be a hill on the bank of the Rio Grande. Just as the polished wooden prow touched the muddy grit of the submerged hill-top, the back end of the boat wallowed below the surface of the inter-national waters. The skids on the bottoms of each big motor settled firmly into the muddy bottom.

Jack chopped the throttles to save the props from the rocks.

We'd sunk the dang boat! (Several other colorful descriptions of the maneuver were offered.)

The wind was pushing wave after wave over the sunken stern of the boat. With each wave shove, the bow was grinding on rocks of the submerged hilltop. But, the bow and most of the boat was above water and -- by golly -- we weren't sinking further!

Jack pushed the brim of his cap down over his left eyebrow, stepped over the side into the oozy mud, and said, "OK, everybody out! Three on each side. Let's turn the bow into the wind so we bail out the boat!"

We all piled out into the water. Into the mud. I groped in the jumbled gear in the water in the boat for something to bail with. No bailer. If the boat had had one, it had washed out or sunk.

That hill top had only recently been a dry, rocky, cacti-encrusted protrusion overlooking the international border between the U. S. of A. and Mexico. Please note the reference to cacti!

Water up to our arm pits. Mud up to our knees. Unstable rocks mucking in mire under our feet. Now we had to cope with cacti!

Except Jim. Jim was a kicker (that's one description for a West Texas cowhand or sheep rancher) and a motorcycle rider. He had on a pair of long-legged ropers. Those boots had twelve-inch tops. But, the mud under the boat was that deep or deeper.

With three of us on each side, we heaved and strained to lift the boat's suddenly transformed bulky hulk off the rocks so we could turn the bow into the wind and keep the waves from unceasingly sloshing into the boat. With all that water in the boat, we just couldn't do it.

Then -- inspiration! One of the ice chests was an old Scotch-cooler. We emptied the ice and drinks and began to bail with it. Only to discover that the bottom of the thick-walled, barrel-shaped container had long ago rusted out, the insulation was by then thoroughly water-logged, and each time we bailed a gallon, we lifted a five-gallon weight!

On top of all this, it humbles me to tell you, that some agitated numskull -- in the throes of the swamping and sinking -- had left his tackle box open in the bottom of the boat. You know what happened! Some lures in that tackle box were floaters. And, sure 'nuff, danged if Jack didn't manage to get a treble hook jabbed into the calf of his leg way over the barb.

"Not to worry, Jack", I assured him. I dug around in my fishing vest pocket and retrieved the taped razor blade I always carried for just such a dire and distressful need. Just snicked a little slit in his hide, pushed the point and barb through, cut the shank of the hook with a trusty and not too rusty pair of pliers, sponged the area with some of his Texas Tea, slapped on a band-aid, and The Skipper was good for the next round.

During this lull, salvage operations ground to a halt while we rounded up other floating, sharp-pointed fishing stuff. And then, . . .

Jim waded up to the shallower water at the front of the boat and took off one of his boots to shake out the gravel that had worked in as he was wallowing in the mud.

Quicker than I can tell you, Jim was persuaded to sacrifice. Off came the other boot. Two volunteers got in the boat and with the combined efforts of two enthusiastic boot-bailers and an alternating Scotch-cooler coolie, the water level in the boat was lowered far enough that we were able to horse our stricken water craft around and turn the bow into the wind.

When Jack deemed the water in the boat down enough, he cranked up, and without any other crew on board, goosed the motors, and, just like he said, bailed out most of the water in the boat.

The skipper eased up to his wet, muddy, cold, and bedraggled would-be bass busters and bade us climb aboard for the ride back to the campsite. I suggested that, since the trip back was against the wind and into ever- bigger waves, he might take part of us and come back for the rest. He vetoed that while he mixed up another big glass of Texas Tea from ingredients he had plucked from paraphernalia pulsating in the shallows still shifting in the bottom of the boat.

"Solo trip back," he said. "Ship now or swim."

I didn't argue with the Cap'n any further.

The return trip was also not totally devoid of excitement.

We had to hug the shallows along the eastern shore to avoid open-water waves. Cautiously, we crept in and out of rocks, tree stumps, and submerged but not yet rotted south Texas brush. Just past half-way back, we struck a snag and sheared a pin of one of those big motors.

There was no joy in Mudville! One of our super slugger motors had struck out!

I know you know before I tell you.

In all that garble of gear strewn about in the here-to-fore Argonaut of Falcon Lake -- a boat just miraculously extracted from the jaws of Davy Jones' locker -- nary a shear pin to be found!

The remaining long mile or so back, with only one motor, was a voyage of apprehension. We sulked along the in lee of the shore, through the specters of stalking shallows and sunken stumps and other sea specters. With no spare shear pin!

But the deepest hurt of all came when we limped up to the camp site in the calm little cove, expecting the crew waiting in the protected environment to welcome us back with sympathy for our plight and astonished admiration at our skill and resourcefulness in effecting our own rescue.

A single look at our butt-dragging state should have evoked warm expressions of sympathy and understanding.

Not hardly.

Where the heck had we been? Selfishly living it up while they were left on the bank?

Our woeful tale of boat floundering and our razor-thin escape from disaster was just a big windy!

Plus! While we were away, a mean little mini-tornado dust twister engendered by afternoon heating in South Texas had come spiraling along the inlet shore, swooshed right over the top of the camp, collapsed the tent, and scattered those aluminum dishes and pots and pans to hell and back. In and out of the water.

Dorothy fixed Jack a strong swig of Texas Tea.

She and Bette and Jim joined him.

Barnie and the kids had a coke.

The rest of us had a cold beer.

Julie's Hunt

Julie Block, young bride of my brother Lee, had a yen to hunt in the hills and canyons of the West Texas wilds -- in Val Verde County -- in the ranch country bounded or bisected by Devils River and/or the Pecos. So, Lee set it up.

Of all the Block, Baker, and Hinds boys exposed from the cradle on to romanticized, epic yarns spun around evening firesides, Lee was the single solitary holdout not severely infected by the hunting and/ or fishing bug. But, true to at least some of his ancestral genes, he was a good story teller. And Julie, an outdoor gal whose avocation was training winning show horses, was an attentive listener. She wanted to bag a whitetail buck!

Lee was the Episcopal rector in Junction at the time. Julie was a stem-winder in a busy medical clinic. In the fall -- deer season, of course -- not long after they were married, they scheduled a quickie visit in their new car to our neck of the woods.

The plan was for them to be in Del Rio, visiting with us on Friday. Early Saturday morning, Wayne and I would accompany them to the ranch of Lucious and Beth Hinds northeast of Comstock. At the time, Uncle Lucious was recovering from an ailment and not up to a hunt. Lee was to spend the day visiting with Uncle Lucious and Aunt Beth while Wayne and I shepherded Julie. After an early evening supper in Aunt Beth's small, savory kitchen, Lee and Julie would drive on up to

Baker's Crossing, touch base with Papo and Uncle Jim, and then scoot on to Junction so Lee could do his Sunday morning preacher chores.

Based on Lee's vivid descriptions of the rocky and thorny country we were to hunt, Julie had a brand spanking new pair of thick-soled hunting boots and some stiff and sturdy denim jeans. She was well-prepared for the Texas sun with a long-sleeved corduroy shirt and well-insulated for the nippy fall day by a hip-length, big-collared coat. Good gloves. Plenty of ammo. Sharp, fixed-blade hunting knife on her belt.

As I recall, she had borrowed the rifle she carried from the doctor with whom she worked. She had personally sighted-in the variable-powered scope on the .257 in preparation for the trip.

Wayne and I drove out in our VW. Lee and Julie followed in their shiny new buggy. Thirty miles to Comstock, then eight miles to the county road turnoff, and another nine unpaved miles through the seven gates we opened for them on the way to the Hinds ranch house.

Uncle Lucious had the Ford Bronco gassed up and ready for us when we got to the ranch, and, after hugs and a relatively small amount of palaver, we hustled off. Aunt Beth, Uncle Lucious, and Lee gave ample assurance that they would not allow themselves to be so immersed in dominos, cards, and story-telling that the pot of Aunt Beth's "special" chili and her larrupin'-good peach cobbler would not be waiting for us at suppertime.

Wayne and I had carefully mapped out a considerate, thoughtful, easy, enjoyable, and productive hunt for Julie. We truly wanted her to have a good, successful hunt. We also wanted her to see a good sampling of The Wonderful Country which Lee had been telling her about.

From the house, we drove up to the barn, went through the pens, and headed northwest. Out on the divide. To work the headers that dropped off into Dark Canyon. One of the pastures in the canyon was simply called "Dark Canyon". Another pasture, closer to the river, was named "Rough". Every bit of that canyon was rugged as all get out. Beautiful country.

We would drive out on a point -- but not too close to the edges in order not to spook the deer with vehicle noise -- and one of us would get out and walk Julie to a good spot on the rimrock overlooking the area where the header emptied into the canyon. Then, the other of us would drive or walk, well-back on the divide, and ease up to the rimrock just over the upper end of the header and toss some rocks into the brush below to jump deer so they would move toward Julie.

We spent the rest of that lovely morning doing that. Sweet hunting. Worked all the way down to Devils River. Got up does, spikes (not legal game then), some javalinas, and a distant buck. But nothing for Julie to shoot at. Fun for us, even if not productive. However, at lunch, Julie moaned some about her boots and seemed to think we might be pushing her a little hard.

We lunched up on the divide at the East Mill. Uncle Lucious watered stock at the pens and troughs at this windmill. He had fenced his ranch and run pipes from the big water tank at the mill down to watering troughs in multiple locations in both Dark Canyon and Dead Man Canyon. Of course, deer and other wildlife slaked their thirst at these waterings also.

Sitting in the sun on the lee side of the big water tank, Wayne and I were perplexed that Julie was picky about the lunch we brought. It was our usual hunt menu. Washed down with good cold river water or fresh water the mill was pumping into the tank, crackers and canned sardines, smoked oysters, and Vienna sausage was easy to prepare, easy to pack, easy on the palate -- we thought. Julie differed. She did eat a couple of Snickers and a Granny Smith apple.

Well, sir, after lunch we took another hunting tack. We drove back to the barn on the divide, went around the chicken house, and took the new road Uncle Lucious had carved down into Dead Man Canyon. Hand-made with shovels, sweat, and crow bars, this long-needed road now gave him vehicle access all the way down Dead Man from the house end of his ranch to the river.

"Vehicle access" meant four-wheel drive, mostly in "Grandma" (lowest available gear). Dead Man Canyon on that ranch for the first dozen or so years Uncle Lucious and Aunt Beth owned it had to be worked on horseback or on foot. In those early days, except at its head and at the river, there were only a couple of places you could get a horse down into the canyon from the divide.

That delightful, crisp afternoon, in the Dark Canyon pasture called "Paradise", we worked the headers from their open end. You climbed up a point on one side of the header to where you could see the trail or trails that entered and/or exited the top end of the header. Then you used home-made leather slings to lob rocks up into the brush and run stuff either "out the top" or around the other side of the header.

Julie was showing some weariness. But she still was eager to hunt.

Not far after driving southwest into Paradise, we stopped. The three of us walked together up into a small header. Unexpectedly, we jumped a buck. He was leaping up rock ledges and thru a stand of sotol and was almost over the top when Wayne shot and dropped him.

We looked at Julie. She said, "I was waiting for him to stop."

After dressing the deer, we climbed over a saddle and back down into the next header. Julie was about spent. She and I went down and got the Bronco. Wayne went back and dragged the buck down to us in the canyon.

We decided we would not do anything more that would make Julie have to walk far.

We jockeyed the Bronco down the canyon almost to a place where we knew there was an unusually long header -- a short feeder canyon, really -- coming into Dead Man from the southwest. That long header almost always had a buck laying up in it.

I told Wayne and Julie I'd cross Dead Man, climb the ridge between Dead Man and the feeder canyon, and then walk down the feeder to its juncture with the main canyon. Wayne was to drive down Dead Man below the juncture and take Julie a few short steps up to a position on the far side of the canyon where they could wait and watch for anything coming to them.

I eased up the ridge until I could see over into the feeder draw. And -- great gobs of goose grease -- there were TWO bucks on the far side; standing with heads high and ears cocked. They either heard me coming up to the ridge line or the Bronco going down Dead Man. But they weren't moving yet. Just listening and maybe scenting.

I decided to shoot one and send the other to Julie and Wayne. Dropped him where he stood. When I fired, the second buck bolted down the feeder draw toward the waiting Julie and Wayne.

I heard a shot. Just one. Couldn't tell whether it was Julie's .257 or Wayne's .250.

I gutted my deer, draped him over a rock to drain, and walked hurriedly on down toward the place Julie and Wayne were to have taken a stand.

As I neared where they should have waited, I saw them ahead, moving into Dead Man. Wayne was leading and looking like he expected to jump something. Julie was following, rifle "at the ready". I called, and Wayne said, "He's hit and ran into the thicket in the bottom of the canyon."

The deer had run almost right at them and then, when he saw them, he darted off at an angle, passing not more than 20 yards in front of them. Wayne hesitated, but Julie was waiting for the buck to stop so she could have a standing shot. When Wayne realized she wasn't going to shoot, he shot. The buck stumbled, but ran on down the hill.

At first, we followed a good blood trail. Then it began to peter out. A few more blood-sprinkled rocks and then none. We went back to the last drop, marked it, circled, and then circled wider, while Julie stood to the side, watching ahead, ready to shoot. No buck.

It was getting late. The sun had long left us in the canyon shadows. Supper was waiting. Lee and Julie had a long way to go. Hated to lose a wounded buck, but we already had bagged two.

Reluctantly, we gave up. Wayne and I went to my buck, dragged it to the road in Dead Man, loaded it in the Bronco. We low-geared it back up and out of Dead Man Canyon to the house.

Julie was quiet. She was really tired. And disappointed.

At the ranch, Julie went in to wash up and help Aunt Beth set the table.

Wayne and I dressed the two deer, sacking the back straps for Lee and Julie to take with them. We told Uncle Lucious about the day's hunt and apologized for the wounded deer that we couldn't find. (He later found its carcass not far from where we gave up the search.)

At supper, details of the day's quest ebbed and flowed along with hearty servings of chili. Julie quietly said she enjoyed the hunt, but her feet hurt. She was ravenous, explaining that her hunger was due to both Aunt Beth's exceptionally delightful "special chili" and the awful "jail-house" noon-time rations. Uncle Lucious and Aunt Beth had a good laugh at her tart description of our lunch while she was wolfing down more than a child's portion of Aunt Beth's chili. Topped it off with big bowl of cobbler, of course.

Much later than planned, Lee and Julie left for Baker's Crossing and then on up Highway 163 as it follows the winding, twisting, dipping, curving route to Juno and Junction.

As soon as they left the Baker ranch, Julie worked those new boots off her punished feet. Lee put the pedal down on that new car on the drive home. He knew all the dips and curves of the road past the Hudspeth ranch and beyond, and, remember, he had to preach and conduct Sunday Services early the next morn.

In time, from first one family member and then another, we learned that, on the way home, Julie began to mutter that we might have "staged" a difficult hunt for her. That kind of dark thinking probably wormed into her tired mind during the three stops Lee had to make. For her to open the door of that brand new car so she could hang her head outside to upchuck.

Oh, she cast nary a single verbal stone at Aunt Beth's chili. Certainly not at the cobbler. Just belabored Lee's mentally deficient driving on those dips and curves. And gritted out some weird, absurd, irrational, and illogical ideas about sardines and oysters and Vienna sausage and a scalawag brother-in-law and his wayward son.

Monday morning she hobbled to work. Returned the borrowed gun. Hung up her boots.

Never hunted deer again.

And she still grimaces and groans about that hunt and grimly swears that Wayne and I -- in cahoots with her conniving husband -- planned it that way!

The Short Golf Game

Bob Poole talked me into it. I was reluctant. But he thought he could make a golfer out of me.

When I went to work for the school district, I lacked a few hours of degree credit at Texas and to meet teaching certification requirements, I had to do some additional course work. So I spent a couple of summers back in Austin. Bette, Candy, and Wayne stayed in Del Rio while I was soaking up those higher, mind-warping levels of knowledge, understanding, and comprehension.

So, we joined the country club -- primarily to have access to the swimming pool for the kids during the summer.

Bob was a self-made, scratch golfer. He figured if he could fashion himself into an accomplished player, he might be able to introduce me to the thinking man's sport.

Jack Moon got wind of the project and jumped on the band wagon. He had an old set of clubs gathering dust in a corner of his garage. He insisted that I borrow them. Bert Lynch, then the high school golf coach, dug up a bag of used but not too terribly abused golf balls which he contributed to the scheme. Thus, with most of my protests for naught, my links career was launched.

Now you must realize, considerate reader, that even in the beginning, it was a dubiously daunting task. Nobody was aware of it more than old me. Every peek in the mirror revealed not the slim, trim, lean and lithe torso of a model golfer. I was a bunch chunkier than Arnold Palmer. By that time I had mostly gotten over my indignant response to Gayle Burton -- a doctor friend in Woodville. Several years before when he casually observed that I was "slightly obese" my dignity had drooped for days. Let's just say that for any aspirations of superior golfing achievement, I recognized I had a serious built-in handicap.

Never-the-less, with copious quantities of mesmerizing and cajoling sweet-talking, Bob enticed me out to the practice areas of the country club.

The hand-me-down clubs were most welcome. But they were more than a tad too long, of course. Jack was six inches taller than me and, if anything, his arms were longer than average for his size. I had to short-grip to compensate.

Golf books and magazines galore abounded in Bob's house. Both he and Susan, as professional educators, believed in the power of the written word -- as well as constant practice. If a new golfing gimmick or gizmo -- process, practice, or procedure -- came on the horizon, they wanted to at least understand it, even if they did not adopt it. I was "encouraged" to do my homework as well as practice.

Nearly every day for several weeks of an otherwise lovely fall season I was out in one of the rather rudimentary practice areas -- putting or chipping, or lofting or loafing -- sometimes even laughing -- at myself, out there trying -- as my granddad used to say -- to make a silk purse out of a sow's ear.

Gargantuan gobs of garbled golf gobbledygook -- along with the hearty servings of basic and sound instructional info -- were offered. Some were somehow absorbed and digested. About the face angle the clubs -- the theoretical distance each and every one was designed to cover (if the swing was right) -- hooks and slices -- rules and regulations and etiquette -- when to fish and when to cut bait -- all those seemingly infinite and unending details and techniques -- crunched into my neophyte noggin. Did I tell you a delightful creek twines thru the SFCC course?

On that practice tee, I worked on grip and stance and swing with a seven iron. Then moved up and labored with a nine iron. And danged if those balls didn't start falling closer to the pin in that little ole hole. Not all of them. But it began to bolster my confidence.

I planned to work on drivers and long clubs later. The practice area was small and I was too reclusive to get out on the course and display my ineptitudes at this stage of my development.

At the putting practice area, I felt less inhibited. Enough grown folks and an ever-present snarl of kids were bumping little balls into the practice holes all the time and I could get lost in the shuffle there. Perceptible progress came on the putting. Not great. But better most every day!

I began to think maybe I could play golf, after all.

Every so often, someone would ask if I was ready to play. Quit practicing and play!

I avoided those invitations and temptations as long as possible.

One bright and shining afternoon, Bert, the friendly, jocular, helpful high school golf coach, ambled up. I was quite adroitly, I thought, allowing for windage and ball spin to cast those little age-yellowed golf balls up respectably close to the practice driving hole.

Bert simply stated: "Come on, Walt. You've practiced long enough. Let's play ball!"

"Just you and me?" I cautiously gulped?

"Yep. No one is playing on the first holes right now. Let's go."

So we sauntered over to Number One Tee, a par three.

Now, friend, if you don't already know, on San Felipe Golf Course Number One, the distance from the tee box to the hole is almost exactly the same as the yardage from the tee to the hole on the practice area. Get the picture? That location of lo my many days of persistent and devoted toil and effort. With one slight modification.

Number One tee is on the east side of one of the branches of San Felipe Creek that flows so harmoniously thru the golf course. Number One hole is on the west side of that creek branch. Moreover, the tee on the east side and the Green on the west side both lie about forty feet higher than the surface of the gurgling creek running betwixt and between.

In other words, although the tee and the hole are about on the same plane, there is a sharp incline down and away from the tee to the foot bridge over the creek and an equally sloping climb up to the green and the hole.

Need I tell you that oft times the mossy and graveled bed of the twisting waterway curving between, in front of, behind, and/or beside most of the several tees and greens on the SFCC golf course is semi-paved with golf balls? A thriving adolescent industry abounds with kids diving for those balls and returning them to wayward wielders of wretchedly wicked golf sticks.

Bert teed off first. Lofted his ball over the creek and soared over most of the green to a nice lie comfortably close to the cup.

Trepidaciously, apprehensively . . . I punched my wooden tee peg into the turf, settled the little white ball on it, and heaved a big sigh. Craftily peering around from under the brim of my jaunty golf cap to make sure there were no peeping peekers, I stepped up to judiciously choose the club for my first auspiciously official golf shot.

Since the distance from tee to green on Number One was the same as I had been practicing with a seven iron, I calmly extracted from my bag of clubs -- a seven iron.

Assuming the appropriate stance, I laced the fingers of both hands in the short-grip adjusted location and swished the club head deftly back and forth over the top of the ball. Then, ignoring the telltale pops of my twisted spine, I stretched around on my back swing, hauled with my left arm, herded the club head with my clenched right fist, and smacked the ball a solid whack.

Now right here, dear friend, I know you expect me to be tee-totally honest and tell you about the gyrations and outlandish behavior of that little white ball. But I want you to know the absolute truth.

My shot soared sweetly thru the serenely beautiful Texas sky, across the gurgling creek below, dropped gently onto the green, and rolled . . . to a stop five feet short of the pin, mas o menos.

Bert looked at me. I coolly bent and retrieved my peg. We walked down to the creek, across the narrow foot bridge, up to the green. Nary a word was said.

Amazingly, Bert was away. He two putted for a par.

I managed to jab my putter into the grass just behind the ball. It was close enough to nudge the object of my momentary disaffection into motion. Awesomely it wobbled unsteadily and unevenly right up to the lip of the cup -- and slid on beyond.

But it was close enough for a gimmy!

I had parred my first hole of golf!

Bert looked at me real hard like. And muttered something like: "Why you sneaky snake in the grass. Just been lying in the weeds waiting for the suckers!"

Well, sir. I'll have you know it was with a bit more confidence that I teed up on Number Two.

Number Two is a par four, dog-leg to the left. First shot normally has to lay up short of the creek and a stand of trees. Second shot is a short iron over the creek to the green.

I waggled that faithful ole number seven iron, hit the ball almost exactly where I wanted it to go . . . short of the creek and the trees. And . . . I simply could not get over the creek.

It wasn't my normal practice range distance! My nine irons either bounced short of and into the creek or plopped directly into the water. Or caromed off the trees. When I switched to the seven iron -- other than the putter, those were the only two clubs I really knew -- I drove first into the mud of the far bank of the creek and then out of sight over the green! By the time I got a ball in the cup I only had five balls left in my bag!

I struggled thru the next two holes in similar manner. The air was besmirched with foul words. Every rotten tee, fairway, rough, and/or green is beside or over that miserably meandering creek.

Then came Number Five. The fifth hole offers a lovely vista from tee to green. Such deception! A much broader creek at that point. Bounded on both sides of the water with menacing, ugly stands of cat-tailed reeds. A ball hit into those reeds was a gone gosling.

I finished off my stash of golf balls on Number Five. From there on out at Number Nine I was borrowing balls from Bert.

Number Nine is a par three uphill shot from the tee down on the east side of the creek up to the green just in front of the clubhouse. The clubhouse, you know, where bug-eyed watchers sit around with a cool one and giggle at golfing wanna-bees exposing their talents.

I was grimly confident that I was going to fly the green and smash a window of the clubhouse or conk one of those gawking galoots.

Instead . . . caution overcame me. It only took five shots to get up that hill. Golf shots, that is.

Even before I got up to where ole hound-dog friendly Bert was sympathetically waiting for me with by-then gentle, clucking, consoling words, I knew what my future in golf was to be.

At that stage in the development of the Block family fortunes, I quite easily determined I could not financially afford the game of golf. I was already in debt to Bert for more balls than I could count.

I just flat out didn't have the balls for it!

As I told you in the beginning, it was a short golf game.

The New Hunter

Bobby Mohan was a hunter of a different cast. Southern style, that is! After Bobby hatched, the mold cracked. A lot of Bobby's friends called him: "Mo".

Deer stalkers from his neck of the woods must have all done it in tennis shoes. That's exactly the way Bobby snuck up on 'em -- even in West Texas where the southern edge of the Balcones Escarpment meets the Rio Grande. Dog cactus, horse crippler, lechuguilla, and rattlesnakes, be damned.

He was a US Air Force transportation officer assigned to Laughlin AFB. Graduate of one of Mississippi's distinguished institutes of higher learning. You didn't know Bobby long without learning of his hunting zeal. He considered it fortunate that his military assignment was to a prime Texas deer hunting country location.

Bobby was a mighty friendly cuss. He liked people. They liked him. You knew him on a first name basis real quick. Ergo, he received numerous invites for hunting jaunts.

On this sparkling and spectacular occasion of which I am about to relate, one of Bobby's many friends --a civilian employee at Laughlin -- set up a weekend hunt, with Bobby included, on his small ranch in Kenny County a bit north of Brackettville. Then some unforeseen happenstance prevented the part-time rancher-host from going. He urged ole Bobby to make the trip anyway.

Gregarious Bobby always wanted companionship. Besides, as you know, most walking hunts in our part of Texas fare better with more than one hunter working the brushy hillsides, headers, and draws. Happily, he asked me if I would like to go with him. I jumped at the chance.

It was a bodacious hunt!

On a coolish fall Friday afternoon, before the scheduled Saturday hunt, Bobby and I were in Russell Hardware, obtaining doodads for anticipated needs on the Brackett outing, and Bobby ran into an old buddy. This old pal, whom I'll dub, "Mack", for the purposes of this tale, had recently traded his Air Force blues at Laughlin for the khaki shirts and denim jeans of Del Rio's plebeian way of life.

Bobby and Mack were, loudly and happily, long-lost cronies outstandingly well met. It mattered less than none that Mack was a clip-tongued talker originally from somewhere up New York way and Bobby was probably the slowest talking Boy of the South you ever in your born days might run in to. They back-slapped and jaw boned about past escapades in Uncle Sam's winged service to the smiling amusement of gawking Russell Hardware shoppers.

Mack hustled us out to his car in the parking lot to show off a buscadero-type pistol holster and belt he had purchased in Ciudad Acuna. The still-stiff, pungent-smelling scabbard was a slick fit for his new, nine-shot .22 caliber Hi-Standard revolver. Cartridge loops all the way around the two-inch wide leather belt were each filled with bright, brassy, hollow-pointed .22 ammo.

Right off, Bobby clued Mack in about the Kinney County hunt. And danged if it didn't turn out that Mack and our part-time rancher host had ALSO been amigos at Laughlin. Southern rascal that he was, Bobby spontaneously asked Mack if he would like to go along -- if Bobby could contact the host for an ok.

It was one of those hardly said before done things. Mack 'fessed up that he'd never in all his born days hunted whitetails before, would like absolutely nothing better, but -- alas -- he had no rifle. He doubted either his recently acquired pistol or his unpracticed hand gun skills were up to taking a whitetail buck. We hurdled that PDQ. I had a worn but trusty old 30-30 to loan him. Back in Russell's, Mack got a hunting license and ammo. With a whole lot more friendly palaver, arrangements were worked out to meet the next morn.

It was a mite cold for our clime the next day. In pre-dawn wisps of fog, while driving from Del Rio to Brackettville and then north to the ranch, Bobby gave us the lay of the land and his proposed plan for the hunt.

The ranchero was small. The road we used entered via a southwest gate. Fenced off on that side were: a small house, barn, windmill, tank, and cedar-stay sheep and goat pens. Except for a small trap, the rest of the place was divided into two pastures. At the time, it was not stocked except for a couple of horses in the pricky-pear choked trap.

Rising up immediately behind the house and pens was one of the outlaying foothills on the southern edge of the Texas Hill Country. What we could see of it in the dissipating morning mists was a rather sharply sloping, inverted cone. Its top was still obscured in the last tendrils of fog. The fence dividing the two pastures sloped from the house enclosures up and around the left or western side of the hill. Our hunting area was on and around the eastern side of the little mountain. We would be moving from south to north, going up the brush-choked draw scoured and eroded by waters of the infrequent rains flowing down from the escarpment.

Bobby set Mack up on the side of the hill. About a third of the way up, the brush thinned out on up to the rimrock. Mack was to slowly move around the hill, just high enough above the denser brush to keep both of us in sight as much as he could. Bobby would walk along the flats just above the draw on the side away from the hill, to spook out deer in the bottom. Since the fenced pasture did not include much of the next hill to the east, I was to work the hillside across the draw from Mack, higher than Bobby, but not as high as Mack.

Bobby would be swinging an arc around Mack. I was to make still a larger circle. The plan was to jump deer out of the brush so they would, hopefully, pause or run in front of Mack where each of us could possibly have a shot.

Mack, the new hunter, was cautioned by Bobby -- with soft, southern, diplomatic emphasis -- that we should walk along in that relationship until we got to the ranchero's north boundary fence. Then, we would get together and plan the rest of the hunt.

After Mack reached his position on the hill and I fanned out on my side of the draw, we started our circuitous trek, with Bobby tossing an occasional pebble into the denser thickets of the draw.

We had only gone a short piece when a nice little buck jumped out of the draw ahead of Bobby, trotted up to a tiny opening on the flat ahead of and below Mack, and stopped to look back.

Whereupon ole Mack swings his "thirty" to his shoulder and shot him down. He did! One shot!

We all heard the .30.30 slug whack the buck. He flopped over into the brush and we couldn't see him. But he didn't run off. We could hear him scuffling in the brush.

Calling softly to Mack, Bobby told him to ease on up, since the deer was on his side. We would watch and be ready to pop the buck if he got up. Bobby couldn't see very well from his position low in the draw. But from my higher spot, I witnessed a mighty amazing scenario.

I could not see anything of the wounded buck. But suddenly . . . Mack hunkered down behind a big rock, then slowly raised up, drew his pistol from the buscadero belt rig, thumbed the hammer back, aimed, and shot! Then he jumped back to his left, and crouched down again behind that big boulder. I still couldn't see the deer.

In a second or so Mack cautiously poked his head around the rock, raised up on tip toe, reached way out with his right arm, aimed his hand gun, and shot. I couldn't see what he was shooting at!

Again, he immediately ducked right back behind the rock.

Bobby couldn't see Mack. Couldn't see the deer. Didn't know what the heck was happening!

I couldn't see the buck, but Mack was . . . hiding . . . shooting . . . hiding . . . shooting again!

I tell you truly, I was teetotally mystified!

I looked down at Bobby. He gawked up at me. I shrugged my shoulders. He lifted his arms.

Finally, after about the fourth pistol shot, Mack holstered his pistol, stepped up higher where Bobby could see him, and called out in a long, slow, plaintive tone:

"Mowwww???"

Bobby Mohan answered, "Yeah, Mack, did you get him?"

"Yep! He's down and he finally quit kicking! He kept trying to get up. I think he's dead now."

"OK, Mack. Cut his throat and gut him. Walt and I will work on up the draw to the fence and come back to you on that side."

Well, sir, way further on -- almost at the fence line -- Bobby slipped along through the cactus and catclaw, tennis-shoed up on a nice buck, and killed it.

We field dressed that critter quick as we could and tossed him over a bush to drain. Then, we hustled back to Mack and his deer. As we walked along together, I told Bobby about Mack's Cowboy and Indian routine with the pistol.

Bobby chuckled that we'd probably hear a big windy from Mack and, since he hadn't killed a deer before, we'd probably have to help him with the field dressing. He was right!

Back as the scene of the Wild West six-gun action, Mack had his coat hanging on a tree limb, rifle stacked beside it. His hat was on the ground and his buscadero rig and his shootin' iron were laid carefully on it -- well up out of the dust. Mack had his sleeves rolled up and his jaw muscles were bulged out from gritting his teeth. He was grunting some, sweating a lot, and swearing more. A strained and strangled mixture of Yankee and Air force cuss words!

You have to believe me when I tell you this: The cut in the buck's throat -- why, . . . you could have covered it with a big band-aid. Hardly any blood. Worse -- with his pocket knife, Mack had cut a slit not more than five or six inches long in the buck's belly and was trying his damnedest to pull the innards out through that little hole!

Mack allowed as how he was mighty glad to see us, started apologizing for not knowing how to gut a deer, and wasn't at all hard to persuade to let Bobby and me finish the field dressing.

While we opened up the body cavity and cleaned the deer, Mack breathlessly described the mystifying happenings after he shot the deer with the .30.30.

Apparently, the rifle shot broke the buck's back. The wounded critter kept trying to get to his feet, but each time he got his fore legs under him and then tried to work up on his hind legs, he fell back. Of course the buck had his eyes on Mack and the hair around his neck was bristled out and he was gasping and snorting with effort. Every time the buck got his front end up, Mack thought he was about to be charged by the enraged deer. As he aimed and fired, the buck fell just before the hurried pistol shot, except the last time, when Mack timed it right. Close up, the .22 hollow-point broke his neck.

Then, by golly, as we picked up the buck to spread him over a bush to drain, here came some rocks and pebbles rolling down the hill behind us. Seemingly right out of the clear blue Texas sky, up walks this smiling young fellow with a rifle slung over his shoulder. Accompanied by as comely a young blond lass as ever you did wish in your fondest imaginings to see.

Just like back in Russell's the day before, it was sorta like "old home week". The new nimrod was ANOTHER Laughlin buddy who was ALSO a friend of both Bobby AND Mack. He, too, had been invited by the property owner to hunt on the place. He and his girl friend had gotten there before we did that morning, entering the place from another gate on the north side. They had been up on the top of the hill and had watched us from the time we left the house!

Except for the introductions, all during the animated and jovial hail-fellow-well-met mini-reunion, the blue-eyed young lady with the soft blond hair was strangely silent. She might have been Scandinavian -- very blond. And she was almost continually blushing.

After a bit, the young couple left. Bobby, Mack, and I began hoofing it back to the house; to have lunch, then get the horses out of the trap and come back for the deer.

As we walked along, Bobby, in his appreciative Southern drawl, spoke reflectively about the uniquely coincidental meetings of all these air force compadres.

"And how about that sweet-darlin' gal? She's so good lookin' you could eat her with a spoon! But, did you notice how embarrassed she seemed? I think she was blushing the whole time we talked. You could tell every time her heart beat."

"Oh, well," Mack said. "I can probably explain that."

We looked askance.

"You remember how you told me to be sure to stay high out on the side of the hill in a position where I could keep you and Walt in sight as you walked around? Well, this was my first hunt -- my first kill -- you know. And I was more than some worked up and excited. But I remembered what you said."

"You think the girl was agitated by the pistolero action and the deer killing?" I asked.

"Well, maybe. But . . . As I tried to dress that deer . . . I had this urgent 'call of nature' . . . climbed up on that big rock where I could still keep you guys in sight . . . dropped my britches . . . squatted . . . took a dump . . . right up there . . . on top of the rock . . .!"

After lunch we tried to get a bridle on an old raw-boned, wall-eyed, hip-shot mare out in the horse trap. Every time we got close to her in one of those narrow, overgrown, prickly pear trails, she would snort, throw her tail up, pass some gas, and trot off to another strategically chosen vantage point in the maze of thorns. Bobby tried to sweet-talk her into submission -- called her honeyed names. Mack cussed her with Northern lingo and Flyboy phrases. Finally, I picked up a dry sotol stalk, broke it loudly over my knee, held the heavy, jagged end up where the she could easily eyeball it, and, using some slow, deliberate, and singularly appropriate Southwestern Tex-Mex linguistic verbiage, told that old girl what her fate was gonna be if she ran off one more time. She batted her eyelashes around those big bulging eyes and stood quivering as I looped one of the reins around her neck and slipped the bit between her teeth. Then we caught the other horses and went back out and packed in our venison.

Always wondered just how ole Mack told the tale of his first whitetail hunt!

The Two Turkey Tale

Back in the fall of '66 or '67, I forget exactly which, when Wayne was 13 or 14, he and I made a hunt at Uncle Lucious and Aunt Beth's place on Devils River. It was a week or so before Thanksgiving and we had hopes of bagging a buck or two for some tenderloins and back strap.

Wayne had a "new" Buck Knife. Four-inch blade, folding, brass bolsters and pins, hardwood finger grooved handle, snap-fastener sheath to go on his belt. He had gotten it for his birthday in May, I think. Might have been a gift the Christmas before, but the remembrance that this was the first hunt with his new, so earnestly coveted knife is vivid.

He had that knife about as sharp as a guy can get it in those months between taking possession and taking it on a hunt. He had whetted and honed and stropped that blade just about a shade better than perfection. Most all the hair on both forearms had been shaved off more than once, testing the blade edge.

Wayne was about as keen as that knife edge to harvest a white tail buck and field dress it.

Well, sir, Uncle Lucious, in his usual thorough, thoughtful, and considerate manner, had a special plan for us. He wanted us to hunt down in the river end of Dead Man Canyon. Some Spanish goats had infiltrated that part of his country. Fences had been pushed down by the passage of wetbacks. Those broken fences were on the east side of his ranch in really rugged places where it was mighty difficult to get to them to check and repair damage.

In those days, the illegals traveling through from Mexico in search of employment were usually mindful of things that would irritate ranchers. There was a measured degree of respect, consideration, and courtesy between the landowners and the transient travelers. Unless the trespasser was in extreme haste, fences were pulled back up and gates were not left open.

But not always.

Uncle Lucious wanted only pure-bred Angora goats on his place. Angora mohair brought top prices during and for some time after the war-time era. Unfortunately, his neighbor ran some Spanish goats in a pasture that abutted Uncle Lucious' river country.

Spanish goats are nimble-footed. They easily traipsed and romped the rough and rugged canyons where horses and horsemen couldn't get down from the rim rock or up from the headers to the caves and ledges. On foot-back, you couldn't keep up with them as they clambered over the steep narrow trails and shale-covered slopes. Uncle Lucious and Aunt Beth had not been able to round them up to get them back to their owner. If Spanish billies bred his Angora nannies, the resulting cross-bred kids would not mature into profitable mohair producers.

So, Uncle Lucious made a deal with us. For every deer we harvested, we were to make an effort dispose of at least one Spanish goat. Not a bad deal, considering the eating quality of goat meat. Carne de chivo tamales are doggoned hard to beat.

It just made our hunt more challenging and we left the ranch house with high hopes and sweet expectations.

After going thru the pens at the barn, we followed the laboriously hand-crafted ranch road northward into the cold wind blowing across the divide. At the East Mill, we went thru the gate and out of the house pasture, into the river pasture. At the rim rock overlooking the awesome vista of a couple of miles of Devils River winding below, we stopped and scanned the brushy areas below us with binoculars. Then we nosed the old faded blue VW onto THE ROAD OFF.

(THE ROAD OFF will be the subject of another separate tale.)

We nursed our way along in low gear -- right fenders scraping the bluff, left tires kicking rocks off the "road" edge. Went down thru the rim rock cut, around the blind curve, hair-pinned around, and scraped the left fenders some. Massaged caliche gouged out by the front bumper dipping into and the back bumper climbing out of a wicked draw, and started breathing normally when we reached the slopes at the foot of THE ROAD OFF.

There we left the worn and weary vehicle. It needed to recuperate for the climb back out when the hunt was over.

Light whiffs of wind swirled and eddied along the foot of the hills. It was not as cold as up on the wind-swept top, so we peeled off a layer of coats and began a walking hunt toward Dead Man Canyon.

The first brushy draw we came to, we jumped a nice six-point buck and killed him.

Usually field dressing a deer is a necessary chore. Part of the hunt, but not the best part.

But for Wayne, field dressing this deer was special. Out came his new Buck Knife. He had at it with gusto. That sharp edge slit the belly hide slick and neat -- hardly a hair fell into the gut cut. All I had to do was hold the buck's feet while Wayne relieved him of his circulatory, respiration, digestive, and reproductive works. I don't think we ever did a neater or quicker job of shucking a buck of his innards and tossing him over a big rock to drain.

In short order, we were walking eastward, to cross the mouth of Dead Man Canyon and hunt up a narrow steep header that the eastern boundary fence of the ranch ran down.

'Twarn't long before we spotted a little bunch of those vagabond Spanish goats. But they had seen or heard us and were moving out of the thicket just below the rim rock of that skinny header. We watched them high-tail it over the top and out of sight.

Just about then, Wayne discovered he didn't have his Buck Knife.

The leather sheath on his belt was not snapped and the sheath was empty!

Wayne was sick. I think I felt almost as bad as he did.

We talked it over. He couldn't recall if he had put the knife back in the sheath after cleaning the deer and failed to fasten the snap and the knife had come out of the sheath as he jumped some of the rock ledges. Or, perhaps he left the knife where we cleaned the deer. Or maybe . . .

Well, we just didn't know. But that knife -- the one so long yearned for and so often dreamed about before it finally was his -- was so dear and meaningful and important to him that it was a "no brainer" to decide to backtrack and try to find it.

We knew where we were and where we had cleaned the buck and how we had walked between those points. Or so we thought.

Although we had been hunting along together, neither had followed exactly the same route. As we walked back, each looking at the ground, the rocks, the cacti, the catclaw, the tesajilla, the guajillo, the sheep and goat and deer droppings, Wayne tried to follow as best he could the route he had taken. I ranged back and forth behind him, trying to cover the flanks of the way we had come.

We hoped the knife would be where we had cleaned the deer. When we got back there we made a slow, thorough, meticulous, and diligent search. No knife.

Soooo, after a quick lunch on the grub we had brought along, we reversed our search and, at a much slower pace, retraced our way back to the area we were in when Wayne became aware of his loss. Still no knife.

Disappointed and down, we opted to go on with an abbreviated version of the planned hunt. Maybe after we told him about it, Uncle Lucious or someone else would later find the knife.

We climbed up higher, walked back around a point and up into Dead Man Canyon. We worked a few headers on the east side of the canyon without any luck.

326

The shadows of the western edge of the canyon were crawling almost to the upper edge of the eastern side of the canyon. We cogitated about how long it would take to hunt along the dips and draws and washes in the canyon bottom and across the hilly flats on the way back to the VW, decided it was getting late, and started back toward Devils River.

I was walking almost in the bed of the canyon, to jump possibles laying up in the thicker bush growing there. Wayne was to my right, walking parallel to me, but higher. He could see anything I spooked out of the bed of the draw. I watched for game getting up ahead of him and circling around into the next header.

Quite unexpectedly, not deer, but turkeys flushed ahead of me, running and dodging away through the brushy bottom of the draw.

In those days, there was no Spring turkey season. But in the Fall buck deer season, you could harvest gobblers. Toms only. No hens. So you had to peel your eye for bearded birds.

I saw that Wayne and had seen the turkeys. I yelled for him to shoot a tom if he could.

Then I heard wing beats. Tho I couldn't see them at the moment, I knew the turkeys were flying.

When the big dark birds went airborne, they were flying away from me, parallel to Wayne's route, down the canyon, just over the top of the brush.

Wayne aimed his scoped .250 Savage, tracking the fly turkeys. He shot once. Levered another round into the chamber. Shot again. Lowered his rifle and waved his hand overhead.

"Did you hit one?" I called.

"Got two!" he answered.

"Two? You got two?"

"Yep, two on the wing," he responded.

"On the wing?"

"On the wing! Two gobblers!"

When we found the first tom, he was blasted into a bunch of bloody feathers hanging together with some strips of hide. Flying broadside to Wayne, the .250 slug had hit him dead center. Wasn't a decent eating piece left.

"Didn't lead him enough," Wayne groaned.

But that second gobbler! Lead him almost perfectly! His shot hit the flying bird in the neck close enough to clean his crop. Just took out a touch of the front of his breast. A butcher couldn't have dispatched him much better.

So we dressed that turkey, picked up the buck killed earlier, agonized the VW back up The Road Off, called it an almost perfect day and went home. No knife. No Spanish goats.

But how often do you shoot a flying turkey out of the air with a scoped deer rifle? Two turkeys on the wing?!

But, wait. There's more.

The Monday before Thanksgiving, Bette and I were talking to Bob Poole at the school administration building. Bob was a scratch golfer and he had won a frozen turkey in a golf match at the country club over the preceding weekend.

Bob suggested that, since he had a turkey and we had a turkey, we should get our families together for Thanksgiving. A two-family, two-turkey Thanksgiving.

So we did. Bette cooked Wayne's turkey gobbler and some lip smacking fixings. Susan Poole thawed and cooked the frozen turkey hen Bob had won and made some mouth watering good things to go with it. Bette, Candy, Wayne, and I took our contributions over and joined Bob, Susan, and their children, Renee and Doug.

Renee Poole was a Del Rio High School senior that year. Candy and Doug Poole were juniors. Wayne was a sophomore. Bob, Susan, Bette, and I all worked for the school district. We had been friends for several years.

That Turkey Day table was a sight to see. The aromas swirling over it twanged your taste buds and got your juices flowing!

Bob carved his turkey and it was on a big platter at one end of the spread. Wayne's sliced turkey was presented on another platter at the other table end. Dressing, mashed potatoes, green beans, cranberry sauce, green salad, Bavarian salad, hot rolls, giblet gravy, etc., in between!

Everybody got some of each of the turkeys and a rich sampling of each of the delicious dishes on their first serving. And the eating and the fellowship were purely copasetic!

Amidst a pause as plates were being passed for seconds, Renee commented that the two turkeys were both simply outstandingly great, but wondered why Bob's was a little bigger and had more white meat and Wayne's was somewhat smaller and seemed to have less breast meat? What was the difference?

Bob said, "That's because the larger turkey is the frozen Butter Ball I won at the golf meet and the smaller gobbler is the one Wayne killed."

Renee paled. "Killed?" she gasped.

"Yes", I told her. "Actually, he shot two gobblers on the wing -- with a rifle, not a shotgun --right out of the air. One was sorta pulverized, but he made an excellent shot on this one!"

Renee slowly edged her plate a bit away from her.

We had not known of her aversion and distaste for killing wild things -- especially eating them. It just plain scuttled her appetite. She even passed on both the pecan and the pumpkin pie.

After the meal, as I told about the loss of Wayne's cherished knife and how that deflating experience palled the otherwise successful hunt for us, Renee began to thaw a tad as her normal gentle and sensitive nature resurfaced.

In time, Wayne and I eventually climbed back up out of the Neanderthal/
anthropoid, sub-human status to which in she had mentally relegated
us and were accepted back in Renee's good graces.

Once Upon A Train In Mexico

We shanghaied Jim . . . and Joanna missed the train.

Bette and Joanna had heard about, read about, studied about this bodacious railroad that crossed the Chihuahuan desert, climbed up from sea level to 8,000 feet, had at least 75 tunnels, almost 40 bridges, and skirted the edge of the grand canyon of Mexico.

So they got on the phone and rustled up "first class" tickets for the four of us: Fred and Joanna Rose, Bette and me. Fifty-four bucks -- each -- roundtrip.

All we really wanted to do -- in the beginning -- was to ride the train from the Texas-Mexico border across the desert to Chihuahua City and over the storied route through the mountains to the Golfo de California. Just to eye ball the engineering marvels and soak up the scenery.

And return, of course.

It was such a simple plan.

We were nearing the end of June and since Bette, Joanna, and I worked for the school district, we were ready for the work break that usually came about then. Fred could flex his ranching and feed supply chores.

The train schedule was such that we could drive from Del Rio via Alpine to Presidio and Ojinaga on the border to board the train on Friday afternoon, arrive in Los Mochis Saturday afternoon, rest and relax Sunday at Topolobampo, hop on the train at Los Mochis early Monday morning, get back to Ojinaga late Monday night, and drive back to Del Rio. Be back at work Tuesday morn!

The early part of that last full week of June 1971 we began to get ready. Got in high gear with our fixin's Thursday afternoon after work. Joanna and Bette made up a batch of sandwiches. Fred filled a large ice chest with essentials of the journey -- beer. (We seriously thought we had enough cervezas to last 'til we got to the Baja de California.) I serviced our old Pontiac. Gassed it up to the brim. Got extra film for the Kodak.

We each packed a small bag of duds and gear for the four-day trip.

As we did a final review of our plans Thursday evening, our friend Jim Latham rode up on his motorcycle. He was looped to the gills. Plumb pie-eyed. Jim had attained 34 or 35 sprightly years of maturity at the time. He worked for the school district also.

When we told him we were leaving early the next day for a Mexico train trip, Jim allowed as how if he had a bag packed, he'd just go along with us.

We knew Jim's mom sometimes supervised the gathering of his gear when he was off on a cycle trip or a sailboat outing. Couldn't Leita pack a bag for him?

Well, yeah, but there were a couple of other minor problems. He had no train ticket and he didn't have much cash in his pocket.

"No problem", Fred assured him. We could stop at a bank in Alpine. Jim could cash a check there on our way to Presidio.

The train ticket? Well, there were always last minute cancellations. Jim most likely could get a ticket at the train station in Ojinaga.

Jim said to pick him up on our way out of town the next morn, waved as he hopped on his Yamaha, and zoomed off.

Darned if he wasn't ready, bag in hand, when we stopped at his house the next morn.

During the drive to Alpine, Jim began to fret about the contents of his "war bag". He was wary about what his mom had packed for him -- what he might or might not find when he opened his bag. His biggest fear was whether Leita had packed his tooth brush.

The Alpine bank cashed Jim's check. At the Ojinaga railroad station Fred and Jim together mustered up enough Spanish to wheedle a ticket from the doubtful lady behind the bars of the ticket booth.

We found a shed we could rent to sorta protect the Pontiac while we were gone and climbed on the train.

Our railroad car was like the old air-conditioned Pullman cars that were standard for years on the Southern Pacific trains that ran through Del Rio from New Orleans. Cooling was accomplished by loading blocks of ice in bins under the cars. Fans blew air over the ice and into the cars. It worked -- as long as the ice held out, the electric voltage for the fans was not impaired, and the old fan motors didn't give up the ghost.

Fred, Joanna, Bette, and I had tickets that provided not only seats on the air-conditioned railroad car, but also four berths. Joanna had a lower berth. Fred's was up over hers. Across the aisle, Bette and I had a similar set up -- my berth was directly over Bette's.

But, although the ticket seller in Ojinaga had come up with both a seat and a berth for Jim on the same car with us, his berth was up over another seat further down the car.

There was no room in the coach seating area for our beer-laden ice chest. But when Joanna and Bette obtained our tickets, the travel agent said it would be ok to leave our ice chest in the men's restroom on our car. It was a necessary and respected travel custom.

Still, we stashed our beer chest with more than moderate apprehension!

We were aboard one of the world's fabled railroads, The Orient Express of Mexico.

Near the end of the U. S. Civil War, an American named Kinsey Owens dreamed of building a railroad link through the Sierra Madres of Mexico to reduce the shipping route from Kansas City to the Orient. He got a concession from General Manuel Gonzales, the president of Mexico, in 1880. Owens had hard luck. Finally lost his contract when the Mexican government enacted the Railroad Law of 1899.

Another group headed by Enrique Creel and Alfredo Breedlove made a stab at it with little success.

Then Arthur Stillwell, who had been a successful railroad builder in the U. S., formed a company called the Kansas City, Mexico, and Orient.

Stillwell's plan was to lay over 1,600 miles of tracks through Kansas, Oklahoma, and Texas to Presidio. Entering Mexico at Ojinaga, they would cross the desert to Chihuahua City, climb to the 8,000 foot level at Creel, then build through the rugged mountains and gorges to Los Mochis and Topolobampo. Between 1910 and 1914, Stillwell's company completed the rail line between Ojinaga and Chihuahua City.

One of the contractors who built parts of the railroad for Stillwell was Pancho Villa. Stillwell directed construction from his private railway car but never invited Villa into his car. During the 1914 Mexican Revolution, Pancho Villa led an armed group which attacked a rich silver mine that Stillwell owned near the railroad. Villa could have captured the mine and operated it, but he destroyed it.

All railway work in Mexico was halted by the revolution.

The tracks, tunnels, and bridges through the mountains were finally finished by the Mexican government in 1961. At that time the line was named the Ferrocarril Chihuahua al Pacifico. Most U. S. travel agents referred to it by that more romantic and quixotic moniker: The Orient Express of Mexico.

A rail line from Presidio to Alpine, completed in 1930, joins the Southern Pacific Railroad at Alpine and thus connects to the U. S. rail network. But no railroad bridge spans the Rio Grande between Presidio and Ojinaga.

While most of the occupants of our rail coach were Mexicans, we found we were not the only turistas. Among our fellow travelers were two joyfully noisy couples from Louisiana and a pair of "December and January" honeymooners from Houston.

Our meeting with these folks demanded, of course, that we toast the newly weds. Nearly one whole case of beer evaporated PDQ.

During the first several hours of our trip after leaving Ojinaga, the country was drab. Very dry. Sparse vegetation. Scattered livestock. Few people. A sprinkling of rustic ranch dwellings.

As shadows lengthened over the desert, our train slowed and stopped at a barren and lonesome place. There were no structures. No windmill or water tank. No road. Just caliche and cactus. When the train began to go on, a plainly garbed man with a wide-brimmed hat, a woman with a colorful shawl, and a young boy were standing beside the track. Each had a suitcase or bag. They waved. And began walking away on a dim and dusty trail. Out into the gathering gloom.

After sun down, we began climbing to the 5,000 foot level of Chihuahua City. By dark-thirty, we had wiped out the sandwiches, so we moseyed forward on the train to the diner. The meal was a happy one, since we gained assurance that there was a moderate supply of cooled (but not icy cold) Mexican cervezas available. We had begun to be concerned about our diminishing ice chest supply.

Returning to our railway car, we found some passengers were having their seats converted into berth configurations so they could retire. Fred and Jim made a little huerte back through the train to the last car. When they returned after that scouting inspection, the five of us relocated to the vestibule on the tail end of the last car.

The vestibule at the end of each passenger coach has a door into the car which is closed while the train is moving. That door allows passage from the inside of the car out onto a covered area. On each side of the sheltered part, steps descend about two or three feet so people can get on or off the train. While the train is moving, a metal plate covers the steps. When that plate is lowered on each side of the car, it creates a flat area that extends the total width of the car. Above this flat area, a window on each side, which can be closed or open, provides a fine observation deck.

The spaces over the couplings that hold two cars together are constantly flexing and adjusting as the train follows the curving track. A person out on the vestibule of the last car usually has only a railing between them and all the country moving off behind. On a passenger train, there was no caboose. The last car has large red lights attached to its back vestibule so trains coming from behind can easily see the rear end of the train ahead.

When we adjourned to the vestibule on the end of the train, we first were a cozy group of six: the five of us and the brakeman.

The brakeman frowned when we came out into his nook. Fred offered him a can of cold beer. The scowl became a wide grin.

After a spell, Jim went back to the men's restroom on our coach to replenish the drinks for the six of us. He returned with our four Cajun acquaintances in tow. He also brought the ice chest. Said it was too much trouble to hike back and forth. And, besides, the chest was by then a lot lighter.

Our now larger group of ten, plus other occasionally curious passengers, was a mite crowded on the tail-end vestibule, but the eastern Sierra del Carmen got well splashed with lusty swamp-water lyrics and old-time western country singing. The initially reluctant brakeman added lines in Espanol now and then . . . especially the "ai, yi, yis".

Camaraderie flowed. Until the ice chest was empty. And until Bette began to worry . . . that the brakeman might be getting too foggy to wave his signal lantern to flag down any unexpected train that might loom up behind us.

So we went forward to our coach. The porter had our berths ready. The ladies disappeared behind their curtains. Fred and I made our way up into our uppers. Jim toodled happily off down the dimly lit aisle in search of his upper berth.

The mesmerizing clickity-clack of the train wheels crossing the rail joints doused the glim for me very quickly.

Then . . . Jim was shaking me and growling to: "MOVE OVER!"

From time to time, train conductors the world over probably conjure up extra pesos or shekels by peddling empty berths in the coaches to sleepy folks in the chair cars. We just kept Jim up too late.

The guy snoozing in Jim's berth was big. Hairy. Bushy black mustache. Bunch of grizzly whiskers and a mess of snaggly teeth. Ole Jim said when he opened the curtains of his berth and this guy snarled at him, he thought he was face to face with the original magombo-magombo. Jim figured that since he himself might possibly be at least three sheets to the wind, it was the better part of valor not to start another Mexican revolution.

It is a rare experience to spend half the night in a narrow berth jammed between a big guy like Jim and the cold, bare metal side of a lurching Mexican railway car. Jim swore he had the worst of it, since he had to hang onto the curtains to keep from making a six-foot dive into the aisle when the train went around a curve the wrong way.

We were up at daylight. Stiff. Sore. Coffee hungry. Fred and the ladies said they had a nice night. Jim and I hustled off to the men's room and tried to wash off some of the diesel-smoke grime we were gifted the evening before on the vestibule by the three big red locomotives hauling the train up into the mountains.

Huevos rancheros in the dining car helped our recuperation.

When we got up, the train was lugging through the mountains. I did a double take through those diesel-smoked windows at what appeared to be a lot of naked women we were passing. After a bit of pulsating excitement, Fred said he had already been introduced to those gals and they were really just madrone trees.

Madrone trees have thick, papery bark that flakes away like patches of sunburned skin. The cream-colored new bark then changes in color to peach, to coral, to Indian Red, to Chocolate, and then peels again. The

337

Tarahumara Indians make "tesguino", an alcoholic beverage distilled from fermented red madrone berries. The hard and durable wood of the small trees has many uses, one of which is in making balls for the Tarahumara running games.

About that time, one of the Cajun damsels looked up from the guide book she had been studying and said we were approaching the first of the reported 75 tunnels the track went through between Creel and the western edge of the Sierras. I dug out my camera. Right off I found the soot-streaked windows just too dirty to allow taking good photos. So, I and others took up semi-permanent residence on the train vestibules. We could lean out, crane for better shots. Diesel smoke from the laboring engines was bad, but endurable.

Gawking passengers and zealous photographers jockeyed back and forth, switching from one side of the train to the other as the terrain changed and new vistas were exposed. Warning shouts kept the unwary from intimate meetings with the rock facings of tunnel openings. There was not a lot of clearance between the side of the rail cars and the tunnel arches and walls.

There are not 75 tunnels. There are at least 85, some say 87. But a few of those may be some of the shed-like structures which are built on precipitous mountain sides to keep loosened rocks from sliding down onto the train tracks.

Most of the tunnels had a number painted on the rock wall entrance. After I had shot a slew of photos, I took one of the tunnel entryway that was marked "75". As I came back into the car, smugly reporting that I had taken the picture that would verify to all the folks back home that this amazing train track had 75 tunnels -- we entered another tunnel. I staggered back down the darkened aisle to the vestibule, fumbling another roll of film into my Kodak.

There are also 36 bridges . . . at last count. The longest one, over the Rio Fuerte, is 1,837 feet long.

That someone had the audacity to imagine that a railroad could be built through those mountains is mind boggling. But about one hundred years after the dream, this fabulous railroad was really there.

The engineering is fantastic. The work is almost unbelievable. You do have to see it to believe it.

One of the tunnels is 5,966 feet long -- over a mile.

The most incredible tunnel makes a 180 degree turn totally inside the solid rock of the mountain.

The west-bound train approaches high up on the mountain side. Looking down, one sees an amazing horseshoe-shaped bridge crossing a large river below. The river is flowing westward, toward the distant sea. The train and its awed passengers enter the black bowels of a tunnel. When the train emerges from the tunnel it has descended down near the river bank and is heading east. Without being aware of it, the passengers have been transported down several hundred feet, are now traveling upstream and nearing the beautiful crescent-shaped bridge. After crossing the bridge, the train is once more heading west along the other bank of the river.

In the mountains, the train climbs from Chihuahua City to San Isabel, to San Andres, to Anahuac, to Cuauhtemoc, to La Junta, to San Juanito, to Creel, and up to Ojitos. Then begins descending to Divisadero, to San Rafael, to Cuiteco, to Bahuichivo, to Temois, to El Descanso. On the western foothills of the Sierras it goes from Loreto, to El Fuerte, to Sufragio, to Los Mochis. None of the villages are more than 35 miles apart, some much closer. There are more than 50 "flagged stations" where stops can be made at passenger request, to deliver goods, or pick up cargo.

At the time of our 1971 trip, we saw almost no motorized vehicles in those towns in the mountains. The occasional pickup or truck had been brought in on a railroad flatcar. There were very few roads. No paving. Horses, mules, burros, wagons, and carts aided in transporting people and objects.

The train was the principal conveyance. At each stop, people with small amounts of luggage got on or off. Women carried small cloth-wrapped bundles. Some toted produce -- eggs, chickens, even a piglet.

Old box cars were on sidings near the main track. People living in them stood watching in their doorways as we went by. Washing was hanging outside to dry. Kids stopped their play to watch the train.

It was always surprising to round a curve and view in the distance a solitary rustic cabin audaciously attached to a steep hillside or tucked neatly in a cozy gap . . . now and again in the midst of small green fields carved out of the side of a mountain. Some of those cultivated plots looked like the farmer who slipped and fell in his corn patch might take a several hundred foot fall.

Some of the canyons are over 5,000 feet deep. At the lower depths, lush tropical plants -- sugar cane, citrus, etc. -- abound.

In contrast, high up in the canyons and gorges, clouds from the Pacific and the Baja, overriding some of the mountain passes, occasionally poured gently down to lower levels. There were often distant vistas of striking beauty. The craggy cliffs and bluffs were sometimes bisected by the slender vertical plumes of silvery water falls. The distant colors faded and blended into shades of green and ocher and lavender.

We traveled westward that Saturday out onto the plains of the west coast of Mexico at the tag end of the dry season.

The brown western mountain slopes and upper canyons gave way -- first to cacti and dry desert growth, then to increasing greenery as we descended lower and nearer the coast.

In the roughly 110 miles -- from the highest point of the railway just west of Creel at Ojitos to El Descanso -- the train had descended from the cool 8,000 altitude to about 1,200 feet above sea level.

As we reached lower levels, it became more humid. And that fabulous air-conditioning of our train car failed. Just quit.

It became muggy and hot in the Pullman.

When we asked the porter to crank up the AC, he shrugged his shoulders and said it usually happened that way. The bins under the cars were out of ice . . . or the voltage was too low for the fan motors . . .

Passengers tried to open windows. In vain. They were stuck tight by multiple layers of paint.

But then Jim put his back to it. He grunted and strained. Got most of the windows open. And diesel smoke poured in.

As we moved over the coastal plains, the vegetation shifted from cacti to verdant broad-leafed greenery. Increasingly frequent farms and livestock. Creeks and rivers. The rails followed the Rio Fuerte and adjacent fields and groves on into the railroad depot in Los Mochis.

John Steinbeck called the Gulf of California the Sea of Cortez. Los Mochis is twelve miles inland from the sea, gulf, gulfo, bay, baja, or whatever name is appropriate at the moment.

We took a short bus ride to from Los Mochis to Topolobampo and checked in at the Yacht Hotel. First order of business for each of us was a shower. Bette still marvels, almost 37 years later, about the amazing rivulets of black diesel gunk that streamed from her hair, down her body, across the tile to the shower drain.

During a sumptuous seafood supper, our plans for Sunday were altered. We had considered fishing in the Baja, but figured the price for a chartered boat would be too stiff. But when the honeymoon couple wanted to join us, the seven-way boat cost split altered our outlook.

The hotel cooks had boxed lunches ready for us early Sunday morn. Before sunrise, the larger than expected boat -- with the seven of us, a boat captain and mate, and our partially replenished ice chest -- shoved off and headed north up Topolobampo Bay.

At first the bay surface was only disturbed by the dawn riffles. We met and passed a small fleet of shrimp boats, one behind another, bringing in their night's trawling catch. Beautiful sight as the little ships with dripping nets hanging from masts and spars passed between us and the rising sun.

As we got out into more open water, the waves were rougher. The young Houston bride succumbed to wave after wave of nauseating seasickness.

She retired to a bunk, her anxious husband by her side. She was out of it for the rest of the boating trip.

About 14 miles out into the Gulf of California we approached Farallon Rock. The captain and his crew rigged a chair bolted to the aft deck and hauled out deep water fishing gear. Our friend from Houston, Fred, Jim, and I took turns buckled into the chair with a monster-sized rod and reel trailing artificial lures in hopeful enticement of sailfish.

During a whole morning of that, we got one strike. The gent from Houston hooked a fish and graciously turned the rod over to Fred. Fred hauled in a nice sailfish. Jim and I gave copious advice.

So we took in our heavy fishing gear and cruised over to take a gander at Farallon Rock. This massive granite chunk impressively pokes its bluffs and crags up out of the azure waters. Lapping wavelets on the windward side splashed and foamed against it. Along its nooks and crannies at or just above sea level, clumps of seals basked and barked. Jim said they were laughing at our frustrated and futile fishing.

The box lunches were box lunches.

It must have been the Baja sun, but our supply of Mexican beer was too scanty. By early afternoon we were paying ridiculous prices for luke-warm beer the boat crew had brought for their own use. The crew kept their beer in the same metal container with a few chunks of ice and the live bait. Their tepid beer tasted mighty dang fishy!

After the sun moved westward enough to cast a shadow in the sea east of Farallon Rock, el capitán broke out smaller fishing rigs, baited hooks with live bait that had been swimming in that metal tank with his tepid beer, and Jim and I began trolling out on the fan tail of the boat.

Wham! We each had a fish on at almost the same instant.

Jim squalled, "I've got Moby Dick down there!"

The capitán chopped the boat throttle and the boat wallowed as we wrestled and tugged, lifted and reeled, cussed and scrambled.

Fred and Bette and Joanna were yelling encouragement and instructions.

Joanna, trying to take photos, was perched up on the top of the after cabin. The boat rolled down into the trough of a small wave. Joanna slid across the cabin top toward the rail. Fred grabbed her just as she slid off on a flight that would have sailed her into a cool dip in the drink. She never missed a camera click.

My fish swam right. Jim's went left. Our lines crossed. Jim's line was on top, so he climbed up on the after cabin and back down while I moved over. Jim's biceps bulged and his rod bent. He hauled his fish up to the surface. The mate snagged it and pulled it on board. Right after that we got mine in also.

The fish -- jacks or yellowtails -- weighed 25 to 30 pounds each. Just a fraction of what we thought we had on our lines down there in the briny deep.

Back at the Yacht Hotel, we headed for the showers again, had a fine supper in the restaurant, and sacked out for the early Monday morning bus ride into Los Mochis to catch our return train home.

The eastbound Orient Express pulled out on time Monday morning, but when we got to the foot of the mountains it was raining. The rainy season had begun.

As the train began climbing up into the mountains, it was slowed by the necessity for a small motorcar to go ahead to find and remove fallen rocks from the track or repair damage from such.

As we wound our way up into the canyons, the contrast with our trip two days earlier was remarkable. Stalks and leaves of previously dry and wrinkled plants on the lower slopes had already begun to enlarge. The dusty gulches under the frequent small bridges we had passed over were by then gushing torrents. Those formerly slender white vertical waterfalls were bigger, wider, browner, and fuzzier due to the spray and the sometimes misty, often pelting, falling rain.

Just before dusk, our eastbound train chugged into Divisadero, then the 8,000 foot high switching stop on the line. We halted on the siding to wait for the westbound train coming in on the main track.

At this major switching point where the trains routinely pass, the native Tarahumara Indians, famed for their long distance running, had a trading center which many train passengers visited during the brief stops. Purchasers of hand-made craft articles especially prized the wooden balls the Indians carve from the hard wood of the madrone trees. The balls are used in the infamous Tarahumara running games.

Joanna had a compelling urge to get one of those wooden balls as a memento of the trip.

As she got off the train in the misting rain, Fred cautioned her that the main track which the arriving train would be coming in on was between our train and the trading shop. Our eastbound train would leave as soon as the westbound train cleared the main line tracks.

In aisles of the trading shop, absorbed in her shopping, Joanna failed to hear the whistles of the approaching train. Suddenly she became aware of people leaving the shop and dashing back toward the waiting train.

Shoving money to the vendor, grabbing her wooden ball, Joanna sprinted for our train. Too late. The incoming train pulled into the station. Between Joanna and our train. And our train began leaving for the downhill leg of its journey on to Chihuahua.

Jim, Bette, and I were in the dining car, waiting for Fred and Joanna to join us for supper. We looked up as Fred walked rapidly up the aisle toward us.

"Joanna missed the train," he almost, but not quite calmly stated.

We tried to question him, but he hurried on, snapping back: "I've got to stop the damn train!"

Jim and I jumped up and ran back to the vestibule at the end of the train. As we got there, our train, which had not gathered much speed yet, seemed to be slowing.

Fred first asked the dining car waiter to stop the train. The waiter sent him to the porter. The porter said he had no authority to stop the train. But the conductor could. Fred asked where the hell the conductor was. The porter pointed forward. After dashing through three cars of wide-eyed travelers, uncounted chickens, and some squealing pigs, Fred found the conductor in one of the engines, with the engineer.

By then Fred had morphed . . . from his normal, easygoing, everyday, laidback, slow-talking kicker version . . . back into that B-Battery Field Artillery Commander Ogre characterization he used so effectively at A & M to figuratively eviscerate, disembowel, and gut underclassmen when necessary over on the great, grey-green banks of the Brazos River.

The train stopped.

The last car of our train had just come out of a sloping downhill cut carved out of a solid chunk of one of the Sierra Madres. We could only see a few yards up into the darkening gloom between the high rock walls of that cut.

Two brakemen lit flares and ran back from the end of the train toward the dark cut. Mandatory emergency procedure to warn any other rail traffic of the stopped train.

Fred and the conductor rushed out onto the vestibule platform. Above the throbbing sounds of our train, we began to hear -- faintly at first and then more distinctively -- the "crunch-crunch-crunch-crunch" sounds of someone running -- heels digging into the rock ballast between the rails -- coming down that cut toward our train.

In a moment, Joanna materialized out of the darkness.

She was picking them up and laying them down and calling: "Fr-e-e-e-ed" every step.

One of the brakemen running toward her with a burning flare asked, in Spanish, "Are you the lady from the train?"

Joanna collapsed. Fell in a pile in the middle of the track. She knew she was saved.

345

Fred jumped down off the vestibule and ran to her. Picked her up. Together they staggered to the waiting train. Jim and I, a concerned conductor, and a wide-eyed porter aided them up the steps onto the vestibule.

Joanna was shaking, crying, and breathless. In the dining car, she sank wearily into a seat. Between the tears, the sweat, and the rain running down her face, she gasped out a vivid description about stumbling along, looking up and seeing a stoic, cross-armed Indian standing on a bluff staring down at this crazy woman running down the railroad track. She said that apparition gave her a jolt of energy she needed to keep on running to catch the train.

But then . . . she knew Fred would stop the train for her.

Well, sir, when we finally got to Chihuahua City we had a long layover. Some kind of mechanical difficulty, they said. It was mid-morning Tuesday before the train pulled out to take us back to Texas.

As before, after the train left the cooler mountain climate, the blasted air conditioning of our old Pullman could not cope with the heat of the desert. Hot and tired, short on sleep and rest, we were yearning for home.

On the way back across the desert, I worried and fretted about our old Pontiac squatting under that shed in Ojinaga. But when the train finally got to the border, we found the old buggy waiting for us. Covered with dust. As per norm, no rain on the east side of the desert.

We drove back to Del Rio via the road running south along the Rio Grande to Lajitas and Terlingua, through the Big Bend Park, Marathon, and Sanderson. It was a long old haul.

We were a rag-tailed, bleary-eyed, bone-tired, but happy band of vagabonds when we got home.

But we had tales to tell.

Made in the USA
Lexington, KY
16 October 2013